Shared & Satisfied: 12 Howife Quick Reads

A Collection of Smutty Short Stories

January Hotwife
February Hotwife
March Hotwife
April Hotwife
May Hotwife
June Hotwife
July Hotwife
August Hotwife
September Hotwife
October Hotwife
November Hotwife
December Hotwife

Lacey Cross

CONTENTS

January Hotwife

Hotwife of the Month Club 1

Lacey Cross

CHAPTER 1

My phone beeps with an incoming text message, and I swipe to read it just as I hear the front door open.

DEBRA

I've got the craziest story to tell you. Call me ASAP.

Yeah...sorry, Debra. I've got a husband that I haven't seen in five days to kiss, so I don't have time to indulge in her drama. Debra's the wife of one of my husband's friends from college. I don't know her that well, but she likes to gossip. I'll text her later.

Henry calls out, "I'm home, baby."

I raise my voice and try to sound seductive as I stretch languidly on the couch. "In the living room."

My body's been buzzing with anticipation all day for Henry's return, and I could hardly focus on the book I was trying to kill time with. He told me he wanted me as soon as he got home, and I'm ready for him.

When he finally appears in the doorway, my heart skips a beat at the sight of him. He drops his bags and coat, and I stand up so I can run my hands over the sun-kissed skin of his arms. "Mmm, someone got some sun. You look so good after a trip," I whisper, pulling him closer for a kiss. "Did you have a pleasant flight?"

Every year, Henry joins his old college frat brothers on a trip to Aspen. I don't mind that the wives aren't invited; I'm not much of a skier, and the nights are just filled with poker and cigars for the men. It works out perfectly since I can plan my own girls' weekend getaways without any complaints from him—like the trip I'm taking next weekend. It's a win-win situation.

Henry sighs and hugs me. "Flight was fine, but traffic around the airport was a beast. I'm glad Will was driving and I got to relax. How've you been?"

Just being near him again warms my heart. "I missed you so much. I hate waking up without you so many days in a row."

Henry nuzzles my neck, and I shiver a little at the prickly stubble on his jawline.

"I'm so sorry I missed our morning ritual. I was thinking about you every day at seven in the morning. Every. Single. Morning." He punctuates his last three words with kisses along my neck, and it makes me giggle.

My husband loves to tease me right before he goes to work every day. He kisses me until I'm breathless and longing for more. Then he either plays with my nipples or rubs my pussy until I try to convince him to come back to bed...only to have him leave me panting as he goes to work. If he does his job well enough and gets me all hot and bothered, I run for a sex toy as soon as the front door clicks shut behind him.

I smile at him before shimmying my hips and rubbing against him. "You better not start anything you don't plan on finishing."

Henry groans and scoops me up in his arms, carrying me bridal-style up the stairs into our master suite. Ooooh, guess he's not going to get me worked up and leave me wet and needy tonight.

While Henry may not look like the guys you see on the covers of the romance novels I read, he knows exactly how to rock my world. He stays in shape and between his broad, muscular shoulders and deep brown eyes that make my insides melt, he's the perfect person for me. We just passed our ten-year anniversary, and we both feel lucky to have found each other.

Henry sets me on the floor of our bedroom, and we strip off each other's clothes, kissing as we reveal more and more skin. I'm down to just my bra and panties, but he's still got too many clothes on. I'm suddenly frantic to feel his naked skin against mine.

I struggle to get his shirt off, and he laughs as he helps me. "I think someone missed me."

"Less talk, more stripping."

I reach for the fly on his jeans, and he pushes my hand away. "Patience, my love."

Damn him. My entire body is tingling, and I just need his cock inside me. I step back from him a bit and unclasp my bra behind my back.

"You sure you want me to be patient?"

I slide my bra down my arms and let it drop on the floor before leaning forward to slip my panties off my ass. When they reach my ankles, I step out of them. What my husband doesn't know is that I had a spa appointment while he was gone and got a Brazilian bikini wax.

When I straighten up, his eyes drop to my smooth, bare mound, and the pupils in his eyes dilate with desire. I can see his erection jump in his jeans, and I try not to smile.

I climb up on the bed on my hands and knees with my ass facing him and look over my shoulder.

"So..." I purr at him and wiggle my ass. "Are you going to fuck me or not?"

Henry rips his pants off like a madman and climbs on the bed behind me. He grabs my hip with one hand, but as soon as I feel the tip of his cock pressing against my opening, he pauses.

"Baby?"

"Hmmm?" What game is my husband playing at now? My body trembles in anticipation, and I groan out, "Henry, don't tease me. I've been dying for your cock for days."

It's true. We usually have sex twice per week, fairly routine, so going five days without his cock isn't common.

He asks in a deep voice, "You're going to get what you want, but you have to answer a question for me first."

Henry gives my ass a quick spank and I let out a surprised squeak. It stings a little, but it only adds to the intense desire that's already coursing through me.

My voice drops an octave. "If you know what's good for you, you'll fuck me first, and then ask questions later."

He laughs and totally withdraws even the tip of his cock from me. "Someone doesn't want my cock that badly tonight."

"Fuck, Henry! You know how turned on I am. Put your cock inside me right now before I make you regret it."

My pussy aches with emptiness. I'm desperate to be filled by him, and when his cock brushes against my inner thigh, I mewl out in frustration. He's driving me crazy, and he knows it. I'm seconds away from begging for his cock, and he's enjoying drawing it out as long as possible. Damn my man and his excellent self-control.

With a finger, he draws a line from my clit, along my wet seam, and stops at the entrance of my pussy. He slides his digit inside me and slowly finger fucks me. My clit throbs and his tender touch sends sparks through my entire body. My head spins because it's not enough.

"So answer my question, and I'll fuck you as hard as you want." His voice is soft but commanding, and the authority it holds has my pussy contracting around his finger.

I'm desperate for release, but the delay is also driving me wild. I moan out, "Fine, what do you want to know so badly?"

He's still using his finger in slow, measured strokes, and I rock my hips back towards him.

He gives a throaty laugh. "Do you ever think of fucking someone other than me?"

My face flushes, and I'm suddenly glad I'm not looking at him. He's kidding, right? Why is he asking this?

I don't want to tell him that sometimes I imagine fucking some random hot guy I saw while I was out and about. It's never anyone he or I knows, so it's just a hot body without a real personality—it's fantasy.

Henry thrusts two fingers into me, but my thoughts are everywhere and I barely register it.

"Tell me and I'll give you my cock." His tone has lost its earlier playfulness.

I gasp out, "N...no."

Yes, yes, yes, a thousand times, yes. I want to scream out to my husband, but I keep it inside.

He stops moving his fingers and demands again, "Give me the truth, baby."

The raw lust in his voice shocks me to my very core. He wants me to have thought of fucking someone else. My mind spins, and I feel myself getting wetter. This is so fucking hot.

Something inside me cracks open, and I whimper out the truth, "Yes."

He moves his finger to my clit and rubs circles around it while holding his cock with the other hand and pressing against my opening, dipping the head just inside but pulling out again.

Henry croons, "Is your pussy soaked right now because you're thinking of fucking someone else?"

I wasn't thinking of anyone else until he said that, but suddenly I imagine there's a massive guy behind me—some biker-gang type with tattoos who looks like he'd make a woman sit in his lap all night being a cock-warmer while he chats with his friends.

I can't keep up with my husband, and my head whips around to look over my shoulder. His expression is smug when we lock gazes, and his fingers don't miss a beat as he continues to rub my clit.

"Come on baby, admit it."

He's pushing me farther than I ever thought he'd go, but I decide to go for broke and just blurt it out. "I imagine fucking other guys all the time. Happy?"

Henry plunges into me to the hilt, and I cry out in pleasure as he bottoms out.

"That's so sexy." Henry smacks my ass, and the stinging pain reverberates through my entire body.

Ohhhhh, god, he might be insane. I don't know what's gotten into him tonight. He's never this enthusiastic after a trip, but I'm loving it.

He fucks me in a punishing rhythm. Each stroke knocks me forward while I moan in ecstasy. The pleasure builds in layers, and I'm not going to be able to stop myself from coming. I briefly imagine he's the biker guy fucking me, but everything about what's happening is familiar, so the fantasy is short-lived. I don't really want to fuck someone else; I just want my husband.

When he spanks my ass again and picks up speed, I explode with an orgasm, crying out with pleasure. My entire body shakes as waves of bliss ripple from my core, and my climax triggers his. His cock spasms deep in my pussy as he bathes my walls in thick ribbons of his warm cum. I swear I can feel every spurt.

I'm still on my hands and knees, and I give a soft grunt when he pulls out and falls onto the bed next to me on his back.

When he holds out an arm, I settle against his side and rest my head on his shoulder with one hand on his chest and a leg thrown across his.

My brain is a jumbled mess as I whisper out, "What was that all about?"

Henry chuckles and wraps his free arm around my shoulder, holding me tightly against his chest. "The guys were talking in Aspen. One of the guys' wives fucks other men with his permission."

Huh. I trace patterns in his smattering of chest hair and say nothing. It's a pleasant fantasy.

Henry squeezes me and nuzzles his nose into my hair, breathing deeply. "I liked the idea more than I thought I would. If you ever want to try it, I'm game."

A small flutter of pleasure zaps my clit, but I don't want to sound enthusiastic about the idea, because I don't think I'd ever do it. "After tonight, who needs other men?"

He kisses my forehead. "Well, just know if you ever want to, you have my blessing as long as you tell me before and afterwards—like on your trip next week."

I laugh lightly. "Uh-huh, okay. I'll fuck my way through the entire resort over the week."

A low rumble comes through his chest. "Why don't you just start with one guy, and we see how it goes, okay?"

An erotic thrill flares through me at the idea of having sex with another man with Henry's approval. I never thought this was even an option, and I need time to think about it.

"Okay, honey." I snuggle against him and we both relax, lost in our thoughts.

CHAPTER 2

Felicity, my best friend in the entire world, pokes me from the lounge chair next to me. "January, did you notice how many hot guys are at this resort?"

It's shortly after lunchtime on the second day of my girls' trip, and Felicity and I came down to the pool to sunbathe. I crack my eyes open to look at her, and she tips her head to gesture across the pool deck. A smile curves up the sides of my lips as I spot three men hanging around the poolside bar. All three men look delicious.

When one tall, blonde-haired guy in blue swim trunks turns around with his drink, I suck in a sharp breath. Yummy. His face is classically handsome, with sculpted cheekbones and perfectly trimmed facial hair around his jawline and chin. He's fit with an incredible build—in fact, he's massive. He towers over the other guys, and my pussy hums to life.

My mouth is practically watering, and I have a sudden urge to fuck this man even though he's definitely the biggest man I've ever looked at in the flesh. If his cock is as big as the rest of him, that's one challenge I'd love to accept.

The giant turns back to his friends, and my gaze flickers to Felicity. I try to make a joke to hide how hot and bothered I suddenly am. "Yep, we're in heaven. Can it get any better than this?"

We're at a posh retreat on a private island for a long weekend. It's an exclusive getaway that caters to adults twenty-one and older. It's the ultimate paradise, with activities, a beach, bars, a hot tub, a pool, and, of course, a spa. We had massages and mani/pedis yesterday, and tonight is a huge bonfire down on the beach.

"Oooh, speaking of hot, check out those two." Felicity raises her sunglasses to peek at a couple of guys walking by and gives them an approving nod.

Those guys are attractive, but they can't hold a candle to the massive blonde guy. Felicity says something, but my mind wanders as I watch the hot blondie with his friends out of the corner of my eye. If given the chance, would I fuck him? Nah, I wouldn't go through with it. The fantasy is fun, but I'm not really that kind of woman.

I'm suddenly thirsty, and I take a sip from my bottle of water to quench my dry throat as Felicity catches my eye and says, "Did you hear Marilyn fucks other guys and James lets her?"

I sputter, and liquid goes down the wrong pipe and I have a coughing fit. Felicity looks worried for a minute before my fit dies down. The giant must have overheard me choking because when I sneak a glance over in his direction, he's looking directly at me with a concerned expression. I flash him a quick smile and then glare over at my friend.

"Are you trying to kill me?" I hiss out as quietly as I can so I don't attract any more attention.

My bestie just grins. "Debra's got her panties all in a wad over it, but if my husband would let me, I'd take a guy in each hole and thank them afterwards."

I'm glad I'm not taking another drink. Just imagining her husband, Edward, wanting to share her is pretty hilarious. He's the stuffiest dude I've ever met. How he scored a hot-blooded, sexy wife like Felicity, I'll never know, but she seems happy.

I guess I also now know what Debra wanted to talk about last week. I kept forgetting to text her back. Hopefully she'll forgive me when I message her after the trip.

I swing my legs off the lounger and face her. "I need to go back to the room. I've got to call Henry and take a nap before dinner and the bonfire. You coming with?"

"Nah." She shakes her head and stares off towards the group of men by the bar. "You head up, I'm going to enjoy the eye candy some more."

"Okay then, see you at dinner." I grab my bag before heading up to my room. I don't like to share rooms when I go on these vacations, because I want to have private conversations with my husband easily and I sleep better when there isn't someone else with me. It works out fine since Felicity enjoys her privacy as well.

In my room, I'm a bundle of excitement for no real reason. My hands shake as I hold the phone and dial my husband to video chat with him. He's got poker tonight, so hopefully I catch him before he leaves.

When Henry answers the call, he's shirtless, which makes my mouth water. They say distance makes the heart grow fonder, but next year I don't think I'm going to schedule a trip so soon after he gets back from Aspen. I needed at least another week of sex before being separated from him again.

Henry flashes me a charming grin. "You have good timing. I'm changing and heading out for poker. How's my wonderful wife today?"

The sight of his smile tugs at my heart, and my voice comes out a little husky. "Your girl's horny and wishing you were here."

My husband sits down on the edge of the bed and winks at me. "I bet there are plenty of guys around to help with that. Remember what I said."

As if I could forget. "They aren't you."

He chuckles and stretches his arms out wide, flexing his biceps, before dropping his hands. "Come on, tell me, did someone catch your eye?"

I bite my bottom lip and consider telling him the truth about the enormous guy at the pool.

"Wait." Henry sets the phone down on the bed before I say anything. A moment later he picks it up and aims it at his naked and erect dick. "Now tell me."

He holds the phone camera directed at his cock and slowly starts stroking his length with his other hand. Holy shit. Watching his shaft turn shiny from pre-cum has me so wet I can feel my bikini bottoms sticking to me.

"Show me your pussy, January."

My core pulses and my stomach clenches with desire as I untie the strings of my bikini bottom and spread my legs, pointing the camera so he can see between them.

My pussy lips are glistening, and when I run a finger down my slit, I moan and lift my hips off the bed to meet my fingers. I roll my clit under the pads of my index and middle finger. It feels so good that I know I could come quickly, but I also like the torture.

Henry groans. "Baby, I've got to go. I'm picking up dinner on the way. But promise me something."

"Anything," I breathe out as my fingers continue working their magic on my swollen clit.

"If you meet a guy you like, you have my full blessing to do whatever you want, okay? Promise me you won't hold back out of concern for me."

The muscles deep in my abdomen seize, and my orgasm teeters on a razor's edge. I barely manage to whisper, "Yes, honey."

My husband blows a kiss and then ends the call.

I remove my hand from between my legs and slump back on the bed, shivering from how close I was to coming. When the image of the blonde-haired guy pops back into my head and I picture him above me on the bed, fucking me, I almost start rubbing my clit again. Will I see him tonight, and could I get him alone?

Oh god, am I nuts? I'm starting to actually consider fucking someone else.

Crawling up to the pillow, I settle in and close my eyes. I'll get my nap, and I'm sure the feeling will disappear once I'm no longer horny.

CHAPTER 3

There are more people at the bonfire than I expected, and the laughter is infectious as it swirls around me. This party is such a different vibe when it's all adults on vacation. It almost seems like a college party.

The beach is dark, but it's a warm night, so I'm just wearing a sundress and sandals. I put my long blonde hair up in a ponytail, and I know I look sexy. I tried to tell myself it wasn't for the blonde guy the entire time I was getting ready, but it was.

I came down here with Felicity, but we quickly separated to get drinks and flirt with other guys. You'd think we weren't two married women, but I'm not going to judge her, since my husband actually wants me to fuck someone. That's way beyond flirting.

I see the massive blonde guy several times and we keep catching each other's eyes. Every time our gaze connects, a tingle of awareness runs through my body. There's always an appreciative look on his face, and knowing he finds me attractive makes me even more turned on than I was earlier when I was daydreaming about fucking him.

Shit, I need a drink. He's going to keep me thirsty all night at this rate. Since I want a clear head, I grab a soda instead of anything alcoholic and wander off the main beach area to walk the shore. The sand is wet and firm beneath my sandals, and the foamy crest of each wave that hits the shore flows over my toes before receding back into the ocean.

I close my eyes and tilt my head back, soaking up the gentle breeze washing over me. A moment later, I hear a man clearing his throat. I whip my head toward the noise and see the giant standing a short distance away, looking at me. I'm not surprised it's him.

Since he has a can of soda in his hand, he gestures with his head towards the path. "May I walk with you?"

This is it, the opportunity my husband is encouraging me to take advantage of. The strange thrill from earlier comes rushing back, and I hope my voice doesn't sound breathy when I say, "I'd like that."

His face lights up with a smile, and the brightness of it fills me with a mixture of nervousness and excitement.

He offers his hand to me. "I'm Adam."

I give him my customary greeting that I've perfected over the years whenever I meet someone new. "I'm January—like the month. It's nice to meet you."

I slip my hand into his massive one. His grip is firm as we shake, and my brain short circuits. The masculine strength that emanates from him sends shivers to my core, and a delicious ache of longing for him builds inside me.

He drops my hand and we fall in step with one another. Neither one of us speaks as we make our way further down the beach. I glance at him out of the corner of my eye, and his broad shoulders seem to brush the stars. Besides being impressively sized, the top of my head barely reaches mid-chest on him. I'm not a tall woman, but he'd tower over almost anyone. Hell, how would I even fuck this guy? I imagine riding him, and the mechanics of that send a tingling spark through my pussy and I have to shift to ease the ache.

"So, have you ever been here before?" Adam finally breaks the silence.

I startle out of my mental daydream of riding him. "Um, yeah, every few years I come with my friends. You?"

He shakes his head. "First time here for me."

We're getting close to the end of the beach section for the resort, and we angle towards one of the wooden docks on the outskirts where boats come to deliver goods and take guests to and from the island. I never come down to these docks other than when I first arrive at the resort or when I leave. I've never had a reason.

As we walk, the beach becomes darker around us. The sounds of laughter from the bonfire fade into the distance. We are surrounded by the ocean on one side and sand dunes on the other, with the dock looming ahead. In just a few steps, we will have to turn back.

I don't want to go back. I'm here with him, and I have a choice to make. Stopping in my tracks, he pauses also with a curious look on his face.

The moonlight reflects in his eyes, and he gives me an encouraging smile. "So, what made you want to come for a walk with me? Not that I mind the company."

My pulse flutters as I swallow and lick my suddenly parched lips. "My husband said I could have sex with someone on this trip. He gave me his blessing."

Adam chuckles, a mischievous glint in his eyes. His gaze is intense, and I can't remember why I didn't want to fuck someone else when he says, "Well then, that changes things."

What does it change? Before I can gather the courage to ask, Adam steps closer to me and tilts my chin up with a gentle touch. "But do you want what your husband wants?"

I hesitate for a moment, my mind filled with doubts. But then I remember how turned on I've been thinking about fucking him, and how Henry is encouraging it. This is my chance to do something wild and crazy, and I'm going to take it.

I take a deep breath and confess. "Yes."

My stomach lurches like I'm falling and when Adam slides his arm around my waist, it's only his grip on me that keeps me stable. "Have you been thinking of fucking me?"

I'm tongue-tied as his closeness and the warmth of him fries my brain. He must read the answer from my face. Adam brings his lips down to my neck, brushing lightly against my skin, and it's so tantalizing that I sway towards him.

His voice is a dark whisper. "What do you want me to do to you?"

I can feel his cock harden through his pants, and I press closer against him. The size of him both thrills and intimidates me. A shudder runs through me, and I gasp out, "Make me scream so loud that if anyone walks past, they'd hear."

He shifts and pushes me closer to the dock until my back runs into one of the wooden support beams. He takes my soda can from my hand and sets both of our cans on the edge of the dock before lifting me off the ground effortlessly. I wrap my legs around him as a pleasurable tingle zips through me. Holy shit, he's holding me like I weigh nothing.

"Lean back and grip the edge," he says in a husky voice as he tugs my dress up to my breasts, exposing my panties and stomach.

My hands scramble to find purchase on the wood. It takes me a second, but I finally grip it while leaning my back against the dock. The air is cool on my exposed skin but feels refreshing with the contrast of the heat radiating off him. I'm a trembling, aching ball of need, but I force myself to maintain eye contact with him.

Adam drags my underwear to the side before reaching for his zipper. He frees his cock from his pants, and I look down to see how big he is. Wow. That is one hell of a cock. My inner muscles clench with hunger as I eye his length. I suddenly feel powerful and sexy in a way that I haven't felt in a long time. I know my husband loves and desires me, but to have this effect on a guy I just met is a heady experience.

His dick is impressive. Long with a broad crown. The ridge around his cockhead is thick, and my stomach clenches with anticipation. I'm wet and needy, and he hasn't done more than just show me his cock. My senses are overwhelmed with anticipation, and a shiver runs through me. Yeah, it doesn't matter. I want him. My nipples strain against my dress, needing attention, and every inch of me aches.

Adam growls out a demand. "Ask me to fuck you."

I love how commanding he's being, and I feel a jolt of desire. My heart hammers as I whimper, "Please fuck me."

"Ask again and use my name."

My pulse quickens even more. I need him in me, and the tip of his cock brushes against my center, taunting me with how close he is to me. He's so hard, but the softness of the velvety smooth skin drives me crazy with lust.

I arch my hips closer to his and grind against him, trying to find some friction for my aching clit. "Please fuck me, Adam."

He holds me stable with one hand while he pushes my dress and bra up over my tits, exposing them to the night air. Imagining what I'd look like if someone saw us from the beach has my blood boiling in my veins, and I tremble in his grasp, nearly frantic to get his cock inside me.

He pinches and pulls on my nipples roughly before releasing them. The sting is slightly painful and turns me on even more. If he doesn't fuck me soon, he's going to have a crazed woman in his hands.

"Keep your eyes on me while I fuck you, and say my name when you come," he demands in a tone that leaves no argument.

"Yes," I mewl out and try to tighten my thighs around him to get him to shove his cock inside me. He's clearly got something about me using his name, and it's hot. I'll scream his name out if he gives me an amazing orgasm.

Adam aligns himself at my opening and slowly starts to push in, giving me every inch in slow, steady movements. Holy fuck, he's thicker than I realized. Once he's in as deep as he can go, I can't hold in my cry of ecstasy. This feels incredible.

"God, you're tight." Adam grits out the words while he pauses for a minute to allow me to adjust to him—if I even can adjust to him. His cock is stretching me out farther than I've ever been before.

I lock my eyes on his and feel every twitch of his shaft buried deep within me. He starts to pull out, and it feels like my core tries to cling to him on purpose to prevent him from withdrawing. Oh fuck, this feels so good, I'm going to be thinking about his cock in the future. I'm not sure my husband realizes what he's unleashed inside me.

Once he pulls back until just his cockhead remains lodged within me, he pushes forward with one fluid movement, and I cry out in pleasure. Every nerve ending is alive, and for one moment it's like I'm hovering above my body, staring down at how raunchy it is to fuck a guy I don't know on the beach. As he fucks me, I return to my body, mentally let go of all the "what-ifs and doubts," and embrace my sluttiest side. I'm ravenous for his cock, and I need him to fuck me hard.

He sets a grueling pace, and my moans reach higher in pitch as I keep up with his thrusts. My hands lose their grip on the pier, and I wrap them around his neck instead as he fucks me into a frenzy. Each time he spears into me, the base of his cock rubs my clit and sends sparks up my spine. The stimulation is maddening, and I'm desperate for whatever is going to make me come. I try to bounce against him and fuck him like he's a standing sex toy. His cock is so fucking amazing I could impale myself on it every day and climax.

Oh yeah, I'm such a slut and my husband is the most amazing man in the world for letting me do this.

He bends his head forward and captures one of my nipples with his lips, sucking hard until it reaches the threshold between pleasure and pain. His words rumble out of him against my breast. "You fucking love this, don't you?"

A tremor passes through my body at the sheer need in his voice, and I pant out a response. "Yes, I love being a slut."

Adam bites my nipple in retribution for my brazen comment and then lifts his head and focuses on his thrusts. The pleasure builds deep in my core, and I'm crying out every time he hits a magical spot deep inside me.

I throw my head back and squeeze my eyes shut while every muscle in my body begins to tense, ready to explode. The pressure builds, and when my eyes snap open again, the passion in his gaze locks on to mine. I can tell by the harsh tone of his breathing and the deep flush spreading on his cheeks that he's as affected as I am by what we're doing. We are like two animals mating on a public beach without shame.

This isn't me—or it wasn't. This is not who I thought I was when I came on this trip. Yet I've embraced it, and I wouldn't stop it for anything. The physical connection is too addictive—he's too addictive. Everything about him sets me on fire.

When he thrusts harder, I see stars, and my muscles clamp down on his cock when the tension finally breaks.

"Ooooh, god!" I scream as I come undone.

My nails dig into his shoulders as my walls pulse and squeeze him as the orgasm rips through me. I cry out his name in a rising crescendo as all my senses explode in bliss.

He fucks me through my orgasm, prolonging the pleasure, and just when I think he's going to come with me, he unhooks my legs from around him and sets my feet on the sand.

What's going on? My brain is too fuzzy to understand anything while he leans over and brushes his lips against mine before pulling me against him. His kiss is full of passion and lust, and I savor the taste of him. My arms creep around his shoulders as my head spins. I don't care what happens next.

He rips his mouth from mine and orders, "Turn around and bend over."

I can't think beyond obeying him, so I turn and place my hands on the wooden beam, dipping low until my ass is in the air. I gasp when he tears my panties off with a sharp jerk and tosses them aside before stepping close and kicking my feet wider apart. Wetness drips down my thighs, and I'm curious if he can see it.

When he drops to his knees, I'm surprised and then almost giggle. Yeah, I bet he can see exactly how wet I am.

When he traces his fingers along the seam of my pussy, he groans. My pussy aches to be filled again, and I push backwards, trying to tempt him to fuck me again.

He toys with my opening for a moment, swirling a finger in circles around my slick heat before plunging two digits deep in me. I moan and rock against his hand, loving how his fingers feel as he pumps them in and out of me. My knees threaten to buckle, but he stills behind me.

"Promise me you'll tell your husband every detail about tonight and let him know how much you enjoyed fucking me."

The demand in his voice surprises me, and a thrill runs down my spine. I don't have a problem sharing the details of tonight with my husband, since that was our agreement.

"I will," I promise.

He stops fingering my pussy. "Stand up and turn around."

When I do what he says, he shifts his position in the sand to stretch his legs out in front of him and reaches for my hand, tugging me down, facing him. I straddle him, and the sand cushions my knees. Yeah, we're going to be a mess when we're done.

My dress is still pushed up above my tits, and my bra is holding the fabric up. Adam plays with my nipples as I position his cock so I can rub up and down the length without him being inside me.

Adam's breathing increases, and he grits out in a gravelly voice, "Fuck yourself on me and make me come."

His dirty command has my pussy contracting in anticipation as more wetness slips out and coats his shaft. I consider teasing him some more, but I want his cock back inside me too much to wait.

I lower myself onto his shaft while he rolls both of my nipples between his fingers. Pleasure heads straight to my clit, and I cry out as he fills me again. After his entire length is seated inside me, it's like a switch is flipped on in my brain and I go wild.

I ride him, rolling my hips, and he moves his hands down my body to put one on my hip while the other dives between my legs. He caresses my clit, flicking the swollen nub as I try to drive him deeper and harder inside me. I lean back, putting my hands on the sand so I can change the angle of his cock as it moves in and out. I slam against him to the hilt repeatedly as he continues to brush circles around my clit with his finger.

Nothing matters but the pleasure. I'm moaning continuously as I hurtle towards another orgasm, lost to the rapture.

When he rubs my clit faster, I detonate into bliss with a drawn-out mewl that transforms into an "Oh, Adam!" as my entire body shakes and shivers. White-hot pleasure cascades through me.

He bucks into me as I ride the orgasm out while circling my hips, rocking my pussy against him while my inner walls contract again. A hard thrust from him, and fireworks go off in my head. I come a third time as I cry out loudly and my entire body quivers.

His cock pulses inside me, and his own groans of ecstasy reverberate in the air as I collapse forward and his warm cum floods my inner depths. His thigh muscles quiver as he finishes unloading, and I kiss him softly as he comes down from his orgasm.

When I can tell he's done, I slump onto his chest while my brain blanks out for a few moments.

Holy shit, I just fucked someone on the beach where anyone could have seen us.

After a few minutes, he stirs beneath me and helps me pull my bra and dress down. I'm giggling as I stand up and he joins me and adjusts his clothes and picks up my panties, pocketing them. Yeah, he can toss them. I'm going to walk back to the hotel with his cum dripping down my inner thighs to feel like the ultimate slut.

When our clothes are straightened, he pulls me against him for a hug. "Was that good for you?"

I laugh. "As if you couldn't tell. That was amazing."

"Yes, it was." His voice is deep with appreciation, and I know he means it.

We kiss tenderly for a minute until it threatens to get hot and heavy. I don't want Felicity to worry, so I step back from him. He grabs our soda cans, and I hook my arm through his as we head back up the beach.

When we get close to the bonfire, we pause and I look at him. "Thank you for a fun evening."

He winks at me. "No, thank you. Have a wonderful rest of your trip."

We split up as we get to the group of people. Felicity finds me shortly afterwards and gives me a long, questioning look. I'm sure I look like I was just fucked. She opens her mouth to say something, and I put my finger to my lips. "Not now. Let's talk tomorrow."

She nods, and I go to find another soda. I need something to drink after that workout. For the next hour, I can feel Felicity's eyes on me, and I have to stop myself from giggling. She's going to be shocked when she finds out what I did, but my husband deserves to be the first one who hears it.

CHAPTER 4

I told my husband everything that happened before bed that night and then Felicity the next day. She took it better than I expected and kept calling me a slut in an admiring way, but my husband's response was all that really mattered to me. When I told him, he got quiet and said to expect to be fucked hard when I got home.

And now I'm home.

My entire body is humming with desire as I walk in the front door.

"Hello, baby." Henry steps into the hallway as I set down my luggage, and my heart skips a beat. He was clearly waiting for me.

I rush over to him and fling my arms around him, inhaling deeply as his scent floods my senses, a mix of warm skin, musky cologne, and the familiar scent of our laundry detergent. God, I missed him.

When he nuzzles my neck, a shiver runs through me, and my nerves dance with electricity as I look at my husband and giggle. "So what now?"

His voice is a sensual whisper near my ear and his breath tickles me when he replies, "I want to hear all of it again—every naughty thought or deed—leave nothing out."

My husband wraps his arm around me and leads me to the bedroom. I don't have time to take off my clothes before he pushes me on my back and peels off my pants and panties.

I sit up on my elbows and stare at Henry. "I can't believe I'm turned on by the thought of telling you what I did with another man."

"I'm excited too. Now start talking." His voice is hoarse, and I hear his belt buckle clink before it drops on the floor.

I stare up at Henry. He's more handsome than he's ever been, and he's looking at me like he owns me, like I belong to him, and I do. A deep craving twists in my stomach, and my body calls out for him.

Henry pulls his jeans off, and his cock bounces out. God, I need him inside me. I spread my legs as he climbs up on the bed and crawls to me, pushing my shirt up so that he can capture a nipple in his mouth. I cry out when his cock slides inside of me.

The look on Henry's face is primal. "You like getting your pussy filled with cock?"

"Only yours," I sigh as he bottoms out.

He smirks. "Liar. Now talk."

It's hard to form words as he starts fucking me vigorously. "It started when I saw a sexy guy at the pool..."

I pause when Henry slams his hips into me, but I love this side of my husband. So while he fucks me, the entire story tumbles out. Every thrust and groan from him tells me he loves my slutty side.

Henry fucks me in a steady rhythm as my climax builds. Right before I orgasm, I whisper the last bit to my husband. "I liked getting fucked by someone else, but you're the one I love and nothing will change that."

Henry kisses me passionately, swallowing my moans as he gives a deep, possessive thrust that tips me over the edge, and I climax while clinging to him. The pleasure washes over me, and I moan loudly while he groans that he's coming. The pleasure swells and spreads as Henry gives a shuddering thrust and bathes my inner walls with his cum. His release triggers a series of mini spikes of bliss, and I writhe beneath him.

My husband is the perfect man for me, and he holds me in his arms as my mind clears. All I want is him. No one else matters.

After we come down from our high, I curl up into a ball next to Henry with a contented sigh and run my fingers through the hair on his chest. "So I guess I'm now officially a hotwife."

My husband laughs and wraps an arm around me, pulling me tight to his side. "You mean you're *my* hotwife, and I *might* agree to share you again if you beg good enough."

My core hums to life again with the promise of more adventures to come. When the time is right, I'm going to beg like he's never seen me beg before.

The End

February Hotwife

Hotwife of the Month Club 2

Lacey Cross

CHAPTER 1

As soon as I step through the front door, my body is on fire with pent-up desire. My husband, Edward, is at work, and I'm back from my girls' trip with my best friend January. On the trip, January fucked someone else with her husband's permission, and now I'm envious as hell.

I've been buzzing with sexual energy all weekend, and if Edward were here right now, he'd find himself on the couch with me riding him hard. My body pulses with pleasure at the thought. Hell, that's what I'm going to do as soon as he gets home. I just have to get out of my head and stop daydreaming about having all my holes stuffed at once...or at least understand it's a pleasant fantasy but not reality.

Sighing, I wheel my luggage to my bedroom and unpack. It was a great weekend, but nothing seems fair in life. January is my second friend now with an open marriage. Our other friend, Marilyn, recently became a hotwife. I'm the one who never wanted to be monogamous in the first place when they were both ecstatic to pledge their entire sexual lives to their husbands.

Edward knew from the beginning that I had my doubts about monogamy, and he had to convince me...with lots and lots of orgasms. We've had a wonderful marriage, so I've never regretted marrying him, but I'd be lying if I said that January and Marilyn aren't making me wonder what I'm missing. I'm so totally in love with Eddie, and I'd never cheat on him, but this dumb green-eyed monster is my constant companion since January told me she fucked some dude on the beach.

I guess I should just be glad it was one guy and not three since she didn't get my ultimate fantasy. I joke around about having a cock in every hole, but I'm only a slut in my head. That's all it will ever be since Eddie made it clear he wasn't interested in an open marriage from the beginning, and he's worth it.

With my suitcase emptied and the dirty clothes in a pile for me to take to the laundry room, I lie back on the bed and close my eyes. It was a great trip, I just wish I felt refreshed and relaxed instead of keyed up and horny for multiple cocks. I might explode as soon as I get Eddie's cock inside me tonight with how turned on I am.

When my phone trills with a text message, I smile, assuming it's from Eddie.

DEBRA

> I can't believe you sat there while January cheated on her husband. If you had invited me along, I could have kept her in line. She's such a loose cannon.

The text shocks me, and my stomach churns with unease. I'm not sure how to reply or if I even should. Debra, the wife of my husband's friend, isn't someone I trust or confide in easily. She's known for her sharp tongue and love for gossip, and this message proves it.

I knew January was texting Debra earlier today, but I didn't realize how much January had told her about our trip. Debra needs to calm down and stop with the slut-shaming. This is exactly why she's never invited along.

Ooh, wait. I know exactly what to say. I snicker as I type my reply.

FELICITY:

> Sorry, I was too busy flirting with a bellhop to stop her. I offered to give him an extra tip if he slipped me his tip. Sadly, he declined.

As soon as I hit send, I turn the sound off on my phone and lay it facedown next to me. After her nasty comment about January, she can chew on that all night. My phone suddenly rings, meaning whoever is calling dialed twice in a row to break through my phone's silence feature.

If that's Debra...

After four rings, I look at the screen to see who's calling. It's Debra. Of course.

I send her to voicemail and haul myself off the bed. I'm going to make sure I'm showered and clean when Eddie gets home, so I can entice him to fuck me. Despite being disgruntled over the lack of multiple cocks inside me, I still desperately want my husband. After an orgasm or two, I'll forget all this nonsense about fucking other guys.

"Where's my baby at?"

Eddie calls his customary greeting when he gets home, and I don't reply. He doesn't realize it yet, but he's on a treasure hunt with me as the prize. I'm on the living room couch, draped lengthwise on my side, in my sexiest black teddy with a garter belt and thigh-high stockings. My brown hair is in a ponytail, and I'm hoping the sight of me puts him in the mood.

I listen to the floor creak as he hunts for me, and I try to hide my smile when he walks into the living room.

"Hey, there you—"

He stops short, his eyes widening with lust as he becomes transfixed on my body. Eddie works out at the gym regularly, and he's my handsome, sexy man. Knowing that, after eight years of marriage, he still wants me as much as I want him makes my body hum with desire.

I trail my fingertips from my thigh up to the peak of my breast and toy with the nipple poking through the delicate fabric of my sheer lingerie. I trace circles around the sensitive flesh, giving him an enticing smile.

"Did you miss me?" I purr, my voice low and seductive.

His eyes hungrily devour every inch of me, lingering on my breasts for a few seconds before roaming down to my legs. The thin fabric of my lingerie leaves nothing to the imagination as it hugs my curves in all the right places.

I pull on my nipple and moan softly. "See something you like?"

Edward draws a ragged breath. "Very much."

"Excellent," I say with a satisfied grin as I swing my legs off the couch and sit upright. "Take off your clothes and get over here. We need to fuck."

The eagerness in his eyes is palpable as he starts stripping, revealing his toned chest and tiny love handles that endear him to me. All I can think about is how badly I want him to dominate me tonight. My submissive heart thrills at the thought of being completely at his mercy. My husband may not be a hard dom, but he knows exactly how to satisfy me.

Within seconds, he's naked, and he stands in front of me, stroking his hard cock. I resist the urge to praise him and call him a good boy, knowing that it might lead to me being across his knees for a playful spanking. I can't risk him edging me tonight and prolonging my delicious torture. All I want is for him to fuck me until I forget about all the imaginary cocks I'll never have.

He clears his throat, and he sounds slightly amused. "Is this all because you missed me?"

Giving him my sweetest smile, I point to the cushion next to me. "Maybe...now sit here. I want to ride you tonight."

The best thing about this teddy is that it's crotchless, and when he sits, I straddle his lap. The anticipation builds as his cock slides between my folds and presses against my clit. With one hand on his shoulder for support, I use the other to guide him inside me.

As I sink down the length of his shaft, I moan in pleasure as his cock's broad mushroom-shaped head massages every inch of me. His cock throbs as I grind against him, and my inner muscles clench tightly. I'm ready to fuck him hard, but it's time to tease him a little first.

January told me I could tell Eddie what she did on the trip, so I brush my lips over his before murmuring, "Guess what? January fucked a guy on the trip with her husband's permission." I exaggerate my next words in the hopes it will make him feel bad for me. "She left me *all alone.*"

When I roll my hips and lean in to nibble on his collarbone, he grunts. It almost sounds pained when he rasps, "Yeah? Did that make you want to fuck another guy?"

Mmm, oh yeah...but there's no freaking way I'm admitting that. The thought makes me bounce on his cock harder as bliss swirls in my core.

"Nope, you're all the man I need."

He groans and holds onto my hips, pistoning upwards so he can fuck me. "Admit it, Felicity...admit you're desperate to fuck someone else. You want some guy with a massive cock splitting you open."

The growl in his voice makes me quiver around his shaft, and my head spins. Damn it, he's pushing all my buttons. I bite down on his collarbone before dragging my teeth to the base of his throat, tasting the salt on his skin and feeling the vibration of his next moan. I roll my hips again as his fingers dig into my waist and he pulls me roughly against him.

I can't stop playing with fire. "Maybe you married a slut who wants you to watch her get all her holes filled."

"God," he groans as my words send him into a frenzy.

He thrusts his hips up, forcing the head of his cock to nudge repeatedly against the pleasure point deep inside me. I claw at his shoulders while I circle my hips, grinding against him as ripples of pleasure run up my back. Fuck, this is wild tonight. I should go on a girls' trip more often.

He pulls me close and kisses me deeply, our tongues tangling as my body responds to his every thrust. I edge closer and closer to my orgasm as the pleasure builds.

"Baby..." he moans, and I can feel him swelling inside me. "I want to watch someone else fuck you."

His words send a jolt of pleasure through me, and I explode. I cry out as I climax, my inner muscles convulsing and throbbing. My orgasm triggers his, and he groans as he unloads deep inside me. My pleasure seems never-ending as I continue to ride him through the waves of bliss.

When I finally come down, the pained look on his face tells me he's sensitive. Oops.

I slump against him, and he whispers, "That's a good girl."

Giggling, I kiss his neck, and he strokes my back gently. There's no way he really meant he wants to watch someone fuck me, but it was a nice fantasy in the moment. I rest my head against his shoulders and revel in the feel of being wrapped in his arms. I have my guy, and I'd never really want to act on those fantasies, right?

Right.

I run my hands through his silky chest hair and breathe a happy sigh. One guy is all I want...for real.

"So," he says thoughtfully, interrupting my post-orgasmic haze. "I take it you and January found out that Marilyn is a hotwife?"

His words make me laugh. I shouldn't be surprised that he knows. January's husband, Henry, probably told him. Our friends' group is large, and it's a bunch of guys who were in the same frat together in college, and they probably gossip together just as much as the wives do.

"Yeah. That's what prompted January's fun on the trip. I guess the idea turned Henry on."

My husband tucks a loose strand of hair behind my ear and caresses my face with a gentle touch before he pushes me upright so we're looking at each other.

"What are your thoughts, baby? Would you want to fuck another guy if I was there with you?"

He searches my eyes for an answer as my cheeks flush and my head spins. Is this really happening? I keep my tone light so he doesn't know how interested I am. "If you want me to be a slut for you, just say the word."

"How does Saturday sound?"

I jerk my head back, uncertain of what to say. Holy shit, is he for real? His spent cock twitches, and I can feel it growing hard inside me again. My eyes snap up to his as a pulse of desire makes me slowly grind against him. I need to make sure we're talking about the same thing before I get too excited.

"As in, I fuck someone this weekend...while you're watching?"

He chuckles. "Yes."

My entire body grows hot and my heart pounds as I think of fucking someone else while Eddie watches. I want this. The prospect of becoming a slut excites me more than it probably should, but this is an offer I can't refuse.

I continue to ride his cock as pings of delight make my nipples harden.

"Who would I fuck?"

That makes him laugh again. "Why don't you leave that to me? I have an idea."

My pulse speeds up, and I speak in a soft voice. "Okay. I trust you."

"Good," he growls, and tips me over on the couch so he can fuck me roughly.

By the time we both orgasm again, my brain is mush from pleasure and I don't think to ask him again who he wants me to fuck.

Chapter 2

Eddie makes me wait in suspense for a couple of days until he comes home on Thursday and tells me he wants me to fuck two guys he knows from the gym. My inner slut wants to dance around the room at the thought of two guys. This is better than I imagined. Eddie has talked about Russell and Lance before, but I've never met them. My dear husband claims Russell and Lance are going to be perfect for me, which causes me to raise an eyebrow, but I don't question why. I like the mystery of it all.

When Saturday rolls around, I'm a wet mess all day just thinking about tonight, and I spend extra time in the shower making sure everything is neat and tidy. It's been years since another guy has seen my pussy, and it's going to be two extra pairs of eyes. Oh god, is this nuts?

Shit, I need someone to tell me it's okay to be a hotwife. I briefly consider calling January, but I already know what she would say. January would tell me to hop on board the train to pound town. I need a neutral opinion, so I give my friend Mia a call.

She answers on the first ring. "Hey, I was just thinking of you. How was your trip?"

We chat for a few minutes about the trip last weekend, and I leave out anything about January fucking another guy. Mia's husband was on the

Aspen trip with my husband, so she might have heard the hotwife news, but I'm not going to tell her January's personal business.

When there's a natural lull in the conversation, I bring up the burning topic. "Did you hear Marilyn is now a hotwife?"

"Oh my God! I know, isn't that crazy?"

Ugh, she's going to think I'm an idiot. I'm about to laugh and agree when she continues. "I told Larry I'd fuck other guys for him, but he didn't seem impressed." She sighs dramatically. "Too bad."

Her response makes me laugh, and I can feel my anxiety easing. "Eddie liked the idea, and I'm actually fucking two guys tonight."

She squeals so loudly I have to pull the phone away from my ear before she demands, "Tell me everything!"

We spend a few minutes discussing the upcoming night, and by the time I get off the phone, I'm calmer. She was the perfect person to call.

I daydream the rest of the afternoon, and my mental thoughts swing between thinking this is a horrible idea to being so turned on I'm ready to stalk my husband down and fuck him just for arranging this for me. Eddie knows I won't share him, and he said he's not asking for that, but that doesn't mean he shouldn't get a week's worth of imaginary blowjob tokens. I might actually let him cash them in this time, too.

When the guys get here, I'm in the bedroom getting ready and my head is spinning with everything that's about to happen. Eddie is in the living room talking with Russell and Lance like they're all hanging out after a workout. Knowing they're out there and waiting for me makes me shiver. If everything goes right, I'm about to have an amazing workout while Eddie watches.

Studying my lingerie options, I try to decide what to wear. I'm not sure why I didn't think about this before now, but excitement has been scattering my brain. I want to feel sexy while Eddie enjoys the show. What's going to say "I'm a slut who wants to be stuffed in two holes at once?"

Eventually, I pick what seems like just the right thing. The lingerie set has a sheer red bra that laces up the back and a matching thong. I bought this lingerie set last month because I knew Eddie would like it, but I haven't had the time to model it for him. Now whenever I wear it in the future, we'll both remember tonight. It will be the gift that keeps on giving.

I'm almost ready. Butterflies swirl in my stomach, and I press on it to calm my nerves as I slip into my red heels. When I check myself out in the mirror, I get a pleasant jolt from how sexy I am. Damn, I'm smoking hot. My nipples are barely covered, and the thong offers plenty of access to my pussy and my ass. My clit pulses in pleasure as I imagine taking both men at once—which holes will they use? I hope they at least spit roast me. What's the fun of two guys if I don't get two cocks at once? Of course, the ultimate dream is having all three holes filled like a greedy slut, but there's no way I am going to protest about only having two. Like...poor me, I only get TWO holes filled!

I spend a few extra moments on my hair, leaving it long and curly, and I make sure my eyeliner and lipstick are perfect. It's all probably getting completely destroyed, but they'll get a few minutes to enjoy the sexy presentation.

I really wonder how they're going to use me. One of them better take the lead. I won't know what to do with myself, and I'll end up standing around like an idiot if they don't. The logistics of taking two men at once will be awkward if I have to direct the show.

The thought of two cocks sliding inside me makes my pussy flutter, and I shiver in pleasure. My mind flits again to the chance to have all three holes stuffed—maybe after tonight, Edward will consider doing it again with a third guy? Oh god, this is going to turn me into an insatiable slut. It's amazing.

This whole thing has happened so fast. Five days ago, Eddie told me he wanted to watch, and now there are two men in the living room ready to make it happen. My husband loves me and always tells me he'll do anything for me. I've never doubted him, but now I believe him even more.

But the most important thing is that Eddie is here with me. I couldn't do this without him. Knowing he'll be watching me with these two men is both nerve-wracking and so much hotter...and it's time to see how many times two men can make me come tonight.

CHAPTER 3

I gather my courage and strut out to the living room, where I find three sexy men. Eddie works hard at the gym, so I shouldn't be surprised that his two friends are buff. They probably all hang out in the free-weight section, grunting and being manly together. My nipples harden as I imagine their sweaty, hard bodies. Yeah, okay, I need to focus.

We have an L-shaped couch, and Eddie is on one side while the two visitors sit on the longer section. I can easily guess which guy is Russell based on Eddie previously mentioning that Russell was over 50. He's what I'd call a silver fox. His hair is dark brown but threaded with just enough gray at the temples to make my knees go a little weak. He has broad shoulders and biceps that make my toes curl. I know he could hold me down and make me never want to get up again. That's definitely Russell.

Lance, the younger man, looks like he's in his mid-20s. He's just as muscular as Russell, but with a leaner look. He probably logs more hours on the treadmill than lifting weights. His sandy-blond hair is long enough for me to tangle my fingers in, and he's just as good-looking as Russell. Both men are wearing t-shirts and jeans—as if they've come over to watch a movie and relax.

As I stand in front of the men, my confidence wavers for a split second. My revealing lingerie and towering heels suddenly feel out of place in this room filled with powerful men. Then I look at Eddie, and everything falls into place because he's grinning, clearly enjoying himself already.

All three men eye me hungrily while I shiver from pleasure. Russell lifts his eyebrows as he appraises me, and I can tell he appreciates my lingerie, while Lance lets out a low wolf whistle.

"Hi, guys," I say in my best seductive tone, trying to mask my nervousness.

I can feel my pussy getting wetter from the way they're staring at me, and it's like a switch gets flipped in my brain as all my fear drains away and is replaced with excitement. "Thanks for coming over."

Lance chuckles, and Russell's voice is a sexy rumble that punches me in the gut with lust and makes me tremble as he says, "That's quite the outfit."

I'm so turned on I'm practically vibrating, and I give him a coy smile. "I wanted to look pretty."

Russell's deep laugh gives him a dominant aura, and my pussy clenches in response. Oh yeah, we like Russell.

He appraises me with a smirk and asks, "Is pretty really the look you were going for?"

I bite my lip, uncertain how to answer. Should I tell him I wanted to be a gorgeous slut? He's looking at me like I'm a treat he's going to devour, and my core tightens as my body responds.

Before I say anything, he continues. "Because you look like a slut who wants both her holes used. Isn't that right?"

I gasp, and my eyes fly to Eddie. He's got a tiny grin on his face, and I can tell he told Russell what to say to me. The submissive part of my brain kicks in from the double dose of control from Eddie pulling the strings, and it turns me into the sluttiest version of myself. The world gets fuzzy around the edges, and I can feel all my mental reservations dropping before I finally respond.

"Yes. I want you to fuck any of my holes. Whatever you want. I'm yours to use."

My answer seems to please Russell. His eyes sparkle as he growls, "Good girl. Now come over here so we can use you."

I instinctively reply, "Yes, sir," and put a little extra sway in my hips as I walk to him. I'm ready to be an obedient toy and do whatever they say.

Russell takes my hand and pulls me into his arms so he can kiss me. He starts out soft as his lips brush against mine before groaning and nipping at my lower lip. When I open my mouth for him, he claims what I'm offering, sweeping his tongue inside to dance with mine. Heat spirals through my body, and I sigh into him.

When he lets go of me, Lance is there, pulling me into his lap. I straddle him, and there's nothing soft about Lance's kiss, not even for a second. He forces my mouth open with his tongue and groans into me. He palms my breast and teases at my nipple, making me moan.

He grinds me against his hard cock through his jeans as he grabs a handful of my ass. "Your husband said you were our toy for tonight. We're going to enjoy using you."

My head spins, and I think I fall more in love with my husband in that second. How did Eddie know how much I'd want them to treat me like a toy?

"I'm your toy," I agree and look over at Eddie.

Eddie is relaxed against the couch cushions, and his hard cock is creating a tent in his pants. I flash him a grin, and when he smiles back at me, I can tell he's dazed from lust. Knowing Eddie likes this relaxes me. The most important thing tonight is that we both have fun, and he's clearly enjoying me being a slut.

Russell takes my attention as he stands up and strips, and Lance tips me off of his lap and onto the couch so he can get up and remove his clothes as well. I stop worrying about anything other than the two cocks I'm about to have inside me.

Their cocks are both completely gorgeous. Russell's is just like him; thick and long, with veins bulging along the length of it. He's not fully hard yet, and I have a moment of doubt as I watch it growing before my eyes. Am I going to be able to take all of him? The thought sends a lightning bolt of pleasure to my clit. Who knows, but I'm up for the challenge.

Lance is also impressive. His cock is longer than Russell's, but not as thick. It's still more than enough to make me whimper and squirm with need. He's fully hard, and the bulbous head is already glistening with pre-cum.

I've always loved Eddie's cock, and he's got nothing to worry about in that department. But seeing these men and knowing I'm about to have two of my holes stuffed while my husband watches makes me even wetter. Neediness shoots through me, and I whimper a little. I'm really about to become a hotwife.

I don't know where to even start. Do they want me to suck on them—and if so, which one?

I don't have to debate long. Russell hauls me off the couch, pushes me to my knees, and steps back. "Open wide, slut."

Yep, I know which hole is getting used first. Lance steps into my line of sight as I open my mouth for him. I reach for his legs to steady myself as he slides his cock between my lips. I expected him to give me time to adjust, so I'm surprised when he slides straight down into my throat.

"You're just holes for us to use," Lance says, and I moan around his cock. "A fucktoy desperate to be covered in cum."

Ooooh. I am just a desperate fucktoy who wants their cum everywhere I can get it. I try to mumble yes around his cock as he pushes in further. He's stretching out my mouth, and he's so long that he's pushing at my gag reflex. He's going slow and not being rough, but it's still work to take him all the way in. I'm loving every moment.

Russell doesn't seem satisfied with Lance's slow pace. He places his hand on the back of my head and guides me, forcing me to take Lance's cock deeper as Lance's hips touch my face. I think for just a moment about that lipstick I carefully applied. It's going to be smeared all around my mouth after this. If my mouth wasn't full of cock, I'd laugh.

And we're just getting started.

Lust pings through my brain, and I moan loudly as I bob my head eagerly with Russell's hand guiding me. Each time Lance is buried to the hilt, it makes me crave even more debasement. This right here is what Eddie never gives me. He can't use me like this, and I don't even know how he knew I needed it.

Lance groans, and for a second, I think he's going to come down my throat. I'm eager for it, desperate for his cum, but he pulls out, panting. *Dammit!*

Before I have a chance to catch my breath, Russell kneels in front of me, his massive cock in my face. I lean forward on my hands and knees as he slides between my lips. Lance felt big in my mouth, but Russell is a whole new world. It's a tight fit, and he's not being gentle.

As he fucks my face, he's the perfect amount of roughness that I thought would only happen in my dreams. I can barely keep up, but I do my best, sucking and taking him as he threads his hands in my hair and holds onto my head to hold me right where he wants me.

I feel Lance move in behind me, his cock hard against my ass cheek.

"Good toys get what they want," Lance murmurs as he caresses my ass.

I moan around Russell's cock, and the vibrations make Russell murmur, "Fuck," as I throw myself on his cock more eagerly.

Russell groans, "Is our fucktoy ready to get it in two holes?"

I manage to nod as Russell continues to fuck my face. Lance responds by sliding his hands around me, one hand pulling on a nipple while the other hand moves between my legs. He slides my thong to the side and plays with my clit. He sets up a rhythm, brushing circles around my clit seemingly in tempo with Russell fucking my mouth.

My brain shuts off. All I can do is let these men use me, and I feel an orgasm building in a wave. I peep out tiny moans as the pleasure builds in layers, and when my climax hits, I come fast and hard, screaming around Russell's cock.

Russell swears and keeps thrusting into my mouth while Lance doesn't let up on my clit, drawing out the pleasure until I sag between them.

"Oh god," I whimper when Russell finally pulls out of my mouth.

Lance snickers and Russell reaches down to tilt up my chin. "Our fuck-toy better not be tired. That's only one hole. We've got more to use."

My head spins as I breathe out, "Yes...more."

"Good girl," he says as he stands up. "Come here."

I stumble to my feet, and Russell pulls my panties down my legs. I go to step out of my heels, but he stops me.

"Keep those on," he says as he sits down on the middle cushion of the couch and pulls me into his lap. I'm kneeling over his enormous cock, red stilettos on my feet, and I'm not sure I've ever felt filthier...or sexier.

I take a quick second to glance over and make sure Eddie is okay. My eyes go wide, and I giggle. He's more than okay; he's rock hard. He hasn't taken his cock out, but he's palming himself lightly through his pants.

I whimper with delight as Russell plunges a thick finger into my pussy. I'm wet enough that I know my juices are coating his hand. My body is eager for more, and I buck my hips against him, trying to grind down a little.

He slaps my tit hard enough to sting, and I gasp from the pleasurable pain.

"Dirty little slut," he growls. "Be a good girl and don't move. I decide when you get pleasure."

He punctuates the end of the sentence with a second finger pressed into me, and I groan. My leg muscles shake as he starts to finger fuck me, stretching his fingers wide apart. I cry out from the sting as I imagine his fingers are his cock. I'm practically in a frenzy, and I can't stop my hips from moving, but this time he doesn't try to stop me.

When he removes his fingers, I cry out, frustrated at the sudden emptiness. I must be pouting because he laughs at me and tweaks my nipple. "Poor greedy slut just wants cock. How about we both give it to you?"

My pussy clenches with eagerness, and I moan, "Yes, please."

This is all I've been wanting since my husband offered me two men. I want them to fuck two holes at once until I'm mindless from pleasure and can't even speak.

Russell's eyes narrow, and he presses his wet fingers against my mouth. I know what he wants. I open my mouth, and he slips them in. I suck on his fingers, cleaning my own juices off him. The saltiness of his skin mixed with my unique taste is delicious, and I moan, gripping his wrist and sucking his fingers as if he's offered me the finest ambrosia. I'm such a slut.

"Good girl."

He pulls his fingers free of my mouth and lines his cock up with my pussy. I have barely a moment to adjust before he pulls me down, spearing me on his gigantic cock.

"Ohhhh, god!" I cry out.

The stretch is incredible and overwhelming. I feel myself soaking him as he bottoms out. I'm so tight around him I can feel every single inch of him. He flexes his hips, forcing me to fuck him and barely giving me time to adjust to his size. I whimper and moan as I work to meet his thrusts. He holds onto my hips and rocks me against him.

He's so thick he almost hurts, but when Lance comes behind me and wraps his hand around me and moves it between my legs to play with my clit, everything suddenly feels amazing. I've never felt this full. My body feels invaded, but in the most amazing way.

Heat builds in my core, and I moan as it spirals through me. I rotate my hips harder, my tits bouncing. The cups on my bra are already so low that they slip down, exposing my nipples. Russell groans and reaches forward, pulling one into his mouth as he continues to pound into me. At the same time, Lance pinches my clit and I scream as a sudden orgasm hits me.

White-hot pleasure ripples through me, and stars sparkle along the corners of my vision. They fuck me through it, drawing out the pleasure as my pussy clenches on Russell's cock.

Russell slows down, rocking against me gently and in my post-orgasmic haze, I hear the flip-top of a bottle from behind me a second before I feel Lance's fingers between my ass cheeks. The lube on his fingers is cold, and I tense up for a moment as I feel him press at my hole there.

"Relax," he says in my ear. His voice is firm but not commanding the way Russell's is. "You want this, don't you?"

I'm not sure I can form words, but I'm able to say, "Mmm hmm."

"Then let me in."

His finger probes at my ass, and I force myself to relax. Russell keeps rocking in me slowly, just enough to keep pleasure rippling through me. There is a disorienting moment when Lance's finger presses past my rim, and then the sensation of fullness overwhelms me. I whimper and fight my instinct to push back against the feeling.

"Oh, good girl," Lance says, his voice full of praise that makes me want to wiggle and whimper with happiness. "But there's a lot more. You're going to take more like a good little slut, aren't you?"

"Yes," I moan.

I need this. Oh god, how I need this.

He doesn't respond as he removes his finger. I hear him add more lube, and then a second finger is pressing into me. I cry out, craving this more and more as he strokes his fingers in me.

"Give me more," I whimper. "Fuck me. Fill me with your cock. Please, please, please, fuck my ass."

I hear Eddie moan, and I focus enough to look at him. Eddie has his cock out now, and he's stroking. His eyes are wide, and the expression of bliss on his face matches how I feel.

Then Lance grants me my wish. There's a cold sensation of more lube before I feel his cock pressing my ass open. It's so much bigger than his fingers, and I'm already stretched full by Russell's massive cock.

I cry out, whimpering, trying to take his cock in my ass. I want to be a good fucktoy for them, but I'm so full. This is even more than I expected.

"Breathe," he says, stroking his hand down my back.

I exhale shakily, and I can hear him smile as I loosen up around him. "Good girl, taking everything we give you."

He pushes into me farther, and I can feel the stretch, but it's bearable now. He drills into me slowly until he's buried all the way in my ass.

Holy fuck. This is amazing. I'm so grateful that they did it this way because if I had to manage Russell's extra-large girth in my ass, I don't know how it would have gone.

"Does this feel good?" Russell groans as both men move in me.

I'm so stuffed and aching that the room spins. "Can't think," I whimper.

"You don't have to think," he chuckles. "Dirty sluts just have to get fucked."

His words make me moan. He's right. I don't have to think. I just have to let them fill me.

The men move together and find their rhythm. They pace their strokes so I'm caught between them, always full as they press in and out of me. The pleasure is so intense I can't do anything but cry out as I race towards another orgasm. This one is going to be big.

I can feel my pussy and my ass gripping at them, eager for them, desperate for more. I hold on to Russell's shoulders so they can stroke into me faster. With my body so stretched, they're both hitting spots deep inside of me that are sparking waves of pleasure. I'm crying out gibberish, begging for release but knowing that they aren't stopping me from coming. I don't know what else I need, but I'm desperate to come.

I sense movement by my side, and when I look, Eddie's right next to me. He's stripped, and his thick cock is out, aimed towards me. I've never seen him so hard.

Letting go of Russell's shoulders, I lean over and cry out as he grips the back of my head and pulls my mouth onto his cock. Both Russell and Lance groan in unison, and Eddie curses as he pushes my mouth down the length of his shaft, farther than I usually take him.

This is everything I wanted. I'm stuffed in all of my holes, and I've never been so full. My husband, my wonderful husband, is here, filling the last hole and making my dream come true. This is what was missing.

Russell's thrusts get sharper and shorter, and I know he's close to coming. Lance has an iron grip on my hips, and I think he's holding on by a thread. And Eddie has never fucked my mouth like this, this urgent, this needy, this fucking hard.

I feel like the biggest slut ever as Eddie comes in a surge, firing down my throat. I can barely keep up. Some of his cum dribbles down my chin and chest as I try to gulp it all down. The men in my other holes move faster, making it even more difficult.

The feeling of being coated with his cum is the last thing I need. The orgasm slams into me like a ton of bricks, and I turn into a wild woman, riding the cocks inside me, chasing the pleasure as it spikes and recedes. I'm moaning and crying out, unable to think of anything as the rapture overtakes me.

My husband's cock is still in my mouth, and I barely hear Russell groan out a curse as he slams into me and explodes. He paints my cave walls with his warm cum, which sets off another full-blown orgasm as Lance empties ropes of sticky cum deep into my ass.

The three men fuck me through my orgasm and theirs until we collapse into a sweaty heap. There's cum leaking out of me from everywhere. I have no way to know whose is where, and I giggle deliriously from pleasure. I've never been happier.

Eddie settles down next to me, and Lance and Russell slowly pull out as cum drips and coats my thighs. I whimper at the emptiness, painfully sore and already wanting more of everything.

Russell and Lance get up from the couch and slump down onto the cushions while Eddie strokes my hair. When the men are cleaned up and dressed, they take turns bending down to kiss me. I have no energy to even lift my head, and I let them come to me.

"You're fucking gorgeous," Russell says. "Thank you."

I murmur my thanks, and when he moves away, Lance is there, kissing me just as fiercely as that first time. "Thanks," he says. "That was fantastic."

Eddie tells me he'll be right back, and he ushers them out of the living room.

When they're gone, I lie on the couch grinning and completely at peace. I'm coated with cum, sore, and blissfully in love with my husband. I close my eyes and drift while I listen to him say goodbye to the men at the front door.

I don't know how long I'm out of it before Eddie comes back and lifts me into his arms. He carries me into the bathroom and sets me on my feet, removing the last of my lingerie. He's naked, and I barely have time to think before he's lowering me into his lap into a warm bath. Oh wow, I was so out of it I didn't even hear him running the water.

We soak together, and he cleans me gently with a washcloth.

"How do you feel, baby?"

"Wonderful," I say with a smile, knowing he can't see it.

God, tonight rivals any sexual experience I've ever had, but it was only this amazing because of Eddie.

When he laughs, he sounds so delighted that it makes me giggle with him. After he quiets, he asks, "Do you really mean that?"

I turn in the tub so I'm looking at him, and I can see he honestly needs to know. I get goosebumps realizing just how thoughtful my husband is. Smiling at him, I wrap my arms around his neck as the words come from my soul.

"I'm more than wonderful, and tonight was absolutely perfect."

His eyes twinkle. I can tell he's happy as he beams at me with love. "It really was, wasn't it? I can't believe we just did that. It was…"

When he trails off, I ask, "What?"

His grin widens, and I swear he's blushing a little. "Wild."

"Wasn't it?" I ask him as I settle against his chest again. "We're both filthy. What does that say about us?"

"That we're incredibly lucky and perfect for each other."

He kisses my head, and we let the steam and warmth of the bath soak in and ease our bodies. I don't want to move. I feel safe and loved.

He kisses my head again and whispers, "Are you going to want to do this again?"

A zing of delight runs through me as I reply. "How about just one extra cock next time? Three at once should only be for special occasions."

He laughs. "Deal."

Oh god, in the morning I'm calling Mia. She'll never believe I took a guy in each hole.

The thought makes me giggle, and Eddie asks, "What are you thinking about?"

I laugh again. "I've decided I really like being your slut, and I have the best husband ever."

"Good." He gives a contented hum that I can feel through his chest.

Yep, I really do have the most amazing husband.

The End

March Hotwife

Hotwife of the Month Club 3

Lacey Cross

CHAPTER 1

My heart races, blood pounding in my ears as Felicity's words sear into my brain. "Oh God, it was incredible," she gushes through the phone, her voice practically giddy. "The most mind-blowing sex ever. Two hard cocks ravaging me while Edward watched, stroking himself."

"Fuck," I whisper, squirming in my kitchen chair. Wetness pools between my thighs as I picture the scene. Strangers roughly taking my friend, using her, as her husband looks on with dark, hungry eyes. "I...I don't know if Lawrence would..." The words lodge in my throat.

"You'd be surprised," she says with a salacious giggle. "Men have needs–filthy urges. The key is unlocking them. It's not for everyone, though. I'm just grateful Eddie wanted it. Whatever James told the guys about Marilyn being a hotwife got them all riled up."

I laugh because it's true. Every year, our husbands take a trip to Lake Aspen, staying at James's family's huge-ass mansion. No wives allowed. Probably so they can drink and play poker all night, pretending they're still in college and aren't middle-aged men. But this time, James shared sordid stories about letting other men plow his wife Marilyn and how it's reinvigorated their sex life. Fuck. The thought alone has me dripping and craving something so wrong but so delicious.

My pussy throbs as I hang up the phone, Felicity's words echoing in my mind. The idea of being a hotwife, of having Lawrence's blessing to fuck any man I want, sends shivers straight to my aching clit. I squeeze my thighs together, trying to ease the growing need.

Closing my eyes, I let the fantasy consume me. Strange hands roaming my body, pinching my nipples, spreading my legs. A hard, muscular body crushing me into the mattress. The delicious burn as a thick, unfamiliar cock sinks into me. I gasp, rubbing my thighs together again as my imagination runs wild.

I whimper under my breath, so turned on that I'm almost desperate. If Lawrence knew the filthy things I picture when I touch myself sometimes. How I use my biggest sex toy and pretend it's another man's cock. How I moan as I come over and over again to thoughts of new lovers taking me in every hole.

I'm so lost in my daydreams, I don't hear Lawrence come in until his deep voice snaps me out of it.

"Hey beautiful." He sets his briefcase down and eyes me. "What's got you all hot and bothered?"

I blush, knowing my face is flushed and my nipples are poking through my thin shirt. I'm hyper aware of every nerve ending in my body.

"Oh, nothing." I lie breathlessly, forcing an innocent smile. "Just gossiping with Felicity."

Lawrence chuckles, his eyes twinkling with mischief as he walks over. He plants a soft kiss on my forehead and I shudder at his touch against my fevered skin.

"You sure, baby?" he murmurs. "Cause you look like you'd come if I rubbed up against you."

Oh God. If he keeps talking like that, I just might come without him even touching me. I'm so fucking turned on I can barely think straight. I want to blurt out all my fantasies, beg him to let me be the slut I crave to be. But I chicken out.

"Hah, you're so full of shit." I laugh, trying to will my body to calm down. "I'm just hungry. Let's eat."

Lawrence smirks knowingly but lets it drop. He has no idea what I'm imagining. How badly I need to be filled and fucked senseless. My whole body is vibrating with pent-up arousal.

Someday, maybe I'll work up the nerve to tell him. But for now, I'll have to settle for my wild imagination and a drawer full of toys to satisfy my cravings.

We decide on grilled chicken and pasta for dinner. I can't keep my eyes off Lawrence as we move around the kitchen, preparing our food. His broad shoulders strain against his shirt, and that dimple in his cheek when he grins sets me on fire. Six years of marriage and I'm still crazy for him.

As I watch him chop vegetables, all I can think about is Felicity's confession. The idea of getting fucked by a stranger with Lawrence's permission has me dripping into my panties. I shift on my stool, the seam of my jeans rubbing my swollen clit. Am I a slut for craving this? Would Lawrence be disgusted if he knew about my depraved fantasies?

"You're awfully quiet, baby," Lawrence sounds worried as we sit to eat. "Everything all right?"

Fuck it, I need to tell him. I suck in a breath, my nipples pebbling to stiff peaks. "I'm good. Just thinking about something wild Felicity told me."

Lawrence quirks an eyebrow, fork pausing halfway to his full lips. "Oh? What has Edward done now?"

I can tell by his tone that he thinks Edward did something bad. I laugh and choose my words carefully. "Well, apparently, she and Edward have been experimenting. In the bedroom."

"Experimenting?" He takes a bite, chewing slowly, and then licks his lips. Fuck, I want that tongue on my clit.

I nod, feeling the desire simmering in my core. "Mmm hmm. She's been fucking other guys while Edward watches and gets off on it."

Lawrence chokes on his water, slamming the glass down. When he recovers, he sounds amused. "Jesus. This is James and Marilyn's fault for starting this hotwife shit."

I shrug and my tank top strap slips down. He eyes my bare shoulder and I keep my tone light. "Come on, it's not like they're forcing anyone. If people are exploring, it's because they want to."

He shoots me a speculative look, his blue eyes narrowing. "But why the hell would any sane man want to watch his wife get fucked by someone else?"

"Maybe it turns them on," I suggest, playing with the rim of my glass. Imagining Lawrence stroking his cock, watching me get split open on another man's dick. "It's taboo. Risqué. An exciting way to spice up a marriage." I peer at him over the glass rim as I take a sip. "They're both getting off on it."

Lawrence barks out a laugh. "I bet SHE'S the one getting off."

Shit. This isn't going how I'd hoped. Time to be direct. "I know it sounds wild, but Felicity said it's brought them closer than ever. That it's the best thing they've done for their relationship."

Silence stretches, his jaw twitches. "Well, good for them, I guess. Whatever works."

Fuck. He's not jumping on the idea like I'd fantasized. But did I really expect him to? I shrug again, twirling pasta on my fork. "Yeah. Have you ever fantasized about trying new things? Spicing up our sex life?"

A blush creeps up Lawrence's neck, and he clears his throat. "I mean, sure, who hasn't? But there's a big difference between fantasies and actually fucking other people in reality."

Yeah, okay. Time to change the topic. "Of course," I agree, reaching over and squeezing his hand. "I'm not saying we should run out and find a stranger who wants to fuck me. But maybe we should roleplay, or talk dirty, or share our fantasies."

I gaze up at Lawrence through my lashes, a hunger coursing through my veins. His eyes darken with lust as he leans in close. "You holding out on me, baby?" he growls. "Got some naughty fantasies you haven't shared with your husband yet?"

Fuck. A moan escapes my lips. "Oh, the filthy things that run through my mind." My voice is a silky purr. "You have no idea how I think about being used like a slut."

Lawrence pulls me out of my chair and into his lap. He slants his mouth over mine, his tongue delving deep. I melt against him, my body on fire. His roaming hands ignite sparks across my tingling skin.

"Tell me," he commands between kisses. "Every detail. Because I'm going to make all those nasty fantasies come true."

Oh God. Promises, promises.

When he makes a move to slide his hand up my shirt, I push him away and stand up. "Last one naked has to go down on the other!"

He's up from the table in a flash and chasing me to the bedroom. A trail of clothing litters the hallway behind us. We're both naked by the time we tumble onto the bed, laughing. I'm not sure which one of us won, so we call it a draw.

He covers me with his body and he trails kisses down my neck to my tits. "So, what are Felicity and Edward up to?" he murmurs, sucking a stiff nipple into his mouth.

Oh? Someone wants details, does he? He looks up at me and I flash him a coy grin. "Apparently, she had a night with two of his gym buddies. Said it blew her mind..." I moan in bliss as he positions himself between my legs and presses the tip of his cock against my entrance.

"And what did you say after she told you that?" Lawrence asks as he rubs the swollen head through my slick folds.

"Mmm, not much." I moan louder as his cock slides inside me. "I just listened. Though I must admit..." I arch against him and rock my hips, dropping my voice to a seductive lilt. "The whole idea is hot."

Lawrence groans and speeds up his thrusts. Pleasure ripples from my fingertips to my toes and I convulse beneath him, every nerve ending alight. Holy hell, what's got into him? This is fantastic.

"You like the idea of some other guy fucking you?" he growls, his words make me quiver in delight.

"Yes! Fuck, yes." I whimper. He rams deep in one swift thrust, and I nearly come on the spot.

Pinned beneath him, I'm lost in ecstasy. His heavy balls slap my ass as he pistons into my pussy. I lock my ankles around him, pulling him deeper. Harder. Faster.

"Want to pretend I'm some random guy dominating this prime piece of ass?" His words make me clench tight around him.

"Uh huh," I pant. "Be rough. Use me like a fucktoy."

He pulls out, and as soon as I unhook my legs from around him, he flips me over onto my knees. I cry out as he slams back into me. I don't know what is making my husband so crazed right now, but I love it.

Grasping my hips, he rails me into the mattress and the headboard bangs against the wall. I surrender to the forbidden fantasy. He's not my husband but some well-hung stranger. He's a large, tattooed guy, fucking me with his powerful strokes. Ruthlessly pounding my slutty cunt into submission.

My mind goes blank, overwhelmed by the obscene pleasure. Tension builds with each hammering thrust as I rush towards my orgasm.

I dig my fingers into the bedding and my thigh muscles quiver with every thrust. His cock is hitting all the right places, and I'm so close, dangling on the edge. I moan and gasp as the joy intensifies with each passing second. This is a wonderful fantasy.

He holds my hips steady while he drills into me. My clit throbs and every thrust hits the magical spot deep inside me that sends tendrils of bliss up my spine.

"God, you feel so good. Don't stop," I moan as I feel myself about ready to explode.

He slams into me harder and rumbles, "You're a dirty little slut who likes it rough, don't you?"

When he reaches beneath me and rubs my clit, the delight makes me cry out, "Yes, oh yes!"

I'm amazed he's talking dirty to me, and the surprise skyrockets me into my climax. I moan loudly, and my clit pulsates from a zing of delight.

The fantasy of another guy fucking me is still playing out in my mind—it's another man thrusting into me as his cock slides in and out of my wet pussy. I can feel his hard length stretching me, filling me completely. Lawrence's pounding becomes the rhythm of that other man's relentless thrusts. When Lawrence finally comes, it's someone else filling me and coating my pussy with his hot, sticky cum.

When my body finally stops shaking from the pleasure, Lawrence rolls off me and lies on his back, panting. I snuggle against him, sighing contentedly as he wraps an arm around me. He's my husband again. The man I love. Jesus, I think I enjoy roleplaying.

We lie there quietly for a while, basking in the afterglow. When my heartbeat finally calms, I break the silence. "That was intense."

He laughs. "Is it wrong that I enjoyed imagining you fucking someone else?"

"Not at all. It's sexy as hell." I grin as I kiss his cheek and rub his chest.

Lawrence props himself up on one elbow, his blue eyes questioning as they lock onto mine. "What if I wanted it? You know, you being with someone else."

My breath hitches, arousal spiking through me. I don't want to sound too excited, so I try to aim for casual. "Oh?"

He nods. "I thought it would make me crazy, picturing another man touching you. But it's like a switch was flipped on in my brain, and now I want it. I want you to fuck someone else and come back to me so I can prove to you, over and over, that no one can make you feel as good as I can."

My affection for my husband warms me. "You know you have nothing to prove. I'm yours, always."

"I know, baby. But something in me still wants to stake my claim." His wandering hand dips lower, and I buck against his skilled fingers as they find my still-sensitive clit. "I want to ruin you for anyone else."

"Yes," I hiss, grinding shamelessly against his fingers. "I'm yours, only yours." He can ruin me like this any day of the week.

His mouth crushes down on mine in a searing kiss as his fingers bring me to the peak again. I'm still quivering through the aftershocks when he pulls back, something unreadable in his expression.

"I want to try it. At least once, just to see."

It takes my pleasure-fogged brain a moment to catch up and I need to make sure he's serious. "You mean me actually sleeping with someone else for real and not roleplay?"

Lawrence swallows hard, his eyes searching mine. "If you want to. You can fuck someone else and then I can remind you who you belong to."

He shudders, and I feel the evidence of his arousal twitch against my thigh.

I can hardly dare to believe it. "Are you sure you'd be okay with that?"

He kisses me again, hot and hungry. When he breaks it off, he says, "More than okay. In fact, I want you to choose the guy. If you could fuck one other man, just once, who would it be?"

Holy fuck, he's serious. "I...oh wow, I don't know," I hedge, my mind reeling. "That's a big question."

"I know. You don't have to decide right now." Lawrence pulls me into the curve of his body, spooning me from behind. "Just tell me when you do. Because the second you pick him..." He nuzzles into my neck, his cock hardening against the cleft of my ass. "I'm going to spend hours fucking you until you forget any name but mine."

God, that's hot. I press back against him with a needy whine. My head is spinning from the conversation. This is a massive step, one that could change our marriage irrevocably. But my wonderful, doting husband wants to share me and then reclaim me afterwards–how can I possibly say no to that?

Chapter 2

A few days pass and all I can think about is choosing someone to fuck. It's St. Patrick's Day, and I have to go to the gym and run some errands before we meet up with friends tonight at a pub. Maybe when we get home later, I'll get him to roleplay with me again.

I'm just about to head out the door to the gym when my phone rings. It's my friend Debra, and from the tone of her voice, I can tell she's got something juicy to dish about.

"Oh my God, have you heard about Felicity?" she blurts before I can even say hello. "Apparently, she's sleeping with other men while her husband watches! Can you believe it?"

Ugh, this might take a while. I wander into the kitchen and put her on speakerphone as I start unloading the dishwasher. "Yeah, she mentioned it to me the other day. Sounds like she and Edward are exploring some new things together."

"Exploring?" Debra scoffs. "More like fucking up their marriage! I can't imagine Vincent ever letting me sleep around like that. It's just wrong."

I bristle at the judgment in her tone. "Is it though? I mean, if they're both on board and it's making them happy, who are we to criticize?"

She argues, "Oh, come on. This is just an excuse for them to cheat."

I don't enjoy her slut shaming, so I choose my words carefully. "Every couple is different, Deb. What's right for you and Vincent may not be right for me and Lawrence, or Felicity and Edward."

"Fine, but I still think it's weird," she grumbles. "Anyway, did you see the drama going down on the group's social media page with Ana and Max? I swear, some of our friends are crazy."

Ugh, I need to call Ana and find out what's going on. I don't want to hear it secondhand. I'll call her tomorrow.

As Debra launches into the latest gossip, I tune her out as my mind drifts to thoughts of me choosing a guy. Debra would throw a fit if she knew I was going to be a hotwife as well. I'm not going to tell her and will just imagine being pleasured by other men while Lawrence waits to fuck me afterwards.

Heat floods me and I feel my skimpy spandex shorts I'd thrown on for my workout growing damp. I'm so lost in my fantasies that I don't hear Lawrence come in until his arms are wrapping around my waist from behind. I startle, nearly squeaking in surprise as his lips find the sensitive spot behind my ear.

"Hey, I gotta run," I say hurriedly to Debra. "Talk to you later, okay?"

I end the call without waiting for her answer and spin in Lawrence's embrace, my breath catching at the intensity in his blue eyes. "Well, hello there," My voice drips with honey as I loop my arms around his neck. "To what do I owe this pleasant surprise?"

His hands skim down to my spandex-clad ass, and he kisses my neck. "Couldn't resist. You're sexy when you're fired up and passionately defending our friends."

Shit, how long had he been watching? I mold against him, tilting my head to give him better access to my neck. "Mmm, you like seeing me get all worked up, huh?"

"You know I do," he groans, sucking on my pulse point. "Especially when you're worked up in more ways than one." He presses his hand against my pussy, rubbing me through my shorts.

Hmm, do I have time to convince him to fuck me now? I don't want to wait until later. He kisses me deeply as his tongue delves into my mouth, staking his claim. I wrap my arms around him, and calculate how long it will take to get his cock inside me.

We're breathless when he finally stops kissing me. "I'm going to fuck you so hard once you choose a guy." He punctuates his words with another firm rub against my pussy.

I shudder from longing, and my body is disappointed that he's not bending me over the kitchen table. "I guess I better decide who I want to fuck, then."

Lawrence holds my gaze a moment longer before stepping back, smoothing his hair. "Yep. Now I need to mow the lawn, and you get that sexy ass to the gym before I decide to keep you home and remind you who you belong to."

Wait, is that a threat? I almost try to be sassy and get him to fuck me, but I decide to be good because the pleasurable pain of waiting is giving me a nice buzz.

"Yes, sir," I give him a sassy salute and twitch my ass at him as I grab my bag and saunter out the door. His responding groan makes me smile.

Jesus, I don't even need to fuck someone else. How possessive Lawrence gets by just thinking about sharing me is amazing.

I definitely can have some fun with this tonight when we get home from the pub.

CHAPTER 3

While I'm at the gym, I realize who I want to fuck when my thoughts keep drifting to Heath, Lawrence's devastatingly handsome boss. As I move around the circuit, I can't shake the image of his chiseled features and those piercing blue eyes that seem to see right through me whenever I talk to him at one of my husband's work parties.

Hmm, I wonder if he's got a huge cock. I snort to myself. Well, he's got a massive ego, so at least something of his is big. He probably isn't even that great in bed and expects the woman to do all the heavy lifting while she worships him. But maybe he's got something worth worshiping?

When I'm done at the gym and back home, I try to distract myself by scrubbing the bathtub, but all I can think about is how my husband would respond if I told him I wanted to fuck his boss. I need to stop fixating on someone off-limits. I doubt Lawrence would be happy to share me with Heath. Yet, I still can't shake the thought.

I'm wound up and horny when it's time to get ready for our night out. Lawrence and I rarely go to the pub since we don't drink anymore, so this feels like a special occasion. I'm excited to chat with our friends and relax before coming home and fucking my husband's brains out.

When I select my black lace panty and bra set, I have a brief daydream about someone other than Lawrence removing them. When that person turns into Heath, I shake my head to dispel the vision, determined to think of anyone else. It doesn't help. Yep, I'm a dirty girl.

I take extra care getting ready, slipping into a curve-hugging black miniskirt and an emerald green blouse. A pair of sky-high stilettos complete the look, making my legs look a mile long. I feel sexy and desirable.

The pub is packed when we arrive, a sea of green with everyone already well on their way to a good time. The air is thick with laughter and lively Irish music. We easily find our friends at a round table in the back, and Lawrence and I order sodas to go with our fish and chips.

When the server brings us our drinks, I sip mine, feeling restless. I've been turned on all day, and I can already feel my panties getting damp just from my slutty thoughts of fucking someone else. What would happen if I told Lawrence I wanted to fuck his boss? Would he pull me into the bathroom and take me against the wall in a fit of jealousy? Mmm, that sounds good to me. Maybe I should find out.

Lawrence rests his hand on my knee under the table and I force myself to stop fidgeting as I lean into him, my lips brushing his ear. "I have a confession to make," I murmur, emboldened by my buzzing pussy. "I've been thinking about who I would fuck."

Luckily, the pub is noisy enough that no one else can overhear what I'm saying. Lawrence's eyes sparkle, his fingers tickling up my inner thigh. "Oh really? Who does my slutty wife want to fuck?"

I'm about to answer when a familiar figure catches my eye across the room. It's Heath. He looks yummy in a fitted green button-down shirt with his sleeves rolled up to reveal his toned forearms. My mouth goes dry at the sight of him. Holy shit, what are the chances of him being here?

My mind freezes and all I can think about is fucking Heath. Right now.

Lawrence follows my gaze, and I can tell the moment he figures out what's going on because his body goes taut. "My boss? You want to fuck Heath?"

I swallow hard, my heart hammering. This is it, the moment of truth. "Yes, but only if you agree to it. I want to see if I can seduce him tonight and fuck him somewhere private."

Lawrence is silent for a long moment, his expression unreadable. Then, slowly, a sexy grin spreads across his face. "You naughty minx. Do you think you can?"

I'm about to answer him when he leans in close, his breath warm against my ear. "I want you to do it. Bring him to his knees. But you have to promise to tell me every detail afterwards."

His words make me even more aroused. Wow, he's agreeing to this! I give him a quick, hard kiss before standing on shaky legs. "I promise. Now watch me, babe. I'm about to make you proud."

Ignoring the butterflies rioting in my stomach, I undo the top buttons of my blouse as I make my way to the bar where Heath is waiting for a drink. I sidle up next to him and give him my best flirty tone. "Fancy meeting you here, stranger."

Heath's eyes widen as he takes me in. "Mia, wow. I almost didn't recognize you. You're stunning."

I preen a little under his appreciative gaze, leaning forward to give him a better view of my cleavage. "You don't look so bad yourself. Green really brings out those baby blues."

He chuckles. "Just getting into the holiday spirit. What're you drinking?"

"Oh, I'm not here to drink," I reply, holding his gaze meaningfully. "I'm more interested in the company. Especially tall, dark, and handsome company."

Heath's brows shoot up at my forwardness, but I don't miss the way his gaze dips to my cleavage. He shifts closer and murmurs, "Is that so?"

"It is. I was actually thinking about you earlier, and now here you are. It's like fate."

He looks amused. "Were you now? And what were you thinking about?"

I lean in closer and coo at him, my voice soft and inviting. "Well, I was wondering if your cock is as big as your ego."

Heath barks out a laugh and I can tell he didn't expect my response because his eyes widen in surprise. There's a flicker of desire in them as he responds. "Mia, I'm flattered, but you're Lawrence's wife. I'm not going to fuck you."

I give him a coy smile, placing my hand on his arm. "Are you sure? Lawrence and I have an arrangement. He's okay with it. Just look at him."

I tip my head towards where my husband is sitting. Heath's eyes dart over to Lawrence, and Lawrence gives him a small nod of approval.

This is so damn filthy to be propositioning Heath while my husband watches. I'm so turned on, I'm practically dripping.

I trace my fingers along the neckline of Heath's shirt, my voice sultry. "So what do you say? Are you going to satisfy my curiosity? Just one fuck. No strings attached."

My pussy throbs and I struggle to suppress the urge to press up against him.

His gaze smolders. "If that's what you want, I'm going to make you come so hard, you'll be begging for more."

A sudden surge of excitement courses through me as I slip my hand into his. "Then take me somewhere private," I breathe, my eyes sparkling.

Without another word, he rises from his seat. His touch is firm as he guides me out of the pub. My inner slut is ready for whatever happens.

The cool night air nips at my flushed cheeks as Heath leads me around the back of the building. Distant streetlights cast a faint glow over the area, but it's mostly cloaked in darkness. The rhythmic click of my high heels echoes off the concrete walls, sounding overly loud, like it's announcing to the world that I'm about to get fucked in an alley.

A thrill races up my spine as I follow Heath deeper into the shadows. I can't believe I'm actually doing this—sneaking off to fuck my husband's sexy boss while Lawrence waits inside and imagines what I'm doing. It's so wrong but feels so deliciously right.

Heath stops and turns to face me, the sharp angles of his chiseled features outlined by the faint light. The shadows make his expression difficult to read.

"Mia, are you absolutely certain about this?" he asks, his deep voice is tinged with longing. "If we cross this line, there's no going back."

I gaze up at him, my pulse racing as a reckless hunger overtakes me. For days now I've fantasized about fucking someone else, craving another man's touch, his kisses, and his thick cock. Now that it's within reach, I refuse to let anything stop me from taking what I want.

"I need this. I need you. Please?" My voice is breathy but certain. "Give it to me rough and tell me how slutty I am."

I blush at how I'm demanding he talk dirty to me, but it's something that Lawrence isn't always comfortable doing. I need more of it. If I'm going to fuck someone else, I want it to be different from what I can get from Lawrence, or else there's no point.

My stomach flutters when he gives me a slow, wicked grin. "Well, in that case..." He leans in close, his minty breath caressing my ear. "Get ready to be thoroughly fucked, you naughty little slut. I'm going to wreck you for any other man," he promises darkly. "By the time I'm done, your greedy cunt will only crave my cock."

Mmm, yes. He takes direction well. His words make me shiver as he walks me backwards. The rough brick wall presses against my shoulder blades through the thin silk of my blouse as his tall, muscular frame cages me in.

He grabs my chin, his grip firm as he tilts my head up. His mouth claims mine in a searing kiss, his tongue delving past my parted lips to stroke against mine. The taste of mint makes me whimper into the kiss, my fingers curling into the fabric of his shirt. Desire pulses between my thighs, and I can tell my panties are soaked.

He trails kisses along my neck. "Mmm, you taste so sweet," he murmurs against my skin. "I could devour you."

"Please," I breathe. I'm desperate for his hands on me, his cock inside me, to be filled and used for his pleasure. "Fuck me. I'm yours tonight."

He chuckles, the low sound vibrating against my throat and making goosebumps prickle my overheated flesh. "Just wait. I'll give you exactly what you need."

The cool air soothes my fevered skin as he shoves my skirt up around my waist. His fingers dig into my inner thigh, his grip just shy of painful as he hitches my leg up and around his waist. He groans appreciatively as he rubs his fingers over the damp lace of my skimpy black panties.

"Fuck, Mia. Did you wear these for me?" he asks, his voice a low rumble. "Did you hope I'd rip them off and stuff that pretty little pussy full of cock?"

I moan at his words, my head falling back against the bricks. Oh god, did I? I didn't know he'd be here tonight, but when I was getting dressed, I thought about him and how it would feel to have another man peel these panties off me besides Lawrence.

Instead of answering him directly, I push against him and beg. "Fuck me, please. Don't make me wait."

"Dirty slut," he says approvingly, eyes flashing with lust. "I'm going to wreck you."

The delicate lace of my panties disintegrates beneath his powerful hands. He carelessly tosses the scrap of fabric aside, and I gasp at how quickly it happened. A new rush of wetness floods my core as I roll my hips forward, seeking more friction against my aching clit.

He presses two thick fingers against my slick, swollen folds, circling my entrance and making me whine.

"You're absolutely dripping." There's a hint of masculine pride and satisfaction in his voice. "So wet and ready for my cock, aren't you?"

Slowly, maddeningly, he circles my clit with the rough pad of his thumb. Pleasure streaks through me like lightning.

"Heath, please!" I practically sob, my nails digging into his broad shoulders. "I need you inside me. I can't take it."

"Since you asked so sweetly..."

He sinks his fingers into my tight channel, and I cry out, clenching around him. He starts pumping them in and out, finger fucking me hard and fast. Obscene wet sounds fill the alley as his thumb rubs circles on my clit and he slams his fingers inside me.

Pressure builds low in my stomach, coiling tighter with each thrust. My thighs start to shake as I rapidly approach my release, his fingers driving me closer to ecstasy.

"Such a good little slut," he murmurs, his voice strained.

Just as I'm about to fly apart, he withdraws his fingers. I almost scream in frustration, my hips rocking helplessly as the delight from the stolen orgasm fades.

"Not yet, my greedy girl," he admonishes with a wicked grin. "I want to be deep inside this hot cunt when you cream on my cock."

Jesus, his dirty talk is filthy. I love it.

He spins me around to face the rough brick wall and uses his foot to kick my legs further apart, making me present my ass to him. The bricks scrape my palms as he bends me over, manhandling me into the position he wants. The minor pain only heightens my raging desire.

I hear the telltale rustle of clothing and the clink of a belt buckle behind me. I know he's freeing his cock. My heart pounds wildly in anticipation, and I groan when I feel the broad, swollen head of his cock against my soaked entrance. I push my hips back in silent invitation, begging him to take me.

"I'm going to fuck you so hard, you'll still be thinking about me tomorrow," he promises savagely.

His sinful words echo in my pleasure-hazed brain as he slams forward, impaling me on his thick cock in one brutal stroke. I scream, the sound reverberating off the bricks. Oh god, his ego isn't the only thing that's huge. He's splitting me open, stretching me to the limit. The sweet burn of it is exquisite. Shit, I wasn't expecting him to be this big, and my body struggles to accommodate him.

He sets a punishing pace, pulling nearly all the way out before driving back in balls deep. The sheer force of his thrusts rocks me forward, the coarse bricks digging into my cheek. His pelvis slaps obscenely against the globes of my ass as he rails me, grunting with the effort of fucking me so savagely.

"Fuck, your cunt feels like heaven. So tight and wet. Is this what you need? To be fucked in an alley so you'd know how much of a slut you are?"

"Yes," I mewl shamelessly, too lost in the sensations to care how debased I sound. "Don't stop!"

His fingers bite into the flesh of my hips hard enough to bruise as he roughly yanks me back onto his cock. He's hitting spots deep inside me that I didn't know existed, sending shockwaves of pleasure radiating through my entire body. My inner muscles ripple around his shaft as I rapidly spiral towards my orgasm.

His harsh breaths mingle with my high-pitched keens, and anyone walking past the alley would know exactly what we were doing in the shadows. The thought of being caught is almost enough to make me come, and my thigh muscles quiver from the impending explosion.

"Play with your clit," he demands. "I want to feel you come."

I obey mindlessly, snaking a hand between my legs to rub frantically at the swollen nub. The tension coils tighter and tighter as he pounds into me.

"Come for me, Mia," he commands, his deep authoritative tone sending shivers to my toes. "Now."

His order pushes me over the edge. I detonate with a silent scream, colors bursting behind my eyelids as my pussy spasms almost violently around him. Delight crashes through my veins, and my entire body quakes from my orgasm.

To my surprise, Heath doesn't stop his relentless thrusting, hammering into my pussy without missing a beat.

"You didn't think you were only getting one measly orgasm, did you?" he taunts. "Oh no, you're going to come again so you can tell your husband how much of a slut you were for his boss's cock."

Fuck, that's hot. His words only turn me on more as he pulls out and flips me around to face him. My back collides with the rough bricks once more. I barely have time to register the position change before he's pushing my thighs further apart and sliding his thick cock back inside my slick channel.

I close my eyes and moan as he fills me again, fresh waves of rapture making my mind blank. He lifts me effortlessly, hands cupping my ass as he encourages me to wrap my legs around his waist. I cling to his broad shoulders, fingers clutching at his shirt, as he fucks me again.

The new position allows him to sink even deeper, the head of his cock knocking against a pleasure point with each powerful thrust. All I can do is hang on for dear life as he sets a relentless pace, his hips crashing against mine again and again.

"How does that feel, Mia?" Heath asks, his voice husky. "You like having your pretty little pussy stuffed full of my cock?"

"Oh god, it feels amazing," I gasp, my hips bucking against his in response. "Please don't stop."

Heath's fingers dig into the soft flesh of my ass as he grunts, "I'm not stopping until you come on my cock at least one more time like a needy slut."

Each drive of his hips is harder than the last, and the small of my back scrapes against the rough bricks with each thrust. I know I'm going to be deliciously sore tomorrow, but I don't care. The minor pain only enhances the pleasure. All that matters is the feel of Heath's thick cock sinking into me and the buzz I'm getting from being a slut.

He changes the angle of his hips slightly and grinds against me, stimulating my clit with the base of his cock. The added friction sends jolts of delight through my body. I can feel a second climax rapidly building, my slick inner muscles clenching around him. I cling to his shoulders as I hurtle towards another release.

His grunts fill my ears, driving me closer to coming. "Say my name. Let everyone hear what a filthy slut you are for my cock."

Imagining people hearing me sizzles my brain, and I cry out, "Heath! Oh god, fuck me!"

It feels wrong to call out another guy's name, but this is what I wanted—what Lawrence wanted.

"That's it, Mia," Heath pants harshly against my ear. "Squeeze my cock with that sweet little cunt. Milk me dry. I want to fill this pussy with my cum."

I come undone in his arms, my pussy clamping down on his shaft as wave after wave of dizzying rapture crashes over me until I'm limp and boneless.

My spasming pussy triggers Heath's release. With a low, guttural moan, he buries himself to the hilt one last time as he pulses inside me. I can feel the hot spurts of his seed coating my inner walls as he empties himself, each twitch of his cock prolonging my bliss. He rocks his hips almost lazily, fucking me through the lingering aftershocks.

Eventually, he carefully lowers my feet back to the ground. He keeps me pinned against the wall, his softening cock still nestled inside me, as we both struggle to catch our breaths in the aftermath. I feel wrung out from delight. I love it. This is easily one of the top five sexual experiences of my life, and I'm married to the most remarkable man ever to give me the opportunity to do this.

When Heath finally slips out of me, I feel the warm trickle of his cum slide down my inner thighs, and it makes me feel like even more of a slut. He helps me straighten my clothes with surprising tenderness as he smooths my skirt back into place.

He sounds satisfied when he speaks. "That was incredible. You're a goddess."

I practically glow at the praise and grin at him. I feel like a goddess, powerful and sexy. When more of his cum drips down my thigh, I almost laugh. Yeah, okay, I'm a dirty goddess, but it's wonderful.

"You weren't so bad yourself," I tease, reaching up to straighten his collar. "Thank you for making my first hotwife experience so amazing."

I can tell he wasn't expecting me to say it was my first time when his eyes flicker slightly. "Glad to be of service. This was a pleasurable surprise."

"It was." I giggle because he's right.

As we make our way out of the alley, I'm energized. I've taken control of my own desires, and it feels glorious. I've embraced my inner hotwife, and there's no going back now.

CHAPTER 4

As Heath and I make our way back into the pub, a grin spreads across my face. I've just fulfilled a fantasy I never thought I'd have the chance to experience. My heart is still racing, but now it's not just from the excitement of what I did or possibly being caught, but from wondering how Lawrence is going to react.

The noise of the pub hits me like a wave, and I take a deep breath, steeling myself. I can't let anyone know what just happened, so I need to pretend everything is normal. I glance over at Heath, and he gives me a wink, as if he knows exactly what I'm thinking.

I desperately need to talk to my husband and I want to do it without Heath, so I turn to him. "Thank you for satisfying my curiosity. That was memorable."

He laughs. "It's going to make the company picnic this summer a little more enjoyable. You know I'll be thinking of you."

My nipples harden as a dark thrill zings through me. Oh shit, I didn't even think of that. There's no way I won't be thinking of what just happened every time I see him.

"Well," I give him a saucy smile. "Nothing wrong with good memories. It'll be our little secret."

"A very pleasurable secret." He winks at me, and I say goodbye to him as we part ways.

When I get back to the table, Lawrence's eyes glitter with lust and I get an illicit rush. He knows what I did, and he's turned on by it.

I slide into the chair next to him, and he immediately wraps his arm around me, pulling me close. I can feel the heat radiating off him, and I know he's just as desperate for me as I am for him.

"Did you have fun?" Lawrence murmurs into my ear.

I turn to him with a smile. "Oh yeah, you're going to love hearing this story."

He leans in, capturing my lips in a kiss that sends a jolt of electricity straight to my clit. The kiss leaves me breathless, and before I know it, we're saying goodbye to our friends and he's pulling me towards the exit. My heart races, and I can feel the wetness of Heath's cum mixed with my juices between my legs as we make our way out of the pub. The cool night air makes this all seem more illicit.

I just fucked his boss behind the pub. I'm such a slut.

We make our way to the car, and I can feel the tension between us growing with every step. Lawrence opens the passenger door for me, and as I slide into the seat, I notice the bulge in his pants. I lick my lips in anticipation. Oh yeah, he's going to fuck me hard.

As soon as Lawrence is in the driver's seat, he turns to me, his eyes flashing with a burning fire. His voice is low and husky. "Tell me everything."

I bite my lower lip, my mind racing as I try to think of where to start. "Heath was amazing," I begin, my voice barely above a whisper. "He was so dominant, and he knew exactly what he was doing."

Lawrence's hand slips between my legs, inching its way up my inner thigh. "What did he do to you?" he asks, his voice strained.

I close my eyes, remembering the feeling of Heath's hands on my body, his lips on mine. "He fucked me against the wall of the pub," I say, my voice breathy.

Lawrence's fingers reach my pussy and his hand stills a moment as he realizes I'm not wearing my panties. Yeah, they're in the alley somewhere. I almost giggle, but it turns into a gasp as he slips his fingers into my wetness to brush against my clit. "Did you like it?" he asks, his voice thick with lust.

"Yes," I moan, my hips moving in time with his fingers. "It felt so wonderful."

Lawrence's fingers move faster, and I can feel myself getting closer to another orgasm. Jesus, I'm insatiable. His breathing gets heavier, but without warning, he pulls his fingers away.

I whimper in protest, but he silences me with a quick kiss. When he pulls away and starts the car, my mind whirls. Holy shit, he really is turned on by me fucking his boss.

The car ride is a blur. All I can focus on is Heath's cum dripping out of me and the desire radiating off Lawrence. I'm going to get fucked so hard when we get home.

Before I know it, we're pulling over to the side of the road on a deserted street. Wait, this isn't home.

Lawrence turns the car off and looks at me with lust. "I need you. Now."

Without waiting for a response, he gets out of the car and comes around to my side. He opens the door and pulls me out, and runs his hands all over my body. He's crazed, and I love it.

He pushes me backwards until I'm up against the hood of the car, his lips crashing down on mine. I can taste his need for me, and it only serves to fuel my own desire.

His kiss is demanding, and I reach down, fumbling with his pants. I need him inside of me. He groans as his cock springs free.

Lawrence lifts me up onto the warm hood of the car, spreading my legs and positioning himself between them. I put my hands flat on the hood to stabilize myself. He thrusts into me hard, and I cry out in pleasure. The feeling of him inside of me, combined with the thrill of being out in public, is erotic and I almost come right then.

"Tell me everything," Lawrence growls into my ear, his breath hot against my skin.

I moan as he fucks me, my mind racing as I try to remember everything. "He took control immediately by pushing me up against the wall and kissing me."

Lawrence's thrusts become more frenzied as I continue, his cock pulsing inside of me as I tremble from pleasure. "He made me come so hard my legs were jelly."

Lawrence's hand finds its way to my throat, his grip firm but not tight. "Say it. Tell me how much you loved another man's cock inside of you."

The dirty talk only serves to heighten my delight, and I can feel myself getting closer and closer to my climax. "I loved it," I gasp. "I loved him coming inside of me, filling me up."

Lawrence's grip on my throat loosens as he explodes, his body shuddering. I follow right behind him, my orgasm crashing over me in waves. It's like a never-ending roller coaster of rapture as Lawrence rocks against me, unloading ropes of sticky cum inside me to mix with Heath's cum.

When we both finally come down from our highs, he gives me a gentle kiss. "I love you," he murmurs against my lips.

"I love you too," I reply, my heart filled with love and gratitude for this man who has let me fulfill my fantasies.

My mind is still reeling from the intense connection I feel with my husband, and it creates an overwhelming sense of euphoria.

"So, what do you want to do next?" Lawrence asks.

I raise an eyebrow, feigning innocence. "What do you mean?"

He chuckles, shaking his head. "You know exactly what I mean, Mia. Do you want to explore this more?"

"How does next weekend sound?" I tease him.

When he replies, "We'll see," pleasure pulses through my core.

We climb into the car, and it hits me. Holy shit, I really am a hotwife now. I'm flying high and eager to sing it from the rooftops. Maybe when I call Ana tomorrow, I'll tell her how much of a slut I am.

This is fucking awesome.

The End

APRIL HOTWIFE

HOTWIFE OF THE MONTH CLUB 4

LACEY CROSS

CHAPTER 1

"Another margarita?" Marcela asks as she brings the pitcher over.

"Hit me." I grin, holding out my glass. The tart lime and sweet Triple Sec hit the spot perfectly. "God, I needed this."

"Duh, that's why I invited you over." Marcela laughs, her dark eyes sparkling with mischief. "Well, that and to give you the latest dirt."

I raise an eyebrow. "Ooh, do tell."

When I married my husband Max, he came with a large circle of friends that he stayed in contact with from his frat in college. I'm the youngest wife of all his friends, and everyone has known each other for years. I'm always intimidated at the parties they throw throughout the year, but I've grown close to a couple of the wives.

Marcela leans in, her voice dropping to a conspiratorial whisper. "So, apparently Felicity and Edward are trying the hotwife thing now, too."

"Shut up!" I gasp, nearly choking on my drink. "Felicity and January both?"

I had heard about January through the grapevine, but Felicity surprises me.

"Right?" Marcela laughs gleefully. "I guess Eddie boy decided he wanted to share."

I shake my head in disbelief. It seems like everyone in our friend group is hopping on the hotwife train these days, letting their husbands watch them screw other guys. The mere thought sends a forbidden tingle down my spine, settling between my thighs. I'd never have the confidence to fuck someone else, even with Max's permission.

Marcela sighs dreamily, stretching out on her lounge chair like a contented cat. "Can you even imagine? All the thrill of someone new, but still having your man to come home to? Talk about the best of both worlds."

I chew my lip, my mind wandering to dangerous places. Faceless hands roaming my body, a hard chest pressing me into the mattress, Max's eyes burning into me as he watches...I squirm, heat rushing to my cheeks.

"Earth to Ana!" Marcela giggles, waving a hand in front of my face. "Where'd you go just now?"

My face flames red as I blurt out, "Nowhere! I mean, I could never actually do it. I'm not bold like you."

Marcela rolls her eyes. "Oh please, you're a total smoke show. Once you got a little taste of it, you'd own it."

I fiddle with the hem of my sundress. "I've only been married a year. Isn't the honeymoon phase supposed to last longer than that?"

"Honey, there's no rulebook." Marcela shrugs. "Variety is the spice of life and all that jazz."

I force a laugh, but my mind is racing. Is there something wrong with me for even daydreaming about this? I love Max. He's sweet and funny and sexy as hell. I shouldn't need more than that, right?

Except...sometimes I wish Max was more dominant in the bedroom, and that he would call me a filthy slut while fucking me hard. My man is a sensual lover, through and through. He always wants to make sure I'm comfortable as he worships my body. It feels dumb to even mentally complain about a sex life with a husband who makes your pleasure a priority.

I sigh and force myself back to just enjoying the moment with Marcela. She's the best thing that's come from dating Max—other than Max himself—she's in her early 30s, and compared to my 25 years, she seems so much more worldly. She gives great advice and is a genuine friend. I hope in seven years, I'm as confident in my skin as she is instead of feeling all awkward and naive whenever I'm around Max's friends.

When I get home, Max practically pounces on me, his grin a mile wide. "Welcome home, gorgeous."

I can't help but smile back. "Someone's in a good mood."

"Well, I might have a surprise for you." He waggles his eyebrows. "How does five days in Cancun sound?"

I squeal, throwing my arms around his neck. "Seriously? When? How?"

"Next weekend. And I have my ways." Max winks, his hands settling on my hips. "I thought we could use a little adventure."

Something in his tone makes me pause. "What kind of adventure?"

Max's eyes darken, his voice dropping to a husky murmur. "Well, I was thinking...what if we used this trip to explore some fantasies? You know, the stuff we've never tried before."

My mouth goes dry. "Such as?"

He leans in close and whispers, "Such as...maybe you want to be a hotwife and let me watch."

I jerk back like I've been scalded, my heart hammering. "You want me to sleep with another man?"

Max holds up his hands. "Only if you want to. I just think it could be insanely hot. Seeing you all wild and uninhibited, knowing I'm the one you'll come back to..."

I sputter, "I couldn't! That's not me, Max. I'm not like Marcela and the other girls."

My pussy buzzes, almost as if she's calling me a liar. Yeah, just because I don't think I could do it doesn't mean the idea isn't hot.

"Okay, okay." Max soothes, drawing me back into his arms. "No pressure. It was just a thought. When I was in Aspen with the guys, James told us about how hot it was to watch Marilyn fuck other guys. I've been thinking about it, but it's not something I want if you aren't into the idea."

As he kisses my forehead, I try to quiet the swirling thoughts in my head. My sweet, adoring husband wants me to fuck someone else? The filthy images flood my brain—a huge, dominant man pinning me down, fucking me senseless while Max watches.

It's everything I've secretly craved but never dared to ask for. The depravity thrills me as much as it terrifies me.

Pulling away, I paste on a bright smile. "You know, I should start packing for this trip. Cancun, here we come!"

Max grins, but I can see the wheels turning behind his eyes. He's planted a seed in my mind, and now it's going to grow, whether I like it or not.

As I rifle through my closet, I can't ignore the need pulsing between my thighs. The skimpier bikinis and shorter dresses call to me, begging me to pack them. Maybe Max is right. Maybe Cancun is the perfect place to shed my good girl persona and walk on the wild side.

The question is...am I brave enough to actually do it?

Chapter 2

"So, I had a thought." Max corners me in the kitchen, his eyes gleaming with mischief. "About Cancun and your...adventures."

I nearly choke on my coffee. It's been a few days since he first brought up the idea of me sleeping with someone else on our trip, and I can't stop thinking about it.

"Oh?"

Max leans against the counter, his arms crossed over his broad chest. "Well, I know the idea of jumping straight into bed with a stranger is a little daunting. So what if we started smaller? Like, flirting with a guy online. Just to test the waters."

"Online?" I echo, my mind whirling. That definitely sounds easier than fucking a stranger, but still. "I wouldn't even know where to start."

Max's fingers toy with the hem of my shirt, grazing the skin beneath. "That's the beauty of it. You can be anyone you want to be. Create a profile, chat with a few guys, see what all the fuss is about."

I worry my bottom lip between my teeth. I'm not hating the idea. "And you'd be okay with that? Knowing I'm talking to other men?"

"More than okay." Max's eyes darken, his voice dropping an octave. "It's hot as fuck imagining you driving some poor bastard crazy when I'm the one who gets you in real life."

A shiver runs through me, my thighs clenching. When he puts it like that... "All right. Let's give it a whirl."

Max whoops, smacking a kiss to my cheek. "You won't regret this, baby. I promise."

Famous last words.

An hour later, I'm perched on our bed, agonizing over which photos to use for my dating profile. I finally settle on a few flirty selfies that show off my curves without giving away too much. I swear I look like a nerd with my glasses, but Max is always telling me I'm crazy and guys love girls with gorgeous eyes and glasses.

Well, here goes nothing. I take a deep breath and hit submit.

The response is immediate and overwhelming. Within thirty minutes my inbox is flooded with messages, each one bolder than the last. I scroll through them, completely flattered.

"Well, well, well. Looks like someone's a hot commodity." Max flops down beside me, peering at my phone. "What about that one? Dominant-Teddy. Sounds promising."

I tap on the message, my pulse speeding up as I read it aloud. "You're gorgeous. I'd love to make you scream my name as I fuck you senseless."

I glance at Max, my cheeks burning. "Jesus. He doesn't mince words, does he?"

Max grins. "I like him already. What're you going to say back?"

My fingers hover over the keypad, my mind racing. Fuck it. In for a penny... "How's this? 'Promises, promises. You'd have to earn the privilege of touching me first.'"

Max groans, his hand sliding up my thigh. "Perfect. Hit send."

The reply is instantaneous. "'Or maybe you'll have to earn it. Get on your knees and open wide, baby. It's time to play.'"

Liquid heat pools in my core, my breath catching. This is insane. I'm sexting a total stranger while my husband eggs me on. But god, it's intoxicating. I can feel myself slipping under the stranger's spell, craving more.

The messages fly back and forth, growing filthier by the minute. DominantTeddy paints vivid pictures of all the depraved things he wants to do to me—spanking me, making me beg, fucking me until I can't remember my own name.

Max is riveted, his eyes glued to the screen. Every so often, he'll point to a particularly dirty message and growl, "Fuck, baby. Would you let him do that to you?"

By the time DominantTeddy links me his social media page, I'm a writhing mess. I nearly combust when I see his photos. He's a personal trainer, all rippling muscles and cocky smirks.

"Holy shit." Max palms himself through his jeans. "If that guy railed you, I might have to send him a fruit basket afterwards."

I smack his chest, giggling. "Down, boy. It's just flirting, remember?"

"For now." Max gives me a seductive smile. "But in Cancun? All bets are off. We could find you another smoking hot guy."

My entire body tingles at the thought. My husband is nuts, but I love him. When I finally say goodnight to DominantTeddy, I can barely type, my fingers shaking with need.

"Shit, that was intense." I flop back onto the bed, my chest heaving.

"I take it you enjoyed yourself?" Max smirks as he starts nuzzling into my neck.

"You could say that." I laugh breathlessly and pull him closer as his hands creep up under my shirt and squeeze my breasts gently. "Is it weird that I'm this turned on by a total stranger?"

"Baby, that's the point." Max whispers in my ear before wrapping his lips around my earlobe and nibbling softly. "And it's so fucking hot knowing you're doing it for me."

Our kisses become frantic, and I'm getting more desperate by the second. I want to feel his skin against mine.

"I can't wait," I pant between kisses. "I need you inside me."

I start tugging his clothes, and Max laughs at how turned on I am as he peels my panties and shorts down. It doesn't take long before we're both naked.

He positions himself between my legs, and I feel the tip of his cock teasing my wet opening. We're both eager and ready for each other. He kisses me passionately while he slides his cock into me, and I moan loudly from the pleasure. I know I'll never tire of the feeling of him inside me.

I whimper as he moves in deeper. His pace is deliberate and slow, sending waves of pleasure through my body. My mind goes blank, and I'm consumed by sensation. I wrap my legs around him tightly, wishing this moment could last forever.

Each thrust brings me closer to climax, and I let out a constant stream of passionate moans. He matches my rhythm as we move together, both of us in a frenzy, fueled by my flirting with the sexy trainer online.

When his cock massages a particularly sensitive spot, I cry out as my orgasm hits and the waves of bliss wash over me. My pussy contracts, trying to get Max to come at the same time.

As the ecstasy spreads from my fingertips down to my toes, I can feel his cock pulsing inside of me. With a deep groan, he explodes and fills me with his warm seed. I can tell he's giving me a big load tonight, and I'll have a thoroughly satisfied and dripping pussy.

Afterwards, we collapse into a sweaty, sated heap. I can't stop grinning, my body still buzzing. I could get used to this.

But of course, the universe has other plans.

The next morning, Marcela's ringtone jolts me out of a sex coma. I'm alone in bed, and I fumble for my phone, my stomach sinking as I see the string of missed calls and texts.

"Shit. Marcela, what's up?"

Marcela's voice is annoyed. "Debra is losing her shit in the group chat, calling you a homewrecking slut."

Ice floods my veins. "What? Why?"

"Apparently, she saw you thirsting over some beefcake online. Now she's telling everyone you're cheating on Max and your marriage is a sham."

Bile rises in my throat. This can't be happening. "It's not...we were just..."

But how do I even begin to explain? That my husband was sitting next to me and getting off on me flirting? That we're exploring a taboo kink that could blow up our entire lives?

Tears burn my eyes as Marcela keeps talking, her voice softening. "Hey, I know you and Max are solid. And frankly, Deb needs to get laid and mind her own business. I just didn't want you to go online and get a bad surprise."

I manage a weak laugh. "Yeah. Good call."

I'm shaking as I hang up, panic clawing at me. Max finds me curled up in bed, crying into a pillow.

"Baby, what's wrong?" He gathers me into his arms, alarmed. "Talk to me."

The whole sordid tale spills out of me—Debra's snooping, the group chat, my sudden terror that we've made a horrible mistake.

"She thinks I'm cheating on you!" I wail. "What if she's right? What if this means I'm a terrible wife?"

Max sighs as he rubs my back. "Ana, what we're doing is our own business. You're not cheating, and you're not a terrible wife."

I blink at him, sniffling. "But our friends are going to think that."

"No they won't. When I was with the guys in Aspen, I told them if I could get you to fuck someone else, I'd watch it in a heartbeat."

"You told them that?" My tears instantly dry up and he gives me a firm kiss.

"Yep. You're exploring a fantasy, with my full blessing. Debra can frankly fuck all the way off with her sanctimonious bullshit."

A surprised giggle bursts out of me. "Max!"

"I mean it." He cups my face, his eyes shining with conviction. "I love you. I trust you. And if this is something you want to pursue, I'm all in. Fuck what anyone else thinks."

I search his gaze, looking for any hint of doubt or hesitation. I find none. Only love, acceptance, and a heat that makes my insides buzz.

"Okay," I whisper, leaning in to kiss him softly. "Let's do this."

Max grins against my lips. "Damn right. Now, let's get packing for Cancun. I have a feeling this is going to be a trip we never forget."

As I start tossing bikinis and sundresses into my suitcase, a thrill zips through me. Maybe Max is right. Maybe this is our chance for me to shed my inhibitions and indulge my wildest fantasies.

Look out, Cancun. This good girl? She's about to be very, very bad.

CHAPTER 3

The sun practically blinds me as we step out of the airport into the chaotic bustle of Cancun. I slip on my sunglasses, drinking in the sights and sounds. This is my first time here, and anticipation buzzes through me. I wasn't much of a traveler before meeting Max, but he's quickly showing me the delights of the world.

Max drapes a possessive arm around me, pulling me close. "Welcome to paradise, baby," he rumbles in my ear. "Ready to let loose and get wild with me?"

I plaster on a smile, trying to ignore the flip-flop of my stomach. After the incident with Debra and her snarky comments about my online flirting, I'm still not sure I'm ready for anything wild. Maybe attempting the hotwife lifestyle will be a huge mistake. Maybe I'm just not cut out for this level of adventure.

When we arrive at the resort, my breath catches. It's stunning. Majestic palms wave in the balmy breeze, white sand beaches beckon seductively, and the sprawling buildings gleam like polished pearls. The opulent lobby stuns me with its soaring ceilings and glittering chandeliers.

"Wow," I breathe, spinning in a slow circle. "This is incredible."

"Just wait until you see our suite," Max winks as he smoothly checks us in.

When we get up to our room, we discover one of our keycards doesn't work.

He gives me a quick kiss. "I'll run down to the front desk, babe. You explore and get settled in. I'll be back."

The suite blows me away. Posh, stylish, with a sinfully large bed and a jacuzzi tub built for two. Floor to ceiling windows frame a breathtaking view of aquamarine water. I could happily stay in this luxurious haven forever.

Max is gone longer than I expect, and I wander onto the balcony, entranced by the picture-perfect view. The sound of the waves and the cry of gulls lulls me into a trance. I'm so lost in the beauty of it all that I jump when his arms snake around my waist from behind.

"A penny for your thoughts?" Max nuzzles my neck, sending shivers cascading down my spine. "What's on the agenda first—beach? Pool? Margaritas?"

The thought of parading around in my new bikini and feeling self-conscious if I catch guys gawking at me makes me tense up and second guess myself. Debra's hurtful remarks about me being unfaithful make me want to hide in the room. "Maybe we should take it easy up here for a while," I suggest, attempting to keep my voice carefree.

Max turns me to face him, his expression soft with understanding. "Hey, don't let that bitter harpy ruin our trip." He tips my chin up, forcing me to meet his eyes. "You're stunning, Ana. Sexy as hell. I'm the luckiest man alive, and I love you."

"I love you too," I whisper, a tiny smile tugging at my lips. His praise makes me feel all gooey inside.

He kisses me softly. "I want you to have the time of your life here, baby. Whatever you're comfortable doing."

I melt into his embrace as my fears dissolve. "You're right. I can't let her pettiness hold me back. Let's hit the pool."

The sprawling pool area dazzles like a tropical oasis. Sparkling water, cushy loungers, swaying palms—it's paradise. I feel daring in the red bikini Max coaxed me into buying since it barely covers my tits and ass.

"Damn, I knew it would look gorgeous on you," Max whistles as I shimmy out of my sundress. He palms my ass appreciatively. "Every man out here is going to wish he was me."

I feel deliciously on display. Pleasure simmers in my core at his blatant admiration. "Yeah?" I bite my lip coyly. "Prove it." I sway my hips as I saunter to a prime poolside spot, relishing his groan behind me.

As I settle on a lounger, Max plops down beside me. "First things first—I'm getting us drinks. Don't go running off with any cabana boys while I'm gone."

He kisses me hard, a blatant display of ownership, before heading towards the bar. Alone again, I fidget self-consciously, hyper aware of my barely-clad body. Maybe this suit is too much. I'm not the type of woman who can easily show off her body. When I look in the mirror, all I see are my flaws, and it makes me self-conscious when other people look at me. Yeah, this was a bad idea.

I'm about to reach for a towel when a rich, accented voice stops me cold. "Well hello there, beautiful. I don't believe we've had the pleasure."

I glance up, prepared to be annoyed at the cheesy opening line, but when I see the guy, my mouth goes dry. The Adonis smiling down at me looks like he just stepped out of a cologne ad—mid-forties, chiseled jaw, tanned skin, dark hair artfully tousled. Even with his eyes hidden behind sunglasses, he radiates blatant sexuality.

"I'm Javier." He extends a hand, and I take it numbly, tingles racing up my arm from the contact. His skin is warm, his grip strong and confident.

"Ana," I manage to say, my heart playing a drum solo against my ribs. "Nice to meet you."

"The pleasure is decidedly all mine." His gaze drags over me, slow and scorching, leaving my skin flushed. He makes no attempt to hide his blatant appreciation of my body. "Tell me, Ana, what brings a goddess like you to Cancun? Only pleasure, I hope?"

I swallow hard, fighting the urge to squirm under his penetrating stare. "Just a little couple's getaway with my husband."

I risk a glance at Max, finding him watching our interaction with hawk-like intensity. But there's no anger or jealousy in his eyes, only...excitement?

Javier draws my attention back to him. "Your husband is a very lucky man."

My cheeks flame, and arousal pulses between my thighs. The way he looks at me, the way he speaks, it's so bold, so direct. I'm not used to such brazen flirting, and it flusters me.

"He certainly thinks he's lucky," I quip, trying to control my reaction to him.

Javier laughs. "As he should. Though I must say, if I were lucky enough to call you mine, I'm not sure I'd be able to let you out of my sight." He leans closer, his voice dropping to a sinful murmur. "Or out of my bed."

I nearly swallow my tongue, desire licking through me in molten waves. Did he really just say that? "I...is that so?"

I'm half scandalized and very turned on.

His smirk is pure satisfaction. "A woman like you deserves to be worshipped and pleasured until she's a puddle on the floor."

Each word of his is a promise, and my clit throbs in response. I'm saved from combusting on the spot by Max's return, a drink in each hand.

"Making friends, I see?" His grin tells me he knows exactly what effect Javier is having on me.

"Your wife is definitely gorgeous." Javier drawls, angling his body towards Max in a way that feels strangely conspiratorial. Realization clicks into place. They know each other. This was a setup.

Max sets our drinks on the side table and sits down next to me with a grin. "Don't I know it. I'll never understand what she sees in me."

"You're just as much of a catch as I am," I protest, head spinning from their strange camaraderie. Are they really bonding over how hot they find me? Is this normal?

"I'll leave you to enjoy your time together," Javier says, his smile turning wicked. "But Ana, if you find yourself craving some extra attention, I'd be more than happy to...entertain you. Max knows how to get ahold of me."

With a wink, he saunters off, leaving me slack-jawed and overheated. The second he's out of earshot, I whirl to face Max.

"You set this up," I huff, torn between whether I should be angry or whether I should kiss him for being so sweet. "You planned for him to flirt with me!"

Max just grins, completely unrepentant. He leans over and captures my lips in a kiss that makes my toes curl. His tongue delves into my mouth, stroking and claiming me, until I'm boneless and ready to beg him to take me to our hotel room and fuck me.

"Guilty," he admits when he finally comes up for air. "I ran into him when I was getting the new key card. We got to talking, and I could tell you'd find him attractive." His eyes gleam with mischief and something darker. "Baby, if you want to fuck him, you have my blessing."

I blink at him, certain I've misheard. "You want me to sleep with him?" My pussy clenches at the thought, and I force myself to calm down. We're just talking about it, and it might not actually happen.

Max frames my face in his hands, his expression open and earnest. "Flirt, kiss, fuck. Whatever you want, I support you. I love you, and your pleasure is my pleasure."

Tears swim in my eyes, and my heart feels full for this wonderful man I married. "I don't know what to say. I love you so much."

"You don't have to say anything. Just answer one question." His grin turns downright devilish. "Do you want to be a hotwife?"

My body pulses with need as I think of Javier...the way his eyes devoured me, my husband's eager encouragement. The forbidden thrill of it all.

I know my answer.

"Yes," I breathe, capturing Max's lips again. "Yes, I do."

CHAPTER 4

The bar is buzzing with energy as I sip my club soda, scanning the crowd for Javier. Butterflies swirl in my stomach, anticipation humming through my veins. I'm wearing a blue dress that hugs my curves and accentuates my figure. The deep V-neckline shows off my cleavage, and the short hemline reveals my toned and tanned legs. I'm wearing sexy high heels with a strap around my ankle, and I make sure to cross my legs and perch on my bar stool in a way that shows off my outfit.

I caught the appreciative glances of a couple of men as I passed their tables, and I haven't felt this sexy since my wedding day. I can't believe I'm actually doing this, meeting a near-stranger for a hookup, with my husband's blessing.

Speaking of Max, he's at the other end of the bar, keeping a watchful eye on me. The heat in his gaze every time our eyes meet sends shivers down my spine. He's getting off on this just as much as I am.

"There you are." A now-familiar voice says, making me jump. "I was starting to think you'd stood me up."

I turn to find Javier grinning down at me, looking good enough to eat in a crisp white button-down and dark jeans. The lust simmering in my core makes me brave as I check him out. "Not a chance."

He chuckles. "Glad to hear it. I've been thinking about you all day." His eyes linger on the plunging neckline of my dress. "I couldn't get the image of you in that bikini out of my head, but this dress might put the bikini to shame."

I flush, and I can feel my panties growing damp. This guy is a smooth talker, but I kind of love it. "Is that so?"

"Mmm." He leans in, his breath tickling my ear. "Though I have to say, as incredible as you looked, all I could think about was getting you out of it."

I press my thighs together and hold in a moan. Fuck. If he keeps talking like that, I might beg him to fuck me right here.

As if reading my mind, Javier says, "What do you say we get out of here? Somewhere more...private?"

I nod frantically, taking one last sip of my club soda. "Yes. Please."

He puts his hand on the small of my back and leads me over to Max. Standing next to my husband with another guy's hand on me feels so damn naughty.

Max stares at me, and my stomach flips at his heated gaze while Javier talks to him. "I'm taking Ana up to your room. Are you joining us?"

Max nods once, and his eyes look dazed as he stands up. We move together, weaving through the crowded resort towards the elevators.

The moment the elevator doors close, Javier pushes me against the wall, his mouth crashing down on mine. His tongue delves deep as he grinds against me. I gasp into the kiss, desire spiking through me like lightning. Holy hell, is Max still okay with this?

Javier nibbles down my neck, and I'm able to look at Max. He's smiling, and the lust is clearly written all over his face. He nods at me, giving me the silent go-ahead. Jesus, this is crazy.

"Fuck, I want you." Javier growls against my throat, his hands roaming my curves. "Tell me you want this too."

"I do." I pant, arching into him. "I want you."

The elevator dings and we stumble out. I giggle as we make our way down the hall to our room. Every step fills me with more confidence. I've got one of the sexiest guys I've ever met planning to fuck me while my husband follows us, desperate to watch. When I pull out our keycard, Javier takes it from me. When he fumbles with it, cursing, I smile. The effect I'm having on both of them gives me a nice self-confidence boost.

When the door opens, we tumble inside, a tangle of groping hands and desperate kisses. We pause long enough to move to the bedroom and wait for Max to sit down in a chair facing the bed. My entire body is thrumming with pleasure, and I'm desperate to get Javier's cock inside me, but I feel the need to check in with Max.

Moving in front of my husband, I bend down and give him a deep kiss. He holds onto my hips as our tongues twirl together. When we break apart, I rest my forehead on his and whisper, "Are you sure you want this?"

"Yes, baby. I need it."

I'm not totally sure I understand his need to watch another guy fuck me, but the look in his eyes says he's telling the truth.

When I straighten up and look over my shoulder at Javier, the desire in his eyes gives me a jolt. I'm a sensual goddess tonight, and both these guys could be putty in my hands.

Suddenly, every last reservation about fucking Javier fades. I don't want to lose this sense of power. No matter how many times Max told me how gorgeous I was, I never really felt it until right now...and it's not just because Javier wants me. It's realizing that I'm in control of my choice, and I'm not doing this just for Max. I want to feel Javier's hands all over my body and know what another cock feels like.

And I need a massive orgasm.

I reach for Javier, pulling him into a kiss. Our lips lock, and I slide my hands under his shirt, feeling the muscles of his chest jump as I explore every contour. He has more chest hair than Max, and the difference fascinates me. He groans and presses his hard cock against my hip. I'm still feeling gloriously in control, and I push Javier away, taking a step back from him. I want to give them both a show.

I start working my dress down my shoulders, revealing a matching blue push-up bra that accents my ample bosom perfectly. When the dress slides to the floor, I stand still and let the men admire me. My nipples poke out from the satin of my bra, and my entire body vibrates with desire.

The men's eyes gobble up my curves, and I smile softly to myself. Why has it taken me a year of marriage to realize the power I have over my husband? Instead of hiding my body and feeling self-conscious, I should have been flaunting it and driving him crazy. Both men clearly appreciate my assets. It's time to give them a better view.

Reaching behind my back, I unhook my bra. The straps slide down, and I hold the fabric against my breasts briefly before letting it fall. I slide my panties off, being careful to step out of them and not get my high heels tangled up. I'm naked other than my heels. Their eyes take it all in, and seeing both of them hard through their pants sends a rush of wetness between my thighs.

I have their undivided attention as I sit on the edge of the bed and lift my foot, pointing it at Javier. "A little help, please?"

Javier wordlessly unbuckles the strap around my ankle and slides my shoe off, revealing my pink toenail polish. The gentle touch of his palm along the sole of my foot makes me shiver. He bends down and kisses the top of my foot, leaving his lips close to the skin where I can feel his breath, he looks up at me. "Want me to take off the other?"

"Yes, please."

He lowers my foot, and I raise the other, my breath catching as he does the same ritual of unbuckling the strap, taking my shoe off and then kissing the top of my foot. He caresses the arch, and I almost moan from the pleasure.

His voice is husky as he continues to massage my foot. "What would you like me to do now?"

My head feels like I'm swimming through a fog of lust, and I blink, trying to think straight. "Take your shirt off."

His eyes flash with amusement as he rises and follows my command. I watch Javier remove his shirt, revealing a sculpted chest with the hint of a softer belly that makes him human and not some chiseled statue. I'm humming with lust, and I want to pull him to me and touch him everywhere and really see how different his body is from Max's, but I wait to see what he does next.

Javier takes the opportunity to undo his pants and let them fall to the floor, standing in nothing but boxer briefs, his erect cock straining against the thin cotton. I can't keep my eyes off of the length and size of it. Max is nothing to sneeze at, but Javier is obviously well endowed.

Javier moves closer and cups my chin, forcing me to look up at him. I see a change in his eyes, and my core throbs in response.

"Ana..." His voice is husky. "Your husband told me a secret."

"Mmm?" I'm practically lost in his eyes, uncertain where this is going and not caring as long as it ends with his cock inside me.

"He told me that he thinks you want to be called filthy things in the bedroom, but you'd never ask for it. Is this true?"

How did Max know? I never told him. My eyes dart to him, and he's leaning forward, rapt. I'm not sure how to answer Javier, so I play coy. "Maybe. Why don't you tell me what you're thinking of saying."

The corner of his mouth twitches. "Well, I'll start with easy things like slut and toy. But I'll call you a fucktoy. Or a cum dumpster slut if you like. Anything to make you know I mean what I say, and it's all for you. It's for your pleasure."

Fuck.

My breathing is ragged as he leans into my ear and whispers, "Deep down, you know you want to be used for pleasure like a good little fucktoy. You just have to ask for it."

A small moan escapes my lips, and he pulls back, giving me a fierce look. "Tell me what you want."

It's too dirty to admit it—to speak it aloud.

I can't say anything, so I look at Max. My husband watches our exchange with hunger. That look alone, his green eyes burning bright with lust, makes my pussy spasm, and it gives me the confidence I need.

I turn back to Javier. "I want it."

"What do you want?" His smirk makes my head spin. "Say it out loud. Let your husband hear how much of a slut you are."

My eyes are on my husband when I say, "I'm a filthy slut who wants to be used."

Oh god, I said it. My eyes snap back to Javier, who seems satisfied by my response.

"You're right, you are. What do you think should happen next?"

I'm speechless. I just told him I wanted to be used, and now he's asking ME what should happen next? Isn't he supposed to just do something? I'm so confused.

Finally, I'm able to respond. "I...I think you should fuck me."

He shakes his head. "Not a chance, my dirty little slut. You haven't earned that privilege yet. What you're going to do is suck my cock with that beautiful mouth of yours."

Oh...my mind goes blank, and suddenly, that's all I want. I need to taste him. "Yes. Yes, please." The words come out as a moan, and I actually feel like a dirty little slut.

Javier removes his boxer briefs. I stare at his cock in wonder and curiosity. It's been several years since I've seen a cock that's not my husband's. His is slightly longer, though not by much. It's the girth that makes all the difference. He's so thick I'm not even sure he can fit in my mouth. What will that monster feel like in my pussy?

It's pink with a prominent mushroom cap, and it has a vein running down the underside. I reach for it, and he swats my hand away. "Ask permission, slut."

It's embarrassing how turned on that makes me.

"Can I touch your cock?"

Javier smiles. "Yes, but start slowly."

His penis is a thing of beauty. I explore him, stroking his shaft slowly and cupping his balls. They're soft and spongy and larger than Max's. I'm fascinated by their differences, and I want to taste him.

When he slides his fingers around my head, my pussy tingles. I'm about to get that taste.

"Open wide," he demands, and I immediately obey.

I'm still not sure if he's going to fit, but I'm desperate to try. He slides the tip past my lips, and I have to open even wider. I swirl my tongue around his shaft as he pushes into my mouth. His salty precum tastes different than my husband's, and the unique flavor and smell of him makes me feel even sluttier. I moan around him, and to my surprise, I'm able to take most of him in.

He grunts as I use my tongue on the underside of his shaft and he swells up a little. I'm drooling as I run my lips up and down his shaft, wanting to please him. Javier groans and pushes my head down on his shaft until it hits the back of my throat.

My hand is busy massaging his balls as I hum around his shaft. I feel Max's eyes on me, and knowing that he's watching me in such a filthy position sends a fresh flood of moisture to my already dripping core. I've never been more turned on in my life.

I continue to suck on Javier's cock as he thrusts in and out slowly. The world goes fuzzy around the edges, and I feel like I'm floating as he uses my mouth. I feel myself sinking down to a place in my mind that I've never been before...a warm place where I really am a fucktoy for him, and by extension, a fucktoy for my husband. I'll do whatever they want of me tonight. I'm just a toy for their pleasure.

"Stop."

Javier says it so firmly that I pull off and lean back.

"How should I use you next?"

My brain is frazzled, and I barely know what I'm saying. "Use me any way you want, I'm yours. Fuck me, whatever, just use me!"

I'm so horny for this man, and he's giving me an experience I've never had before. This is amazing.

His hands grip my tits and the squeeze is rougher than I'm used to. The contrast to Max's gentler approach makes it hotter.

Javier growls, "I could just fuck these tits and come all over your face. Do you want that, slut?"

Do I want that? If he had asked me an hour ago, I would have said 'no way,' but now the thought of his cum spurting over my lips while I'm desperate for his cock inside me is a delicious kind of torture. "I would love that."

A mischievous smirk creeps across his face. "But I don't want that. I'm not going to miss my chance at that sweet pussy."

He pushes me back onto the bed, and I gasp as excitement zips through my veins. Oh thank god, he actually is going to fuck me.

He pulls me down the bed by my legs so that I'm laying across it at an angle. I'm confused for a minute until I realize that this gives Max a better view. Has Javier fucked for an audience before?

I barely have time to wonder as Javier roughly spreads my legs and climbs on top of me. He slides the tip of his cock through my wetness, not pushing in, just teasing me.

I writhe under him, clutching at his shoulders and trying to buck my hips and force him inside me. "Oh god, please fuck me. I need it. Please?"

The sensation of his cock pressing against my entrance, but not going any further, drives me insane.

"What?" Javier's voice is rough. "Does the slut want my cock inside her?"

"Yes!" I cry out, rocking against him some more.

"Hmm...I don't know if you're desperate enough yet."

He presses the tip in slightly more, and I gasp, thinking he's going to push all the way in, but he pulls out instead.

"Noooo," I whine and try to reach down for his cock, hoping that I can move him into me.

He grabs my hands and pins them above my head with one hand. "Now don't be a bad girl. Maybe I really should fuck those sweet tits and come everywhere but your pussy. Would you still like that?"

"No, no," I shake my head, and the idea of not having his cock inside me makes me frantic. "Please, I'll be good. Just fuck me. I need your cock. I'm a good fucktoy."

I don't even know who I am right now, and I'm too far gone to wonder if Max is shocked by how I'm debasing myself.

"Very good, now you're ready."

Without any more warning, he thrusts inside me, driving deep. I cry out from the pleasure as my pussy stretches and molds around him. His cock feels like a steel rod as he sets a brutal rhythm, fucking me hard.

I'm pinned in place by his hand, but I can still move my hips in time with him, and the angle is perfect for his cock to rub against the pleasure point inside me. My vision blurs as the intense bliss makes me moan and chant, "oh god, fuck me...fuck me."

With how long he toyed with me, I can tell I'm going to come quickly.

Javier growls, "You better ask for permission or you'll get punished."

Punished? My brain buzzes, and that's it. I explode. My cry of bliss is so loud the hotel room next to us can probably hear it, and my vision darkens around the edges as my body quivers and contracts around Javier. He fucks me harder as the ecstasy rolls over me.

When I come down, I gasp and say, "I'm sorry...oh god, I couldn't stop it."

He continues to pound into me. "What am I going to do with you, you disobedient little slut?"

Uh...am I supposed to pick my punishment? I'm barely able to concentrate on any thought, and each thrust sends ripples of pleasure down my spine.

I buck my hips to force his cock in deeper. "Please forgive me. I didn't mean to. It was so good...so fucking good."

"Maybe I can give you another chance?" His tone is menacing, but his smirk is playful. He's enjoying this. "I could finish in your mouth instead of in that gorgeous pussy. How does that sound?"

That's the choice?

"No. I need your cum inside me. Please? I'll be a good slut. Oh god, I want you to cum inside me!"

He laughs warmly, like he's amused by my desperation. "Then I guess it's good that I want to fill your pussy full of my cum too."

He lets go of my wrists and pulls out, and I'm confused. What is he doing? He has to be inside me to fill me up. He rolls me over and yanks my hips up, forcing me onto my knees. Oh god, yes...this is what I need.

I raise up on my hands to steady myself. Javier grips my waist with both hands and slams his cock into me.

I cry out, "Oh fuck!" and almost come again. My pussy clamps around his cock, and I can tell I'm not going to last long.

Javier pumps in and out, his breath ragged and his fingers digging into my flesh. He's merciless as his balls slap against me.

"Who's a little cum slut?"

"Me! I'm a cum slut, I'm a slut, oh, oh, oh...." I'm babbling and have no control over what I'm saying. Words are flowing out of me as I race to my second orgasm.

"Do you want my cum, you little slut?" Javier sounds like he's panting too.

"I want it so bad."

I'm about to lose my mind with how much I need it.

"You know your husband is watching me turn you into a complete slut right before his eyes."

What's this? Oh god, I am being turned into a slut. I'm not sure I'm ever going to be the same again.

Javier continues. "He's listening to you beg for another man's cum. You know what that makes you?"

Oh, it's so deliciously dirty when he talks like this. My pleasure ratchets higher and higher, and I can feel the edge right in front of me. I want to go over it so badly.

"Say it." He whacks against my pussy, and I cry out from the sharp pleasure. "Tell your husband what you are, and then you can come."

A string of filthy words comes out of my mouth in desperation. "I'm a cum slut. I'm your fucktoy. I just want to be fucked and filled with cum. I want your cum, I want Max's cum. I want all the cum. Ohhh, fuck, please can I come? I can't stop it!"

Javier groans. "You beg so beautifully. Yes, come for me, little slut."

His command sends me hurtling over the edge. The world stops as my orgasm explodes through me, sending my mind into orbit and my body into convulsions. It's one of the strongest orgasms I've ever experienced. I distantly register Javier's grunting as he rides through his own pleasure, but all I'm focused on is the cascading bliss coursing through me.

Before I can even come down, his relentless pace triggers another orgasm. Pleasure crashes through every part of me, all the way to the tips of my toes and fingers.

Eventually I hear a groan and feel Javier shudder as he releases ropes and ropes of sticky cum deep inside me. Feeling his cum makes me climax again. My arms are too weak to hold me up, and I scream into the bedding as the ecstasy consumes me. This is heaven, or at least I think it might be.

When my mind reforms itself, I'm collapsed on the bed. I lie there gasping for air as Javier leans down and plants a soft kiss on my lower back.

He slips his fingers down and strokes through the valley between my legs, playing with the cum leaking out of me.

I groan with approval. His cock just gave me one of my top five orgasms ever. I barely register what is happening, but Javier pulls his hand from between my legs and brings his fingers to my lips.

"Taste it," he says. His voice isn't harsh anymore. Now he's just...commanding.

I obey without question, tasting us mixed together. His fingers dip back to the source, then return to my lips again. I swirl my tongue around the digits and moan at the mixture of our juices. I never knew this could be sexy, but right now, I'm mesmerized. Javier does this another time or two, feeding me his cum.

At some point, he lets me be and I sink into the bed, closing my eyes and I float as the men talk. I hear Max thanking Javier and saying he'll text him, and then I hear the hotel door open and close. It's time to face my husband.

CHAPTER 5

When Max joins me on the bed, I can see the bulge in his pants. He's still desperately turned on. He lays next to me and brushes his fingers down my back. "Are you okay?"

I peek at him, and the love I see in his face makes me know everything is going to be okay. I relax and giggle. "I'm fucking awesome. Javier was fantastic. You picked a winner. Did you hear how dirty I was? I called myself a cum slut."

Max chuckles softly. "I was really surprised at the direction that went, but I enjoyed it. He was quite the entertainer."

I turn my face to his, and he leans in, capturing my mouth with his. His tongue slips into my mouth and explores me. Suddenly, it feels like the first time with him. Everything feels the same and yet wonderfully different. This is the man I love, but I've never been more attracted to Max than right this moment. He has a wild side that I never knew existed.

I lean up on my arms, staring down at my husband.

He raises his eyebrows. "Why are you looking at me like that?"

There's so much I want to say to him, but instead, I climb up onto my knees and open his pants. As soon as his cock is free, I straddle him and sink down onto his length. We both sigh as his cock fills me.

We take our time exploring each other's bodies and sharing kisses. His hands massage my back as I gently ride him, our hips rocking together in perfect unison. Our movements are languid and unhurried as I savor every movement, every touch.

I gaze into his eyes, feeling my soul connect with his, and I know this is the man I will share my life with forever. Being with Max is such a different experience than what happened with Javier, and the deep love I feel for Max shows me that I can be a filthy little slut with other men but still be the same Ana with my husband that I always was.

This experience changed things for me, but it only made me freer. There's nothing wrong with having needs that I can fulfill with other people as long as we have trust and honesty with each other.

Max cradles me to him as his hips begin to move faster, and I lift and lower myself to match his rhythm. The intensity between us builds, and we lose ourselves in pleasure, both of us so close to the edge.

I shatter before he does. As my orgasm rolls through me, he groans and I feel him pulse and empty himself deep inside me. I lean down and kiss him, rocking against him as we both shake from the force.

When the intensity fades, I climb off him and cuddle against his side. "I love you."

"I love you, Ana. I love you so much."

I trace figure eights on his chest and giggle. "You still want me to be a hotwife?"

He kisses my head. "Oh yeah, there's no way I'm going to miss a chance to hear you call yourself a filthy cumslut again."

"Hey!" I slap his chest playfully with no malice and giggle. "Yeah, he really got me going."

"Mmm hmm," Max's voice is heavy, and I can tell he's close to falling asleep as he mumbles, "But maybe next time you'll get even filthier and call yourself a cumdumpster whore."

"Yeah...maybe."

And now that he's put that thought in my head, it's for sure going to happen. I think I'm going to love being a hotwife.

The End

May Hotwife

Hotwife of the Month Club 5

Lacey Cross

Chapter 1

I take a sip of my chardonnay, savoring the crisp flavor as I relax on the plush sofa in my living room with my four closest friends. Our husbands are downstairs in the gaming room playing their monthly poker game while we enjoy our treasured girls' night upstairs. The conversation flows freely, punctuated by frequent peals of laughter and spicy details about our lives.

June's phone trills loudly and she hushes us with a grin and a wave of her hand. "Hold up, ladies, it's the babysitter."

I look over at my best friend Ana and we both giggle conspiratorially as June shoots us a playful dirty look and gets up from the overstuffed armchair, chatting animatedly with the babysitter. She's saying goodnight to her two young kids. This is also part of our monthly ritual, so I know that next she'll take the phone downstairs so her husband Mark can say goodnight to the little ones as well before rejoining the poker crew.

When June returns a few minutes later with a refilled wine glass, she plops down on the sofa and says in a stage whisper, "I think our husbands are up to something. When I walked into the room, they all completely stopped talking."

Ariel raises one perfectly-shaped eyebrow and leans forward. "Ooh, you think they're hiding some juicy secret from us?"

"Definitely," June confirms with a nod. "They only get super secretive like that when there's some really good gossip they don't want to say in front of us. I wonder what it could be this time..." She takes a long sip of wine, eyes sparkling mischievously over the rim of her glass.

I glance over at Ana, sitting cross-legged on the sofa next to me, and notice her cheeks are pink and she looks distinctly uncomfortable. She's picking nervously at a cocktail napkin and refusing to make eye contact with any of us. Hmm, I wonder what's gotten into her all of a sudden.

"Okay, Ana banana, spill it, girl. What scandalous thing is going on with you?" I coax teasingly, reaching over to poke her leg. "You look guilty as hell right now."

Ana takes a big fortifying gulp of wine, clearly nervous. She hesitates, tucking her hair behind one ear, before blurting out, "Um, well...I gave Max permission to tell the guys what happened on our trip to Cancun last month. I...I slept with someone else. And Max watched me do it."

Holy shit. Shy, sweet Ana is a hotwife now? I'm stunned. Right before her trip, she claimed she could never sleep with any other man besides Max. I feel a surprising twinge of jealousy deep in my gut at her unexpected revelation. So many of our friends are experimenting with the lifestyle these days, and I'm starting to wonder what the hell I'm missing out on.

"Oh my god!" Juliet squeals, bouncing excitedly on the sofa across from us. "What was it like? How did it even happen? I need all the dirty details!"

Ana fidgets with the stem of her wine glass. She has a small secretive smile playing as she remembers. "It was actually Max's idea, if you can believe it. He said he thought it would be really exciting and erotic for both of us. And honestly...it was incredible. A total rush. Scary but thrilling, like riding a roller coaster for the first time."

June scoffs, "Well, I'm guessing you aren't the home-wrecking slut that Debra was claiming when she saw you flirting with that trainer online, huh?"

Debra is the prudish wife in our larger friendship circle and she's been a mega judgmental bitch lately, slut-shaming all our friends who are dipping their toes in the lifestyle. She totally blew up at Ana a few weeks ago on our social media group page after seeing Ana posting some thirsty, flirtatious comments to a handsome male bodybuilder online.

Ana blushes an even deeper shade of pink at the memory, and grins bashfully. "Yeah, about that...Max was actually egging me on to sext with the other guy. He got really turned on watching me do it and telling me what to say."

Well, that's shockingly hot. My body hums in delight as I imagine my sweet, submissive husband Jackson doing the same kinky thing—encouraging me to flirt and sext with a hot, ripped guy online while he watches and gets off on it. There's no fucking way that would ever happen in a million years, but I still get a forbidden little thrill shooting up my spine at the naughty thought.

We all pepper Ana with more questions, fascinated by this peek into her newly adventurous sex life. But soon enough, we hear the men clomping up the basement stairs, the poker game apparently over for the night.

As our friends leave, Jackson stands in the open doorway with his arm wrapped around my waist as we wave goodbye to everyone. He exudes comforting strength, reminding me why he's so perfect for me. He and I have our share of problems and disagreements, just like every other couple, but we've been together since college and it's been a damn good ten years.

As Jackson and I get ready for bed, I can't stop thinking about Ana's confession. I wait until we're under the covers to bring it up.

"So, apparently Ana is now a hotwife," I say cautiously, gauging his reaction.

Jackson grins. "I heard the story. Ana seemed the least likely to go for it of all our friends–well, other than Debra." He snorts. "Can you imagine? Debra would probably complain the entire time and slut-shame herself."

My husband's blunt words send an unexpected yearning straight to my core. But instead of picturing Debra, I vividly imagine that it's me in the scenario—crying out what a dirty cock-hungry slut I am while some gorgeous mystery man with a huge cock rails me... with Jackson watching and stroking himself a few feet away. My entire body flushes with heat and I feel slick wetness between my thighs. Fuck.

I almost laugh out loud at myself and my outrageous fantasy as I pull Jackson closer, encouraging him to lay his head on my breast while I play with his hair. Jackson and I may not have a vanilla relationship behind closed doors, but we've never been open to anything wild outside the bedroom. We initially hooked up in college because I thrilled him by taking the dominant role. He was eager to be my sexy little toy and submit to me. It was never supposed to be a permanent dynamic, but we became addicted to each other and the incredible D/s sex, and well...here we are a decade later, still kinky as ever, and also very much in love.

I'm a switch when it comes to BDSM, and while I adore dominating my sexy submissive husband, over the years I sometimes miss the heady thrill of simply being told to get on my knees and worship a big hard cock—of obeying filthy commands and being used like a willing fucktoy. Occasionally, Jackson takes the dominant role, and I love him for doing it, but it's just not in his nature to do it often, and he doesn't fuck me as hard as I crave. I wouldn't trade my relationship with Jackson for the world, though. He's the peanut butter to my jelly, my perfect match.

We lay in comfortable silence for a few minutes, and all I can think about is the fantasy of Jackson watching another man fuck me hard while I surrender to the erotic bliss of being someone else's fucktoy. Jackson's shirtless, the comforter bunched around his waist, and I enjoy the view of his chest. Jackson could easily overpower me physically if he really wanted to, especially because I'm petite at 5'2" and not exactly Wonder Woman strong. But there's nothing sexier to me than bringing a powerful, masculine man to his knees and knowing that he's choosing to let me control and dominate him. The ultimate act of loving submission.

I'm too turned on to sleep and I boldly slide my hand under his pajama pants, heading straight for his semi-hard cock. He chuckles, his eyes crinkling at the corners, as I grab his hardening member and give it a possessive squeeze.

I caress his length and whisper, "Time to earn the privilege of making me breakfast in the morning, my sexy boy toy."

This is an erotic game we like to play on weekends. He always cooks me a delicious breakfast on Sundays, and I like to make him earn the right first. I lightly run my thumb across the head of his cock, massaging the bead of pre-cum into his shaft as it swells in my hand.

Jackson squirms, his breathing picking up. "What would you like me to do, my gorgeous Mistress?"

I trail my fingertips lower to cup and fondle his balls before running my short fingernails teasingly along the sensitive skin of his inner thighs. "First, my sweet slut is going to get naked and then I'm going to give you something to think about," I promise seductively.

I swear I've never seen him get up and scramble out of his pajama bottoms so quickly before. Someone is very excited to play. I stay in bed and shimmy out of my panties and remove my nightgown. I toss them carelessly to the floor. I'm going for maximum efficiency, and pesky clothing will just get in the way of ravaging my man.

When we're both naked and he's back in bed, I give him my most devilish smile. It's time to test the waters and see what my kinky husband really thinks about so many of our friends trying out the hotwife lifestyle lately.

His breath catches as I wrap my fingers around his shaft and slowly start caressing him. His eyes roll back in bliss and he closes them, surrendering to the pleasure.

"That feels so good," he moans, his voice gravelly from desire. "Don't stop, please."

I still my hand, holding his cock against his stomach, and nuzzle his neck as I squeeze the shaft. Biting his earlobe, I whisper, "You're my sweet slut, and you're using such nice manners today. I think you deserve a reward for being so good."

In one graceful movement, I throw my leg over his broad chest and straddle him, pinning his upper body to the bed. I reach over to grab the hot pink fuzzy handcuffs from our toy stash in the nightstand drawer.

I give him a stern order. "Put your hands above your head, my sweet boy. Don't you dare move them."

"Yes, Mistress. Anything you say," he agrees breathlessly, his eyes shining with worship.

He obediently raises his arms, and I feed the fluffy cuffs through the wrought iron bars of our headboard and secure them snugly to his wrists, immobilizing him. I'm briefly tempted to scoot up and ride his talented tongue until I'm screaming in ecstasy, but the ache in my core tells me I really want to feel his cock inside me. I move back down his body until his shaft is trapped between his body and my wet, swollen pussy.

I glide my pussy along the length of his cock, savoring the delicious friction against my throbbing clit. Throwing my head back, I groan loudly in pleasure. "Fuck, that feels amazing, baby."

I undulate my hips, working myself up into a frenzy as I use Jackson like my own personal sex toy. But as wonderful as this feels, I'm ready to kick things up a notch and really blow his mind. First though, I need to tease him a little and see how he reacts to the idea of watching another man fuck me. I'm curious to see his uncensored reaction.

Leaning forward and bracing myself with one hand splayed on his chest, I dangle my tits enticingly in his face, the dusky pink nipples puckered and just begging to be sucked. I keep them maddeningly just out of range of his eager mouth as I roll and pinch one sensitive peak between my thumb and index finger. Jackson moans helplessly, straining against the cuffs, as I continue to slide my drenched pussy up and down his shaft.

"Tell me something, my sweet, slutty boy," I purr, finally bringing one nipple to his parted lips. He immediately latches on hungrily, sucking it and making me gasp. I let him worship my tits for a minute before cruelly pulling them away. "Have you ever fantasized about watching another man fuck me? Letting some hung stud rail your wife right in front of you?"

It's a risky, bold question, I know. He and I have never seriously discussed bringing another person into our bedroom before. But every time Jackson talked about our various friends exploring the hotwife lifestyle, he always sounded more curious and intrigued than disapproving or turned off.

His eyes widen in shock at my question, but I also see an unmistakable spark of hunger flare in their depths as he breathes out, "Jesus, Marcela. Do you...is that something you want to try?"

I grind my hips down harder against his cock in response. "I'm the one asking the questions here, slut," I remind him sternly, before letting my voice go all breathy and seductive again. "Have you ever imagined watching me get railed by a massive cock?"

"God, yes, I have," Jackson admits with a strangled groan as his face contorts in pleasure. "Someone who will fuck you hard while I watch. I want to see you fall apart on another man's cock, Mistress. Will you do it for me someday, please?"

Holy shit, what? I wasn't expecting him to admit it and then ask me to do it. Searing hot pleasure ripples down my spine at his confession and my entire body lights on fire. This is beyond my wildest dreams, and so insanely hot I can hardly think straight. But I know he and I need to have a discussion about this when his mind isn't totally fogged with lust.

I give my voice a singsong lilt. "Maybe I will, if you keep being such a good boy for me."

There's a hunger written all over his face as I move my hand down and grasp the base of his shaft. I slide it against my pussy lips, teasing the entrance and making us both crazed. He jerks against the handcuffs, flexing his hips upward, and I can tell my sweet slut is desperate to feel my pussy around his cock.

I line up the head of his cock in the perfect spot and sink down on him. The moisture between my thighs helps him slide inside easily, and I moan at the exquisite pleasure as my pussy molds around him.

He groans loudly once he's balls deep in my pussy. This right here is always my favorite moment. I enjoy it when my slut services me, but I get a bigger sexual thrill from watching him take pleasure.

I rotate my hips slowly, feeling every inch of his cock massaging my inner walls. "If I let you come, are you going to be a good boy and make me breakfast in the morning?"

He lifts his hips, trying to force me to ride him faster. "Yes," he pants. "Anything you want."

Bracing my hands on his chest for leverage, I start to bounce on his cock, angling my hips so he hits that magic spot inside me just right. My body thrums with excitement, and I close my eyes. The only sounds in the room are our combined moans and the squeak of the bed as we surge together. I can feel my orgasm building, and I know that he'll be a good boy and wait for me to come.

As I fuck him hard and fast, I imagine another guy in the room filling my ass. I'm so surprised at the double stuffed fantasy that it tumbles me into my orgasm.

I cry out, "Oh god, I'm coming!" as wave after wave of toe-curling pleasure crashes over me.

My vision swims as I quiver around his cock. My entire body is wired as I slam my pussy down and grind against him, seeking out the last bits of pleasure.

I take a few moments to recover, and when I can think again, I can tell how badly Jackson needs to come. He's still hard inside me, his shaft pulsing with the force of his denied release.

I kiss him slowly as I stroke his cheek, feeling so lucky that I married a man who lets me treat him like a sexual object when I want, and lets me love him tenderly when I don't. "Thank you for your service, my sweet boy."

His cock jumps with excitement as I move my mouth down to suck on the tender skin of his neck. I'm ready for him to fill me with his cum. I start to lazily rock my hips, squeezing my inner muscles around his shaft. His answering groan is music to my ears.

I tease him one final time. "Beg for it, my sweet boy. Beg to fill my pussy."

"Mistress," he gasps, his eyes snapping shut. I can tell by his expression he's on the brink. "Please, please. Let me fill you. Oh, fuck."

He's so sweet when he's begging, but I put him out of his misery and command, "Come for me."

"Fuck, Mistress! Oh shit, fuck yes!" he moans, his cock twitching inside me with the force of his intense orgasm.

I feel his warm cum bathe my insides and I keep rocking, milking his cock for every last drop. Knowing I gave him pleasure makes me feel sexy and powerful.

After he comes down, I free his wrists from the handcuffs and cuddle with him, enjoying the scent of our lovemaking. He wraps his arms around me and he's quiet for a long time. I smile to myself, knowing that the stronger his orgasm is, the longer it takes for his brain to work.

"Mmm, that was amazing as always, baby. You did so good," I praise him, enjoying the blissful afterglow. "Thank you for letting me use you like that. You're such a good boy for me."

Jackson pulls me closer, nuzzling his face into my hair. "I love being your good boy. You really do deserve whatever you want for breakfast."

I giggle and kiss his chest. "I'm a simple girl; bacon, eggs, and toast, please."

"Your wish is my command, Mistress. I love you so much," he murmurs drowsily.

I smile and hug him tighter, breathing in his familiar, comforting scent. "I love you too, baby. More than anything."

I'll wait until morning when we're both fully awake to discuss what he said during sex. It was probably just the heat of the moment, but I'm not going to complain if my husband WANTS me to fuck someone else.

CHAPTER 2

After a delicious breakfast the next morning, we're snuggled up on the living room sofa watching a TV show. We're relaxing today, and we planned to watch two back-to-back episodes, but to my surprise, he pauses the show after the first one ends, turning to face me with an unreadable expression.

"Is something up, baby?" I ask lightly, trying to keep the sudden unease out of my voice. My mind immediately flashes back to the erotic banter last night, my body warming up at the memory.

Jackson clears his throat, looking oddly nervous. "Um, yeah, actually. We need to talk."

Pasting on what I hope is a reassuring smile, I squeeze his knee. "What's on your mind, love?"

He takes my hand, threading our fingers together. I rub my thumb soothingly over his skin, trying to ease both our nerves as I wonder if this is it—the moment of truth. Is he about to admit that he was caught up in the heat of the moment and he doesn't want me to be a hotwife, or is he going to confess he really does? Am I going to be disappointed if he doesn't?

Jackson studies our entwined hands and the seconds tick by in silence. Finally, I can't take it anymore. I gently remove my hand from his and reach up to cup his cheek, forcing him to meet my eyes. "Jackson, look at me."

His eyes blaze with an intensity that surprises me, and he finally speaks. "I want to watch another man fuck you, but not just anyone," he admits.

Wow. Okay. I'm already nodding because it's an easy request. I don't want it to be just anyone either. If I'm going to fuck someone else, I want it to be mind-blowingly hot and memorable. And if I'm being honest, I'd like someone with a big cock. Not that Jackson is small by any means, but I've always been curious what it would feel like to be split open on a really massive dick, you know?

Mentally shaking myself out of my X-rated musings, I refocus on my husband, who is watching me closely. "I want it to be a guy who can give you what I can't," he continues urgently. "What I'm not giving you."

Wait, what's that supposed to mean? Does he think I'm not satisfied with our amazing sex life and he's not enough for me? The thought makes me feel uneasy.

"Baby, no. You make me happier than I ever thought possible," I rush to reassure him, stroking his stubbled cheek. "I don't need anything or anyone else."

To my relief, Jackson chuckles, his eyes crinkling at the corners. "I know that, sweetheart. Believe me, I do." He leans in to kiss me softly before saying sheepishly, "I didn't phrase that very well."

As if to prove his point, he takes my hand and places it on his denim-clad crotch. I can feel that his cock is already semi-erect and growing harder by the second. Holy fuck.

He grins at me. "That's not what I meant. What I was trying to say is...I've been fantasizing about watching someone dominant absolutely wreck you and do all the things to you that I'm not confident enough to do myself. I want to see the blissed-out, totally fucked look on your beautiful face when he's railing you and making you come so hard you scream. I just...fuck, I want to be there experiencing it with you as you're getting your mind blown by a real Dom guy."

I gape at him, completely speechless. He's been fantasizing about this? Like, specific, detailed fantasies of another man dominating the fuck out of me while he watches? Jesus Christ. A pleasurable shock zings through my body like an electric current, making my nerve endings sizzle and my pussy flood with moisture. My clit throbs in time with my racing pulse as I picture it—Jackson stroking his cock as he sits in a chair a few feet away, watching me get pounded into oblivion by a dominant stranger. The forbidden image is so searingly erotic that my brain shorts out for a minute, lost to the fantasy.

When I finally regain the power of speech, my voice trembles with need. "You've really been fantasizing about this?"

He nods, swallowing hard, and I can see a telltale flush creeping up his neck above the collar of his t-shirt. He's blushing. It's adorable and sexy as hell.

Emboldened, I start to slowly rub his stiffening cock through his jeans, feeling it twitch and swell. He groans low in his throat, hips shifting restlessly as I give him a firm squeeze. "Tell me, baby...have you been stroking yourself while imagining another man dominating me? Picturing him wrecking my pussy with his enormous cock until I'm a writhing, screaming mess? Is that what gets you off these days?"

"Yes," he rasps. "Sometimes when I'm watching porn, I imagine it's you in the video, practically cross-eyed with pleasure. I can't help it."

Fuck me, this is so deliciously dirty and unexpected. Who knew my sweet, submissive husband had such a filthy, voyeuristic side? The revelation makes desire swirl in my lower belly. "Mmm, you naughty boy. Did you stroke your cock faster when the man in the video started groaning as he got close? Did you imagine him blowing his big load all over me while you watched?" I ask breathlessly, rubbing him harder through his jeans.

Jackson's hands clench into fists at his sides and he squeezes his eyes shut, clearly fighting for control. His hips buck up into my touch and he moans, "Yes, Mistress. I did."

I click my tongue in mock disapproval even as my pussy grows increasingly wet. "Eyes open. Look at me when you're confessing your dirty secrets,"

He obeys instantly, staring up at me. "Good boy. Now, why the hell didn't you tell me about this sexy fantasy of yours sooner, hmm?"

Jackson shrugs helplessly, looking flustered. "I don't know. I guess it was just a private fantasy at first. I didn't think you'd actually want to do it for real."

My heart melts a little at his sweetness, even as my body screams at me to strip him naked and ride him until we both pass out. But first, we need to get a few things straight. Letting go of his straining erection, I put my hand under his chin instead, tilting his face up to mine and forcing him to maintain eye contact. I use my normal, everyday voice so he understands this is just me, his wife, talking to him, not his Mistress.

"Baby, listen to me. I would absolutely love to fulfill this fantasy for you. For us. But only if you're really, truly sure you want it too," I say seriously, holding his gaze. "I don't need other men to be satisfied, physically or emotionally. What you and I have fulfills me. You're more than enough for me, always. I need you to know that."

He smiles at me tenderly, his eyes going soft and warm. "I do know that, Marcela. I promise. You're all I need too. I want this because the thought of sharing you, of watching you come undone with another man, is a huge fucking turn-on for me. But only because I know at the end of the day, your heart belongs to me. I'm secure in that. In us."

If I wasn't ready to jump him before, I sure as hell am now. This man! Overwhelmed with love and passion, I surge forward and crash my lips to his in a bruising kiss, moaning into his mouth as I straddle his lap. He kisses me back just as fiercely, his strong arms wrapping around my waist and hauling me closer. We make out for several minutes until we're both panting.

Breaking away with a gasp, I roll my hips against the rigid line of his cock, seeking friction. "Well, in that case…start looking for a well-hung guy to fuck your wife, baby," I grin wickedly. "Because I'm all in."

Jackson grasps my gyrating hips, holding me in place. "Fuck yes," he groans. "Thank you, Mistress."

I kiss him one last time before reluctantly climbing off his lap on shaky legs. I'm tempted to pull his cock out and fuck him right now, but I resist… barely.

Smirking at his dazed, lust-drunk expression, I press one finger to his kiss-swollen lips in a shushing gesture as he opens his mouth to protest the loss of contact. "That's all you get until you find a sexy Dom to fuck your wife while you watch," I tease, tracing the seam of his lips. He nips at my finger, eyes dancing with mischief, and I tap his nose in reproach. "Be a good boy. Just think about how incredible it'll feel when I fuck you after you watch me get absolutely wrecked by a big, thick cock. The wait will be more than worth it, trust me."

Jackson mutters something that sounds suspiciously like, "Evil, cock-teasing succubus," under his breath, but wisely keeps any other complaints to himself. I know I have him exactly where I want him—horny as hell and willing to do anything to get some relief.

"So, you have your orders. Find me a stud to play with, and I'll give you the ride of your life afterwards. Now I'm going to get some water for the next episode."

I sashay out of the room with an extra sway to my hips, grinning like the cat that caught the canary. I have a feeling my kinky husband will have found the perfect guy to dom the hell out of me by this time next week.

This is going to be fun.

CHAPTER 3

I was wrong. He found someone the next day.

I work from home as a transcriptionist and when I take my first break on Monday, there's a text waiting for me.

Jackson

> I got you a guy.

My body tingles from a zing of pleasure and my nipples harden.

Marcela

> Oh? That was fast.

Grabbing a glass of water, some string cheese, and grapes, I settle onto the sofa. This conversation deserves my full attention. I smile and take a sip of water as I see the chat bubbles pop up as my husband is replying.

Jackson

> I actually found three guys. You get your pick, or you can have them all at once.

His words make me suck in my breath, which turns into a coughing fit as I try to swallow the water down the wrong pipe. Holy fuck...Yes, please! I didn't even contemplate more than one man as an option. I mean, I've got three holes...I don't even know what to say, so I type without thinking.

Marcela

> **Do I want that many at once?**

Jackson

> **I think you do.**

Well, hell, if he wants me to have three cocks...

Marcela

> **You're right. I do. Who are they?**

Jackson types out the details while I eat my snack. Victor, one of his work buddies, has always thought I was super hot. When Jackson joked with Victor about fucking me to see if he'd really want to do it, Victor said he had two friends he could bring along to show me a really good time. I guess the guys have done this before.

Fuck, that's slutty, and so damn hot. I type to my husband and tell him to set it up.

I can barely pay attention to work after that as I daydream about fucking multiple men. I love being domme for my husband, but my submissive side doesn't get to play much. This experience isn't just about fucking another man; the idea that I can really become a submissive slut is the best part.

Jackson keeps texting me and we discuss everything. He's checking with his coworker to find out when they're all free. The plan is to have them come over to our house, but after I agree to it, I almost wish we were going somewhere else. My filthy side wants to embrace the naughtiness of what we're doing and I'm not sure our house is going to make me feel like we're doing something illicit.

After lunch, I give up pretending I'm working. I try on some sexy lingerie, debating what to wear. I send my husband a photo of myself from the neck down. I'm topless with a sexy garter belt and lace black thong, and tell him to share it with the guys so they can see what they're getting. Now that I've embraced the plan to be a hotwife, I'm so turned on it's crazy.

As I put away the lingerie tossed in a pile on the bed, Jackson sends me another text.

Jackson

> They just told me they're free tonight. Want to fuck them tonight?

I'm so shocked, I laugh out loud and dial his number immediately. As soon as I hear his voice, an idea comes to me. I don't care that I sound like a total slut when I tell him, "I want it to be at a cheap motel. Make it happen and text me the address and time. I'll meet you there."

My sweet, submissive husband confirms my request. "I'll have the room ready."

I hang up the phone and stare at the wall as my body buzzes. I guess I'm getting all my holes stuffed tonight in a cheap motel so I can feel extra dirty and used.

The idea thrills me to no end, but I'm suddenly overcome by the magnitude of this experience. Am I really doing this? I know it's something I want, but it still feels unreal. My head spins as I change into my sluttiest outfit. The black skirt I pick out is tight and barely covers my ass, and my blouse is a low cut V-neck that I'm practically popping out of. I forgo a bra and I can tell my nipples will pop against the fabric of my shirt. The last item of clothing is a sexy black thong. I decide to wear my long brown hair in a ponytail so it doesn't get caught on all the extra body parts.

I apply minimal makeup, knowing it will be a mess by the end of the night. Yep, I'm a practical gal. I slip on my four-inch fuck-me heels and practice walking in them for a few minutes. Hopefully, I won't be wearing them for very long.

I imagine showing up and stripping in the hotel room in front of everyone, and I shiver from longing. If someone had told me two days ago that I'd be fucking multiple guys tonight, I wouldn't have believed them.

Yeah, I'm really doing this. I'm about to become a hotwife.

Right before I leave, I toss a bottle of lube into my purse. I'm not sure if anyone will want to use my ass, but I'm going to be prepared. There's a certain thrill from knowing I'm not meeting Jackson at a fancy hotel for a romantic rendezvous. Nope, I'm going to a seedy motel where he and I are renting a room for the sole purpose of a hard pussy pounding. The anticipation is exhilarating. I just hope I can relax enough to lose my inhibitions. What if fucking people I don't know is awkward?

By the time I get there, I'm shaking with arousal and nervousness. I park my car, grab my purse, and hurry to the room, eager to get fucked.

I knock on the door, and Jackson opens it with a grin. "Hi."

"Hi." I smile back at him and he steps aside to let me in. We arranged for the guys to arrive after me, so we're alone right now. As the door closes, I scan the room, and it's exactly as I expected: threadbare carpet and mismatched furniture, with an air conditioner unit rattling from the corner. It's perfect for the occasion.

Jackson touches my ass, and I glance over my shoulder and purr at him, "Like what you see?"

"Oh yeah," he laughs, and when I turn towards him, his gaze fixes on my chest.

My nipples harden and I almost giggle as I say, "My eyes are up here, baby."

He's vibrating with desire when he looks up, and I get a nice thrill from knowing he's turned on as much as I am. I press my body against his, sliding my arms around his neck and pulling him down for a kiss. When our lips touch, it's all fire and passion. He's so familiar and comforting, yet exciting at the same time.

When we come up for air, his eyes are clouded with lust. I give him a teasing pat on the butt and say, "Okay, hands off the merchandise. Save your energy for the main event."

There's a large mirror on the wall above a small dresser, and I notice my cheeks are extra pink and my eyes sparkle. Yeah, I'm a horny slut. I set my purse on the dresser and fish out the lube before looking at Jackson with a smirk. "Should I be naked when they get here?"

He doesn't have time to answer because there's a sharp rap on the door. My stomach jumps from excitement. My first foray into being a hotwife is about to begin.

Jackson rushes to the door and opens it to reveal three muscular guys. I swear, as soon as the men enter the room, my pussy grows even wetter. Oh my god, I'm getting dicked down in a seedy motel room by these gorgeous men?

Two of the men are white, one with blonde hair and the other bald, and the third guy is Black with dark hair. They're all extremely good looking and athletic. They're casually dressed in jeans and t-shirts, and I can already see impressive bulges underneath the denim.

Jackson clears his throat to get my attention. "Marcela, this is Victor, Daniel, and Shawn."

I quickly try to memorize their names. Victor is the blonde guy, Daniel is bald, and Shawn is Black.

All of them greet me with friendly waves and smiles, and I relax as I return the greeting. "Nice to meet you."

Victor seems to be the leader of the group, and he takes charge. He moves in close and cups my jaw, tipping my face up. My pulse races as I stare into his eyes.

"This isn't how I normally fuck other people's wives, so I need to hear you say you want it."

The fact that he's worried about consent makes my panties even wetter, and my voice is breathy. "I want all of you to fuck me."

He studies me, and apparently he's satisfied with my answer. A slow, devilish smile curves his lips. "Good to know. We're going to have fun toying with you."

His words and tone of voice immediately start making me feel submissive, and I can already tell this is going to be fabulous. It's been so long since I've felt the delicious mindlessness of being someone's fucktoy, and I'm ready to embrace my sluttiest side.

He takes my hand and leads me to the center of the room. My chest is heaving and I'm having a difficult time catching my breath as his fingers ghost down my throat. "One last detail to work out. Your husband wants us to dominate you and turn you into a wet puddle. What do you want?"

A deep longing grips me, and I almost forget to breathe. Holy hell, I'm already a wet puddle. Mission accomplished.

When I realize they're all staring at me and waiting for my answer, I say in a rush, "I want that. Dominate me. Treat me like a dirty slut who's only here to satisfy all of you." The longer I talk, the faster the words spill out, coming from deep within me. "Break me down until I can't think. Just fuck me senseless, please. I'll do whatever you want."

Victor shares a look with his friends. "In that case, slut, get on your knees and open your mouth."

I tremble with excitement as I awkwardly kneel next to the bed. My damn high heels are already getting in the way, but the struggle just makes me feel dirtier. Looking up at them ready to use me and knowing they could fuck my mouth all night and I wouldn't complain is the final piece that snaps me into my most submissive self. I'm completely ready to be used.

Jackson sits in a chair facing the bed, and the other guys remove their shirts. My gaze lands on their taut stomachs and chiseled chests. My body buzzes as I imagine how their skin is going to feel against mine. It's been over ten years since I've intimately touched a man other than Jackson, and I'm curious to explore the differences between the men.

My heart flutters when I hear a zipper lowering right behind me, and my scalp prickles as my ponytail is taken by a fist and my head is pulled back. I blink to clear my vision and focus. It's Daniel. He's leaning over me, his expression fierce.

"Do you know what a mouth is for, slut?"

I manage to murmur, "For sucking cocks."

"Show me, whore," he demands.

It's so hot to hear a stranger call me degrading names like that. He moves in front of me and guides his cock to my mouth. I shudder with pleasure as I lick the underside of his shaft.

Daniel's hands wrap around my head, and the pressure he applies intensifies when I part my lips to take him into my mouth. His steel rod slides past my lips and I curl my tongue around the tip before opening wider. His cock is bigger than my husband's and I daydream of how it will feel inside my pussy as I suck on him, swirling my tongue across his velvety skin.

I feel another man behind me and I hear the sounds of a zipper and the rustling of fabric. My heart races with excitement.

Daniel's grip on my head tightens as he thrusts deeper into my mouth. I can taste his pre-cum, and it makes me even more eager to please him. I moan around his cock, and the vibrations make him groan in pleasure.

Victor interrupts. "Let's put the slut on the bed. I need to use a hole."

Oh, wow. Daniel pulls out of my mouth and helps me to my feet. I kick off my heels in relief, and suddenly three pairs of hands are all over me, tugging and pulling at my clothes. It's like a whirlwind, and before I can blink, I'm standing naked while all eyes are on me. I feel a rush of vulnerability and I want to hide my tits behind my hands, but I force myself to stand tall and let the men examine me.

Victor takes charge again and pushes me onto the bed. "Get on your hands and knees."

I scramble to obey and position myself at an angle that gives Jackson a side view of the action. Daniel stands in front of me while I eagerly suck on him. I wasn't done with my treat.

Victor climbs on the bed behind me and grabs my hips, and his hard cock presses against my ass. I tremble with desire as he rubs the tip of his cock, poking at my asshole, teasing me. Shit, should I tell him to get the lube? Not that I really can, since my mouth is busy.

When the tip of his cock probes the entrance of my pussy, I relax—yeah, okay, that hole is nice and wet for him. He thrusts forward, filling me in one swift motion. I cry out around Daniel's cock as Victor starts to fuck me hard and fast.

Ooooh, he's not wasting time. I throw myself into the blow job as delight ripples through me from Victor's hard thrusts. I can feel myself getting wetter as the bliss swirls in my core. At this rate, I'm going to come quickly. Victor's cock is hitting all the right spots in my pussy, and the room spins from the pleasure.

I start to move my hips in rhythm with Victor, meeting him thrust for thrust. I can hear the sound of our bodies slapping together and it's so fucking hot.

Shawn moves in front of me, his cock already hard and ready. He grabs my chin and pulls me away from Daniel's cock. "It's my turn."

I eagerly open my mouth. He's bigger than Daniel, and it takes me a moment to adjust to his size as he slides in. I'm determined to please him, and I suck and lick his cock with abandon.

Victor is still fucking me hard, and I can feel myself getting closer and closer to my orgasm. Every time I moan around Shawn's cock, it makes him inhale from pleasure. Being used in two holes at once pings the part of my brain that loves being a fucktoy. I'm on cloud nine, and knowing Jackson is watching makes it so much better.

When Victor reaches underneath me to rub my clit while he fucks me, the sensation shoots me over the edge. My body goes rigid, and I come apart as I shake with pleasure. When my pussy seizes around Victor's cock, he hisses and pulls out before he comes.

My head is whirling from delight when Shawn pulls out of my mouth and lies down on the bed. I'm woozy from the pleasure of my orgasm as Victor and Daniel lift me up and set me down on Shawn's cock. Being moved around like a sex toy is so damn hot.

I moan loudly as I sink down on Shawn's shaft, his thick cock stretching me. His hands wrap around my waist and he thrusts up into me. Holy hell, he feels amazing. It's like he's pinging every nerve ending inside me and I mewl out little peeps of delight.

"Fuck her harder," Victor demands, and Shawn complies without hesitation. His hands tighten on my sides as he forces me to move with him and grind against the base of his cock. It's borderline painful, but it's a glorious pleasure. My husband picked some fabulous guys.

Daniel comes up behind me. "Get ready for some serious ass pounding."

He presses on my shoulder and I lean forward. Mmm, yes, please. I gasp as Daniel applies the lube to my ass, working it in with his finger before his cock slides into my ass. Ooooh, god. I've never had two cocks at once, and I moan as the pleasure threatens to overwhelm me.

Shawn grunts as he thrusts deeper into me, and a tingling sensation zips through me, straight to my pussy. How did I not do this in college when I was going through my slut phase and experimenting? It's sensory overload and I've never felt as full as I do right now.

"You're so fucking tight," Shawn growls, and Daniel agrees. "God, she is. I could fuck this ass all night long."

Out of the corner of my eye, I can see Jackson watching everything. He's stroking his cock over his jeans with a rapt expression on his face. Thank god he's enjoying this.

Victor kneels next to me, moving his cock towards my face. A delicious ache between my legs makes me almost smile. Mmm, yes... all holes will be stuffed. I open my mouth eagerly as he slides in.

My body is on fire and I'm lost in a haze of pleasure. This might be heaven right here—assuming it's filled with massive cocks. My heaven would be.

I moan and writhe with pleasure between the men as they fuck me. I'm their sex toy to use, just a bunch of holes...and I love it. Every part of me zings with euphoria and I feel like I'm going to explode as I'm barreling towards another orgasm. This one is going to be intense.

Victor grips my hair, pulling me closer to him as he thrusts into my mouth. I can feel his cock hitting the back of my throat, and I gag slightly, but I don't care. I want to please him and make him come as hard as his friends are about to make me.

Daniel's fingers dig into my hips as he fucks me harder, his cock hitting that perfect spot inside me. I moan around Victor's cock, my body shaking with pleasure.

Shawn's hands are on my breasts, squeezing and pinching my nipples as every thrust into my ass forces me down harder onto his cock. I'm lost in the moment, my body being used and pleasured by three men at once. It's everything I've ever fantasized about, and it's even better than I imagined.

Victor suddenly pulls out of my mouth, his cock glistening with my saliva. He strokes his cock, aiming the tip towards my face. Oh god, is he going to give me a facial?

When Shawn's cock hits a particularly pleasurable spot, I gasp and open my mouth. Victor rubs the tip across my lips. I try to lick on him and suck on the head of his cock, but he pulls it away.

I'm spiraling closer and closer to my orgasm, and I cry out as my body shudders, my pussy contracting around Shawn's cock as he pounds into me.

Daniel spanks me and the pain adds to my pleasure and tips me over the edge. I scream out with my orgasm and Daniel growls, "That's it, come for us. Such a dirty slut, letting all of us fuck you at the same time."

As I ride out the waves of my orgasm, Victor pushes his cock deep into my mouth. I gag on his cock again, but he doesn't pull out. Instead, he holds me in place, making me drool around his shaft as he fucks my mouth. Somehow, he knows exactly how much I can take. It's the perfect roughness, and I love it.

As my orgasm subsides, I'm left breathless and weak, but the guys aren't done with me yet. Daniel speeds up his thrusts into my ass, and the pleasure builds. There's no way I'm not going to want to do this again—maybe next time I can have a cock in each hand as well. Five at once... the ultimate slut.

Since I can think a little easier now, I try to focus on my husband and make sure he's still okay. He looks dazed, like his mind is fuzzy, but I can tell he's entranced by the scene. He probably didn't know how big of a slut he married. After this experience, I'm ready to take on an entire sports team.

When Jackson realizes I'm looking at him, he smiles at me and continues stroking his cock through his pants. If my mouth wasn't full of cock, I'd blow him a kiss.

I'm brought back to what's happening to me when Shawn sucks on a nipple. As he massages my other breast, a zing of pleasure heads straight to my clit. Having both guys in me, someone sucking on a tit, and a cock in my mouth is too much.

I explode.

The orgasm that rolls through my body is unlike any I've ever experienced before. My legs shake, and I'm overcome with waves of pleasure as I cry out. I'm suddenly in a place where I can feel everything all at once and my vision blurs from euphoria.

Victor pulls out of my mouth, but Daniel and Shawn keep going, driving me to another peak as my mind splinters from pleasure. Stars burst behind my eyelids as my orgasm seems to go on and on. A dark thrill winds its way through me and I know I'm just a fucktoy for them to use all they want. I'd give them anything. I don't know how much more I can take, but I know I don't want it to end.

I lose track of how many times I come. My mind is reeling, and my body is completely spent. I feel like I'm floating on a cloud, and I have a hard time focusing as they continue to use me.

Eventually, it's as if time speeds up, and everything happens at once. Daniel groans a moment before he blows his load in my ass. I feel his cum filling me, and the sensation is exquisite. I clench around Shawn's cock in my pussy and he hisses as I milk his cock for all he's worth. Shawn's entire body spasms as he comes deep inside me. Ropes of sticky cum coat my inner walls, and I imagine it gushing out of me when he pulls out. I've been filled in both holes, and I look around for Victor. Where did he go?

He's standing next to the bed, stroking his cock, and after Daniel pulls out of my ass, Victor pushes me off of Shawn and rolls me onto my back.

I've barely come down from the last orgasm before my pussy is being filled with Victor's cock. Oh god!

"You still like it hard, right?" Victor asks.

I nod and brace myself for his relentless pace as Victor pounds away at my pussy. Within moments, I can already feel another orgasm building. Can someone pass out from bliss?

I don't have time to think about it too much as Shawn climbs onto the bed and kneels by my head. He grabs my hand and wraps it around his shaft, and he moans as I stroke him. I love the way he's taking control and using me for his own pleasure.

Shawn's cock is wet from my juices, and it pulses in my hand as he gets closer to another release. I run my thumb over the head of his shaft and it's like flipping a switch. He shudders and explodes, aiming for my tits. Three shots of cum hit me.

I close my eyes and concentrate on the sensations. When Victor brings a hand down to my clit and brushes circles around it, I detonate. I cry out, my body writhing in ecstasy as the orgasm pulses through me.

I'm still trembling and twitching as the last drops of come drip down onto my chest. Victor groans and jerks several times. I can feel his warm cum filling me up and mixing with Shawn's previous load.

When Victor rolls off of me, I assume everyone is done with me, but Daniel walks out of the bathroom and he's hard again. He pulls me to the edge of the bed so my head is hanging off and he guides his cock into my mouth. I can tell he cleaned up in the bathroom as his shaft sinks into my throat.

He leans over me, bracing his hands on the bed while he uses my throat as his fleshlight. I've never been treated this way, and it's absolutely amazing. Someone at the other end of the bed spreads my legs and starts rubbing the cum dripping out of me around my clit. They aren't finger fucking me, they're just playing with the combined wetness between my legs. It's almost dirtier this way, and I moan around Daniel's cock.

The vibration of my moan sets Daniel off and he blows his load deep in my throat. When he pulls out, cum and saliva smear across my cheek and I almost giggle. I'm sure I look wrecked.

I glance down at the guy playing with my pussy and get a shock when it's Jackson. Oh fuck. My husband is playing with the cum in my pussy. When he sees me look at him, he smiles.

"You're so wet."

I'm too mentally fucked to do anything but moan in pleasure as he continues to swirl his fingers around my clit. My husband briefly stops playing with my pussy to pull me all the way back up onto the bed, but then he resumes his fingering as he talks to the guys. I close my eyes and I'm vaguely aware of the men getting dressed.

I can barely move a muscle, but I also feel more satisfied than I ever have in my life. I let out a contented sigh as the men gather up their things and leave with a collective, "Thank you."

The door shuts and I'm alone with my husband. I muster the energy to pat the bed next to me.

"Take your clothes off and come cuddle, baby."

I'm not sure what I have the energy for, but I desperately need contact with him. I need to feel him inside me and hear him say that he still loves me after watching me be such a filthy slut.

Jackson gets undressed and when he's next to me, I can't help but chuckle.

He raises his eyebrows. "What's funny?"

I grab his still-hard cock. "This. You still want me."

He smiles. "I'll never stop wanting you, not in a million years. How do you feel?"

My whole body aches in a pleasant way, and I don't want him worrying about that. This is now his time. I kiss his nose and squeeze his cock. "I'm sore in all the right ways, and I really, really love you."

His grin is so bright it warms my insides. His fingers trail up my arm and he moves them to my nipple, tweaking it. "I really, really love you, too. It was so hot, watching you get dominated."

When he massages the sticky cum into my breasts, I realize he's staring at his hands. He's definitely fascinated with the fluid. I can't blame him for it since I enjoy it as well. I moan as his hand returns to my pussy and his finger runs between my folds.

I hum with pleasure and murmur softly, "So you liked that?"

He chuckles. "More than I expected."

My pussy is getting too sensitive, and I give him a gentle order. "Stop toying with me and get your cock inside me. I need you."

He hesitates. "You're sure? I could wait. You've been through a lot."

My heart warms from how sweet he is. I can see how desperately he wants me, and I bet he'd wait if I asked him to.

"I want you, baby."

I open my arms to him and he covers my body with his. He's gentle as his cock fills me with one stroke, and I moan as he bottoms out. It feels different. I'm stuffed full of the other guys' cum, but Jackson's cock feels new. I need this, this connection with the love of my life after fucking other men.

"You feel so good," he murmurs against my shoulder as he slowly fucks me.

When he tries to kiss me, I hold his cheek to stop him. "You sure you want to kiss your wife after she sucked on two cocks?"

His nostrils flare, and I know I've turned him on with the dirty talk. His voice is gruff when he says, "That makes me want to kiss you even more."

The desperation in his voice is thrilling. I'm a slut, and it's sexy to be his slut. His lips descend to mine, and we kiss deeply, our tongues twining as we rock together. I love the way he makes me feel. It's like electricity crackling between us, and I can't get enough. The steady rhythm of his cock makes me sigh. I let go and float along, enjoying the moment. He's worshiping my body with his hands and cock, and it's lovely to feel like I've come home. He's mine and I'm his, and no one can ever take that away from us.

When his breath quickens and his moans get louder, I whisper to him. "You can fuck me harder. I need you to come."

Jackson kisses me and I arch my hips so he can fuck me deeper as his thrusting grows more urgent. He grasps my hips tightly with both hands and I wonder if there'll be bruises tomorrow. He's my gentle giant, so for him to be using such force means he's consumed with desire.

I can tell he's getting close, so I give him the command. "Come for me. Give me everything."

That's the breaking point. He comes hard.

His muscles strain and his hips buck. I'm wrapped around him, my fingers digging into his shoulders, and I can feel when his control slips and he surrenders to his release. He comes hard, crying out as he buries his face in my neck. I cling to him as he spills his seed inside me. I never want to let go.

His climax triggers a surprise orgasm for me, and I cry out as we both ride the waves of bliss. My mind blanks from pleasure and I'm not sure how long we stay locked together.

When my brain finally starts working, his face is still buried in my neck and his heavy breaths tickle my skin. I can't stop smiling. My heart swells as I run my hands along his back.

He lifts his head to give me a questioning look. "Is it bad that I want to do this again someday?"

I laugh as I push him off of me. "Maybe someday, if my good boy begs enough, I might let him watch other men fuck me again."

He just grins and starts licking the cum off my breasts. I shiver as he lavishes attention on my nipples. Yeah, he's definitely my good boy...but more importantly, a whole new world of opportunities has opened up for our marriage. If he wants to watch a train of guys dominate me and fuck me, I'm open to the idea.

Being a hotwife might just be the best thing that's happened for our marriage.

My friends are going to think this is hilarious. I can't wait for the next poker night to tell them.

The End

June Hotwife

Hotwife of the Month Club 6

Lacey Cross

CHAPTER 1

I smile and wave to our friends as we leave the monthly get-together at Marcela's house. It was a great night, with laughter and chatter from the girls' night upstairs while the guys played poker downstairs. My husband Mark's hand rests lightly on the small of my back as we make our way to our sensible family sedan parked at the curb.

As our friends Ana and Max climb into their car ahead of us, Ana turns back and gives me a wave, her eyes sparkling with mischief. I grin back at her, my mind still reeling from her earlier confession. Sweet, shy Ana is apparently a hotwife now. Her husband watched her with another guy. The very idea sparks a forbidden thrill within me.

Juliet saunters over to me, her hips swaying in her form-fitting dress. She leans in close, her spicy perfume enveloping me as she stage-whispers in my ear, "Call me tomorrow. I've got some tea to spill that I think you'll find verrry interesting."

She pulls back with a wicked grin, giving me an exaggerated wink before flouncing off to her sleek convertible where her husband is waiting. I chuckle and shake my head as I watch her go, wondering what salacious gossip she's eager to share. With Juliet, it could be anything from a celebrity sighting at her favorite spa to a new sex position she swears will "change your life, honey."

As Mark and I buckle up and pull away from the curb, anticipation flickers in my gut. I know it's silly, but a part of me is hoping my husband will take advantage of our precious few minutes left of being kid-free and ravish me in the back seat like he used to when we were first dating. But the rational side of my brain knows that's unlikely. After a long week of juggling deadlines at my marketing firm, his full-time job, and getting our 4-year-old twins to and from preschool, we're both usually wiped out by the weekend.

The drive home is quiet, and I steal a glance at Mark's profile in the dim glow of the dashboard lights. Even after eight years of marriage, my husband is still sexy to me and I find him incredibly handsome. But lately, I've started to wonder if he still sees me as the vibrant, passionate woman he fell in love with or just the mother of his children and manager of our hectic household.

When we finally get home, I pay the babysitter as Mark heads upstairs. I lock up and check on the kids, and by the time I slip into our bedroom, Mark is already sprawled on his back in bed, one arm flung over his eyes. He's down to his boxers, his toned chest and arms on display. I appreciate how sexy he is as I undress.

"Did you have fun tonight?" he mumbles sleepily, not moving his arm.

"Mmm hmm. It's always fun to visit with the girls." I shimmy out of my dress and kick off my shoes, sighing in relief as I wiggle my newly freed toes.

Mark makes a vaguely affirmative noise, already half asleep. I want to bring up Ana's hotwifing bombshell, if only to gauge his reaction. But suddenly, I'm too tired to get into it. My wine buzz is wearing off, replaced by a bone-deep fatigue and the start of a dull headache throbbing at my temples.

Instead, I finish my nighttime routine in silence, washing the traces of makeup from my face and brushing my teeth before crawling into bed beside Mark. He's fully out now, his breathing deep and even. I curl up on my side facing away from him, trying to ignore the pang of loneliness that lances through my chest.

As I lie there in the dark, my mind drifts back to Ana's revelation. What would it be like to be with another man after all these years with Mark? To feel that electric thrill and experience the heady rush of being wanted, craved, by someone new. The forbidden fantasy sends little sparks of heat through my body.

But that's not my life. All I have this week is an endless slog of work, kids, chores, rinse and repeat. Tomorrow, I'll call Juliet and get the gossip. Maybe it will be the diversion I need. And who knows? Ana could be onto something with this whole hotwifing thing. The idea is crazy, but also...intriguing. Not that I'd ever get the chance, but it might be fun to live vicariously through Ana for a bit. To experience that thrill, even secondhand.

My last thought before I drift off is that I hope Juliet's gossip is juicy enough to get me through another monotonous week. I could use something to look forward to for a change.

CHAPTER 2

The next morning, I'm jolted awake by the sound of my phone buzzing insistently on the nightstand. I groan and grope for it blindly, squinting at the screen through bleary eyes. It's Juliet. Of course. She's never been one to let the suspense build.

I glance over at Mark's side of the bed, but he's already up and out for his Sunday morning run. Probably for the best, since I can talk freely and get the scoop. I answer the phone and try to stifle my yawn.

"Morning, Jules. I'm assuming this is about that gossip you promised?"

"Oh honey, you have no idea," Juliet trills, sounding far too chipper for this ungodly hour. "Are you sitting down? Because trust me, you'll need to be."

I roll my eyes even though she can't see me. "I'm still in bed, so yeah, I'm good. Hit me."

"Okay, so you know our favorite little sanctimonious Debra? Well, apparently she's started a secret blog all about—get this—the 'dangers of open marriages and the hotwife trend.'" Juliet practically cackles with glee. "I guess she's appointed herself the morality police of our friend group."

I sit up straighter, suddenly wide awake. Debra is in our larger circle of friends because her husband went to college with our husbands, but she's been slut shaming our friends for becoming hotwives. "Wait, what? How did you even find out about this?"

"Oh, I have my ways," Juliet says cryptically. "Anyway, you'll never believe the shade she's throwing. Listen to this passage."

Juliet clears her throat dramatically. "'In today's depraved society, it seems that the sanctity of marriage is under constant attack. Everywhere I look, I see once-faithful wives eagerly opening their legs—and their holes—to any man who so much as glances their way. It's a tragic epidemic of sluts gone wild, leaving a trail of broken vows in their wake.'"

"Wow," I breathe, torn between shock and the sudden, wild urge to laugh. "She actually wrote that? And published it online for anyone to see?"

"Oh, it gets better," Juliet assures me. "'I weep for the husbands who are forced to witness their wives' wanton displays of lust and selfish disregard for their marital oaths. How can these women claim to be good wives while allowing their most sacred parts to be defiled night after night?'"

A snort escapes me. Shit, I wish I was so lucky to be getting all of that. I get the giggles, and soon, Juliet and I are both howling with laughter, gasping for breath. "Jesus Christ," I wheeze, wiping tears from my eyes. "'Sacred parts,' really?"

"Right?" Juliet giggles. "I mean, I'm all for Marilyn and Ana getting their freak on, but 'defiled' is a bit much."

"Seriously. If anything, they're being 'defiled' by their own husbands, just like the rest of us. Debra needs to get off her high horse and take the stick out of her ass."

"Ugh, can you imagine how boring missionary must be with Vincent?" Juliet makes a gagging noise. "No wonder she's so uptight."

"Poor thing," I say, my voice dripping with mock sympathy. "She's probably just jealous that she's not getting any of her sacred parts defiled by another man. Lord knows I am."

The words slip out before I can stop them, hanging in the air like a naughty confession. Juliet goes quiet for a moment, and I hold my breath, wondering if I've said too much.

"Wait a minute," she says slowly, her voice taking on a conspiratorial tone. "Would you actually...?"

Heat rushes to my cheeks, and I'm suddenly grateful she can't see me. "What? No! I mean...I don't know. It's crazy, right? I could never actually go through with it."

"Hmm." Juliet sounds thoughtful. "The way you were looking at Ana last night, I thought you were considering taking a page from her playbook."

I'm at a loss for words. Was I that obvious? "I was just...curious, that's all. It's not every day you find out your friend is sleeping around with her husband's blessing."

Juliet giggles. "Hey, no judgment here. Honestly, I'd go for it if Arthur wanted to share me. There's something kinda hot about the whole thing, right?"

I'm saved from having to answer by the sound of a cough at the doorway. Mark is leaning against the doorframe, his running shorts slung low on his hips and a thin sheen of sweat glistening on his bare chest. He looks good enough to eat, and guilt stabs at me for the impure thoughts swirling in my head. Shit, how much did he hear?

I smile at him as I talk to Juliet. "Hey, Mark's back from his run. I gotta go. Talk later?"

"Keep me posted on any developments!"

I end the call and flop back against the pillows and try to play it cool. "Hey there, eavesdropper. Enjoy your run?"

Mark grins and pushes off the doorframe, sauntering over to the bed. "It was all right. Not as exciting as the conversation you were just having, from the sound of it."

My face flushes again. Busted. "Oh, that? That was just Juliet being Juliet. You know how she loves to gossip."

Mark sits down on the edge of the bed, his expression turning serious. "About the hotwife thing, you mean? With Ana and the others?"

I nod, not trusting my voice.

He's quiet for a moment, studying my face. "And what do you think about all that? The idea of being with another man while I watch?"

My breath catches in my throat. Is he really asking what I think he's asking? "I...I don't know," I stammer. "I guess I've never really considered it before our friends started trying it."

Mark reaches out and takes my hand, his thumb stroking over my knuckles. "But you are considering it now."

It's not a question.

I swallow hard, forcing myself to meet his gaze. "Maybe a little," I admit, my voice barely above a whisper. "Does that make me a terrible wife?"

To my surprise, Mark smiles. "No, baby. It makes you human. We all have fantasies, desires. It's natural to be curious."

I blink at him, stunned. "So...you're not mad? Or jealous?"

He shrugs. "I mean, the idea of you being desired, wanted by other men...it's kind of a turn-on, in a weird way."

"Really?" I breathe, hardly daring to believe it.

"Really." He leans in and kisses me softly, his lips warm and familiar. "I love you. I want you to be happy, fulfilled. If exploring this kink is something you want, then I'm willing to talk about it."

Tears prick at the corners of my eyes, and I surge forward to kiss him again, deeper this time. "I love you too. So much."

Mark grins against my lips. "If we do this, I have some ground rules."

I nod, willing to agree to anything. "Such as?"

He nips at my bottom lip, his hand sliding up my thigh. "Well, for starters...I get to pick the guy."

A surprised giggle escapes me. "Oh, is that so?"

"Mmm hmm." His fingers dance along the lace edge of my panties. "And I get to watch."

Arousal zings through my core, and I let my thighs fall open in invitation. "I can live with that."

"Good." Mark slips his hand inside my panties, finding me already slick and swollen. "Because you're mine. No matter who fucks this pussy, you'll always belong to me."

I moan as he strokes me, my hips rocking up to meet his touch. "Yes, baby. Always."

Mark kisses me hungrily, his tongue sweeping into my mouth, claiming me. As our passion escalates, I momentarily pull away, breathless. "Wait, where are the kids?"

"They're still asleep, baby. We've got time," Mark growls, pushing me back onto the bed with rough, possessive movements that make me gasp into his mouth as his fingers continue to work my clit. The thought of him watching someone fuck me turns me on. I wrap my legs around his waist, desperate to feel him inside me, but Mark chuckles and withdraws his hand.

He sits back on his heels, grinning down at me, and slowly licks my arousal off his fingers. "Jesus, you're fucking sexy when you're turned on," he says, his voice thick with desire.

I reach for him, aching to be filled again, but Mark bats my hand away with a smirk. "Not yet. Beg me to let you be a hotwife and I'll fuck you."

His words send a shiver of anticipation through me and I whisper with need. "Please, baby, please let me be a hotwife and please fuck me right now. I need you so bad."

His eyes simmers with barely contained desire. "Not yet."

He stands up and slides his shorts off, taking out his already-hard cock. "Make yourself come while you beg to be a hotwife, and then you'll get this." He strokes himself lazily, making sure I see.

Oh god, he's going to drive me insane with lust. My head is swimming as I spread my legs wider, slipping my own fingers inside my soaking wet pussy.

He's watching me, transfixed. "Do you wish your fingers were another man's cock?"

His question turns me on, and I slide a second finger into my pussy, imagining that he's watching someone fucking me. "God yes, I want someone to fuck me hard and make me your hotwife."

My own fingers aren't enough, and I stare at his cock while he strokes it. He's so damn hard. He needs to shove it in me. I'm going to explode if I don't get fucked. "Please, I need your cock."

Mark positions himself between my legs and continues to stroke himself while I start rubbing fast circles on my clit, desperate to come. He's watching my hands, and moans, "Fuck, you look so hot. Do you want to be a slut for someone else? Say it."

I start to unravel. "I want to be a hotwife. Please let me be a slut for you and another man. Let them fuck me however they want. Please!"

Mark slides into me in one hard thrust. He grabs my ankles and lifts them to his shoulders and slams into me over and over.

"Fuck, don't stop. Don't stop!" The world around me fades as the pleasure intensifies and I'm ready to combust. I grab my own breasts, tweaking my nipples hard, which sets me off. I cry out as my orgasm surges through me. "Mark, fuck!"

Mark slows and savors each slow stroke while he whispers, "That's my girl."

I writhe under him as pleasure zips from my fingers to my toes. When my spasms finally subside, Mark picks up speed again, chasing his own release. He feels so fucking good. I whimper, my nerve endings overloading, my mind barely able to comprehend the intensity of everything.

He grunts, "Oh god, I'm coming," as he explodes. He buries himself in me as deep as he can, his hips jerking as he unloads. The warmth of his cum sends a delicious shiver down my spine. Gasping and trembling, we melt into a heap of satisfied exhaustion.

Mark rolls over, pulling me close and pressing a kiss to my forehead. "Thank you."

I smile at him, dazed. "For what?"

He chuckles and nuzzles my neck, his stubble sending sparks dancing across my skin. "For indulging me, for playing along. And for trusting me."

My heart swells with love for him. "I'd do anything for you."

Mark gives me a lopsided grin, his eyes twinkling. "Yeah, and now you're going to be my hotwife."

"Am I?" I raise an eyebrow, trying to pretend I'm not ready to dance around the room in happiness.

"Hell yes, you are." Mark runs a hand down my side, coming to rest on the curve of my hip. "This isn't a game. I really want to share you. If you're up for it."

I study his face, looking for any trace of hesitation or doubt. But all I see is eagerness and desire. "I am."

Mark gives me a fierce kiss. "Just remember, I get to pick the guy."

I grin, anticipation fluttering in my stomach. "Yes, baby. It's your choice."

"Damn straight it is." He kisses me again, his touch soft and gentle this time.

I lie there in Mark's arms, basking in the afterglow and realizing this is the first time I've felt truly connected to him in a while. If this is what being a hotwife does for us, it's better than fucking another guy. I can't believe the turn my life has taken in just 24 hours. Yesterday, I was a bored housewife longing for more. Today, I'm a woman on the brink of becoming a hotwife with a husband who loves me enough to indulge my deepest fantasies. Does life get better than this?

The next few days pass in a blur of work deadlines, preschool pickups, and endless loads of laundry. But through it all, my mind keeps drifting back to my conversation with Mark. I'm surprised he's actually open to the idea of me sleeping with another man. More than open, even—he's genuinely turned on by the thought, and it's a side of him I've never seen before. I'm getting a glimpse of the kinky depths lurking beneath his calm, steady exterior.

Part of me is terrified at the prospect of actually going through with it. What if I chicken out at the last minute? What if the reality doesn't live up to the fantasy? What if it changes things between me and Mark in a way we can't come back from?

But another part of me—the part that's been lying dormant for far too long—is thrumming with excitement at the possibilities. The chance to be someone else for a night, someone wild and wanton and free. To be desired and pushed to the limits of my pleasure. It's a heady prospect, one that has me squirming in my office chair as I try to focus on budget reports.

Mark has been dropping little hints all week, sly comments about a surprise he has for me next weekend, but he's been maddeningly vague on the details. By the time Friday rolls around, I'm a bundle of nerves and anticipation. I don't know what he has planned, but I hope it involves sharing me.

As we're getting ready for bed, Mark comes up behind me at the bathroom sink and wraps his arms around my waist. He meets my eyes in the mirror, a mischievous glint in his gaze.

"So, I have some news," he murmurs, nuzzling into my neck. "My parents have agreed to babysit all night tomorrow."

My heartbeat quickens, and I lean back into his solid warmth. "Oh? And what's the occasion?"

Mark grins, his hands sliding up to cup my breasts through my thin cotton tank top. "Well, I was thinking...maybe it's time to test out this hotwife thing."

I suck in a sharp breath, my nipples tightening under his palms. "With who?"

He pinches my nipples lightly, making me gasp. "I invited Brandon over for dinner."

"Brandon?" I echo, my mind racing. Brandon is Mark's best friend and was the best man at our wedding. I'd be lying if I said I hadn't noticed his rugged good looks or the way his eyes sometimes linger on me. "Are you serious?"

Mark turns me around to face him, his expression soft but intense. "Oh yeah, baby. I trust Brandon, and more importantly, I trust you. If we're going to do this, I want it to be with someone we're both comfortable with."

I search his face for any hint of hesitation or doubt, but all I see is love and a glimmer of unmistakable heat. "And you're sure you're okay with this? With me and Brandon?"

He kisses me hard, his tongue delving deep into my mouth. I melt against him, my body responding instinctively to his touch. When he pulls back, we're both breathing heavily.

"More than okay. Brandon thinks you're gorgeous and says I'm the luckiest SOB in the world. I can't fucking wait to watch him make you come."

His words make me tremble, and my thighs press together against the ache building between them. "Jesus, Mark. Keep talking like that and I won't make it till tomorrow."

He chuckles, his hand slipping into my sleep shorts to cup my mound. "Oh, you'll make it because I have very specific plans for you. And they all involve you being a very, very good girl and saving this sweet pussy for our guest."

I whimper as he circles my clit with feather-light strokes, never quite giving me the pressure I need. "You're a fucking tease, you know that?"

"Yep, and think about this. I told him you've always wanted to be called filthy names, and he said that's his specialty." He nips at my earlobe, making me shiver. "Now get that sexy ass in bed. I want you well-rested for your big debut."

I let him lead me to the bed, my mind spinning with the thoughts of getting the dirty talk I've always craved. Every time Mark has tried to talk dirty, we've dissolved into a fit of giggles. He's just not dominant enough to pull it off. Holy hell, by this time tomorrow, I'll have had another cock inside me for the first time in over a decade. The thought is terrifying and exhilarating all at once.

As I drift off to sleep in Mark's arms, I can't help but wonder what Brandon will be like as a lover. If this is my only chance to fuck another guy, I hope he's rough and just takes what he wants.

Goddamn, I can't wait.

CHAPTER 3

As I get ready for the big dinner with Mark and Brandon, a flurry of emotions swirls inside me: excitement, nervousness, anticipation. I take extra care with my appearance, wanting to look my absolute best. After much deliberation, I choose a stunning yellow dress that hugs my curves in all the right places. The fitted bodice accentuates my full bust before flowing into a playful swing skirt that dances around my legs, ending just below the knees. The vibrant color glows against my brown skin. I style my hair in a braid-out and slip on my favorite strappy sandals. I can't remember the last time I took this much effort on my appearance, and the mirror tells me it was worth it. I look and feel sexy.

I descend the stairs and enter the kitchen to find Brandon already seated at the table. He rises to greet me, his eyes sparkling with appreciation. Brandon is a striking figure—tall, broad-shouldered, with close-cropped hair, strong brows, and a hint of stubble shadowing his chiseled jawline.

"June, you're absolutely radiant," Brandon says, the rumble of his words igniting a fire low in my belly.

Mark comes over and slips an arm around my waist, pulling me close. "Doesn't she? I'm the luckiest man alive." He places a soft kiss on my cheek, his breath warm against my skin. "Honey, why don't you fix some drinks for you and Brandon while I finish up in here?"

I flash Mark a smile. "Sure thing," I reply. Knowing that Brandon has given up alcohol, and wanting to keep my own head clear for the evening, I consider our options. My eyes light up as an idea strikes me.

"I could make us some fruity mocktails," I suggest, turning to face Brandon. "Any preference?"

Brandon gives me a playful grin. "I'm easy, so surprise me. I trust your judgment."

"Careful what you wish for," I joke as I lead him into the den.

As I mix our drinks, Brandon and I chat, catching up on life and work, but an undercurrent of tension simmers between us. The weight of his stare excites me as I move about the room. His gaze is like a physical caress. My fingers tremble slightly as I give him his drink, a telltale flush creeping up my neck.

Dinner is a lively affair, full of laughter and reminiscing as Mark and Brandon trade stories from their younger days. As I join in the merriment, butterflies swirl in my stomach from eagerness and uncertainty of what to expect tonight. I'm hyper-aware of Brandon's presence, the weight of his gaze, the accidental brush of his leg against mine under the table. Each casual touch sends sparks of electricity crackling through me until I'm practically vibrating with desire.

Once we finish dessert, Mark sits back in his chair and looks from me to Brandon and back again, a mischievous twinkle in his eye. "So, are we really doing this? Because if so, I want to see my gorgeous wife beg to be fucked."

Brandon leans forward, his expression intense. "I'm in if June is." He turns the full force of his attention on me. "What do you say? Ready to be a little slut for me and do as you're told?"

My brain blips out for a second at the men's words. Oooh, maybe Brandon really is good at dirty talk. Arousal floods my core, confirming I'm completely on board for tonight's adventure. I take a shaky breath and meet Brandon's smoldering gaze. "Yes, I'm ready."

Mark reaches over and squeezes my hand. "That's my girl," he says proudly. He stands up, pulling me to my feet and into his arms for a deep, passionate kiss that leaves me breathless. Then he releases me and grins at Brandon. "Let's move the party to the bedroom."

Brandon rises from his seat with barely restrained hunger. "Lead the way."

As we head upstairs, excitement thrums through my veins. Mark leads us down the hallway, but instead of turning into our usual bedroom, he guides us to the spare room at the end of the hall. Curiosity mingles with the butterflies in my stomach. Mark seems to have planned tonight out, which tells me he really does want this.

Mark pushes open the door and gestures for us to enter. As I step inside, my eyes widen. Soft, flickering candlelight gives the room a warm, intimate glow. The bed is stripped of the comforter, and there's fresh, crisp white sheets waiting to get messed up. But what really catches my attention is the tall director's chair positioned at the foot of the bed, offering a perfect view of the mattress.

I glance at Mark, a smile tugging at my lips. "Planning on directing us?"

His eyes twinkle. "What can I say? I want the best seat in the house for the show."

As Mark settles into the chair, I'm suddenly struck by the eroticism of having him watch my every move, every reaction. It adds a whole new layer of intensity to the situation. Fuck, this is hot.

Brandon moves to stand behind me. "You've been driving me crazy all night in that dress," he murmurs, his deep voice wrapping around me like a velvet embrace. "I've been dying to peel it off you, inch by delicious inch."

My breath hitches as his fingers graze my shoulder, tracing the delicate strap of my dress. With deliberate slowness, he eases it down, his touch igniting sparks beneath my skin. "Mark's a lucky man, getting to unwrap you every night," he continues, his lips brushing along the sensitive nerves on my ear. "But tonight, you're all mine. And I intend to savor every" —he punctuates each word with a soft kiss along the column of my neck—"single"—another kiss, lower, his stubble rasping deliciously against my skin—"second."

I moan and tilt my head to the side, giving him better access. I didn't expect seduction, but this is wonderful. Brandon slides the other strap down, his movements unhurried, almost reverent. The bodice of my dress loosens and slips, revealing the lacy white bra beneath. For some reason, I expected Brandon to drag me up here and pound into me. The slow and sensual way he's undressing me leaves me wonderfully off balance, and I don't know how to react.

"Gorgeous," Brandon breathes as his hands skim down my arms, leaving goosebumps in their wake. "I love that you dressed up for me. But as pretty as this dress is, I'll like you even better out of it."

In one smooth motion, he unzips my dress and lets it pool at my feet. Cool air kisses my bare skin, and I shiver—not just from the cold, but also the heat of my husband's gaze.

Mark lets out a low whistle of appreciation. "You're a vision, baby. Brandon, don't you agree our June is sexy?"

"Oh, no doubt." Brandon's hands brush up my sides, his thumbs skimming the undersides of my breasts through the thin lace of my bra. I arch into his touch, craving more. "In fact, I'm going to enjoy using your toy."

Oh, fuck. The mix of worship and dirty talk is messing with my head and making me even more turned on. I lock eyes with Mark, and the raw hunger flickering in them as his friend works my nipples tells me I can let go and enjoy myself. My consciousness drifts towards a place of willing surrender...I want to be a toy for both of them.

Brandon turns me to face him, his eyes burning into mine. One hand comes up to cup my cheek, his thumb tracing the curve of my lower lip. "Tell me what you want, beautiful," he urges softly. "Don't be shy. This is all about your pleasure tonight, and I want to make sure you get what you need."

I wet my lips, my tongue darting out to taste the tip of his thumb. Brandon's eyes flare, and he inhales sharply.

Can I really have whatever I want? There's only one way to find out. Emboldened, I hold his gaze. "I want you to use me and do whatever you want to me, call me dirty names, make me mindless so I'll forget anything outside of this bedroom."

When I hear my own words, I realize that being mindless is really what I need—beyond just the dirty talk. My brain is continually working overtime. I want to stop thinking and just experience pleasure. Since Mark and I have been so busy, it's been difficult to get the sense of freedom that only a really good fucking can bring me.

Brandon gives me a wicked grin of approval. "I like a woman who knows what she wants. And lucky for you, you're about to get it."

He unhooks my bra, letting it fall to the floor before he leans down and takes a nipple into his mouth briefly. Pleasure floods through me at the contact. I push my breasts closer to him, aching for more, but he stops sucking and commands, "I want you on the bed, on all fours. Face your man so he can see your reactions."

I immediately comply, the authority in his tone thrilling me to the core. As I settle on the bed, I meet my husband's gaze. He looks beyond turned on, and it makes everything that Brandon is doing so much better.

"Fucking hell, that ass is perfect," Brandon growls behind me. I hear the rustling of clothing as he undresses, followed by the thud of his belt buckle hitting the floor. I steal another glance at Mark and catch him stroking his erection through his jeans. My entire body shudders with longing. This is so dang filthy, and I'm desperate to feel a cock that isn't my husband's.

Brandon kneels on the bed behind me. He slips my panties off and spreads me open. "Jesus Christ, I have to get a closer look at this pussy," he murmurs, and before I can process what's happening, he buries his face in my slick folds with a deep groan.

I cry out at the sudden sensation of his tongue on my clit and the scratch of his beard against my pussy. My head spins from delight as I push back onto his hungry mouth. He moans into me, a noise of pure lust, as if he can't get enough of my taste. Pleasure ripples through me as he licks and sucks on my clit.

He comes up for air long enough to say, "The smell and taste of you are fucking addictive. Your husband is a lucky man to get to eat this pussy anytime he wants."

The filthiness of the comment sends another surge of liquid heat flooding from my core. I didn't know it was possible to be this turned on, to be desired and owned in a way that satisfies some deep, primal part of my brain. My eyes meet Mark's again, and his hooded gaze is filled with fire as he watches Brandon pleasure me.

The whole experience is incredibly hot, and I never break eye contact with Mark as his friend makes me writhe and moan in ecstasy. My breath is coming in shallow gasps and my toes curl as the pressure builds low in my belly, begging for release. Suddenly, one of Brandon's long, thick fingers pushes slowly inside me. I grip the sheets, overwhelmed by the intrusion.

"Fuck, you're so tight," Brandon groans. "This sweet cunt is just swallowing me up."

He starts finger-fucking me at a slow, steady rhythm, and I whimper. When his lips close around my clit, I come apart. "Ooooh, god!"

Mark stands and moves to sit beside me on the bed, cupping my face and kissing me fiercely as I shudder through the aftershocks of my orgasm. Our tongues tangle, and having my husband's lips on mine while his friend's face is buried in my pussy is so damn filthy.

When my spasms subside, Mark pulls back, his expression intense. "Baby, that was the sexiest thing I've ever seen. Seeing you lose control like that—I could watch that all day."

"We're just getting started," Brandon rasps from behind me, rising up and wrapping one arm around my waist to pull me flush with him.

As Mark sits down again, Brandon lines up his cock, the blunt head nudging my entrance, and my breath catches in my throat as I realize just how big he is. "Holy fuck."

He thrusts into me in one fluid movement, bottoming out in one go. I wail as he stretches me impossibly wide, the slight sting of pain adding another dimension to my pleasure. His cock is amazing, like nothing I've ever experienced before. He holds still for a moment, letting me adjust to the new sensation.

Mark laughs, delighted. "Oh, did I forget to mention that Brandon has a big cock?"

My head spins as I slowly rock my hips, gasping, "Yeah, you might have forgotten that bit."

Mark just laughs again as Brandon withdraws fully and then drives into me hard. I lower my head to the bed, crying out and clawing at the sheets as he sets a punishing pace. All I can do is hold on as he fucks me senseless, every stroke of his thick cock rubbing against my inner walls just right. I'm so overcome with pleasure my brain is melting.

"Such a good girl," Brandon says with a groan as he reaches forward and tangles one hand in my hair, tilting my head back and forcing me up onto my hands again. He growls, "Look at you, taking my cock like a champ. Does it feel good?"

"Uh-huh," I pant. The sensations coursing through me are indescribable. Every nerve ending zings with bliss. I'm completely consumed by Brandon, willing to be nothing more than a receptacle for his desire. The depth of my submission sends a wave of heat rushing through me as a second orgasm starts to build.

"I knew you'd like being a slut for my fat cock," Brandon grunts. "Now be a good girl and come for me."

Those dirty words send me over the edge. "Yes!" I wail as another climax hits, and my inner muscles clench down around Brandon's shaft.

"Such a good little cocksleeve," he grunts as he maintains his rhythm.

It takes all my focus to continue riding his cock through the waves of pleasure, and my arms shake as I struggle to keep from collapsing to the bed again. Mark's watching everything we do, and the anticipation building between us is a tangible force. His eyes darken with lust, mirroring my own desires. I can see the rapid rise and fall of his chest as he rubs himself through his jeans.

Brandon's rough hands grasp my hips, his fingers digging into my skin in a way that sends jolts of pleasure mixed with a hint of pain coursing through my body. His touch is commanding, and I don't want this to end.

"You ready to be a good little fucktoy and take all my cum?" His voice, brimming with primal hunger, leaves me weak-kneed and dizzy.

The word 'fucktoy' reverberates through my mind, sending a thrill of excitement through me. I want to be that for them tonight–a mindless, pleasure-filled toy. "Yes, please," I whimper, and Brandon's answering chuckle is dark, almost wicked, as he gives my hips a firm squeeze.

"That's a good girl," he purrs, igniting a delicious warmth throughout my body

Mark's gaze never leaves mine, his expression a mix of desire, love, and a hint of possessiveness. "You're so beautiful like this, baby," he murmurs, his voice thick with desire. "Our very own pretty little slut." His words make my heart race, a flood of warmth spreading through me at his praise, and I moan at how depraved I am.

Brandon joins in. "She's such a pretty little cumslut for us to enjoy." His words burn like a delicious fire, the degradation swirling with the impact of his praise.

The combination of Brandon's rough fucking and the dirty talk from both men sends me spiraling. I can feel another orgasm building, and it's all I can do to keep breathing. I lock eyes with Mark, my gaze pleading for his permission to crash over that sweet edge. He sees it, and a wicked smile quirks his lips upwards. "Come again for us, babygirl," he orders, and my climax slams through me, making me scream in ecstasy.

My cry of pleasure makes Brandon change his angle, hitting a new sweet spot deep inside me and intensifying the bliss. Waves of rapture assault me, and I tighten around him, my body trembling in anticipation of another orgasm.

When Brandon speaks, it takes me a second to realize he's talking to Mark. "You like watching me fuck your wife, don't you? Look at how much she loves my cock."

I'm momentarily shocked, and my eyes fly to Mark to see how he's taking it. Mark's response is a low groan, his eyes never leaving the sight of Brandon fucking me. I can see the desire in his gaze, the hunger, and I know that he's enjoying this just as much as I am. It fuels my own desire, and I thrust back against Brandon, eager for more.

The sound of our bodies slapping together fills the room, punctuated by my moans and Brandon's grunts. I'm continually on the edge, knowing I could explode again at any second. I'm not sure how much more I can take, but at the same time, I never want this to end. Brandon continues to fuck me, hitting that sweet spot over and over again. I close my eyes, lost in the bliss—finally achieving what I wanted. I'm mindless and just a hole for them to fuck.

Right when I'm about to come again, Brandon pulls out and flips me onto my back. With one swift motion, he plunges back into me, bottoming out as I moan. I wrap my legs around him and hold onto his arms. His pace is relentless, driving into me over and over again. My tits bounce in time with his forceful thrusts, leaving me as powerless as a rag doll in his grasp.

His powerful strokes flood me with pleasure, my orgasm building steadily but remaining just out of reach. "Please, Brandon," I beg, my voice trembling. "Please, let me come again."

Brandon slows down, and it's suddenly worse; every stroke is a wonderful agony as he massages every inch of my insides.

"Does our fucktoy want to come?" Brandon's tone is teasing.

I thrash against him. "Please, oh god, please let me come. I need it."

"Then come for us. Do it now before I come, or it will be too late."

What? No? Brandon's thrusts become more erratic, his grip on my hips tightening to the point of bruising. I can feel his cock swelling inside me, the tremors of his impending orgasm evident in his ragged breaths.

Just knowing he's so close tips me over the edge again, and I come undone. I scream out as my orgasm tears through me like a tidal wave. White spots dance along the corners of my vision, and I convulse around him. The pleasure is so intense it borders on pain. My pussy clenches, milking his cock as the waves of pleasure consume me.

As I ride out my orgasm, I can hear Mark's voice, filled with desire and love. "That's my good girl. Our pretty little slut." His words send a thrill through me.

Brandon groans, and with a few sharp whacks against my sensitive pussy, he erupts. His entire body shudders as the ropes of his warm sticky cum fill me. As he continues to unload, his face a mask of pure enjoyment, a sense of accomplishment washes over me for having satisfied him so thoroughly.

When he's finished, he leans down to kiss me, his lips brushing against mine softly. "Good girl," he whispers, and I bask in his praise.

I glance over at Mark, seeing the desire in his gaze, the hunger that mirrors my own. I know that he's next, that he's eager to claim me for himself. I'm not going to feel complete until he's inside me, but I want to enjoy the euphoria a few minutes longer.

My body is humming with pleasure as I listen to Mark and Brandon talk. I'm in a happy, floaty place, and my mind is blissfully empty. I close my eyes and let myself drift.

Chapter 4

The sound of rustling clothing brings me back to reality as I lie sprawled on the bed, still fuzzy from my numerous orgasms. My skin is flushed and sensitive, the cool air from the vent sending goosebumps up and down my body. I sink into the softness of the sheets, my eyes fluttering open to gaze upon Brandon and Mark. Brandon is getting dressed while Mark sits beside me, a feral fire igniting in his eyes. He wants me—desperately. He's just waiting for Brandon to leave.

Brandon leans down and kisses me softly. "Thank you for a wonderful time," he murmurs, his voice low and sexy. "You were amazing."

"You were too," I whisper, and we smile at each other as he gathers his things and heads for the door.

Right before he leaves, he pauses and smirks at Mark. "Take care of our pretty little slut. She deserves to be well taken care of for being such a good girl." He winks at us as he exits the room, leaving us alone.

As soon as we hear the front door shut, Mark's hands are all over me, his mouth crashing against mine as his fingers explore my body. My hands tangle in his hair, tugging at the strands as he groans in pleasure. We undress him in a flurry, our entwined bodies rolling and tangling in the sheets. We're both wild for each other, consumed with passion. I need him NOW.

He pushes my legs apart, nudging his cock against my entrance before teasing my clit with the tip. I gasp, arching my back as he presses inside me, every inch of his cock filling me up. His hand grips my hip as he thrusts hard and deep, each movement sending waves of pleasure from my fingertips to my toes.

"You're mine," he growls, his voice rough and possessive. "MY good girl. Mine to fuck and pleasure. Mine to fill with cum."

"Yes, yours," I moan, my mind reeling with delight. His fingers find my clit, circling the sensitive nub as he continues to thrust. I can feel my body building towards another release, the tension coiling tight inside me.

Our sweat-slicked bodies slide against each other as he pounds into me, our movements growing more frantic. I wrap my legs around him, my fingers digging into his back as he brings me to the edge of my release.

"Come for me," he commands, his voice thick with desire. "Come for your husband. Show me how much you love it when I fuck you."

His words send me crashing over the edge, my body convulsing around his cock as I cry out his name. He follows closely behind, his release filling me up as he groans against my neck. We lie there, tangled in each other's arms, the sound of our panting filling the silence.

As our bodies cool and our breathing returns to normal, Mark gazes into my eyes, his expression filled with love and adoration. "You were amazing tonight. I'm so proud of you for being such a good girl for us."

His words fill me with joy, and I smile at him. "I loved every moment of it," I admit, kissing him softly. "Brandon was the perfect choice. You know me so well. And I'd do this again, just say the word."

There's a wicked gleam in his eyes. "I'm going to want this again, but not until I've had a couple weeks of fucking you and reminding you I'm the only one you love, no matter how many other guys you fuck."

A happy warmth fills me, and I giggle. "You are the only one I love. Forever."

He growls again, possessively, and my head spins as he kisses me deeply. I never expected fucking someone else would bring this side out in Mark, but I can tell our marriage is revitalized. Being a hotwife is fucking amazing.

The End

July Hotwife

Hotwife of the Month Club 7

Lacey Cross

CHAPTER 1

I'm sprawled out on a lounge chair facing the ocean at a luxurious Bali resort. As I inhale the salty tang of the ocean air mixed with the coconut scent of my suntan lotion, I finally relax for the first time in weeks. God, I needed this vacation. It's been a stressful year.

I feel dumb to even have complaints, and sometimes it feels like I have no one to talk to. I'm not sure my friends would understand since I have a fabulous life. I'm thirty-five, and I have a wonderful husband who dotes on me and more money than I need to live comfortably. But I've had a gnawing pit in my stomach ever since I sold my social media company a few months ago. I should be over the moon about it. Selling the company gave me the freedom to do whatever I want with my life. Instead, I feel...aimless.

The easiest answer is to just enjoy Bali and stop being a baby while on an incredible vacation with the man I love. My husband, Arthur, loves to surf, and he's been doing it since he was young. We take a couple of trips every year to different locations so he can play in the ocean while I enjoy the amenities of the resort spa and try to relax.

I sigh and watch the small figures paddling in the ocean. From this distance, I can't tell which one is Arthur, but it doesn't matter. As I watch a surfer catch a wave and ride it expertly to the shore, I feel a twinge of envy. I love that Arthur has a passion and a hobby, but I'm just...lounging. My career was everything, and now I have no purpose, no direction, and it's driving me fucking crazy. I'm usually vivacious and confident about my place in life, but now I'm second guessing everything–everything except my marriage, even though we've been going through a rough patch in the last year.

I turn my attention to the other beachgoers, my mind hungry for distraction. The resort is adjacent to a public beach, and a group of college-aged kids are playing volleyball close by. Their laughter and good-natured trash talk carries over the sound of the waves. I smile at their antics, remembering my own wild days of partying in college. God, when was the last time I let loose like that? I have a wonderful group of friends, but our monthly meetup while our husbands play cards in the basement doesn't exactly count as letting loose.

A young couple strolls by, hand in hand, their eyes locked on each other like they're the only two people in the world. I feel a pang in my chest, a longing for that kind of connection and passion. Arthur and I used to be like that, once upon a time. But now, it feels like we're just going through the motions, living our comfortable, luxurious life.

Yeah, I need to get out of this funk. I need a change, an adventure, something to make me feel alive again...or maybe I just need a good hard pounding from my husband. He's been busy with work too, and other than his desire to surf, we plan on using this trip to reconnect.

Fuck it, no more moping around. Standing up, I adjust my flowing sundress and slip my sandals on. I'm determined to be happy and have fun. I'm going to start by seducing my husband, and then I'm going to do something on this trip that's daring, something that scares me. It's time to live a little.

Arthur is still out on the water, so I climb the rocky steps towards the resort's outside bar. I need to get out of my head and a fruity drink should help. As I approach, I catch my reflection in a mirrored pillar. My naturally tan skin is glowing, my hair tousled by the sea breeze, and my blue sundress is sexy. For a moment, I hardly recognize myself because I actually look relaxed. There's a spark in my eyes that I haven't seen in years, a hint of the wild, carefree woman I used to be before I became Juliet, the business woman and life of every party. Hey, I guess vacation is actually working its magic on me.

I perch on a barstool, and a bartender offers me the daily special drink–it's delicious. I'm enjoying the tropical flavors and having fun people watching...and that's when I spot him: a guy, maybe a few years younger than me, with scruffy blonde hair and a body that screams surfer. He catches my eye and raises his drink in a friendly toast.

Before I know it, he's sauntering over. "Mind if I join you?" he asks, his voice a low rumble that sends a shiver down my spine.

I bet this guy hangs around at bars to pick up wealthy women. He has the demeanor of someone who's just looking for a good time. I can feel my body responding to him. Yeah, he's attractive enough he probably gets plenty of women. I try to play it cool. "Go ahead."

He slides onto the stool next to me, his bare arm brushing against mine and giving me goosebumps. "I'm Kai," he says, flashing a smile that could melt the panties off a grandma. "And you are?"

"Juliet." I'm surprised by how breathy my voice sounds.

"Juliet," he repeats, like he's savoring the taste of my name. "So, what brings a goddess like you to this humble island?"

I can't help but laugh. "Goddess? That's a bit much, don't you think?"

He grins, leaning in closer. "Just calling it like I see it. But you didn't answer my question."

Kai has a fresh linen smell that I enjoy. I swirl my drink and play coy. "Oh, you know, the usual. Escaping reality, seeking adventure. All that good stuff."

I know I'm being flirty, but Arthur and I have a pact. He enjoys it when I flirt with other guys and get worked up for him. He says as long as I eat at home, he doesn't care where I get my appetite. With how sexy Kai is, I'm going to have a nice appetite when I seduce my husband later.

Kai's eyes sparkle with mischief. "Adventure, huh? Well, you've come to the right place. And maybe found the right person."

Damn, this guy is smooth, though I'm sure he knows it. I raise an eyebrow. "Is that so? And what kind of adventures are you offering?"

He leans in even closer. "How about we start with a midnight swim under the stars?"

My heart races at the suggestion, and I suddenly wonder if he has a big cock–not that I'm going to find out. I manage to keep my voice steady. "Tempting, but I'm not sure my husband would approve."

Kai's eyes drop to my wedding ring, but his smile doesn't falter. "Ah, the plot thickens. Well, how about a raincheck then? If you and your husband ever want an adventure..."

He leaves his sentence hanging, and my breath catches while pleasure swirls in my core. Is he talking about a threesome? I refuse to ask for clarification since that would make it seem like I'm interested.

Kai doesn't press for anything more, and we continue chatting. I find myself laughing more than I have in months. Kai's quick wit matches my own, and our banter flows effortlessly. As we talk, I'm acutely aware of the wedding ring on my finger. I love Arthur, I really do. But there's something about Kai that is making me feel more alive than I have in a long time...which means I need to get out of here and find my husband.

Just as I'm debating how to make an excuse and leave, I hear Arthur's voice behind me. "There you are, Juliet," he says, his hand landing on my shoulder.

I turn to face him, my heart pounding. His hair and clothes are still damp from the ocean, and he has a towel draped over his arms. He smells briny, so different from the clean and fresh scent of Kai. Arthur's eyes flick from me to the surfer, a question in his gaze.

Kai takes that moment to excuse himself by saying, "It was great meeting you, Juliet." He gives me one last meaningful look before disappearing into the crowd.

As I watch him go, I can't help but wonder what would have happened if I was single. I'd never cheat on Arthur–never in a million years–but Kai is the type of guy I'd fuck in a heartbeat if I wasn't married. Yeah, I need to stop thinking about that.

I give Arthur my sweetest smile as I stand up and link my arm with his. As we head back to our room, desire simmers in my core and the world seems full of possibilities. Why did flirting with one random guy at the bar suddenly make this vacation anything but ordinary?

I side eye my husband as we get off the elevator to our floor. Arthur is looking mighty sexy right now. It's time to enact Operation Seduce My Husband.

Chapter 2

Our room is just as opulent as the rest of the resort, with a massive four-poster bed draped in white linens, a private balcony overlooking the ocean, and a bathroom that looks like it belongs in a spa. The walls are adorned with local artwork, and a gentle sea breeze wafts through the open windows, carrying the salt-tinged air.

As soon as the door closes behind us, Arthur slips into the bathroom to shower while I kick my sandals off and wander out to the balcony and wait for him to get out so I can get his cock into me.

He's wearing a robe when he joins me on the balcony after his shower, and wraps his arms around me from behind. "I think my wife needs to remember who owns her," he murmurs, his breath warm against my neck.

Leaning back into him, I savor the feeling of his strong body against mine. I love it when he says stuff like this. He and I both know he doesn't really own me, but it's great when he gets possessive and growly. If flirting with Kai brought this out, maybe I need to flirt a lot on this trip.

I turn my head to give him a playful wink. "Babe, you know I only have eyes for you."

His hands slide down to my hips, pulling me closer and I can feel his erection against my ass. His voice is husky. "You know, we should probably test out that bed. Make sure it's up to our standards."

I laugh, spinning in his arms to face him. "Is that so? And how does that test work?"

His eyes darken with desire, and he leans in close, his lips barely brushing against mine. "I'll show you..." he whispers before capturing my mouth in a searing kiss.

He pulls me into the room and as we tumble onto the bed, I giggle. This is great. I didn't even have to seduce him. I pull at the tie on his robe, enjoying the softness of his freshly cleaned skin. His body is so familiar, almost like an extension of my own, and yet still desirable after all these years. Arthur tugs the straps of my sundress down my arms, exposing my breasts. He sucks on a nipple in the exact way I love, and I run my fingers through his hair and arch my back from the pleasurable pull in my core.

He lavishes attention on one breast before moving to the other. Ripples of delight head straight to my pussy the longer he worships my breasts, and I'm so wet I wish he'd get his cock in me. He slides the hem of my dress up and slips a hand between my legs, pushing aside my panties so he can brush circles around my clit. I cry out in ecstasy and almost come undone. Holy fuck, I'm already close to an orgasm. I swear vacation sex always feels better, and I don't know why.

I'm so lost in the joy of the moment that I almost don't understand what he's saying when he speaks. "Did you think about fucking that guy at the bar?"

I can hear the erotic tinge in his voice, and the lustful tone sends my arousal level through the roof. Holy shit, why is he asking about this when his finger is on my clit? He's watched me flirt with plenty of guys in the past, and he's always just smiled and given me that knowing look, secure in the knowledge that he's the only guy I want.

He continues circling my clit, and I moan, "Mmm, Kai? No. I wouldn 't..."

He gives a light pinch to my clit, and I cry out in pleasure and almost climax again. His voice is husky. "Don't start lying to me now. You were thinking about fucking him, weren't you?"

Lust burns through my brain, and I rock my hips against his hand. This might be the most delicious dirty talk he's ever engaged in, and I can have fun with this. I purr at him, "If I was, are you going to spank me?"

He laughs. "You'd like that too much. Maybe I just won't let you come until you admit you were thinking of fucking another man."

The pressure of his fingers on my clit intensifies, and I gasp in delight. My whole body is burning with need, and I'm so close to my orgasm I can taste it. "Oh god, yes, I was. Please let me come, oh fuck."

My toes curl from pleasure as he nibbles on my ear lobe. "Tell me everything you thought about him. Don't make me stop."

"Fuck, he's hot but I only want you," I groan as I try to hold back my orgasm.

He pushes his fingers inside me as he continues rubbing my clit with his thumb. "Juliet..." The warning in his tone of voice sends a shiver down my spine. "You're lying."

He moves his fingers slower, making it so I can't come, and I gasp out, "No, no, I'm not."

He kisses up my neck until his lips are on my mouth, devouring my moans of pleasure. When he breaks off the kiss, his voice is rough. "Lie to me again and you won't get to come."

Oh god, I'll do anything to come. I whine in desperation, "I wondered what his cock looked like."

I feel him smirk against my skin as he rubs my clit in faster circles. "Anything else?"

I'm so far gone I start babbling. "He offered to take me on a midnight swim under the stars and said if you and I both wanted an adventure, to let him know."

He pulls back and studies me for a moment before finger fucking me harder. "Keep going," he rumbles, his voice dripping with lust.

"I didn't just wonder what his cock looked like, I wondered if it was big. Oh, fuck, please don't stop!" My thigh muscles start quivering, and I'm barely able to hold back my orgasm. "Oh god, I'm going to come!"

"Not yet," he growls and removes his fingers right as I start to come.

I cry out from the stolen orgasm. Fuck, why did he stop?

He gives me a deep kiss with a "hold on, baby" and quickly discards his robe. He positions himself between my legs, and when he slides into my aching pussy, I cry out again, this time in relief.

"Whose cock do you want more?" he asks as he hammers into me.

I grip at his shoulders and wrap my legs around him. "Yours!" I'm panting and moaning loudly, already close to coming again.

He pounds me fast and hard. "Yeah? Mine?"

"Yes!"

"Only mine?"

"Oh, fuck, yes! Only yours! Always yours!" I cry out as my orgasm hits.

I dig my fingers into his shoulders, and my pussy tightens around his cock as the pleasure sweeps over me in waves. He doesn't slow down as I shudder beneath him. My climax seems to go on forever, and I can't get enough. When he finally comes, he groans and his cock pulses as he blows his load.

When he's done, he tumbles onto the bed next to me, pulling me into his arms. I nuzzle into him, pressing kisses to his collarbone and throat while he catches his breath. Mmm, this is a great start to our vacation.

His voice is rough when he speaks. "You're really hot when you're thinking about getting fucked by other men."

I swat playfully at his chest. "Hey, I wasn't the one who brought it up! You started it."

He grins at me, his eyes shining. "I like it when you flirt and another guy wants you since I know you're coming home with me."

I prop up on an elbow and draw a fingertip along the ridges of his abs, enjoying the way his body shivers in response to my touch. "Well, good, because I don't really want to fuck Kai."

He captures my hand and brings it up to his mouth, kissing each fingertip, before saying, "If you wanted to, we could talk about it."

I raise my eyebrow at him. "What if Kai's idea of an adventure is a threesome?"

That makes him laugh. "Yeah, I don't know about that, but I'd watch him fuck you."

This time it's me who giggles as I snuggle against him and hide my face in the crook of his arm. "Let me think about that."

"Okay, love." He strokes my back as we both fall silent, enjoying the post orgasmic haze. I'm too content right now to think about fucking another guy. This will have to wait until tomorrow.

Chapter 3

As soon as I wake up in the morning, all I can think about is Arthur's offer to let me fuck Kai. A lot of our friends are experimenting with the hotwife lifestyle, and I've daydreamed about doing it. I've known for weeks that if given the chance, I'd try it, but the thought scares me as well. If he brings it up again, I'll tell him I want to.

After a shower and breakfast, we go for a walk along the beach. We hold hands and he keeps smiling at me. I can tell he's thinking something, but he doesn't voice it. The third time I catch him grinning, I squeeze his hand and ask, "What?"

He's quiet for a long moment before answering. "You're incredible. And I want to give you whatever you need. You know that, right?"

I furrow my brows, confused. "Uh, yeah?"

"So, I really meant what I said last night. If you want to fuck that guy Kai from the bar, I'd like to watch."

His words send a rush of heat through my body, and my heart rate quickens. Oh god, I really do want to do it, even knowing it's scary, and Arthur wanting to watch makes the idea even more appealing. I'm about to tell him I'm interested when I spot Kai on the beach ahead of us, walking our way. My mind goes blank.

Arthur notices the way I freeze and glances in the same direction. His voice is tender as he whispers, "I love you. Nothing changes that, but this is your decision. Don't do anything you don't really want to do, okay?"

"I love you, too, babe." I pull him to me and kiss him passionately, letting all of the emotions I've felt these past few months–hell, the past few years–pour into it. The depth of this kiss is surprising, even to me, but I know that no matter what happens next, he's my anchor. I trust him so deeply, and that helps me relax. "I want to do it if he's okay with you watching."

Arthur hugs me tightly, kissing me once more before we separate, and we keep strolling hand in hand as we near Kai.

Kai smiles at us as we approach. "Hey, Juliet," he says casually, "I wasn't sure if we'd run into each other again."

I smile back at him, matching his casual tone. "I was going to look for you. My husband and I are interested in your offer of adventure."

Arthur pipes up, "Hey, I'm Arthur. Juliet mentioned your offer, but we'd need to discuss me watching her have some fun."

My eyes widen slightly. This is all happening so fast. When I look at Arthur, I see only love and trust in his eyes. And a bit of excitement. So, I turn back to Kai, whose grin grows even wider as he says, "Sure. This won't be the first time a husband has watched me with their wife."

Oh god, he's done this before. Why does that make it even hotter? The guys talk logistics while I daydream about what it's going to be like fucking another guy again after so many years. If I had known I'd become a hotwife on this trip, I would have been bouncing with excitement for days. When I hear them mention tonight, my heart rate speeds up as a wet heat builds between my legs. Holy fuck, tonight?

We agree to meet later on the beach, and the guys pull out their phones and exchange numbers. I'm practically buzzing with anticipation. As we walk away, Arthur is all smiles and holds me close. I can tell he's just as excited about this as I am.

I feel a strange mixture of horniness and uncertainty throughout the day, like I'm at a rollercoaster before I step into the seat. My imagination runs wild as I picture what's going to happen. Will Kai be able to make me come? What if Arthur doesn't like it? What if this ruins our marriage? I push those thoughts to the back of my mind. I trust Arthur, and I know he'll be honest with me if something is wrong. I just need to enjoy tonight.

I dress in a flowy, black dress with spaghetti straps that leave my shoulders bare. My hair is in one loose braid so the sea breeze doesn't mess it up too much. I'm applying a light touch of makeup when my cell phone pings with a message. I pick it up and see it's from my best friend, Ariel.

Ariel

> Hey, if you get bored in Bali, check out Debra's latest blog post. It's hilarious.

Debra is the wife of one of my husband's friends, and she's been getting on everyone's nerves with her slut shaming. With all our friends trying out the hotwife lifestyle, Debra seems to think we're all harlots. I don't know if she's religious, but it definitely seems like she's praying for our jezebel souls. Her latest thing is blogging anonymously to talk about the downfall of marriage due to the hotwife craze, but I know it's her. She got tipsy one night and showed me an article she wrote, so I followed her blog. I don't think she remembers showing it to me.

I'm curious about this post from Debra, but it'll have to wait. I giggle and type a quick reply to Ariel.

Juliet

> Oh, I will, but not tonight. I'm about to go fuck a hot surfer while Arthur watches.

Ariel's reply doesn't disappoint.

Ariel

> OMG, you too? Okay, you have to tell me everything when you get home, and I mean EVERYTHING.

I smile and promise a long gab session when I return. As soon as I set my phone down, Arthur comes into the bathroom behind me and puts his hands on my waist, gazing at our reflections in the mirror.

He murmurs, "I love you," and I lean back into him, resting my head on his shoulder. "I love you, too."

He presses a kiss to my cheek. "Now, let's get out there and have some fun."

I giggle as we leave the bathroom, and I slip on my sandals. It's time to do something daring that scares me.

CHAPTER 4

The beach at night is totally different than during the day since most of the tourists are busy elsewhere. There are a few groups of people, but everyone keeps to themselves and are wrapped up in enjoying their own company. Arthur leads me down the beach, and I realize he has a destination in mind. Hell, I guess I should have paid attention earlier when he and Kai were talking, but I was too busy daydreaming about cock.

Butterflies swirl in my stomach when I see Kai walking in our direction. He's in board shorts, an open white button-down shirt, and sandals. He's such a surfer cliche, and he looks just as amazing as earlier.

He flashes us a smile and falls in stride with us. "So, you all ready for an adventure?"

I'm suddenly shy, and I nod, not sure I trust my voice. Arthur claps him on the back and gives a little chuckle. "That we are, and thanks for the invitation."

We head down the beach together and my anticipation grows with each step. I could ask where they're taking me, but I'm enjoying the mystery. A small thrill travels through me as I realize that very soon, my husband is going to watch another man fuck me.

We round a sand dune and some large rocks, and Kai veers off towards stairs that lead to a stunning private villa with a pool overlooking the ocean. Everything about this place screams wealth and luxury.

"Kai, where are we?" I say with wonder.

He shoots me a dazzling smile and takes my hand as we climb the stairs to the house. "I'm staying here for a few weeks. The view is incredible."

As he takes us through the house, I admire the luxurious decor and view from the floor-to-ceiling windows, and I suddenly realize I misjudged Kai. He's clearly got money. He's not just some guy who hangs out at bars to pick up wealthy tourists.

We head out to the pool where there is a firepit and several lounges. Even though it overlooks the ocean, it's secluded and no one can see us. The moonlight and the flickering lights from the lit torches lend a romantic feel to the space. He prepared for tonight.

Kai releases my hand and waves us over to the loungers. "Have a seat and I'll get us drinks."

I'd love a cocktail, but I want a clear head so I ask him to bring me water. Arthur and I take a seat next to each other, and I grin at him. "This is certainly different than I imagined."

"Good different, I hope."

I'm already so turned on I can't imagine it won't be great. I giggle and give him a playful shove. "Good different. I thought we were going to go to the beach, but this is nice. Like really nice."

He takes my hand and gives it a squeeze. "Just enjoy tonight. Promise?"

"I promise."

My heart swells with love for Arthur as Kai returns with glasses of water. He sets the water down on a table next to me before perching on the end of my lounger. I admire how gorgeous he is while we sip our water and make idle chatter about Bali and how amazing it is here. It's surprisingly not awkward as we all chat, and I learn more about Kai and how he loves surfing and exploring the world.

As the conversation winds down, Kai leans towards me with a flirty smile. "So, I offered you a midnight swim. Are you up for it?"

I nod and flush as Kai stands and offers me his hand. I'm usually the life of the party, but something about Kai makes me feel shy. But then again, I've never been in a situation like this, so should I really be surprised?

I let him pull me to my feet, and Arthur says, "I'm going to be right here, baby. Remember, this is for you to enjoy."

Smiling at Arthur, I blow him a kiss. I didn't really think Arthur would ever share me, and my heart beats wildly as I realize I'm about to fuck someone else for the first time since college, and I'm ready for it.

I turn my attention to Kai and gaze up at him. He steps closer to me and dips his head, bringing his mouth to mine. His kiss is gentle and searching, and I open to him without hesitation, curling my hands into the fabric of his open shirt.

As we kiss, my head spins. Knowing that Arthur is watching makes this oddly romantic and dirty at the same time. The kiss escalates into a deeper, more passionate exploration, and my whole body sings with desire. Kai tastes like cinnamon, and I'm suddenly desperate for him.

His hands slide to my ass, and he pulls me in tight as he devours my mouth. He's a skilled kisser, and as his tongue twirls with mine, I let myself go and enjoy the moment. When he breaks off the kiss and tugs me toward the water, I follow eagerly. Heck yeah, time to get naked and get some cock in me.

We stop at the edge of the pool, and Kai kisses me softly once again, murmuring, "You're so beautiful," and brushing a strand of hair back from my face. "Are you sure you want this?"

I nod, trying to keep my voice steady. "I've never been more sure of anything. Just fuck me already."

He laughs. "Impatient. I like that."

Kai slowly slips the straps of my dress down my shoulders, teasingly baring my breasts. The air is warm, but I still shiver as my nipples harden.

I glance over at Arthur and see he's turned sideways in his chair, facing us with an intent expression as he watches.

Kai slides my dress down farther, and it pools around my feet. All I have on are my sandals and black lace panties. Goosebumps cover my skin as he peels my panties to my feet. I step out of them and kick my sandals off, leaving me completely bare. I expected a hurried fucking on a sand dune; instead, I feel like I'm being seduced while he's driving me crazy.

He grips my hips, and his voice is hoarse. "Before we start, I need to know what you want."

Oh god, I want him to just fuck me and not make me ask for it. I hesitate and when he makes no further moves, I know I have to say it. My mouth goes dry and I lick my lips, whispering, "I want your cock."

Kai smirks and lifts his voice. "I think your husband needs to hear what a little slut his wife is. Say it louder."

Heat rushes through me, and I almost moan. Making me say it aloud is so dang dirty. When I repeat myself, I speak up so Arthur can hear me. "I want your cock."

Kai cups my face and tips my chin up. "Next question. Do you want to be fucked hard or soft?"

Oooh, what? I didn't even consider anything beyond getting his cock inside me. My brain blips out for a moment. Do I dare ask for what I really want? Then it hits me. If I don't ask for it now, when will I? Now's my chance to experience something different.

Tilting my head slightly so I can see Arthur, I respond to Kai. "I want it hard." I take a deep breath and decide to add a plea to my answer. "Please...and I like dirty talk and being called names."

Arthur has a glazed look of lust on his face, but he smiles and nods at me. That's all I need.

Kai pinches my nipple, and a bolt of lust zings through me as I gasp and give him my attention again. He smirks. "Okay, then here's the rules, my little fucktoy."

I can feel my body flush at the word fucktoy. No one has ever called me that before.

His voice is firm and authoritative when he continues. "If you need me to stop for any reason, say red light. Got it?"

I'm already nodding before he's done talking. "Yes, got it. Red light."

The negotiation is making me even more desperate for his cock. Now that I know he's going to fuck me hard, I can feel my inner thighs getting damp.

"Then let's begin."

I'm about to ask what he wants me to do, but before I can say anything, he spins me around until I'm facing a patio chair and he pushes my shoulders down, bending me over. I grab the arms of the chair, confused. Aren't we going swimming?

When his hand lands on my ass in a sharp slap, I yelp in surprise. His voice is gruff. "Keep still. Your husband told me you enjoyed being spanked. He said it turned you into an obedient little slut."

Holy fuck. This is even better than I imagined. I'm guessing the guys were texting today, and I'm sure that Arthur didn't actually say it turned me into an obedient little slut, but I enjoy imagining he did. Kai slaps me a few more times, and my eyes close as I enjoy the sensations rippling through my body. I love Arthur's spankings, but Kai's are more intense.

As Kai spanks me harder, I gasp and wiggle my hips from the stinging pain, enjoying every second of it. I'm going to be a wet mess by the time he finally fucks me, and getting spanked by someone other than my husband makes me really feel like a slut.

I open my eyes to glance at Arthur, and my heart flutters. He's cupping himself through his pants, and his cock is bulging. I drop my head while I try to process the pleasure washing over me while Kai continues spanking me. My pussy is slick and needy, and I can feel myself getting fuzzy-headed. Maybe Arthur really did say it turned me into an obedient little slut because the longer Kai spanks me, the more compliant I get. He could ask me to do anything, and I'd probably do it.

I drift in a haze of pleasure, and when he stops spanking me, I hear rustling behind me. I see his clothes hit the pavement. He grabs my hip and uses his knees to force my legs apart. When the blunt head of his cock presses against my pussy, I suck in my breath. Holy fuck, I guess we aren't going swimming.

Kai plunges his cock into me, and I cry out, gripping the arms of the chair more tightly so I don't fall forward. Oh My God. He's huge. His cock stretches me out, and my head spins from delight as his thickness pings nerve endings I didn't even know I had.

He doesn't give me time to adjust as he starts thrusting hard with each stroke. His balls bounce against my clit, adding a hint of delicious extra sensation. He keeps hold of one hip, and I feel like a doll being tossed around as he fucks me furiously. My tits are bouncing, and my moans get louder as the rapture builds in layers.

Damn, this went from zero to 60 so fast, but I'm getting exactly what I wanted. With his free hand, he twists my braid in his fist, yanking my head back. I hiss from the erotic combination of pleasure and pain. "Oh god, please…" I moan, but I have no idea what I'm pleading for.

"What do you want, my fucktoy?" he taunts, increasing his tempo. The sound of his skin slapping against mine is obscene.

"Harder, I need it harder!"

He still has my hair gripped tightly in his fist, and when he tugs, it sends electric tingles across my scalp. I'm already close to coming, and I try to focus on holding off my orgasm. I whimper as my legs shake, and to distract myself from how good his cock feels, I tilt my head as much as I can so I can look at Arthur. He's resting back on the lounge and rubbing his cock through his jeans while he watches Kai pound my cunt. There's a look of pure bliss on his face. Oh god, I love this.

Seeing Arthur enjoying himself pushes me over the edge. I detonate around Kai's cock and cry out, "Oh fuck, oh fuck!"

Pleasure radiates from my core, and when Kai pulls his cock from my pussy, I'm gasping as the aftershocks of my orgasm tear through me. Without giving me a chance to recover, Kai lets go of my hair and helps me stand. He swivels the chair so it's facing Arthur and then sits down in it.

"Now my little slut, you're going to ride my cock. Face your husband. I want him to see your expression when I make you come again."

I obey immediately, facing away from Kai and sinking down on his cock slowly. His thick girth spreads me inch by delicious inch until he's fully inside me. Mmm, his cock feels so damn good. I've never been with anyone this big, and if I was selecting a guy to fuck based on his cock, Kai is a definite winner.

I raise my eyes to my husband and lock gazes with him. The look of raw need I see in his gaze shoots a bolt of desire through me, and I hook my legs around the outside of Kai's and start to rotate my hips slowly. I'm spread open to my husband's view, and I know he can see the base of Kai's cock before it disappears inside me. Kai's hand snakes around to play with my clit, and I moan loudly while holding on to the arms of the chair to give an experimental bounce on his cock.

Kai rubs my clit in just the right way to drive me crazy, and I speed up my bouncing and rocking as delight radiates from my pussy. I can feel my tits swaying with every movement, and I watch my husband as he enjoys the show. Arthur is rubbing harder against his pants, and I lick my lips, wishing he was inside my mouth right now while another guy was fucking me. My dirty thoughts push me closer to another orgasm, and my cries become needier and louder. I keep eye contact with Arthur, getting lost in the pleasure as I fuck myself on Kai's cock.

"Make him come inside you," Arthur groans out.

"Mmmm, yes," I whimper as I increase my pace.

Kai's fingers brush against my clit faster, and he plays with my nipple with his free hand. When he gives my nipple a sharp pinch, the pleasurable pain tips me over the edge. I cry out in ecstasy and clench around his cock as I'm wracked with rapture so intense stars sparkle along the edges of my vision.

Kai moves both his hands to my waist and holds onto me, forcing me up and down on his length. I'm chanting, "Oh god, oh god, oh god," from the intense joy as I rock faster and harder, trying to get Kai to come like my husband wants. I feel powerful with both men finding pleasure in what I'm doing, even if only one cock is inside me. This is fabulous.

"Ohhhh, god!" I cry out as I'm pushed into a sudden and unexpected orgasm. My legs shake and my eyes roll to the back of my head as Kai groans and explodes inside me. I can feel the warmth filling me, and knowing I'm taking a load of cum that isn't my husband's makes me feel so damn naughty.

I keep rocking on him until I can tell he's unloaded everything, and I slow the movements of my hips. He runs his hands up to cup both my breasts, his thumbs flicking lightly across my sensitive nipples. My breasts feel heavy and full, and I enjoy the moment of softness as I come down from my high.

Assuming we're done, I unhook my legs from him and make a movement to get up. Kai interrupts me.

"Get on your knees slut, it's time to clean up your mess."

Oooh, yes, please. I clamber off his lap, sinking to my knees between his legs. His cock is half hard and coated in our combined wetness. I run my tongue up his length, and he sucks in his breath. I dart my eyes up to his and then lean in to gently kiss the tip. He lets out an audible moan and runs his fingers along the sides of my head, tightening his grip slightly.

I continue cleaning off his cock. The salty tang of our mixed juices is pleasant, and I savor the way it mixes with his earthy aroma. Once he's clean, I turn my attention to his balls, lapping them while he groans in delight. I wish I could see Arthur, but I know he's watching, and I can feel my pussy tingling in excitement again.

The longer I work on Kai's cock and balls, the harder he gets. Mmm, maybe he'll fuck me again. To help make that happen, I take as much of his length in my mouth as I can. He's way too big to fit it all in, but I swirl my tongue along the underside of him and suck for all I'm worth.

He hisses and uses my hair to pull me off of him, groaning, "Such a good fucktoy. Your husband is a lucky man."

I blush at his words, oddly pleased. Arthur is lucky, and yet so am I. Not many husbands would be willing to let their wife play with another guy without feeling incredibly jealous.

Kai cups my chin and brushes his thumb across my lower lip and forces my mouth open. When he pushes his thumb into my mouth, I suck on it. There's something mesmerizing about being on my knees like this, and the world gets fuzzy around the edges again the longer I suck on his thumb.

When Kai speaks again, it takes me a moment to realize he's talking to my husband. "Have you changed your mind and want to do more than watch?"

Ohhhh. Desire courses through me, and I wonder if Arthur wants that. I don't even care if Kai fucks me again, I just want to give as much pleasure to my husband as I'm getting.

Arthur's voice sounds distant, but he seems hesitant. "I don't know..."

"All you have to do is ask," Kai chuckles.

My pulse speeds up, and I desperately want Arthur to say yes.

Arthur clears his throat. "Juliet, do you want that?"

Kai pulls his thumb out of my mouth so I can answer, and I rock back to rest on my heels. I have to look over my shoulder to see Arthur. The light from a torch next to him illuminates his expression. His eyes are dark and intent as he stares at me, and I can see he wants someone to give him permission to let go and take what is being offered.

My voice is throaty as I give him permission to explore. "Babe, I'm so fucking hot right now I need you. Whatever you want. I'm yours."

The tension breaks with my words when Arthur groans, "Then, yes."

When I look back at Kai, his eyes are sparkling and I can tell he's happy with the new development as he speaks. "So man, do you want her pussy or her mouth?"

"Pussy. I want to feel how much you stretched her."

A zing of pleasure ripples through me. Hearing that Arthur wants to fuck me after taking Kai's massive cock is so damn sexy.

Kai grins down at me. "Her pussy it is then. I'll take that beautiful mouth. She needs to swallow my cum this time."

I feel a spike of excitement, and I'm almost drunk on lust as I gaze up at Kai. "Yes, please."

Kai stands up and helps me to my feet. He pulls me over to where my husband is on the lounger. As if Arthur understands what the plan is, he unzips his jeans and pulls out his cock. It's fully erect, and a bead of precum is glistening on the end.

Oh, fuck yeah, I need that in me. No one needs to tell me what to do. I climb on the lounger with my husband, straddling his hips and gazing down at his face as I sink onto his cock. I'm still wet and swollen from so many orgasms, and Arthur's cock feels amazing. He's not as big as Kai, but he's a perfect fit for me. I moan and grind against him as Kai stands next to me, gripping the base of his cock. I turn my head and open my mouth as wide as I can, letting Kai feed me his dick. He slides into my throat as far as he can go while I grind against my husband's cock. My vision swims as the pleasure explodes through me. My body is a live wire of arousal, and I can't control my moans as I go wild on my husband's cock and hum around Kai's shaft in delight.

Kai wastes no time fucking my throat, holding onto the sides of my head for leverage. The added intensity of him face fucking me is perfection as I slam down on Arthur's cock and whimper with joy. Having my husband's cock inside me while my throat is full of another man is the dream I never even knew I had. I could do this all night—hell, I could take on an entire lineup of surfers like this. I'm feeling like a sexual goddess with two holes stuffed.

As I chase my orgasm, Arthur grasps my hips, bucking underneath me and urging me on. He whispers, "Come for me, baby."

His words push me over the edge, and my eyes close as I whine around the mouthful of Kai's cock. Waves of pleasure cascade through me, and Kai's cock muffles my moan. I don't get time to come down from my high before I peak again.

I writhe and explode as I hear Kai talking. "God, your wife is such a beautiful slut. I could fuck her mouth all night long."

Arthur thrusts up into me harder, sending shockwaves of euphoria through me. His fingers grip my waist, pulling me down as he groans, "I know. Fuck, baby, you feel so good. Oh god, I'm going to come."

I try to beg him to fill me, but all it comes out as is a mumble as Kai's thrusts speed up. Arthur's cock pulses, and he hisses, "Fuck!" as his body quivers and I feel his orgasm tear through him. I plant myself on his cock and grind against him as he fills me up. I'm reveling in the sensation of another load of cum in my pussy when Kai groans and spurts of his hot cum hit the back of my throat.

The taste of his seed sends me into overload, and my body shudders and spasms from the waves of ecstasy washing over me again and again. I feel like a mindless pleasure doll as Kai pulls out of my mouth as he finishes. I'm trembling violently as the aftershocks die down and Arthur wraps his arms around me, pulling me against him.

I close my eyes and sink into him, letting myself float in pure euphoria. I'm not sure how long it is until I can think again, but Arthur is rubbing my back gently when I finally can. Kai's sitting on the other lounge chair, drinking water.

I have no energy, but Arthur reaches for my glass of water and holds it for me. "Take a drink, baby."

I do, and the cool liquid refreshes me a little.

"You were amazing." Arthur says when he sets the glass back on the side table, and I can hear the awe in his voice.

I lift my head to meet his gaze. "Thank you for this."

I kiss him softly on the lips and then nestle against him once more. I'm exhausted and satisfied, and I just want to cuddle with my husband. The guys talk quietly as I drift, and when Arthur finally stirs, Kai helps me stand up.

Both the guys help me get dressed again, and I giggle. "We never went for that swim."

Kai laughs. "No, I didn't want your husband to miss any of the action."

Oh damn, I didn't even think about how Arthur wouldn't have seen much if we were in the water. That tells me Kai really does have experience with husbands watching.

Once we're presentable, Kai walks us through his house. I pause at the door and take his hand. "Thank you for a wonderful time tonight."

Kai flashes a bright smile, kissing both my cheeks. "Thank you too. Glad I ran into you at the bar."

I smile back and reach for Arthur, taking his hand. Arthur thanks him for a good night, and once we say our goodbyes, Arthur and I make our way down the rocky stairs and out to the beach.

I'm tired so we walk slowly through the sand, but I've never felt more connected to my husband. I glance up at Arthur. "This was the best adventure."

His answering smile is glorious and he pauses and tugs me against him, kissing my temple. "It was. I loved seeing you enjoying yourself with him, and the ending..."

He trails off and I can tell he's feeling shy about what happened, so I voice what I think he's feeling. "It was incredible."

"It was," he murmurs, and I wrap my arms around him and hold him tightly, understanding that what we did means he trusts me entirely. After a long moment, he leads me down the beach. We don't say another word, but the connection between us is as strong as ever and I know this trip changed the course of our lives for the better.

Chapter 5

Once we get home from Bali and we're unpacked and settled in, I remember the blog post Ariel sent me. I pull it up on my phone and smile at the title and read the rest.

Hotwives Unleashed: A Glimpse into a Taboo World

If you want to know what's wrong with the world, you don't have to look any further than your neighbor. We're surrounded by horny slutwives who are taking a cock in every hole by men other than their husband.

That's right, you'd be amazed at how many people are trying out the hotwife lifestyle. When you walk down the street, it's hard to stop thinking about what every couple you pass is doing behind closed doors. What depraved, filthy things are going on practically in your own backyard?

That friend you meet up with monthly for lunch? I bet she's a hotwife. She probably spends every Friday night on her knees, worshiping the cock of her husband's best friend while her husband sits across the room, stroking and watching. I bet she's feeling like a complete slut as the guy's cum fills her mouth until it's dripping down her chin, knowing that she's going to take another load, and another, and another, until she's nothing but a hole full of cum.

So the next time you're at the mall, think of that. Think of all the filthy, depraved things that are going on that shouldn't be. And you'll start to realize why this hotwife craze is such a problem.

Oh my god. I giggle as I type a message to Ariel.

Juliet

I'm back and I just read Debra's blog. We're getting together this weekend for lunch, no excuses. I have so much to tell you and that post really is fucking hilarious. She sounds thirsty.

Since it's a workday, I know Ariel won't respond anytime soon. I set down my phone and giggle again as I think back to the night with Kai. I guess I'm now one of those depraved, horny sluts.

It's fucking wonderful.

The End

August Hotwife

Hotwife of the Month Club 8

Lacey Cross

CHAPTER 1

I need to start dinner, but instead, I'm standing in front of the fridge, staring at the calendar on the kitchen wall. My eyes land on the circled dates that mark my ovulation window. Ugh. I sigh heavily, feeling the familiar emotional rollercoaster that comes with trying to conceive.

"Hey, Will?" I call out, my voice wavering slightly. The muffled sounds of his engineering documentary drift from the living room.

"Yeah, babe?" he responds, his attention still divided.

I bite my lip, steeling myself. "It's...it's that time again. Ovulation window's coming up."

The TV goes silent. I hear William's footsteps approaching. He pauses in the doorway, and his hazel eyes meet mine, a mix of determination and weariness behind his glasses. I can see the toll this journey has taken on him too, the self-doubt that's been gnawing at him since we found out the fertility issues stem from his side because of a sports injury when he was younger.

"Already?" he asks, running a hand through his hair. "I swear it feels like we just finished the last round."

I nod, my throat tight. "I know."

My mind drifts to the countless doctors' appointments, the endless cycles of hope and disappointment. I want so desperately to be a mother, to fill our home with laughter and the joy of a child. But with each passing month, that dream seems increasingly out of reach.

William crosses the kitchen in two strides and wraps me in his arms. I breathe in his familiar scent, feeling his heartbeat against my cheek. Despite his own struggles, he's always been my rock, my steady support.

"It's just going to take time, Ariel," he murmurs, his voice a soothing rumble in his chest.

I want to believe him. I want to share in his unwavering faith, his analytical ability to see this as a problem we can solve together. But my heart is heavy with uncertainty. I rest my head on his shoulder, letting his warmth envelop me. "I just wish it wasn't so...clinical. Like we're scheduling intimacy instead of just letting it happen naturally."

William pulls back slightly, his hands cupping my face. His thumbs brush away the tears that have started to form in the corners of my eyes. "I know, sweetheart. It's tough. But we're in this together. And who knows? Maybe this time will be different."

I manage a small smile, appreciating his optimism. "You're right. We just have to keep trying." I take a deep breath, composing myself. "So, what's next? More documentaries while we wait for the right moment?"

He chuckles, a sound that lightens the mood slightly. "Well, I think we need to do something fun. How about we go out for dinner tonight? A little date night to remind us that there's more to our life than just...this."

A genuine smile spreads across my face. "That sounds wonderful."

He leans in, pressing his forehead against mine. "Good. Just keep the faith, baby. It will happen."

William and I settle into our seats at our favorite Italian restaurant, and I'm instantly glad we came out for dinner tonight. We needed this.

As we share a bottle of wine, I can tell there's something on his mind. He's got that look, the one where his eyebrows knit together just a fraction, and he's silent for a beat too long while he swirls his wine thoughtfully.

"You know how all our friends seem to be...experimenting with their relationships lately?" he finally asks, his voice low as if he doesn't want the table next to us to overhear.

I give him a playful grin, curious about where this is going. "You mean James and Marilyn? With the whole hotwife thing?" I reference our friends who recently opened up their marriage. Now more of our social circle is trying it, like it's catching. I try not to think about it too much. The idea is very appealing, but we've got bigger things to think about, like baby-making.

William nods, his gaze fixed on the ruby liquid in his glass. "Yeah, well, the idea of watching you with someone is crazy hot." He risks a glance at me, as if he's gauging my reaction.

Um, what? His comment is so unexpected it makes my heart skip a beat. A warm flush spreads across my cheeks as I process his words. William has always been the more cautious one in our relationship, his steady nature a counterpoint to my adventurous spirit. To hear him suggest something so daring sends a thrill through me, igniting a spark of excitement I didn't know was there.

My imagination races at the idea, vivid scenarios flashing through my mind. I picture William watching me with desire as another man's hands explore my body. A delicious tension coils in my stomach. The possibilities unfold in my mind as a newfound energy courses through my veins.

Fuck, I shouldn't want this. I toy with my napkin, trying to ignore how my entire body is awakening with desires I never knew I had.

"So you're saying you're into this?" I try to keep my tone steady so he can't see how turned on I'm getting.

He sets his wineglass down. "I've been thinking about it. A lot. And I wonder if it's something you'd ever consider trying."

A flush creeps up my neck. Given our current situation with trying to get pregnant, it seems like the worst possible timing. But my body doesn't care as my panties grow wet and a longing pulls at me deep in my core.

"Maybe we could discuss this in a few years, once we're past all this," I suggest, gesturing vaguely at my phone displaying the fertility tracking app on the lock screen.

He grows quiet, his eyes searching mine. "What if this could be part of the family planning?"

My heart skips another beat. "What do you mean?"

"I've been doing some reading. There are couples who've struggled with infertility, just like us, and they've found...creative solutions. Like bringing in a third party to help conceive."

I blink, trying to process his words. "You mean like a sperm donor and a turkey baster?"

He gives me a little smile and shakes his head. "Not exactly. More like...a known donor who's also a participant. Someone we both trust."

I'm stunned into silence, my mind whirling with the implications. When I find my voice again, I ask, "And who would that be?"

William looks at me with an intensity I haven't seen in years. "Zandar."

"Zandar?" I repeat while I try to gather my thoughts. Zandar is his best friend since childhood, and has always been supportive of us. The idea of him in this context is unexpectedly arousing. I imagine him stepping into our lives in ways we've never considered, and my body buzzes with illicit pleasure.

I first have to ask..."But not with a turkey baster?"

"NOT with a turkey baster," William confirms. "He's always been attracted to you. If everyone is comfortable, he could solve our problem."

I contemplate the magnitude of what he's proposing. It's unconventional and so damn hot. My nipples harden as I imagine fucking Zandar. I've heard through the grapevine that he's dominant in the bedroom. What would that be like?

William studies me, his eyes sparkling in the dim lighting, and my love for him eclipses the desire to fuck Zandar. As much as my inner slut wants to dance around the room and immediately agree to this, I need to make something clear.

I reach across the table and take his hand. "Don't suggest this just because you believe I'm unhappy. Our life together means everything to me. We can consider adoption in a couple of years if things don't work out."

He laughs and squeezes my hand. "I know, but this could be fun and turn into a win/win situation. But we don't have to decide anything tonight."

Desire radiates through me at his words, and I know I don't need more time. "If Zandar is open to it," I say slowly, trying to not sound like I'm ready for a celebration party, "then I'm interested."

William's eyes darken with lust. "I'll talk to Zandar about it."

Holy fuck, this might actually happen? I guess only if Zandar wants to, but still. William and I stare at each other for a minute, and an overwhelming surge of lust makes me desperate for my husband's cock.

My panties grow wetter and my pulse races as I pick up my fork. "Eat faster. We need to get home."

William grins. "I couldn't agree more."

We both shovel our food down while he signals to the server that we need our check. The drive home is torturous, with his hand on my bare thigh under my dress, caressing soft circles. With how turned on I am, I might come as soon as he slides inside me. There's a visible bulge in his pants, so I know we're on the same wavelength.

We don't even make it inside the house. Once we park and get out, William shuts the outer garage door and stalks me around the front of the car. He presses me against the side and cages me with his arms.

His eyes are filled with a hunger I haven't seen in years, and his voice is rough with desire. "You have no idea what you do to me, do you?"

A shiver runs down my spine, and I arch into him, desperate for more contact. "Show me."

He doesn't hesitate as his lips crash against mine in a searing kiss. His tongue delves into my mouth with a ferocity that steals my breath. I moan into the kiss, my hands fisting in his hair, pulling him closer.

William squeezes my breasts through my dress, his thumbs brushing over my hardened nipples. I gasp at the sensation, my hips rolling against him instinctively. It's crazy that just the thought of fucking Zandar makes me this desperate, but I love it.

He breaks the kiss, trailing his lips down my neck, nipping and sucking at the sensitive skin. "I want you," he growls against my pulse point. "Right here, right now."

"Do it," I moan.

He reaches down, hiking up my skirt, his fingers brushing against my soaked panties. I whimper and my head falls back against the car as he strokes my pussy through the damp fabric.

"Fuck, you're so wet," he groans, pressing a finger against my clit. "So ready for me."

"Yes," I hiss, grinding against his hand. "I need you inside me."

William hooks his fingers in my panties, dragging them down to my knees. I barely have time to register the cool air against my heated skin before he's plunging two fingers into my dripping core.

"God," he pants, his breath hot against my ear. "You feel so fucking good."

I cry out, my hips jerking as he pumps his fingers in and out of my pussy, his thumb circling my clit. My inner walls clench around him, drawing him deeper.

"That's it, baby. Let go. I've got you."

My orgasm crashes over me like a tidal wave, my body shaking with the force of it. I cling to William, my nails digging into his shoulders as I ride out the intense pleasure.

My vision goes white as I sob, "Oh God, William!"

He holds me close as I come down from my high, his fingers prolonging the bliss as he strokes my sensitive flesh. When I finally catch my breath, his eyes shine with pride and satisfaction.

"You're so beautiful when you come," he whispers, brushing a strand of hair from my face. "I could watch you all day."

I laugh, giddy from the pleasure, and tease, "And I'd let you. Now what about you? I need to see you come."

William grins, stepping back and swiftly removing his shirt. Oh shit, we're not moving inside? He kicks off his shoes and lowers his pants, freeing his cock.

"Come here," I beckon, crooking my finger at him. "Get that inside me."

There's a predatory gleam in his eye. "Your wish is my command," he says, lifting one of my legs and sliding his cock inside me.

We both groan from the pleasure as he fills me, and I cling to his shoulders as he pummels me against the car. This is a side of him I've never seen before. It's wonderful.

He sets a relentless pace, each thrust sending waves of pleasure coursing through me. The garage fills with the sounds of our panting and the raw, primal noise of our bodies colliding. Thank god he closed the outer door because in this moment, I wouldn't care if the entire neighborhood watched us.

The idea of me being that much of a slut thrills me, and my voice is breathy and desperate. "Harder. Fuck me harder!"

He growls, a sound that sends shivers down my spine, and his hips move faster, his cock plunging deeper. I can feel every inch of him, every ridge and vein as he strokes my inner walls, driving me towards another climax.

"You're so tight, so hot," he grunts, his face pressed against my neck.

His words and obvious pleasure send me spiraling, and I cry out as another orgasm rips through me. My body clamps down on his cock, pulsing and convulsing around him. He rides me through it, his own breath coming in ragged gasps.

"I'm close," he pants, his voice strained. "I want you to come again, baby."

My body hums with pleasure as he reaches between us, his fingers finding my clit and rubbing it in tight circles. The sensation is almost too much, and my oversensitive body spasms with each touch. He keeps me pinned against the car, his cock still drilling into me, his fingers insistent.

His voice is hoarse with effort. "Come for me. One more time. Let me feel you come all over my cock."

The relentless pressure on my clit sends me over the edge again. I scream his name, my body convulsing as a third climax tears through me. He groans, his hips jerking as his cock spasms, his warm cum coating me, and I can tell it was a powerful orgasm by the way he keeps shivering.

When he stops thrusting into me, we stand there for a moment, our bodies still joined. My mind spins from the pleasure. Holy fuck, that was amazing. Slowly, he withdraws, his hands gentle as he helps me straighten my clothes.

I lean against the car, my legs shaky. "That was..." I start, but words fail me.

"Yeah, it was," he agrees, leaning in to give me a soft kiss.

Hand in hand, we make our way into the house, the weight of our earlier conversation temporarily lifted. Tonight was so unexpected and so needed. I feel more connected to William than I have in months.

As we get ready for bed, I make my way to the kitchen for a glass of water. The calendar on the wall catches my eye. The circled dates no longer fill me with dread. Instead, there's a spark of hope, a glimmer of excitement. Maybe this unconventional path will lead us to the family we've always dreamed of.

As I curl up against William in bed, he wraps his arm around me, and a sense of peace washes over me. Tomorrow, we'll talk to Zandar and take the next step on this wild, unexpected journey.

Chapter 2

The next day, I'm afraid that all I'll be able to think about is my husband's offer, but luckily, work distracts me. It's half days at the elementary school this week, and as soon as my class is finished, the floodgates in my mind open up. I spend a couple more hours at work grading some papers, but I keep wondering what Zandar's cock looks like. He's incredibly attractive, but I've never let myself go there before.

The moment I walk in my front door, I kick off my shoes and curl up on the couch with my phone. I need a second opinion about whether this plan is crazy. It's time to call Sara.

Sara is one of my closest friends, and she knows all about this hotwife craze that is sweeping through our friends group. When she answers, I dive right in. "Hey, I need to run something past you. It's kind of a big deal."

There's a brief pause before Sara responds, her voice filled with concern. "Oh? What's up?"

I take a deep breath, trying to gather my thoughts. "So, William and I have been talking...we're considering something unconventional to help with our fertility struggles."

"Hmm, what do you mean, like a turkey baster? That's not that uncommon, you know. Fertility treatment is expensive."

I snort. Is that the first thing we all think of? "No, no, not a turkey baster...." I'm really not sure how to word what I want to say. Why didn't I plan my thoughts before calling her? After some hesitation, the words tumble out. "Okay, don't judge, but...we're going to ask my husband's friend to help us out."

There's a moment of silence before Sara responds, her voice calm and thoughtful. "But not with a turkey baster?"

Oh jeez. I giggle. "More of an organic insertion."

"Wow." She sounds surprised but also intrigued. "That's quite a step. How do you feel about it?"

I run my fingers through my hair. "Honestly? It's so far out of my comfort zone, but there's something about it that's thrilling."

Sara hums thoughtfully. "Well, it's not the craziest thing I've heard lately. You know how our friends keep saying being a hotwife has revitalized their marriage, and you have a double need."

"I know," I admit, twirling a strand of hair around my finger.

Sara's voice turns wistful. "I could never be a hotwife. I'm too self-conscious. But I really hope you have a wonderful time and get pregnant. I'll be cheering you on!"

Sara's lack of self-confidence has always surprised me, given that she's thin, blonde, and a knockout. But I've known her long enough to know it's not an act.

"Aw, Sara," I say, feeling a rush of affection for her. "I'm going to be hella self-conscious, too. The guys better be ready for one nervous first-time hotwife. Besides, this isn't really about being a hotwife; it's about having a baby."

Sara giggles and then squeals, "Ooooh, that reminds me. Check Debra's blog later. You'll love the latest post."

"I will," I laugh. Debra is another wife in our circle of friends, but she's been acting holier than thou and starting an anonymous blog about the dangers of the hotwife trend.

Just talking to Sara has eased my concerns. She obviously doesn't think me fucking someone else to get pregnant is a big deal.

"Now, promise me you'll keep me updated on how this all plays out," she says warmly.

"I will. I'll fill you in on all the details. Well, maybe not *all.*"

Sara chuckles. "I'll be here for you, no matter what. Good luck."

As we hang up, I take a deep breath. Talking to Sara has helped me sort through my feelings. Now, all that's left is to find out if Zandar wants to fuck me. William better talk to him today. It's almost go-time, and I need a pussy full of cum asap. The thought sends a thrill through me. Oh god, I really hope this isn't a stupid plan.

I'm at the counter, chopping veggies for dinner, when William walks in, a massive grin on his face. He sweeps me into his arms, dips me like we're dancing, and kisses me so thoroughly that pleasure ripples through every nerve in my body. As we straighten up, he pulls me close, his voice a low rumble. "I talked to Zandar today."

"Oh, yeah?" I ask, heart pounding with excitement. "And? What did he say?"

William's grin widens, and he tightens his hold on me. "He's in. Said he's honored we trust him with this and promises to take good care of you."

A wave of relief rushes through me. "Wow, that's...big, isn't it?"

He chuckles. "Yeah, it is. He'll come over tomorrow. We'll have dinner, and then...we'll see where the night takes us."

I nod, biting my lip. "Okay, sounds good. As good as it can be, considering how crazy this is."

His expression softens, and he cups my cheek. "Hey, we don't have to do this if you're not comfortable."

I lean into his touch, feeling a surge of love for this man who's willing to go down this path with me. "I know, but I want to try."

He kisses my forehead. "Good, because I told him to call you filthy names."

What's this? I tip my head up and catch his smug grin. "Oh my god, you did not!"

"Mmm hmm, I told him to call you a dirty little slut and tell you he's going to breed you."

Lust simmers in my gut, and I have a hard time responding. "You're terrible," I whisper, playfully swatting his chest, though the heat in my cheeks betrays my excitement. "But that's...really hot."

William laughs. "I thought you might like that. We need to make this as enjoyable for you as possible, right?" His hands slide down to my hips, pulling me closer. "Zandar is...quite enthusiastic."

I raise an eyebrow, feeling a flutter of anticipation. "Really?"

He hums in response. "Yep, and I think he's the perfect choice."

Oh god, tomorrow can't get here fast enough. I push out of his arms and turn back to the counter, chopping veggies with a renewed sense of purpose. The thought that I might become pregnant makes this plan even more erotic.

The rest of the evening passes in a blur of quiet anticipation. We eat dinner and watch a movie, but my mind is anywhere but the present. I keep imagining what it will be like to fuck someone other than William.

Later, as we lie in bed with William's arm draped protectively around me, I can't help but whisper into the darkness, "William?"

"Mm hmm?" he murmurs sleepily.

"I love you."

His voice is warm and reassuring. "I love you too. More than anything."

I snuggle in closer to him and try to get some sleep. Tomorrow is going to be a big day.

CHAPTER 3

My mind is a scattered mess as I try to work the next day. Thank god it's another half day at school. By the time I get home, all I can think about is fucking Zandar. I'm too worked up to do anything productive. As I change out of my work clothes and put on shorts and a t-shirt, I contemplate my afternoon. Hmm, maybe my husband needs a distraction at work. I plop down at the kitchen table and text him.

Ariel

I can't stop daydreaming about tonight.

He replies immediately.

William

Me either.

Butterflies swirl in my stomach. What would he say if I told him I've been imagining fucking Zandar all day? Let's find out!

Ariel

I have a confession...

William

Yes?

I bite my lip, nervous about what his reaction will be.

Is it bad that I'm getting worked up by the thought of fucking Zandar beyond just making a baby?

He doesn't answer for a full minute, and my anxiety skyrockets. When his text comes through, there's a picture attached. It's of him sitting in our car in the parking lot of his work, but the camera is angled down towards his crotch, showing a very visible bulge in his pants.

Babe, this isn't because I've been thinking about you getting pregnant.

A wave of heat crashes over me as a sudden surge of arousal makes me squirm in my seat. Holy fuck, he really *does* want to share me. My heart hammers as I type.

Oh my god, how are you working today?

It's hard...

Ha ha, I married a funny guy.

I'm so wet right now. If you're going to change your mind, do it now before I get even more worked up.

While I wait for his reply, I can't resist the urge to touch myself, slipping a hand down the front of my shorts. My fingers brush against my already soaked panties as my clit throbs. I feel like such a slut for telling him how wet I am for his friend, but it's also freeing. Is this what our friends mean when they say being a hotwife is revitalizing their marriage? I definitely feel naughtier, and want to tell William all my dirty fantasies.

William

> I'm not changing my mind. I've been thinking about this ever since James told us how great his relationship with Marilyn is now that she's a hotwife.

Fuck, that's hot. I moan as I press down and rub my pussy harder through the fabric of my panties, trying to get the friction where I need it most.

He sends me another message while I'm distracted.

William

> I never told you this, but Zandar's known for having a large cock. All I've been imagining today is seeing him split you open and making you scream as he fucks you senseless.

I picture Zandar, his dark skin glistening with sweat as he drills into me. God, I hope tonight goes well. But beyond that, I'm enjoying this new-found dirty side of my husband. My hand is busy, so I use speech-to-chat for my next message.

Ariel

> What else were you thinking about?

William

> What your pussy is going to look like when it's so full of his cum that it's dripping out of you.

The mental image is so vivid that it short circuits my brain. I don't even realize what I'm doing when I push my panties aside. I'm lost in the fantasy as I rub tight circles over my clit. My orgasm builds in record time...until the ding of another text message brings me back to focus.

William

> You better not be touching yourself. I can't do anything at work, so you have to suffer with me.

Ugh, he knows me too well. I pull my hands out from between my legs and wipe my fingers on my tank top.

Ariel

Now would I do that?

I give him an emoji of a face with a halo.

William

Don't make me call it off with Zandar tonight.

As if. I giggle as I type back.

Ariel

I'm being good. I just need it to be after dinner already.

I sigh at William's next text.

William

Soon, baby. Soon.

Yeah, not goddamn soon enough. We text back and forth for the next couple of hours until I tell him I'm going to take a long shower and I promise to be good. Maybe tonight I'll get an amazing orgasm and become pregnant. That would be a total win.

When William comes home and walks into the bedroom, the look in his eyes tells me he's ready to ravish me. I'm pulling on my favorite hot pink dress, though I'm not really sure why I'm dressing up since it's just coming off again soon. But a big part of me wants to look sexy tonight. William stalks towards me, and I put my hand out to stop him, pressing on his chest so he can't get too close.

"Hey, now," I purr at him. "You can kiss me, but that's all. Promise?"

He and I both know he could have me bent over the bed, my dress at my waist, and him balls deep in me in one minute flat if he really wanted.

He groans, "Such a little tease."

I relent and move into his arms, brushing my lips against his. When he tries to deepen the kiss, I push him back with a laugh. "Hey now, behave."

Putting distance between us, I move over to the mirror to adjust my dress. The way the fabric clings to my curves makes it clear I'm not wearing a bra, and the hem is short enough that the lacy edge of my thigh-high stockings peeks out.

While William changes out of his work clothes, I watch him in the mirror. The bulge in his pants is unmistakable. Knowing William is turned on, along with me being in my fertile window, makes tonight way more erotic than I expected.

I'm about ready to flirt with him some more to torture us both when the doorbell rings. A zing of pleasure ripples through me. It's time!

CHAPTER 4

Zandar brought Thai food with him, but all I can do is sit there and pick at it. The aroma of spices and coconut milk normally would tempt me, but I'm too excited. Across from me, Zandar's vivid green eyes lock onto mine, and heat rises in my cheeks. His gaze is intense, searching, and I find myself unable to look away. I've never paid much attention to my attraction to other people before. Sure, I always thought Zandar was sexy, with his chiseled jawline and broad shoulders, but I'm not going to drool over my husband's friends. At least, I never used to.

Now everything is different, and the air between us is charged. Whenever he looks at me, I get a rush of desire, and my skin tingles with awareness. I shift in my seat, trying to find a comfortable position that doesn't betray my growing arousal.

Zandar takes a bite of his food, and I watch as his lips close around the fork. I swallow hard, my mouth suddenly dry. The simple act of him eating shouldn't affect me this way, but it does. I force myself to look down at my plate, my fingers fidgeting with my fork.

William sits to my right, his hand resting casually on my thigh, his fingers tracing slow, deliberate patterns that send tingles up my spine. His hand is warm, and it's like he's leaving trails of fire on my skin. How can such a simple touch be so distracting? I'm sure he knows exactly what he's doing, and he's just trying to keep me needy.

The conversation flows easily while we eat, but there's an undercurrent, a tension that has my body thrumming with anticipation.

"So, Ariel," Zandar says, his voice a deep, velvet purr that seems to wrap around me. "I've heard you have quite the appetite tonight."

His eyes hold mine, the implication in his words hanging thick in the air. The corner of his mouth quirks up in a small smile, and the flutter in my stomach has nothing to do with hunger. My mind is racing with responses. Three sexual innuendos fly through my brain, each more daring than the last. Why is it so hard to flirt with Zandar? I've never been this uncertain around him before. William gives my thigh a gentle, reassuring squeeze, and his support helps me loosen up a little.

I give Zandar a playful smile. "Well, you know me, always ready for a feast. And I have a feeling you're serving up something...delectable."

Oh god, that sounded dumb. Didn't it? This is what happens when it's been years since you've flirted with anyone but your husband.

Zandar's eyes darken. "Is that right? You have an appetite that needs satisfying?" His voice is a low growl, filled with a promise that sets my heart racing.

Hey now, I guess he appreciates my awkward flirting. I swear, if he keeps looking at me like that, I'm going to melt right here. I try to keep my composure as I whisper, "Yes."

"And what exactly are you hungry for? Tell me. Let me hear you say it."

His eyes never leave mine, the intensity of his gaze making it difficult to think clearly. He's enjoying my reaction to him, isn't he?

I glance at William, who nods encouragingly, his hand inching closer and closer to my pussy. Yeah, he's trying to drive me crazy as well.

My voice is steadier than I expect. "I'm hungry for you to fill me up."

He hums contentedly. "That's what I like to hear. Now eat up. You need your strength."

Like I'm going to be able to eat after that? I give it my best effort, and the guys chat and joke around about their college days while I manage a few more bites. By the time we're finished, I'm practically aching with need. I can't believe what we're all about to do, but god, I want this.

Zandar stands, extending his hand. I take it, and a jolt of electricity passes between us as he helps me to my feet. "Let's go fill that pussy full of cum and make a baby."

I laugh at how direct he's being, and William grabs a chair from the table and follows us to the bedroom. I didn't consider where William was going to sit while he watched, and him bringing his own chair is filthy in such a good way.

In the bedroom, Zandar turns to me. "Are you ready to be a good little slut tonight?" he asks, his voice a deep rumble that sends shivers down my spine.

Oh god, if he keeps talking dirty, he's going to melt my brain. "I'm ready. I'm so ready."

He smiles and cups my chin, his thumb brushing over my lower lip. "Good. Because I'm going to make you beg for my cum."

My brain blips out and my cheeks flush at his words. I can't look away from him. His gaze holds me captive, and honestly, I don't want to escape.

William places the chair in the corner of the room, his presence a silent support, a reminder that he's there, watching, approving. I never imagined I'd be this turned on by fucking someone while William watched, but suddenly I understand why all my friends are becoming hotwives. When your husband is into it, it's fucking amazing.

Zandar's hand slides down, tracing the curve of my neck, the line of my shoulders. His touch is feather light and makes me shiver. He might treat me gently, but I can tell he's fully in control and he could turn demanding at any moment.

He leans in, his lips brushing against my ear, his voice a husky whisper. "First, I want you to show me what you've got. Strip for us. Slowly."

Strip? Right. I can do that. My hands tremble slightly as I reach for the hem of my dress, my fingers toying with the fabric. I want to tease them and drive them crazy, just like they were doing to me through dinner.

I pull the dress up slowly, inch by inch, revealing more skin. I'm breathless and my nipples harden as Zandar's eyes follow every movement, his gaze a tangible caress. William shifts in his chair and hums in approval. I never knew stripping in front of two men would be this erotic, but just knowing I have their full attention is powerful.

When the dress is finally over my head, I drop it to the floor, and I stand there in my panties, garter belt and stockings. I'm feeling an odd mix of vulnerable yet also like a sexual goddess. I've never felt so desired, so wanted.

Zandar takes a step back, his eyes roaming over my body. "Beautiful," he murmurs, almost to himself. "Now, spin. Let me see all of you."

I obey, turning slowly and blowing a kiss at William as I circle past him. I just want Zandar to fuck me, so him toying with me and making me do his bidding is torture. Sweet, delicious torture.

When I face Zandar again, his eyes are dark with desire. He wants me. Knowing that I'm affecting him is intoxicating.

"Now, let's see if you taste as delicious as you look," he growls as he pushes me back onto the bed. He unhooks the garters and slowly rolls my stockings down each leg, his fingers trailing along my skin, leaving goosebumps in their wake. I prop myself up on my elbows, watching him as he tosses the stockings aside and kisses his way up my leg. His stubble scratches lightly against my skin, adding a delicious friction that makes me shiver.

I glance over at William, who is seated comfortably in the chair, his eyes locked on us. He smiles at me, a slow, encouraging smile that tells me he's loving the show and sends a wave of heat through me.

Zandar's mouth reaches the apex of my thighs, his breath hot against my pussy, still covered by my panties. He looks up at me, a wicked gleam in his eyes. "You're already so wet. I can smell your arousal."

He hooks his fingers into the waistband of my panties and peels them down, inch by agonizing inch. I raise my knees to make it easier for him to remove them, and when he tosses them aside, I'm completely exposed to him. Everything we're doing is so fucking naughty–in such a good way.

Zandar pushes my legs further apart and leans in, his tongue flicking out to taste me. I gasp, my hips jerking involuntarily. Ooooh god, I really didn't expect him to go down on me. I guess he's not going to fuck me quickly and unload his seed.

His voice vibrates against my sensitive flesh as he dives in, murmuring, "Mmm, you taste incredible." He explores every fold, every crease, until he finds my clit and circles it slowly.

I writhe under his talented tongue as the pressure builds like a coil tightening in my belly. Zandar slides a finger inside me, then another, pumping slowly in time with the movements of his tongue. I moan, my eyes fluttering closed, the sensation overwhelming as I rush towards my orgasm.

I hear William's sharp intake of breath from the corner, and it reminds me he's there, watching me come undone. I moan in pleasure from Zandar's tongue and the knowledge that William is enjoying this—that he wants this for me. For us.

Zandar's fingers curl inside me, hitting that perfect spot, and the delight is too much. I cry out, my orgasm crashing over me like a wave. My body convulses, my hips bucking against his mouth, but he doesn't stop. He rides out the storm, his tongue and fingers working in tandem, wringing every last drop of pleasure from me.

As I come down from the high, Zandar sits up, his lips glistening with my juices. He grins, a satisfied, predatory smile. "Ready for more, slut?"

I nod, breathless, my body already aching. William is leaning forward in his chair, rapt. He nods his silent approval for us to continue.

Zandar stands as he yanks off his shirt, revealing his muscular, well-defined chest, dusted with a light sprinkling of dark brown hair. His dark skin seems to glow in the soft light, highlighting his features. He takes his time, his movements deliberate and confident, allowing me to appreciate his chiseled physique.

He undoes his belt next, the leather sliding through the loops of his jeans with a subtle hiss. He pops the button, the zipper following with a tantalizing hum. His dark jeans slide down his lean, muscular legs, leaving him in nothing but a pair of form-fitting boxer briefs that cling to his powerful thighs. Fuck, he's driving me insane.

His boxers are the last thing he's wearing, and when he removes them, I have to fight the urge to lick my lips. Mmmm, yummy. His cock is thick and long, the head smooth and slightly larger than the shaft. His balls are equally impressive, hanging low and full. I know that bigger balls don't mean better fertility, but I still get a zing of pleasure at the thought of him unloading inside me.

"On your hands and knees, slut," Zandar commands, his voice thick with need. "I'm going to fuck you from behind and fill that pussy full of cum."

Mmm, about damn time. I quickly get on all fours and wiggle my ass at the guys while looking over my shoulder at William. His eyes are hooded and his hand is stroking his cock through his jeans. I can see the lust in his eyes, the desire. The love.

Zandar positions himself behind me, his hands grasping my hips. He rubs the head of his cock against my entrance, teasing me, making me whimper with need. I try to push back against him, but he pulls back, denying me the satisfaction I crave.

"Please," I beg and rock my hips, wishing he'd slip his cock inside me. "Please fuck me."

He chuckles, a low, throaty sound that sends shivers down my spine. "Oh, you want this cock?" he asks, rubbing the tip against my clit, making me gasp. "Does the slut want me to fill her up?"

Fuck, him talking to me this way is making me even more desperate.

"Yes," I moan, "Please, I need it. I need you."

He leans down, his body covering mine, his lips brushing against my ear. "You need me to breed you?" he growls. "You want me to fill this tight little pussy with my cum?"

His words send a surge of desire coursing through me as the ache in my core grows more insistent. "Yes," I whimper. "Breed me. Fill me with your cum."

He groans, his grasp on my hips tightening. "Such a good girl," he praises, his voice thick with lust. My mind blanks at being called a good girl, and I barely have time to process it before he slams into me, balls deep.

I cry out, my back arching as he immediately begins to thrust vigorously, his hips slapping against my ass. His cock is hitting all the right spots, and another orgasm builds quickly. He's not being gentle, and I glory in the roughness as he quickens his pace.

"You feel so fucking good," he groans. "I can't wait to fill this pussy full of cum...breed you...make you pregnant."

Oh god, that's hot. His words send me spiraling, and I explode, my body convulsing around his cock. As I shudder from my orgasm, he pulls out and flips me onto my back. Within seconds, he's driving into me again.

"I want to see you," he grunts, his hips moving like pistons. "I want to watch you take every last drop of me."

I'm desperate now, my nails clawing at his back, my feet digging into the mattress as I meet his thrusts, urging him deeper. "Please, Zandar," I beg, my voice ragged. "Oh god, please. Fill me. Breed me. I need it."

He groans as he jackhammers into me erratically, his body tensing. But instead of letting go, he slows down, pulling out of me and rolling me onto my side. He lifts my leg, opening me up to him, and slides back in, his cock hitting new spots inside of me.

"Fuck," I gasp, my body shuddering with pleasure.

"You like that, don't you?" he growls, his hand gripping my thigh, holding me in place. "You like it when I fill you up, when I fuck you deep?"

"Yes," I moan, my body trembling with every thrust. "God, yes."

He moves his hand to my clit, rubbing it in time with his thrusts, driving me wild. Pleasure builds in layers as I spiral towards another orgasm.

"Come for me," he commands. "Come all over my cock. Milk me."

His words push me over the edge, and I come hard, my body convulsing around him, my screams filling the room. But he doesn't stop, doesn't slow.

"Fuck, you're so tight," he groans, his hands digging into my hips.

His cock swells inside of me and his body tenses as he gets closer to his own release. But he's not ready to let go yet, not until he's wrung every ounce of pleasure from me.

He withdraws again, flipping me onto my back and spreading my legs wide. He slides back in, his eyes locked onto mine, his body trembling with the effort to hold back.

I'm crazed from the pleasure, and I babble. "Breed me, oh god, please, breed me. Need your cum. Please!"

Right before he comes, he pulls out. Holy hell? How can he deny himself like this? His body shudders from how close to coming he is, and his cock glistens with our combined juices. Wetness leaks out of me, and I know I look well fucked.

"God," he murmurs, his voice still thick with desire. "You're so fucking beautiful when you come."

He leans down and kisses me, his tongue exploring my mouth, tasting me. His cock surges against my thigh, as if protesting that he hasn't come yet.

"I want more," he growls. "I want to fuck you in every position, in every way. I want to fill you with my cum until you're overflowing with it."

Pleasure swirls in my core, and I moan, "Yesss."

He gives me a wicked smile. "Good, because I'm not done with you yet."

He stands up, his cock hard and ready, and I can't help but stare at it. My mouth waters with desire as he reaches down, grabbing my ankles, and pulls me to the edge of the bed. He spreads my legs wide, exposing my pussy.

"You're so wet," he groans, his fingers tracing the edges of my pussy lips. "So ready for me."

My mind is totally fucked and I'm unable to do anything but whimper as he positions himself at the entrance of my eager pussy. With a slow, deliberate thrust, he enters me, his cock filling me up, stretching me to the limit. I gasp, my eyes rolling back in my head as he bottoms out.

Zandar sets a quick pace, his hips driving into mine with a rhythm that sends waves of pleasure crashing over me. I'm lost in the sensation, my body responding instinctively to his touch. Each thrust pushes me closer to the edge, my orgasm building inside me like a storm.

William moves in closer, reaching for my breast and teasing my nipple. The sensation sends shockwaves through my body, and I moan more loudly, my pussy clenching around Zandar's cock.

"Fuck," Zandar grunts. "So good."

I'm beyond caring about anything but getting his cum, and I whimper, "I want you to breed me, put a baby in me."

His eyes darken with desire, and he picks up the pace, his cock pounding into me with a ferocity that borders on primal. I can feel him getting closer, his body tensing as he approaches his own release.

"Oh, yeah?" he grunts. "Think of how full your belly is going to be when I'm done with you."

Oooh, god. I imagine finally being pregnant and my stomach swelling. I want it so badly.

He continues the dirty talk as he fucks me. "You're so desperate for this, aren't you?"

I writhe under him, mewling out, "Yes!"

"I'm going to fill you up. You're going to be such a pretty mess when I'm done with you. His voice is strained with lust. "Here it comes."

With a final, powerful thrust, he groans as thick spurts of cum coat my inner walls. I can imagine all his little swimmers rushing to their destination, and my head spins as his cock pulses, unloading every last drop. The sense of fullness is overwhelming, and I swear his cum is flooding my womb.

He gives one final whack against my pussy and then collapses on the bed next to me, spent. A zing of pleasure ripples down my spine as his cum leaks out of me. God, this is naughty.

When William moves his hand to my stomach, I realize he's still with us by the bed. His palm is warm as he rubs circles on my belly and leans down to kiss me.

"That was fucking hot," he whispers against my lips. "I love you."

"I love you too." I smile, my body humming with pleasure, my heart full.

I'm not sure the last time I was so thoroughly fucked, and I mentally drift as Zandar stirs. He sits up, the muscles in his back rippling as he runs a hand through his tousled hair. He smiles at me before he stands up and gathers his clothes from the floor. I admire his body as he dresses. It's so damn dirty to know I was just fucking him.

When Zandar is dressed, the men help me to the center of the bed and William says, "I'll be right back, babe."

Zandar turns to me and says, "Thank you for everything. Tonight was wonderful."

"It was. Thank you too," I murmur, and he waves goodbye and follows William out of the room.

I'm left alone in the room, the scent of sex and sweat still lingering in the air. I stretch out on the bed, my body humming with satisfaction as their footsteps recede down the hallway. I hear the faint murmur of their voices, and then the soft click of the front door closing.

When William gets back to the room, there's a hunger in his gaze, a possessiveness that makes my heart race. He quickly removes his clothes and climbs onto the bed, his hands reaching for me, his touch gentle yet firm.

He rolls me onto my stomach, his hands tracing the curve of my spine, sending shivers of anticipation down my body. He knows I love this position, and it's just like him to be thinking of me when it's his turn for pleasure.

His cock presses against my ass, hard and insistent. I push back against him, eager for more, my body already coming alive again. He leans down, his lips blazing a trail of kisses along my shoulder and the nape of my neck, his breath hot and ragged.

He enters my pussy, slowly at first, teasingly, before withdrawing slightly, making me gasp with desire. Then he plows into me, fierce and deep, filling me completely. I cry out, my fingers clutching at the sheets, my body already so close to the edge again.

His body covers mine, his weight pressing me into the mattress. His lips brush against my ear, his breath coming in hot gasps. "You're mine," he growls, his voice thick with lust. "All mine."

"Yours," I whimper as he moves, each thrust deliberate and powerful, claiming me. I match his rhythm, pushing back against him.

He continues to kiss my neck, my shoulders, his teeth grazing my skin, each touch sending waves of pleasure coursing through me. Each thrust feels like a declaration of love as the pleasure builds.

"Oh, god, I love you," I moan, my body trembling as I climb higher and higher.

His movements become more urgent at my words, his body driving into mine with an uncontrollable need. Finally, with a cry that echoes through the room, I reach the peak, my body convulsing with ecstasy.

He follows soon after, his body stiffening, his hips pushing against mine one last time as he explodes, filling my pussy with the second load of cum for the night.

We collapse together, spent and sated. Yep, I just got fucked out of my mind. What a way to live.

Right before I fall asleep, he kisses my forehead, murmuring, "I love you so much."

I mumble, "I love you too," and then I'm out like a light.

CHAPTER 5

The next morning, my body aches in such a glorious way. Yeah, I need to take it easy today. When I wander into the kitchen, I pour myself a cup of coffee and sit at the table before pulling up Debra's latest blog post.

Hotwives Unleashed: A New Trend in Baby-Making?

Listen to what I've been hearing through the grapevine lately. It seems like there's a new trend among those desperate to conceive, and it's not just turkey basters and fertility clinics anymore. Oh no, dear readers, it's much more scandalous than that. Women are using the excuse of "needing to get pregnant" to dip their toes into the hotwife lifestyle. Can you even believe it?

I mean, let's consider this for a second. Imagine that sweet couple down the street, the ones who have been trying for a baby for what feels like forever. You might assume they're spending their nights poring over ovulation charts and temperature graphs, right? Wrong! They're inviting other men into their bedroom, all in the name of "fertility assistance." I bet she's spreading her legs wide, offering her ripe, eager pussy to her husband's best friend, begging him to fill her with his potent seed.

Picture this: She's on her hands and knees, her back arched, presenting herself like an animal in heat. Her husband is sitting in the corner, watching with rapt attention as his friend—let's call him Steve—positions himself behind her. Steve's hands grip her hips, his thick cock poised at her slick entrance. "You want this, don't you, slut?" he growls, his voice thick with lust. "You want me to breed you, to fill this tight little pussy with my cum?"

She moans, pushing back against him, desperate to get him inside her. "Yes, please.

I need it. I need you to breed me," she begs, her voice ragged with desire. Her husband's eyes are hooded, his hand stroking his own cock as he watches his wife about to be claimed by another man.

Steve drills into her, his cock filling her completely. She cries out, her body trembling with pleasure. He begins to move, his hips slapping against her ass, his cock sliding in and out of her wet, eager pussy. "Fuck, you feel so good," he grunts, his fingers digging into her flesh. "I can't wait to fill you with my cum, to make you pregnant."

Her husband groans from the corner, his eyes never leaving the sight of his wife being fucked, being bred. He's enjoying this, getting off on the sheer depravity of it all.

But let's not kid ourselves, dear readers. This isn't just about making babies. This is about lust, plain and simple. These women aren't just trying to conceive—they're using any excuse to become hotwife sluts.

To use the act of conception as an excuse for such lewd behavior is truly depraved. I would never, ever, even think about wanting such filthy things. I'm just a concerned citizen, a moral observer, reporting on the scandalous trends sweeping through our neighborhoods. I'm just here to tell you, dear readers, that the hotwife lifestyle is alive and well, and it's hiding behind the most innocent of excuses.

So the next time you see that sweet couple down the street, the ones who have been trying for a baby, just remember: they might be indulging in their wildest fantasies, exploring their darkest desires, all in the name of "fertility assistance." And who knows? Maybe they're crossing lines that should never be crossed. Let us be grateful for our own moral fortitude. I, for one, will continue to buck this hotwife trend.

I nearly choke on my coffee, laughter bubbling up. Oh god, how did she hear the news so fast? William must have told one of his friends. I don't mind that he did, and the whole situation amuses me.

William walks in as I'm chuckling. "What's so funny?" he asks, pouring himself a cup.

"Just Debra being her usual self," I say and quickly text Sara that if I weren't already a hotwife, Debra would make me want to be one. I set my phone down, turning my attention to William.

He joins me at the table, and we sip our coffee in comfortable silence for a moment. Then, my expression turns serious. "Last night was incredible, but what if I don't get pregnant this time?"

William sets down his cup, reaches across the table, and takes my hand. His eyes are warm, filled with affection. "Then," he says, his voice low and teasing, "Zandar will just have to keep fucking a baby into you until you are."

My eyes widen, and I let out a laugh, as a blush creeps up my cheeks. "Is that a promise?" I ask, a playful note in my voice.

"It's more than a promise, Ariel. It's a guarantee."

A thrill runs through me at his words, and a warmth spreads through my body. Baby-making, it turns out, is sounding better and better.

The End

September Hotwife

Hotwife of the Month Club 9

Lacey Cross

CHAPTER 1

I settle into my favorite chair, phone in hand, eager to dive into the latest drama. I click on Debra's most recent blog post. Debra, the wife of Vincent—one of Caleb's college buddies—thinks she's some anonymous crusader online. She's not. We've figured out she's writing them.

Her blog has become an obsession for our entire friend group, but not for the reasons Debra would hope. It's less about her "exposing the dangers of the hotwife trend" and more about how hilariously out of touch she is. Every post is dripping with judgment, thinly veiled references to our friends' personal lives, and pearl-clutching horror at the idea of open marriages.

I can't help but shake my head thinking about how Debra's holier-than-thou attitude is grating on everyone's nerves. At our last get-together, I caught Olivia rolling her eyes so hard I thought they might get stuck. Even Debra's husband looked uncomfortable and was probably wishing he could sink into the floor.

Still, I can't resist reading—I'm addicted. I brace myself for whatever prissy, moralistic tirade she's cooked up this time, knowing I'll be texting my friends about it within minutes. Poor Debra, if she only knew how her secret blog was the laughingstock of our social circle.

Hotwives Unleashed: A Voyage into the Varieties of Vice

Oh, dear readers, I must confess, my research into the hotwife phenomenon has led me down a path of sinful intrigue. I find myself compelled to delve deeper into the depraved world of wife sharing, to explore the different types of hotwives and the lascivious activities they indulge in. Purely for educational purposes, of course.

First, there are the 'Cuckoldresses'. These are not just hotwives but queens who demand their husbands watch as they take other men. Picture this: a wife, dressed in her finest lingerie, parades a well-endowed stud into the bedroom. Her husband, dutifully bound or caged, watches as she seduces this other man, her eyes locked onto her husband's as she slowly descends onto the stud's thick cock. She rides him, her moans filling the room, as her husband can only watch, his own desire growing but unfulfilled. It's a power play, a humiliation, and these women revel in it.

Then, there are the hotwives who engage in solo play. Imagine a wife, dressed to the nines, stepping out alone to a bar. She flirts, teases, and ultimately goes home with her prize. Her husband is left to imagine the scene, to picture his wife being pounded by another man, her screams of pleasure echoing through a stranger's bedroom. He waits, his cock aching, until she returns home, reeking of sex and another man's cologne. She recounts her adventure, every filthy detail, as he strokes himself, his release timed to her wicked tale.

Now, let's not forget the 'Swappers', couples who trade partners. Envision a room filled with writhing bodies, husbands watching as their wives are taken by other men and vice versa. The air is thick with moans, grunts, and the wet sounds of flesh slapping against flesh. It's an orgy, a binge of marital infidelity, all under the guise of 'swinging'.

And finally, there are the 'Stag and Vixen'

couples, where the husband is the hunter, seeking out men for his wife. Picture him, prowling a bar, his eyes scanning for the perfect prey. He finds him, invites him home, and then watches as his wife unleashes her inner slut, taking this new man in every hole. The husband directs, instructs, his cock in hand as he orchestrates his wife's debauchery.

As I explore these types, I find myse lf...annoyed. It's wrong, yes, but also fascinating. What would drive a woman to want another man, and what sort of man would let his wife get pounded in every hole by multiple bulls?

These are mysteries I'll have to ponder some more. Until next time, stay virtuous, dear readers.

I click away from Debra's post as my heart races. Holy fuck, I didn't expect to get turned on. The words, the images...they're all swirling in my mind. I know people actually do these things—my friends are proof of that—but it's hard to imagine doing it myself. Yet, I can't deny how wet my pussy is getting. If all my friends weren't talking about how it's revitalized their marriages, I don't think I'd ever consider doing it, but now...

Without consciously thinking about it, I find myself opening my dresser drawer in the bedroom where we keep the sex toys. Never once since I married Caleb five years ago have I used a toy while thinking of another man, but today my mind is a whirlwind of forbidden fantasies. I rest against the pillows, naked, and a soft buzz fills the room when I switch the vibrator on.

My eyelids flutter shut as I imagine myself in one of the scenes Debra wrote about. I'm in a dimly lit bar, feeling confident and sexy. I'm not the self-conscious Sara anymore. I'm someone who turns heads, who draws men in. I picture a stranger, faceless but enticing, approaching me. His eyes are filled with lust—for me.

My vibrator hums against my clit, sending pings of pleasure through me. I gasp, arching my back, as I imagine the stranger's hands on me, his cock poised to push in while Caleb watches. I'm so lost in the fantasy, I don't hear the bedroom door open.

"Well, this is a delightful view."

My eyes fly open as Caleb's husky tone sends a bolt of pleasure all the way to my toes. He's home early!

I give him my cutest grin. "Hi, there."

Every instinct screams at me to turn off the toy and snap my legs shut, but when Caleb focuses on my pussy with unmistakable interest, I force myself to keep going. The toy buzzes against my sensitive flesh, and I bite my lip, torn between embarrassment and arousal.

"Don't stop." His eyes never leave my pussy as he slowly unbuttons his shirt. The intensity of his stare makes me feel exposed, vulnerable, yet strangely powerful. I didn't expect sex tonight, but a thrill courses through me. God, he should come home early more often.

Once Caleb is naked—how did he manage that so quickly?—he climbs onto the bed, and the mattress dips beneath his weight. He takes the vibrator from my hand and when his fingers brush mine, his touch feels electric.

"Tell me what you were thinking about," he murmurs.

He makes slow circles against my clit with the tip of the vibrator, and pleasure zings through me, making my toes curl. Do I dare tell him? The fantasy feels like a guilty secret, something too taboo to admit out loud. But there's a hunger in Caleb's gaze—a hunger for me, for my thoughts, for my deepest desires. It both terrifies and excites me, urging me to bare my soul to him.

My heart pounds so hard I'm sure he can hear it. I take a shaky breath, gathering my courage. "I...I was thinking about being a hotwife," I whisper. My cheeks burn with embarrassment, but there's a sense of liberation that comes from voicing my secret fantasy. I search Caleb's face, terrified of what I might see.

Caleb's eyes widen, and he pauses the vibrator. The sudden absence of stimulation is almost painful. "Oh yeah, a hotwife?" He's clearly surprised, but there's something more in his expression—a spark of excitement that makes my pulse race even faster.

I nod, my entire body flushed. "I was reading one of Debra's blog posts, and I started imagining...things."

He smiles that slow, sexy grin of his that makes me melt. "What kind of things?" He starts the vibrator again, teasing my clit with it, and I moan.

"I imagined being in a bar, dressed in a skin-tight red dress. A stranger comes up to me and flirts. Then he says he wants me. He wants me so bad."

I feel his hard cock against my thigh as he groans, "And what did you do?"

"I...I brought him home," I confess. Caleb is engrossed in my fantasy, and I feel a spark that urges me on. "I let him fuck me while you watched."

He groans again as he moves more insistently against my thigh. His cock is wet with pre-cum, and I can feel it painting my skin as he rocks against me. He increases the speed of the vibrator and presses it firmly against my clit. I cry out, my hips arching off the bed.

"You want me to watch you fuck another man?" he growls. "You want me to see you being used?"

My breath comes in short gasps. "Yes. Yes, I do."

Caleb's lips crash against mine in a fierce, passionate kiss. I can taste spearmint on his tongue; he usually chews gum on his way home from work. He devours me, as if he can't get enough, igniting a fire deep within me. The kiss is a desperate clash of lips and tongue, each movement charged with a hunger that leaves me breathless. His scent, a mix of cologne and something unique to him, amplifies my lust as I lose myself completely.

When he pulls back, there's a wildness in his expression, as if he's close to losing control. "Fuck, that's hot."

He slides the vibrator inside me, and I moan. Fuuuck, I need to come. He kisses me again, his tongue mirroring the thrusts of the toy. The wet spot on my thigh grows with his pre-cum, and I reach for his cock and stroke him in time with the vibrator's movements.

"Tell me more," he murmurs against my lips. "Tell me everything you want me to see."

Oooh, I like how dirty he's being tonight. "I want to be on my knees while he face fucks me. You watch me sucking on him, knowing exactly how it feels to be in his spot."

Caleb groans, his cock throbbing in my hand. He fucks me harder with the vibrator and asks, "What else?"

"I'll bend over for him, and you can watch me offer myself up. You'll see me scream in pleasure as he fucks me hard." My mental picture is turning me on even more, and my head spins as I continue. "And when he's done using me, I want you to fuck me while I'm full of his cum. I want both your cum dripping out of me."

"Fuck." Caleb's eyes smolder with passion as he pulls the vibrator out and tosses it aside, climbing between my legs with a hunger that sends shivers down my spine. He slams into me, and I wrap my legs around him, drawing him deeper.

"You're mine." His tone is a low, primal sound that resonates in my core. Each thrust is more forceful than the last, hitting deeper, driving us both to a fever pitch. "You're always mine."

"Yes, yours. Always!" I cry out as Caleb hammers into me. I can feel his cock throbbing, and I know he's close to coming.

He groans. "You feel so good. Imagine me watching you, stroking my cock while another guy fucks you."

I can almost see it—and it sizzles my brain. I cling to his shoulders and meet him thrust for thrust.

"Yes," I gasp. "I want you to be there, knowing that I'm yours, no matter what."

Caleb groans, "Damn right you're mine. And I want to see you wild and free, knowing that you'll always come back to me."

His words ignite something within me. I'm Sara, the hotwife, the woman who can drive men wild and still be cherished by her husband.

The pressure builds inside me, and I moan, "I'm close. I'm so close."

He drives into me relentlessly. "Come for me. Think about being full of another man's cum and I'm fucking it back into you."

Oh. My. God. His command short circuits my brain and pushes me over the edge. I cry out, "I'm coming. Oh god, I'm coming!" as my body convulses with pleasure. Waves of ecstasy wash over me until I'm a quivering mess.

Caleb follows soon after. He groans deeply, his body shuddering as his cock pulses and he unloads deep inside me. His body trembles, and he collapses onto me, his head resting on my breasts. He's still gasping as the aftershocks ripple through him.

We're both quiet, and it's difficult for me to gather my thoughts. Shit, I think he just fucked me senseless.

When Caleb chuckles, I look down at him. There's adoration written all over his face as he says, "I love you. Always."

I smile, feeling a warmth spread through me. "I love you too. And I think you should come home early more often."

He laughs loudly. "Me too."

CHAPTER 2

Caleb brings me breakfast in bed the next morning. He has a self-satisfied expression...he clearly enjoyed last night. I sit up, leaning against the headboard, while he adjusts the legs on the tray and sets it over my lap.

When he sits down on his side of the bed, he gives me an impish grin that only spells trouble...hopefully the type of trouble I want to get in on. "So..." His voice is casual, and he winks at me. "Do you really want to be a hotwife?"

Uh...oh god. What do I say? I blush and try to look busy with my cup of coffee. "I don't know. I mean, the idea is exciting. I've been thinking about it because of our friends. But, I don't know..." I peek up at him. "Do you want a hotwife?"

Caleb's smile widens in excitement. "Well, I already have a hot wife," he says, and gives me another wink. "But if you're asking about the lifestyle, I've always thought watching you with another man would be hot. I just didn't think you'd be interested. Last night was so fucking amazing. I'd love to see it for real."

A flutter of eagerness stirs in my stomach. I need to be sure, to hear him say it again. "So, if I said yes, you'd want this?"

He nods. "If you want to, I'm game. It's your call, Sara."

I get a naughty zing of pleasure when I consider the reality of becoming a hotwife. "But how would we do this? How do people find a guy?"

Caleb chuckles softly, his thumb tracing circles on the back of my hand. "Well, your fantasy was you finding someone in a bar and flirting with them."

I try to picture myself doing that, being that confident. If I were Olivia, maybe. But I'm not. "I don't know…" I trail off as the weight of my insecurities settles in. "It's fun to imagine, but I don't know if I can go through with it."

Caleb squeezes my hand. "Hey, it's okay. We don't have to do anything you're not comfortable with. We can figure something out together." He pauses, thinking. "How about if I find someone I know? Someone I trust."

This conversation is turning me on, and I have to force myself not to squirm. "Who are my choices?"

He laughs. "Oh, you want a say in this, do you? Well, you know my friends. Is there someone you're comfortable with?"

The thought of choosing someone makes my stomach churn. What if they said no? I'd be mortified. I shake my head. "No, you pick. Someone you think would be right for this."

Caleb's smile grows, a mix of mischief and tenderness. "All right. I'll think about it. But first, there's something I need from you."

A delicious tension coils in the pit of my stomach. "What's that?"

His grin turns wicked. "Your mouth on my cock. Right now."

Mmm, I'll give him ten blow jobs if it means I can fuck someone else, but I can't give in that easily. I pick up a piece of bacon and make sure it crunches as I take a bite. After I swallow, I give him my best cheeky grin. "But my food will get cold."

"You brat," he laughs and takes the tray from me and sets it on the floor next to the bed. "I'll make you more food when you're done."

Oooh, I love it when he gets dominant like this. It doesn't happen all the time, but whenever it does, I'm more than willing to give him whatever he demands.

"I guess I better get to work then. I have to earn my breakfast."

"Guess so." He leans back, and I snuggle against him, unzipping his jeans and taking his cock out. It's already hard and wet with pre-cum.

He groans as my lips circle the tip and I apply suction. By the time I'm done with him, he's going to agree to make dinner tonight as well.

I'm on the phone with Olivia and filling my bathtub with water, as her excited squeals fill my ear. "Oh my god, Sara! You're actually going to do it?"

I can hear the mix of awe in her tone, and I laugh. "Yeah, I think I am. Caleb and I talked about it, and...well, we're going for it."

"I can't believe it," Olivia sounds wistful. "You know, it's all because of Debra's blog. Those posts are turning us all into hotwives!"

"Right? Debra has no idea she's creating an army of hotwives with her thirsty posts. At the next get-together, maybe we should joke about how some sexy hotwife blog posts someone is writing is making us want to do it. She'd probably die."

Olivia giggles. "Oh my god, Sara, you're terrible! But I love it. We should totally do that." She pauses for a moment, then adds, "Hey, I've got to run. The band's got a gig tonight, and I need to warm up my voice. Talk to you later?"

"Break a leg, Liv," I reply, smiling. "Can't wait to hear all about it tomorrow."

As I hang up the phone, I sink deeper into the bubble bath, letting the warm, lavender-scented water soothe me. My conversation with Olivia lingers in my mind. She always seems to have it all together—gorgeous, outgoing, and living what appears to be a perfect life. I can't help but feel a twinge of envy as I think about how she and her husband, Anthony, share the spotlight in their band. Their relationship seems so effortless, so in sync.

The sound of clattering pots and pans from the kitchen interrupts my thoughts. Caleb's attempting to make dinner, probably wrestling with a box of mac and cheese. I smile to myself, imagining his determined expression as he tackles the 'gourmet' meal.

As the steam rises around me, my thoughts drift to our earlier conversation and the plans we've set in motion. The questions that have been swirling in my head all day resurface: Who will Caleb ask? Will they say yes? And most importantly, can I actually go through with this? Each time I consider the possibilities, a delightful tingle zips through me, making my pussy tingle with desire. Yeah, as scary as it might be, I want this.

A sudden knock makes me jolt, sloshing water over the edge of the tub.

"Dinner will be done in ten," Caleb calls through the door. "You won't want to miss my masterpiece."

"Okay, love!" I call out and drag myself out of the bath.

As I towel off, I catch my reflection in the mirror. Not bad, Sara. The extra time at the gym is paying off—I'm curvier than I was in my twenties, but in all the right places. I wrap the towel around myself and pad into the bedroom, only to stop short at the sight laid out on the bed.

My breath catches. It's my red lingerie set—the one that makes me feel like a total sex goddess—next to that daring red dress I bought on a whim but never had the guts to wear. What's Caleb playing at? Is this his way of gearing me up to flirt with another guy? Then I spot the matching heels on the floor, and a different thought takes hold. If I'm getting all dolled up, he'd better have plans to peel it all off me later.

The lingerie slides on like a second skin, the bustier hugging my curves. I shimmy into the dress, loving how it clings to my body and shows just enough cleavage to be enticing without crossing into trashy territory. One glance in the full-length mirror confirms it—I look hot as hell.

The smell of...wait, I think he actually cooked something? My stomach rumbles insistently as I make my way towards the kitchen, half-expecting to find an empty pot on the stove and Caleb looking sheepish.

"Hey, beautiful," he calls out from the dining room, making my heart skip a beat.

I round the corner, and my jaw drops. Caleb's standing there looking sexy as sin in a blue polo, next to a table that looks like it belongs in a five-star restaurant. Candles flicker in the center, casting a warm glow over two steaming plates of chicken parmesan—yep, definitely not mac and cheese.

"Wow," I breathe, genuinely impressed. "You went all out."

Caleb grins, pulling out my chair. "I can do fancy sometimes. That blowjob deserved it," he adds with a wink.

A wave of heat shoots through me as I settle into my seat. I can't resist teasing him a little. "This looks yummy. And here I was expecting something from a box."

His laugh sends warmth blooming in my chest. "I thought about that," he admits, "but then I figured, why not make something that might lead to getting lucky later?"

My body tingles. Oh, he's definitely getting lucky tonight, but I try to play hard to get. "You think you're lucky enough for sex two days in a row on top of the blowjob?"

I don't know whatever has gotten into him, but so far, this is a great weekend.

He gives me a slow smile. "That depends. After dinner, do you want to go out for a bit?"

I look at him, surprised. "I don't know. It depends on what you have in mind." I assumed this nice dinner was all he had planned—well, and sex because he didn't leave this lingerie out for no reason.

"What would you say if I had a friend I'd like you to meet?"

I take a bite of my chicken and peek at him through the corner of my lashes as I chew, deliberately taking my time and then washing it down with a drink of water before answering. "Just meet, as in...say hello and we leave?" I ask. I was aiming for casual, but I can hear the slight tremor in my voice betraying me.

Caleb's eyes sparkle with mischief. God, I love it when he looks at me like that. "No. As in meet and see where the evening takes us. No expectations."

My stomach does a little flip. Is this really happening? After all our late-night whispered fantasies, are we actually taking this step?

"And who is this friend?" I manage to ask, my curiosity getting the better of me.

"A guy from work. He divorced his wife a year ago and was joking about how he needed to start dating again because his bed is lonely. He's a great guy. Smart and kind."

"And what does he look like?" The question slips out before I can stop it.

Caleb's playful shrug only heightens my curiosity. "You'll just have to wait and see."

I bite my lip, considering. The lingerie suddenly feels more significant, like a promise of what's to come. Can I really do this? The idea both terrifies and exhilarates me.

"Okay," I say slowly. "I'll go."

The way Caleb's expression lights up sends a warmth spreading through me. "Then let's finish dinner and get out of here," he says, and I can practically feel the electricity crackling between us.

Chapter 3

I gasp as Caleb pulls into the parking lot of a swanky hotel. My heart races. "We're meeting him here?"

Caleb flashes me that wicked grin that always makes my knees weak. "I figured this way, there's no expectations. We can meet him for a few minutes, and if you don't want to do anything, we can leave."

My mouth goes dry. "And if I want to do something?"

"Then we have a room available. But no pressure either way."

"Wait." I blink, processing. "You booked a hotel room?"

"I did." His tone is challenging, daring. When I don't protest, he continues. "If we decide not to stay, then we lose the cost of the room, which is no big deal. I'd rather have the option and not use it than regret not getting it."

My mind whirls with possibilities, each more thrilling than the last. God, his preplanning is such a turn-on. He isn't pressuring me, just...opening doors.

"Okay," I manage, trying to keep the tremor of excitement from my voice.

As we walk hand-in-hand up the hotel steps, my stomach flutters with exhilaration. This is really happening. We're about to do something wild, something that will change us forever.

In the lobby, I watch Caleb check in, hyper-aware of his body next to mine. I'm already getting wet just thinking about what might happen. With the key card in hand, he leads me to the hotel bar. My whole body thrums with anticipation.

That's when I see him. A man at the bar, his back to us—broad shoulders, short brown hair, suit jacket slung over his chair. I can't see his face, but something about his presence makes my breath catch. Is that him? God, I hope so.

Caleb stops, and I look at him questioningly. "Baby, do you want to meet him alone and live out your fantasy, or do you want me with you the entire time?"

I blink, confused. "But my fantasy is you watching."

He pulls me close, his kiss soft and reassuring. "Oh, I plan on watching, but I could go wait in the room while you flirt with him and seduce him before bringing him upstairs."

My stomach does a somersault. "Wow..." My mind is racing. Fantasy is one thing, but reality? That's a whole different game.

Caleb's gentle smile bolsters my confidence. I lean up to kiss him, drawing strength from his unwavering support. "Yeah," I breathe, surprising myself. "Let's see if I can seduce him."

He gives my butt a squeeze. "You got this, baby. You're smoking hot in that dress, and rumor has it he needs to get laid."

"Ha ha, funny guy. Give me the room key and go stroke yourself while I do all the hard work."

I take a deep breath as I watch Caleb walk out of the bar. I can do this. The thrill of the unknown makes me tingle. Sure, this guy at the bar understands the game, but that doesn't mean it won't be exhilarating.

I saunter over to the man in the suit, deliberately choosing a seat a couple of stools away from him. The bartender brings me a glass of water, and I feel the stranger's gaze on me. When our eyes meet, my jaw nearly hits the floor. Holy shit, it's Mark. I struggle to keep my composure as a realization hits me. Mark is divorced?

Memories of company parties flash through my mind. I've seen him dozens of times over the years, but never like this. Gone is the slight paunch I remember; in its place is a broad, muscular frame that makes my mouth water. An image of being pinned beneath him flashes unbidden through my mind, and I feel a sudden dampness in my core.

Mark's slow, sexy grin turns my insides to jelly. "Hello, Sara."

I take a shaky breath. "Hi," I manage, trying and failing to sound casual. The word hangs in the air, charged with possibility.

Mark's gaze sweeps over me, lingering on my curves as a warmth fills me. "You look absolutely stunning," he says, his voice low and rich. "What brings a woman like you to a hotel bar on a night like this?"

Oh, so he wants to play it cool? Two can play at that game. I lean forward, letting my dress fall open to offer a tantalizing glimpse of cleavage. "Oh, you know," I purr, surprising myself with my boldness. "Just looking for some...stimulating company." I run my tongue over my lower lip, watching his pupils dilate in response.

As we trade quips, electricity crackles between us. I can't stop noticing his hands–those strong, capable hands. My mind wanders, imagining how they'd feel trailing across my skin. The air around us thickens with desire, and the scent of his cologne makes it impossible to think straight. I want to fuck him. It's time to stop playing games.

"I should probably come clean," I murmur. "This...isn't exactly a chance encounter."

A small smirk plays at the corner of his mouth at my confession. He leans in, his lips brushing my ear as he whispers, "I know, and it's making me so hard right now"

Oooh, god. I suddenly become aware of how fast my heart is beating, and I squirm in my seat. "I've never..."

I'm uncertain what to say. I've never fucked another man while my husband watched? I've never imagined I could be this slutty?

His grin is positively wolfish now. "Don't worry. I'll show you what to do."

My breath catches in my throat as I picture him controlling me. Shit, I want that. I don't want him to just show me. I want him to tell me what to do.

I reach for my water glass, and the condensation is cool against my overheated skin. I take a sip of water, trying to steady myself, but I can't hide the tremble in my hand.

"I think I'd like that," I whisper as a deep longing courses through me.

"Then let's get out of here," Mark says, standing and offering me his hand.

I take it, a tingle of awareness with the contact. As I rise to follow him, anticipation coils low in my belly. This is really happening. I'm doing it. And it's exhilarating.

The hotel room feels like it's way too far away. He could press me against the wall and fuck me right in the lobby, but I keep my thoughts and hands to myself as we approach the elevator. Once we're inside, he positions himself behind me, his hand stroking the small of my back. The touch ignites my skin, and I instinctively lean into him, craving more contact.

As I press the button for the second floor, Mark suddenly spins me around, pinning me against the wall. His face hovers inches from mine, his breath hot on my lips. "Tell me to fuck you," he growls. "I need to hear you say it."

Butterflies swirl in my stomach as I whisper, "Please. I want you to fuck me."

His mouth crashes into mine, urgent and demanding. Our tongues dance as he presses his body against me, his arousal evident against my stomach. A whimper escapes me as I arch into him, savoring his hardness.

The elevator dings, doors sliding open. Mark pulls away, leaving me breathless and aching. He smirks, leaning close to murmur, "Your husband is one lucky bastard."

A giddy smile tugs at my lips. I've never felt so daring, so alive.

In our room, the door barely clicks shut before Mark's hands are on me again. This time, his kiss is achingly slow, deliberate. I melt into him, every nerve ending singing.

As we part, my eyes find Caleb. He's perched on the edge of a chair, and the obvious bulge in his pants makes me wonder if he was touching himself while waiting.

My heart skips a beat as Mark commands, "Strip for us. Show me what I get to play with tonight."

I can barely breathe. Oh god, someone other than Caleb just told me to take my clothes off. It's so dirty, so forbidden. I swallow hard as my mouth goes dry. I step to the side of the bed so both men have a good view. The room is charged with a sexual energy that's intoxicating, almost dizzying. I take a deep breath to steady myself, and my fingers tremble as I unzip my dress at the side.

As I pull it down, the cool air kisses my skin. The material slides off, pooling at my feet. I'm exposed now, standing in nothing but my red lace lingerie. Both men look like they want to devour me, and I feel an odd combo of vulnerable and powerful.

Caleb's gaze is intense, while Mark leans against the wall with his arms crossed and a wolfish smirk on his lips. "You're fucking hot, Sara."

Heat blooms in my cheeks at his raw compliment. Is this real? Am I actually doing this, standing nearly naked in front of two men, one a virtual stranger?

When Mark steps toward me, his presence is overwhelming. I'm acutely aware of every inch of my skin. He reaches out, cupping my breast, and when his thumb brushes over the thin lace, I have to bite back a moan.

"You have beautiful tits," he growls. "Take your corset off so I can see you properly."

My fingers fumble with the clasp. As the corset slides off, I feel exposed, thrilled, and terrified all at once. My nipples tighten in the cool air, aching to be touched. When Mark's thumb grazes one, a bolt of electricity shoots straight to my core.

His kiss is hungry, demanding. His hands roam my body, leaving trails of fire in their wake. When his fingers slip into my panties, I can't help but whimper. He pulls them down slowly, and I'm acutely aware of Caleb's sharp intake of breath.

I glance over and see my husband rubbing himself through his pants. The sight of him getting off on this—on me with another man—sends a rush of heat straight to my core. I never knew I could feel this wild, this free.

Mark's voice is a low, sensual rumble. "Get on the bed and show us your pretty pussy."

I crawl onto the mattress, hyper-aware that I'm the main attraction. As I spread my legs, exposing myself to Mark, I feel wanton and fabulously dirty. His low whistle of appreciation makes me clench with need.

"Touch yourself," he commands.

My hand slides between my legs, and the first brush against my clit nearly makes me come. I'm so wet, so turned on it's almost painful. The pleasure builds, coiling tight in my belly, as I start to rub slow circles. Mark's dominance and Caleb's hunger make everything more erotic. I never knew I'd love being controlled this much, but god help me, I do.

"Look at her," Mark says to Caleb. "She's so fucking wet."

Caleb groans, and I can't help but look at him. He's stroking himself through his jeans, and he looks ready to explode. "Fuck her," he moans. "She loves cock."

Oh my god. A zing of pleasure runs from my fingertips to my toes. If they keep talking dirty to me, I'm going to come without getting a cock inside me first. I moan and arch my back, my fingers sliding over my clit. I can barely breathe. I'm so close to coming, but I want to wait for Mark. I want to come on his cock.

Mark smirks as if he can hear my thoughts and steps closer to the bed. "Does the sexy little slut need my cum?"

Oh fuck, did Caleb tell him I wanted to be full of two guys' cum? My voice shakes with need as I whisper, "Yes."

Mark's eyes darken with desire. "Then first you're going to have to work for it. Get off the bed and get on your knees."

His tone is firm, commanding, and I'm eager to please him. I want this, I want him, and the thought of Caleb watching me, seeing me like this makes me quiver with desire.

I scramble to obey his command. The plush carpet is soft beneath my knees, grounding me as I look up at Mark, focusing on the growing bulge in his pants. There's a yearning deep in my core as I imagine him in my mouth. I want to give him pleasure.

He unzips his pants, and I lick my lips as he pulls out his thick, hard cock. Fuck, he's huge. I can't stop the moan that escapes as I take in the sight of his massive erection.

He smirks down at me, his hand wrapped around the base of his cock. "You want this?"

I feel an intense surge of longing. I want to taste him, to feel him. "Yes."

"Then ask me to fuck your mouth," he commands, and I feel a buzz of excitement.

I swallow hard, looking up at him. "Will you please fuck my mouth?"

I'm not just asking for him; I'm asking for myself, acknowledging the depth of my own need.

He grins and nods in approval. "Open your mouth and stick out your tongue."

I do as he says, opening my mouth wide, extending my tongue. I close my eyes, waiting, the anticipation building inside me like a storm.

The first touch of his cock on my tongue sends a shockwave of pleasure through me. He tastes salty and warm, and the weight of him against my tongue is so erotic it makes my head spin. "Suck it," he commands, and I obey eagerly, closing my lips around his shaft, flicking my tongue over the tip. I can hear his sharp intake of breath as I take him deeper, and it sends a thrill of satisfaction through me. I'm the one making him feel this way, and the power of that realization is exhilarating.

I bob up and down, sucking and licking every inch of his thick cock. His hips thrust forward, and he hits the back of my throat. I relax, opening my throat for him, and he moans, a deep, guttural sound that makes my pussy throb. Then he's fucking my throat hard, and I gag on his cock, tears burning behind my eyes. But I take it, I take all of it, because I want this, I want him.

"That's it," he groans. "You're a good little cocksucker, just like your husband said."

Oh my god. Caleb said that? My pussy throbs at the words. I feel a surge of satisfaction from knowing that I'm pleasing him and that Caleb is watching it all. It's dirty and raw, and I wouldn't have it any other way. I wouldn't want to do this without Caleb.

Mark pulls his cock out, and I cough, wiping my mouth. He chuckles and lets me breathe a moment before grabbing the back of my head, guiding his cock into my mouth. "Touch yourself while I fuck this pretty little mouth."

I take him deep. My pussy is on fire, and I slip my hand down between my legs and rub my clit. Oh fuck, I'm so wet. I look over to Caleb, and he's got his cock out of his pants while he's stroking it. Wow, he really went for it. He looks glazed with lust as he watches Mark's cock slide in and out of my mouth. Fuck, this is so hot.

As Mark continues to use me, each thrust makes my mind go a little fuzzier. I'm so turned on I'm practically dripping onto my fingers as I rub my clit. I can feel his cock pulsing in my mouth as my orgasm builds.

He pulls out of my mouth again and grins at me while he strokes himself. His cock glistens with my saliva, and I can't help but feel a pang of desire, wishing he was still using my mouth. "Time for you to get on the bed so I can see how good that pussy feels. Get on your back and spread your legs."

I comply, my heart pounding as Mark kneels between my thighs. I expect him to slide inside me immediately, but he strokes his cock over my pussy, teasing me. Wait, what is he doing? He better not come until he fucks me!

I whimper, "Mark, please. I need to feel you inside me."

He grins and slaps his cock against my pussy a few times, then slides the tip along my folds without pushing in. "Beg me to fuck you."

I don't hesitate. My voice shakes with lust. "Please fuck me."

I try to reach for his cock, but he grabs my wrists and forces them above my head, pinning them down as he covers my body. His eyes are full of desire as he grins down at me. "You can do better than that. Beg me to fill you with my cum. Tell me how badly you need it."

The tip of his cock is against my pussy, and I squirm underneath him, desperate to feel him inside me. He's so close, yet he's denying me what I need most. "Please, Mark. I need your cock. I need your cum. I want to be dripping with it. Fuck me hard. I need it hard," I moan, feeling crazed.

He sounds amused when he asks, "Oh, the little slut wants it hard?"

Does he know what he's doing to me when he makes me say all these dirty things? My entire body thrills from how much of a slut it makes me feel when I reply, "Yes. Yes, I want it hard."

He chuckles and then slams into me. I scream in pleasure as his thick cock hits a perfect spot deep inside me. Oh god, he's so much bigger and thicker than anyone I've slept with, and the sensation of him stretching me out is overwhelming. I can't help but whimper in ecstasy, my pussy tightening around him as he pounds into me.

"Fuck, your pussy feels so good. You're so fucking tight," he grunts.

He fucks me hard, pounding me with all his strength, and I'm completely at his mercy. I can't think, I can only feel, and the sensation of him using me for his pleasure is driving me wild. "Please, don't stop," I moan, wrapping my legs around him, urging him to fuck me even harder.

"You want to be full of two guys' cum, don't you?" he growls, thrusting deep inside me.

"Yes," I whimper. Now I know Caleb really did tell him what I want.

Mark raises his voice. "Does she really want it, Caleb?"

Oh god, he's asking Caleb? I squirm and glance over at my husband. He stroking his cock slowly, like he's trying to make this moment last forever. The sight of his cock in his hand is so fucking hot.

"I think you better fill her with your cum," Caleb says, his voice thick with desire. "I think she's earned it." My heart swells with love for my husband. He knows exactly what I need.

Mark rocks into me slowly a couple more times, as if he's trying to decide what to do. It's an exquisite torture. "No," he finally says, "I think she needs to come at least twice more first."

Twice? My mind races, panic setting in. It takes me forever to come a second time. Before I can complain, Mark pulls out and flips me onto my stomach.

"On your knees, slut," he growls. "Get that ass in the air."

I scramble to comply as he moves in behind me. When he shoves into me, I cry out, "Oooh, god," as I feel the delicious stretch again.

He whacks against me hard, as if he's chasing his orgasm and using me for his pleasure. It's raw, primal, and so fucking hot. I've never felt like this before—like a sex doll who is just along for the ride. It's wonderful.

My orgasm quickly builds again, the pressure growing with every thrust. His balls slap against my clit, and I'm mewling in pleasure every time he bottoms out.

"You like that, slut?"

"Fuck, yes!" I push against him, meeting his every thrust. My body is on fire as every nerve ending lights up with pleasure.

He pounds into me harder and faster, his hips slamming into my ass. I can't hold on much longer. The pleasure is too intense. My fingers dig into the bedding as my thigh muscles quiver. I'm trying to hold on, to make this moment last just a little bit longer. But it's no use. The orgasm slams into me as I tremble from the force of it. My pussy clenches around his cock, and he groans in pleasure as I milk him.

"Fuuuck," he groans. "You're a good little cumslut, aren't you?"

A fresh wave of arousal courses through me even as I'm still trying to recover from my orgasm. He pulls out and flips me onto my back, pushing my knees to my chest before thrusting into my pussy. He leans forward, capturing my mouth in a fierce kiss. His tongue tangles with mine, and the room tilts from pleasure.

His thrusts are relentless, and I feel like a rag doll just there to pleasure him as he fucks me hard. The pleasure builds in layers again the longer he hammers into me. Oh shit, this next one is going to be massive.

"Beg for it," he demands. "And then I'll fill you full of cum."

"Please. Oh god, please?" I whimper, my voice catching in desperation. "I need you to come inside me. I need your cum. Please?"

"Good slut," he groans and slams into me one last time.

His cock twitches, and he unloads deep into my pussy, shaking from the force of his release. The warmth rushing through me brings me to the breaking point. A white-hot pleasure ripples from my core, and I scream as I convulse from pure ecstasy.

The world fades away as rapture takes me to a higher plane. I'm not sure how long I'm shuddering from pleasure, but I eventually come back to Earth when Mark pulls out. A rush of our combined wetness runs down the crack of my ass, and I shiver as I straighten my legs. God, this is so dirty. I love it.

Mark looks tired but happy as he climbs off the bed and gets dressed. Once he tucks his cock into his pants, he turns to me with a surprisingly tender expression on his face. "Thank you, Sara. That was incredible."

My heart is still pounding as I give him a dreamy smile. "Thank you, too. It was...more than I imagined."

He leans down and kisses me softly, a gentle touch that takes me by surprise. "You're amazing," he whispers before turning to Caleb. "She's all yours. I hope she'll be a good cumslut for you too."

His words are playful, but there's an undercurrent of respect that makes me blush and giggle as Caleb walks Mark to the door. I've always been a good little slut for my husband, but tonight I've taken that to new heights. I'm overwhelmed with longing, and I desperately need my husband. I'm so ready to have Caleb inside me, to feel both of their cum in my pussy.

CHAPTER 4

When Caleb returns, he doesn't say a word and starts to undress. He watches me slide a hand to my pussy as I play with the wetness. I swirl my finger around my clit, knowing that some of this is Mark's cum and some of it is me. The sensation is heavenly, a mix of my own desire and the evidence of another man's lust.

He grins. "Did you enjoy yourself?"

"Yes, that was so fucking hot."

He chuckles as he sets his clothes on the chair he was sitting in while he watched another man fuck me. "It was. I almost lost it twice. You were so sexy."

Oooh, I like knowing he almost came, but I'm glad he didn't. I bite my lower lip as I look down at his hard cock. The neediness is growing inside me again. "Now do I get your cum?"

He climbs onto the bed and rumbles, "Oh yeah, baby. I'm dying to fuck my slut."

Mmm, nice. He settles between my thighs and presses his cock against my entrance. "Is this what you want?"

I moan, "Yes. You know it is. I need you."

Caleb sinks into me slowly, letting me feel every inch of him. He's not as thick as Mark, but his cock is long and hits all the right spots. Somehow it feels different with him now yet still the same. Oh god, this is glorious. I'm still so wet, and his cock is sliding in and out of me easily. I'm dripping with another man's cum and my own juices, and it's so fucking erotic. My pussy spasms, desperate for more as I get lightheaded from pleasure.

"Fuck, this feels good," Caleb groans as he picks up the pace.

"Yes. God yes," I cry out. "Give me your cum. I need it."

He responds by pounding into me harder. The sound of skin slapping against skin fills the hotel room. It's so fucking hot, and I'm already close to coming again. I'm right on the verge.

"Oh fuck," Caleb groans. "Are you ready, baby? Are you ready for my cum?"

"Yes, please," I whimper as my thighs tense and I press my heels into the bed, meeting his punishing thrusts.

Caleb grunts right before his cock pulses deep inside me and I feel the warmth of his cum filling me, mixing with the remnants of Mark's seed. The filthy thought spirals me over the edge. My climax rips through me as waves of pleasure wash over me. We cling to each other as we both shudder from the force of our shared pleasure.

When we finally come down from the high, he collapses onto me, and I feel his body tremble with aftershocks of his orgasm. "Fuck, Sara," he murmurs into my neck. "That was something else."

I wrap my arms around him, holding him close. "I love you so much," I whisper. And it's true. In a strange way, I feel closer to Caleb than I ever have in our entire marriage. I can still taste another man on my tongue and the scent of sex is heavy in the air—not all of it sex with my husband—but none of that matters because I love Caleb with all my heart.

Caleb gives me a tender look. "I love you too, baby," he says, brushing a strand of hair from my face. "So much."

We stay like that for a moment, lost in the intense connection. Then Caleb rolls off me with a groan, pulling me into his arms so that my head rests on his chest. I can hear his heartbeat, strong and steady, a comforting rhythm that lulls me into a state of pure contentment.

"You know," I say, tracing lazy patterns on his chest with my fingertips, "I never thought I could feel this way. So...free. So alive."

Caleb smiles, pressing a kiss to the top of my head. "That's all I wanted for you. For us."

A sense of peace washes over me. This is what it's all about, I realize. Not just the sex, not just the thrill of the moment. It's about growing, exploring, and discovering new depths to our desires and our relationship.

As I lie there in Caleb's arms, I know that this is just the beginning. There's so much more to explore, so much more to experience. And I can't wait to see where this journey takes us...assuming my husband wants to share his cumslut again. But when I peek up at him, the utter happiness on his face tells me he will.

The End

October Hotwife

Hotwife of the Month Club 10

Lacey Cross

Chapter 1

I lean back, swirling the last sip of my margarita. I'm amused at how Debra is flushing an impressive shade of pink. We're tucked away in a corner booth of our favorite Mexican restaurant, and for the past hour, I've been watching the most entertaining show of my life.

"I just can't wrap my head around it," Debra says, twisting her napkin between her red-tipped fingers. Her voice drops to a scandalized whisper. "It's so...reckless. What about the marriage? The trust? Isn't it...dangerous?"

I catch Nicole's eye over the rim of my glass. Her lips are pressed tight, fighting not to let out what I suspect is either a laugh or a confession. She's been unusually quiet today, and I can practically see the gears turning in her head.

"Dangerous?" I echo, amusement coloring my voice. "Is that why we've spent the last hour picking apart every detail of being a hotwife, Deb?"

Debra's cheeks pinken further. "I'm just worried about how it's affecting marriages these days," she insists, but there's a spark in her expression that betrays her. It's curiosity, plain as day, mixed with something else. Something she's trying to hide behind her moral outrage. I recognize it because I've seen it in myself lately—a yearning for excitement, for something to break the monotony of life.

"Sure," I nod, unconvinced. "And that's why you were curious about how it feels to be the center of attention while your husband watches, right?"

Nicole finally breaks her silence with a snort, quickly disguised as a cough. Debra shoots her a look before turning back to me, her expression indignant.

"I'm just trying to understand," Debra says primly, but her fingers haven't stopped fidgeting with that poor, abused napkin. I can see the internal struggle written all over her face.

As we wrap up lunch, my mind is whirling. Not just with amusement at Debra's transparent act but with my own thoughts. Because as much as I'm poking fun at her in my head, I can't deny that a part of me is intrigued. Hell, more than intrigued. It's as if Debra's questions have unearthed a desire I've been suppressing for months.

The drive home is a blur of half-formed fantasies. I step into my living room, and as soon as the front door shuts behind me, I let out a loud laugh. Fuck, that lunch was something else. I sink into the couch, glad to be home. Our daughter is at my mom's for a sleepover, giving me a rare moment of quiet.

I kick off my shoes and stretch my toes, savoring these last few minutes of relaxation before I have to get ready for our gig tonight. My thoughts shift from lunch to my husband, Anthony, and our life. I'm happy, sure. But lately it's been...routine. Predictable. Busy. The kind of life that's stable and reliable, but maybe a little too beige, if you know what I mean.

No offense to beige—it's nice enough. But sometimes, a person needs a little pop of color.

This isn't about being a hotwife, I don't even know if that's what I need. But I want to recapture that spark of excitement we had when we first got together. Tonight, I'll talk to Anthony. There's just too much beige in our life—I need to shake things up. We both do.

I head upstairs to get ready for tonight's gig. Anthony's old guitar case in the corner of our bedroom reminds me of our college days, when we first started playing together. It's almost surreal that our band has endured this long, even if we're down to just a couple of gigs a month now. We've all settled into family life with kids, and those big dreams of rock stardom have faded away. But it was never really about fame—we still love playing together, and that's what keeps us going.

Tonight's different though. We're playing a private birthday party for some rich guy, and my nerves are on edge. As I start getting ready, my body's on autopilot while my thoughts race. The idea of being a hotwife ...fuck, it's making me wet just thinking about it. It's not just the sex—it's about being desired, of feeling like more than just a wife and mother.

I slip into my sexiest black lace bra and matching panties, shivering as the fabric glides over my skin. I normally dress for comfort when we're performing, but tonight I want to feel desirable. The form-fitting black dress I choose clings to every curve, and the fabric is glittery. I turn in the mirror, admiring how it sparkles in the light and accentuates my figure. I put on my favorite strappy flat sandals—my one piece of comfort for tonight. I won't be teetering around on high heels.

I picture myself on stage, all eyes on me as I perform. But it's not just the audience watching—there's a stranger who can't look away. I'd choose him from the crowd as I sing. And in my mind, Anthony is overcome with lust as he watches this stranger become captivated by me.

The fantasy sends a bolt of desire straight to my core. My hand trembles, and I have to pause while applying my makeup. Jesus, I need to get a grip...or just fuck Anthony's brains out tonight. Yeah, I'm going to tell him to save some energy for after the show.

"Hey, baby." Anthony walks into the bathroom and stops short, his eyes twinkling as they roam over my body. "Damn. You look hot."

"Thanks," I say, turning to face him and deliberately brushing against him. "I needed a boost today."

Anthony pulls me close, his hands sliding down to rest on my hips. "Everything okay?"

I lean into him, savoring his familiar scent and touch. "I was thinking about my day. Lunch with Debra and Nicole got me questioning things."

"Yeah?" Anthony says, his fingers tracing slow circles on my lower back. "What's on your mind?"

"Debra wouldn't shut up about the hotwife thing," I admit, watching his face closely and biting my lip. "And...it got me thinking."

Anthony chuckles, but I notice his pupils dilate slightly. "About?"

"About us. Our life. Don't get me wrong, I love what we have, but sometimes I wonder if we're stuck in a rut. If we're missing out on the excitement we used to have."

"Go on," Anthony encourages in a husky tone.

"I can't stop thinking about being a hotwife," I confess, the words tumbling out as I run my hands up his chest. "The excitement, the newness. I know it sounds crazy, but part of me wonders if it could bring back some of that passion we had when we first got together."

Anthony's quiet for a moment before saying, "Liv, I've had similar thoughts."

"You have?" I feel a rush of wetness between my thighs.

He nods, his hands sliding lower to cup my ass. "Yeah. You're gorgeous, and the idea of someone else appreciating that..." His forehead touches mine. "I love you, and I want you to be happy. If this is something you want to explore, I'm in. But I want to choose the guy, okay? It's important to me that we do this together, as a team."

A longing pulls at me, mixed with a deep love for this man who's willing to explore new territory with me. "I'd like that, and I love you too. Thank you for being open to this."

He kisses my nose. "We don't have to do anything you're not comfortable with. But honestly? The thought of you fucking someone else, knowing you're coming home to me, is hot."

I laugh, and the tension eases as I grind against him slightly, feeling his hard cock through his jeans. "Yeah?"

"Yeah," he grins, his hands tightening on my ass. Without warning, he lifts me onto the bathroom counter, spreading my legs wide. "So hot, I'm going to fuck you right now."

He pushes my dress up, revealing my already damp panties. "Anthony, we don't have time—"

"We'll make time." He yanks my panties aside, and I gasp when he slides two fingers inside me. "Mmm, you're so wet already. Is this from thinking about being fucked by someone else?"

I moan as he works his fingers in and out of me. The wrongness of it all—getting fingered on the bathroom counter when we should be leaving—only heightens my arousal.

"Tell me how much you want to be a hotwife," Anthony demands.

"I—I want it," I pant, grinding against his hand. "Fuck, I want it so bad."

He adds a third finger, curling them just right. "Beg for it. Beg to be my dirty little hotwife."

The request sends a jolt of electricity through me, and suddenly, I want to be the sluttiest version of myself. "Please," I whimper, my hips bucking. "Please let me be your hotwife slut. I want to fuck other men and come home to you, dripping with another man's cum. Please, I need it!"

"Fuck," he groans, quickly unzipping his jeans and freeing his rock-hard cock. He slams into me and I cry out in pleasure. "That's it, baby. You're going to be such a good little slut for me."

Ooooh, I am. The room tilts as he fucks me hard and fast. I cling to him as I feel my orgasm approaching.

"Oh god, oh god, I'm gonna—"

"Think about all the cocks you're going to take as my hotwife and come for me," Anthony commands.

I think about a line of guys waiting to fuck me, and I come with a scream, burying my face in his neck to muffle the sound. He follows shortly after, jerking and pulsing deep inside me.

As we catch our breath, he gives me a wicked grin. "So, do you want to be my hotwife slut tonight?"

I laugh. "Well, let's see if you find anyone you want me to fuck first." I'm feeling lighter and more aroused than I have in months.

Anthony helps me off the counter and murmurs, "Maybe we should just stay home and keep practicing your slut routine?"

I giggle, nudging him gently towards the door. "Nice try, mister. But we have a party to get to. Besides, don't you want time to work up your appetite to fuck me again later?"

He smirks. "You're right. I'm going to fuck you so hard when we get home."

"Promises, promises," I tease, running a finger down his chest. "Now shoo, I need to make myself presentable again. *Someone* made quite a mess of my panties."

He steals one more quick kiss. "You know I love it when you're a mess for me, baby."

"Oh, I know. And maybe I'll be an even bigger mess later." I wink and shut the door in his face, hearing his groan on the other side.

Alone, I survey the damage in the mirror. My hair's a wild tangle, lipstick smeared, and I can feel Anthony's cum slowly trickling down my inner thigh. God, it's like we're in college again.

I clean up quickly, dabbing myself with a warm washcloth. My body tingles as I reapply my makeup, adding an extra coat of mascara for good measure.

When I'm done in the bathroom, I saunter into the bedroom. Anthony's sitting on the bed, watching my every move. I toss my ruined panties in the laundry basket, making a show of bending over slowly.

"See something you like?" I ask, glancing over my shoulder at him.

"You know I do," he groans.

I open my lingerie drawer, deliberately taking my time as I sort through the options. I guess my second-sexiest pair is going to have to do tonight. I pull out a scrap of red lace, barely there and designed to drive him wild. I slowly slip them on, adjusting them just so.

He growls, "You're killing me, Liv."

"That's the idea. Now, are you ready to go find some trouble with me?"

I feel the energy between us shift, crackling with sexual tension. Whatever happens, I know one thing for sure—tonight isn't going to be beige.

CHAPTER 2

Holy shit. This place is something else. As we step into the clubhouse, the opulence is unmistakable. Crystal chandeliers throw warm light over everything, making even the leather sofas look inviting. The air holds a subtle blend of mahogany and leather.

Anthony lets out a low whistle beside me. "Damn. Fancy, but still feels like somewhere you could relax with a beer and chat with friends."

I murmur my agreement and think about how some of the couples in our circle of friends are very well off, but Anthony and I aren't. This place is definitely nicer than any of the other gigs we've had. I grin to myself, thinking about the stories I'll have to share with Nicole after rubbing elbows with rich people. She and I are always laughing at how our rich friends don't understand the "commoner's" problems. Tonight, it's time to see how the other half parties—and maybe have a little fun while we're at it.

The guests we pass are in a variety of dress, from cocktail dresses all the way down to casual clothes. I'm suddenly grateful for my slinky black dress. I look glamorous and sexy. I'm here to be a hotwife slut and sing.

As we make our way to the stage area to set up, I feel everyone watching me—or maybe that's just my imagination. Either way, I sway my hips a little more than usual.

"Someone's feeling good tonight," Anthony says with a grin as he starts unpacking his guitar.

"Well, you did give me quite the send-off, Mr. Talented Fingers. I'm still tingling."

"Just wait until later," he promises. "I'll make sure you're more than tingling."

My body hums with anticipation as I remember exactly what his fingers can do, but I force myself to focus. Our band mates, Jake and Darren, join us on the small stage, breaking the moment.

"Ready to rock, lovebirds?" Jake teases, twirling a drumstick.

Darren rolls his eyes. "Let's just hope they can keep their hands off each other long enough to get through the set."

Oh shit, they heard us flirting. We all laugh, and I feel myself relax a little. This is familiar. This, I can do.

As I'm adjusting my mic stand, I notice a man approaching. Even before he opens his mouth, I know this is Ross, the birthday boy. He's got this confidence that practically oozes out of him. His salt-and-pepper hair is artfully messed up. Blue shirt unbuttoned just enough to make you want to see more. When his eyes meet mine, it's like someone's cranked up the heat in the room.

"Welcome," he says, and holy hell, his voice. It's a smooth velvet that does things to me that a voice shouldn't be able to do. "I'm Ross. Thanks for agreeing to play for my birthday. I've actually been following your band for years now, so this is a special treat for me."

I step forward, hoping he can't see how my hand trembles as I reach out to shake his. "I'm Olivia. This is Anthony—Darren and Jake. Happy birthday, and...wow, I had no idea we had such a devoted fan."

His strong hand wraps around mine, and when he lets go, I can still feel where he touched me. "I've seen you perform a few times," he says. "Your stage presence is...captivating. I'm particularly looking forward to your performance tonight."

Heat floods my cheeks, and suddenly I'm very aware of how tight my dress is. "Thank you," I manage to say. "We'll do our best to make it a great show."

Ross smiles and rejoins his friends. When he catches my eye again, he raises his glass in a silent toast. I quickly look away. Damn. Anthony's suggestion about becoming a hotwife has me practically salivating over the first attractive man I see. I take a deep breath, trying to calm my slutty body down. I've got a show to do. But even as I try to focus, I can feel this pull towards Ross that I'm struggling to resist.

The party's in full swing now, and I'd estimate there's about fifty people. As we take the stage, everyone quiets down, and I can feel Ross's eyes on me. The first notes of the song pulse through me, and suddenly the crowd's energy is electric. When I begin to sing, my voice is raw and powerful. With each song, I feel myself shedding layers of inhibition. My body moves with the rhythm as I sway my hips. The audience is smiling, and some are even dancing. Everyone is fully engaged. But all I can focus on is Ross. He's standing at the edge of the dance floor, and his gaze burns into me with an intensity that makes my skin tingle.

During a break, Anthony excuses himself to the restroom, and I go to the bar alone. I'm still buzzing from the performance. As I order a water, I notice Anthony is stopped near the hallway, deep in discussion with Ross. Huh, what're they talking about?

Before I can think too much about it, Anthony joins me. He sits down next to me, looking both excited and nervous.

"Everything okay?" I ask, trying to sound casual.

"Yep, just talking to the birthday boy. You're on fire tonight, babe. I've never seen you like this."

My cheeks flush, and it's not just from performing. "The birthday boy seems to be enjoying the show," I murmur, unable to hide my happiness.

"I can tell. It's fucking hot to watch him lusting after you." Anthony's hand finds my thigh, squeezing gently.

Before I can respond, a familiar voice cuts through the background chatter. "Mind if I join you?"

Ross slides onto the barstool on my other side, signaling the bartender. Up close, I can smell his cologne—something woodsy that makes my head spin a little.

"That was quite a performance," he says. "You have a remarkable talent."

"Thank you," I manage, taking a sip of water to wet my suddenly dry throat. "I'm glad you're having fun."

Ross's lips quirk up in a half-smile. "Oh, I am. Especially now." His gaze flicks to Anthony, then to me. "Your husband is a lucky man."

I feel Anthony shift beside me, and for a moment, I tense. But when I glance at him, he's smiling, his hand still resting possessively on my thigh. "That I am," he agrees, giving me another squeeze.

Ross raises an eyebrow, something unspoken passing between the two men. Then he turns back to me. "You know," he says, his voice dropping to a near-whisper, "Since it's my birthday, I don't suppose I could request a special performance?"

I'm acutely aware how wet my panties are getting. "What did you have in mind?"

Ross's smile widens. "Something private. Just for me."

Before I can reply, Anthony's lips brush my ear. "Why don't you give the birthday boy a special performance, babe? If you want to, that is."

My mind races and suddenly, it clicks. "This is what you were talking about a moment ago?" My eyes dart between them. My husband and this magnetic stranger were talking about me fucking Ross. Well, that's hot.

Anthony's hand finds mine. "We explored the possibility. But it's entirely up to you, Liv. Always."

I turn to Ross, who's watching our exchange with undisguised interest. He's waiting for my move.

My heart pounds as I realize this is my chance, but for some reason, I can't respond. I said I wanted to be a hotwife, so why am I not jumping at this?

I need to think, and it's impossible to do it around the guys. I stammer, "I...I need a moment to clear my head."

I wobble away from the bar. I probably look like I've been drinking, but I've never been more sober in my life. The bathroom door clicks shut behind me, muffling the party noise, and suddenly it's just me and my racing thoughts.

Damn, even the bathroom is fancy. Warm light makes everything glow like I'm in some high-end spa, and it smells like those ridiculously expensive rose-scented hand soaps you're afraid to actually use. I lean against the marble counter, pressing my palms flat against it, and look at myself in the mirror.

Who the hell is this woman staring back at me? Her cheeks are flushed, and her eyes sparkle. The little black number hugs every curve like it was painted on, and the neckline dips just low enough to make things interesting without screaming "I'm trying too hard." She looks...vibrant. Sexy as fuck. Is this really me?

Am I seriously considering this? Am I going to fuck Ross, a guy I barely know, while Anthony waits for me to finish?

For a second, I'm back home. At this time yesterday, Anthony and I were zoned out in front of the TV, half-asleep and barely grunting at each other. It felt safe then, but now? Now it feels like a straitjacket. I need more. I need this.

My hand shakes as I pull out my phone and type a message to Anthony.

Olivia:

> **You sure about this? Like, really fucking sure?**

The wait for his reply feels like an eternity. When it comes, it's short but hits me like a ton of bricks.

His words calm my nerves and light a fire in my belly at the same time. He gets me. He really gets me. And he's not just okay with this—he wants it.

I straighten up, smoothing my hands over my dress. The woman in the mirror looks back at me with a glint in her eye while I touch up my lipstick. I take one last look in the mirror, barely believing this sex goddess is me. But she is. She's who I've always been, I just lost my way for a bit with my adult responsibilities.

When I push open the door, I'm stepping into a whole new chapter. I'm not just Olivia the wife or Olivia the singer anymore—I'm Olivia the woman who knows what she wants and isn't afraid to get it.

CHAPTER 3

The party's a blur of laughter and clinking glasses, and my heart's doing the cha-cha as I weave through the crowd. A few people make comments about how great the band is, and I smile and thank them, but I've got tunnel vision for the bar.

Wait, where is Anthony? I scan the room and find him chatting with Darren and Jake. He catches me looking at him and gives me a thumbs up. His support sends a thrill through me.

Ross's still holding court at the bar when I approach. The second he spots me, it's like I've become his whole world. Damn, if it isn't a rush. His gaze pins me in place, and I swear I can feel the heat of it on my skin. When was the last time I felt this desirable, this powerful? Too long, that's for sure.

"Olivia," he rumbles, that voice of his still doing things to me that should be illegal. "Thought you'd pulled a Houdini on me."

I laugh. "As if. Just needed a sec to...straighten up."

Ross's eyebrow shoots up, and he smiles. "Well, it looks like you've got everything exactly where it should be."

The bartender materializes, and refills our water glasses. When he leaves, Ross leans in close. "I couldn't take my eyes off you earlier while you were singing."

"Oh yeah?"

"Mmm hmm," he hums, his hand inching closer to mine on the bar. "There's something about a woman lost in her passion. It's magnetic."

I have to take a sip of my water. Over the rim of my glass, I spot Anthony across the room watching us. He gives me a nod and smile. His encouragement sends a bolt of heat through me.

I smile at Ross, feeling bolder. I let my fingers 'accidentally' touch him as I set down my glass, "Well, I do enjoy losing myself in...passion."

Ross caresses the back of my hand. Each touch sends little zaps of electricity up my arm. "And what other passions might you enjoy losing yourself in?"

"What if I told you I had a special birthday surprise in mind?"

Ross's hand freezes on my arm. "I'd say that I've never been more intrigued by a gift in my life."

I give one last glance to Anthony, finding him still watching us. He gives me a subtle wink that I can see even from this distance. Fuck, this is dirty.

I slide off the barstool, making sure to brush against Ross as I do. "How about you take me somewhere private so you can unwrap your present?"

Ross doesn't hesitate. He takes my hand and leads me down a hallway, away from the party's chaos. We pause at a door, and he asks, "You sure about this?"

Am I sure? I think of my life and the thrill that's been missing. "Yes, I'm sure."

Ross's smile is slow and hungry. He opens the door, revealing a dimly lit office with a desk and leather couch. I face him, and the way he's looking at me...it's like I'm a feast, and he's starving.

"Olivia," he breathes, and when his lips meet mine, all thought vanishes. The kiss is full of passion, and he presses me against the nearest wall. This isn't like kissing Anthony—it's a wildfire compared to a candle flame. Ross's hands roam my body, leaving trails of fire, and when he cups my breast, I moan and arch into him.

I explore his chest, feeling the hard muscle under his shirt. He deepens the kiss, and I savor his sweet taste, like birthday cake. A surge of boldness courses through me, and I break off the kiss.

"Hold on," I purr, surprising myself with the huskiness in my tone. "Don't you want to unwrap your gift?"

"Fuck, yes," he growls.

I guide his hands to my zipper. "Then unwrap me."

The zipper's sound is loud in the quiet room. I shiver as cool air hits my skin, my dress pooling at my feet. Ross's eyes devour me.

"Damn," he groans, "even better than I imagined."

His gaze makes every nerve ending tingle. I'm desperate for his touch again. Ross's lips curve into a knowing smile. "Your husband gave me some interesting pointers. He mentioned you like dirty talk...and that you enjoy it rough. But I want to hear you say it. Tell me what you want, Olivia."

A thrill courses through me. Anthony told him that? God, my husband is incredible. My voice quivers with need. "Yes. I want it rough, and I want dirty talk."

"That's my specialty."

Suddenly, we're a flurry of hands and mouths, desperate to be naked and entwined.

Right as he pulls my panties down, voices approach. We freeze. Shit, did he lock the door? I count three heartbeats until they pass without stopping. Oh fuck, that was close. Ross must've had the same thought because he locks the door and turns to me. "Now where were we?"

I step out of my panties and unhook my bra. "You were about to take your clothes off."

Once he's naked, I can't stop exploring Ross's body. He's hard planes and lean muscle. He does the same as his rough hands map my curves.

"Turn around," he commands.

I comply, bracing my hands against the wall. Ross presses against me from behind, and I can feel his hard cock at my ass. His hands slide up my body, cupping my breasts. I push back, craving more.

"Please," I whimper, wishing he'd just fuck me right there.

Ross chuckles. "Patience, my slutty gift." The crude word sends a zing of electricity through me. "Your husband was right about you, wasn't he?"

"Yes," I moan, my head falling against his shoulder. "God, yes. Anthony knows me so well."

His hand dips between my legs, and I gasp as he fingers my clit, circling it slowly. My hips buck involuntarily.

"So fucking wet," he groans, slipping his fingers inside me. "All for me."

I cry out, "Yes. Please. I need you to fuck me."

He works his fingers in and out, his thumb still on my clit. The dual stimulation has me climbing higher as the delight coils tight in my core. I'm making soft whimpers and gasps—but I'm past caring if anyone hears. All I can think about is how perfectly filthy this is.

Just as I'm about to tip over the edge, Ross withdraws his hand. I whine at the loss, but then I feel the blunt tip of his cock pressing against me. "Please, fuck me," I whimper.

With a groan, he sinks into me slowly. The stretch feels amazing, and my fingers claw at the wall so I can push back and take him in further.

Instead of fucking me, Ross holds still for a moment and grunts, "Your pussy feels amazing."

I can only moan in response, overwhelmed by sensation. When he finally starts to move, it's a slow, deep rhythm that sends shockwaves of pleasure through me. I'm about ready to combust.

I try to rock against him and moan, "Oh god, don't stop. Don't stop."

He speeds up his thrusts, fucking me harder. One of his hands snakes around to rub my clit, and I nearly scream at the added stimulation. The relentless pounding of his hips and the skilled movements of his fingers send me hurtling over the edge. My orgasm crashes over me, obliterating all thoughts. My body shudders as joy rolls through me. I cry out, "Ooooh, fuck!"

Ross doesn't come with me. In fact, he stops moving as if he's trying not to. For a long moment, we stay like that, both of us panting heavily. Slowly, reality begins to seep in. I'm suddenly very aware of where we are, of the party still going on just down the hall.

Ross pulls out, and I turn to face him. His hair's a mess, and I'm sure I look equally wrecked.

"You're incredible," Ross whispers. "I want more."

Lust races through me at his words. "Then take more."

"You sure you want it rough?"

"Yes." I feel a rush of excitement from how slutty it makes me feel to admit that I want it rough.

His hands slide down to cup my ass. "Good. Because I'm going to fuck you so hard you scream."

He lifts me effortlessly, and I instinctively wrap my legs around his waist. His mouth crashes against mine, and he carries me to the leather couch, setting me down. "You're so fucking beautiful," he growls. "I can't believe I get to fuck you. It's like a dream come true."

I blush at his words. Holy hell, I'm literally some guy's dream girl. "You're the first guy I've slept with outside my marriage."

"Then we better make it good. Get on your hands and knees for me. Let me see that gorgeous ass."

I obey without hesitation, turning around and positioning myself on the couch. My knees are on the edge, and I'm gripping the backrest.

"So gorgeous," Ross murmurs. "You look fucking perfect like this."

His hands slide over my ass, giving it a light spank. I giggle and shake my ass. I love how desired I feel with him. My husband couldn't have picked a better first-time bull for me.

He grabs my hips and pulls me towards him even more so that I'm fully exposed to him. He slides his fingers through my slick folds. "Your pussy is so wet and swollen. You really do love this, don't you?"

"Yes," I moan, rocking against his hand. "I need you inside me again."

He doesn't make me wait. His cock nudges against my pussy a second before he slams into me. I have to clutch at the couch to keep myself upright.

"Oh god, yes," I gasp and throw myself onto his cock. He fucks me roughly, and each thrust sends jolts of bliss from my fingertips to my toes. The wet sounds of our bodies slapping together is almost obscene, and I can feel the pleasure building inside me again.

Ross's voice is strained with effort. "You like being fucked like a dirty little slut, don't you?"

"Yes," I moan. "I love being a dirty slut."

"You're so fucking tight," he grunts. "Your cunt feels like heaven."

His dirty talk gives me a heady rush, and I'm reeling towards ecstasy. My inner muscles clench around him, and he groans in response.

"Fuck, you feel so good." He jackhammers into me. "I want to feel you come all over my cock again."

His words nudge me closer to the edge, and I'm ready to snap. Each part of me buzzes with delight, and I feel like I'm going to orgasm with every thrust.

"Please," I beg, my voice trembling. "Don't stop. I'm so close."

Ross's hands move to my shoulders, gripping them tightly as he slams into me repeatedly. "Come for me," he commands.

He hits a particularly pleasurable spot, and I scream as I explode. White-hot ecstasy blurs my vision, and my pussy spasms around him. He groans, his rhythm faltering for a moment before he picks up the pace again.

"Fuck, yes." His hips move faster, harder. He continues to fuck me through my orgasm, each thrust sending aftershocks of pleasure through my body. When my orgasm finally subsides, Ross pulls out and flips me onto my back.

"I want to see you," he murmurs. "I want to watch you come again. But first, I want to use that mouth of yours."

He shifts, moving up my body until he's straddling my chest, his cock hovering just above my lips. I open my mouth and take him in eagerly. He grips my head, controlling my movements as he slowly sinks his cock into my mouth. The taste of him mixed with my juices drives me wild. I suck on him and swirl my tongue along his shaft, cleaning him up. He's gentle as he fucks my throat, but I know he could speed up at any moment. it makes me feel like a fucktoy that he can use however he wants. I love every second of it.

He doesn't come, but he doesn't need to. This is about control, about him using me for his pleasure. And I'm more than willing to let him.

"That's it, take it all," he growls, his fingers tightening in my hair. "You feel so fucking good wrapped around my cock." His hips move with a steady rhythm, pushing deeper. "You're mine to use, aren't you? Say it."

I can't speak, instead gurgling around his cock, but my eyes meet his, a silent affirmation.

"Good girl," he murmurs, his voice rough with passion. "You're doing so well, taking me so deep."

A part of me doesn't feel like I should like it when he calls me a good girl, but I get an illicit thrill when he says it. I really do want to be a good girl.

After a few minutes, he pulls out and moves down my body, positioning himself between my legs once more. He slides into me, setting a slower, more sensual pace this time. His hands roam over my body, cupping my breasts and pulling at my nipples.

"Oh god, so good," I moan as I wrap my legs and arms around him.

Ross's lips brush against mine. "You deserve to feel this good. You deserve to be worshiped."

His words send a rush of emotion through me, and I can feel tears pricking at the corners of my eyes. He's right, and Anthony knew it too. This isn't just about the sex; it's about reclaiming something inside me.

Ross continues to fuck me with a steady rhythm. Each stroke sends a twist of raw pleasure swirling through my body.

"I'm close," I whimper. "I'm going to come again."

With a final hard thrust, he sends me over the edge. I cry out as my climax hits me. My body goes rigid, and my pussy seizes over his cock as delight zings through me. He groans, his rhythm becoming erratic as he chases his own orgasm.

He buries himself deep inside me, his body trembling as he explodes. I can feel the warmth of his release, and it sends a fresh wave of pleasure through my body. We cling to each other as we both shudder.

When our orgasms finally subside, Ross pulls out and collapses onto the couch beside me. I curl up against him, my head fuzzy from ecstasy.

"That was wonderful," I murmur, my voice filled with amazement. "I didn't know I'd enjoy it that much."

Ross smiles down at me. "Thank you for the birthday gift. You're something special, Olivia."

We lie there for a long moment before getting up. As we put our clothes on, I feel a deep sense of gratitude towards my husband for understanding what I needed and for making this incredible experience possible.

I don't feel ashamed or regretful. Instead, I feel empowered, more in touch with my needs than I have been in years. This experience has awakened something in me, a part of myself I'd forgotten existed.

Ross finishes buttoning his shirt and turns to me. "Ready to face the party?"

I smooth down my dress and link my arm with his. "Lead the way, birthday boy."

As we walk towards the noise and light of the party, I can't help but feel like everything's changed. I'm not the same Olivia who walked down this hallway less than an hour ago—the one who was glassy-eyed on the couch binging shows with her husband. I can't wait to explore who this new Olivia will be.

CHAPTER 4

My body's still buzzing when we rejoin the party, and I look around for Anthony. When I finally spot him across the room, it's like a lightning bolt hits me. His eyes are intense and full of lust.

He's moving towards me like a man on a mission. Right when he reaches us, Ross speaks up.

"Olivia, Anthony. Thank you for making this birthday unforgettable."

I give him a smile. "It was our pleasure," I manage, my voice surprisingly steady. Anthony nods, his jaw tight, and he murmurs, "Happy birthday."

The twinkle in Ross's eyes tells me he knows what's about to happen with me and Anthony. "Goodnight, then. Enjoy the rest of your evening."

As he melts into the crowd, the air is heavy with unspoken words and...s hit, I can still smell Ross's cologne on my skin. Anthony takes my hand, and damn if that simple touch doesn't send shivers up my arm. It's so familiar, but somehow different now.

Anthony pulls me down the hallway where Ross led me earlier. We slip into the same private room, the door closing with a barely audible click. The only sound now is our ragged breathing.

His gaze rakes over me, and I suddenly feel naked.

"Tell me," Anthony growls, pushing me against the wall. "Every. Dirty. Detail."

Oh, god. He wants to know? My fingers tremble as I move them between my legs, tracing the edge of my panties. Anthony's pupils dilate as he follows my hand.

"He touched me like this," I whisper, skimming my fingers over the fabric. "But I was naked. He was urgent. Demanding. He fucked me while I faced the wall."

Anthony spins me around and replaces my fingers with his. My hands brace against the cold wall.

"And then?" he rumbles.

"He pulled me against him," I whimper, pressing my ass back into his hard body. "I could feel his cock."

Anthony's grip tightens, his fingers digging into my flesh. His hand slides between my legs, pushing aside my panties, fingers slipping inside. "Did you like it?" His breath is hot against my ear.

"Yes," I admit, hips bucking against his hand. "It felt so good."

"Good? Just good?" He finger fucks me harder, hitting that spot only he knows. "Did you come hard?"

"Yes," I gasp, my body clenching around his fingers. "So hard...so many times."

"Such a dirty little slut." He pulls his fingers out and flips me around. When he crushes his lips to mine, his kiss is urgent, demanding. "You're mine," he growls against my mouth. "No matter how many others you fuck, you're always mine."

"Yes," I moan. "Only yours." God, I love this side of him.

He yanks my dress up, bunching it around my waist. His fingers hook into my panties, tugging them down roughly. "What did he do next," he demands, eyes blazing.

My mind races. "He had me on my knees, on the couch."

He lets out a guttural moan. "Show me."

I stumble to the couch on trembling legs. I position myself, presenting my pussy to him. Anthony stands behind me, his fingers playing with the wetness of my pussy.

"Did he fill you with his cum?"

Ooooh, god. "Yes!" I cry out and arch my back, desperate for him to fuck me.

The sound of his zipper is the only warning I get before his cock plunges into me with savage force. I moan in joy as he pounds into me, each thrust sending energy screaming through my body.

"Tell me," he snarls, fingers digging into my flesh. "Tell me how it feels to fuck someone else."

"It...it was incredible," I moan. Cries of pleasure punctuate my words. "So. Fucking. Good."

Anthony's hips slam against me with bruising force. "You belong to me," he groans. "Every fucking inch, every goddamn hole."

"I do. Oh god, I do," I cry out as pings of bliss radiate from my core. The rapture builds to the breaking point, and I'm teetering on the edge, lost in a haze of lust.

"Anthony!" I scream, desperate. "I'm going to come!"

"Come for me. Show me how much you love my cock."

His words ignite an inferno within me. My orgasm detonates, obliterating all thought. I convulse, my body wracked by waves of mind-shattering ecstasy. I scream as my vision goes white, and I surrender to the bliss completely.

Anthony fucks me through my orgasm, and as soon as he can tell I've come down, he lets go. He roars as he comes, and his entire body tremors as he unloads deep inside me. He whacks against my pussy a few more times before collapsing on the couch and pulling me with him. We're both panting, and we stay like that, basking in the afterglow of pleasure.

"Holy shit," I whisper.

Anthony chuckles. "Yeah, holy shit is right."

"Are we okay?" I ask softly, suddenly feeling vulnerable. I look up at him, searching his face for any sign of regret or jealousy. But all I see is love and a hint of awe.

His hand cups my face, thumb stroking my cheek gently. "We're more than okay. This was incredible. I've never been more turned on in my life."

Relief washes over me. "I love you so much." My voice is thick with emotion. "Thank you for giving me this."

Anthony kisses me softly, tenderly. "I love you too, Liv. Always."

We clean up as best we can and straighten our clothes. As we prepare to rejoin the party, Anthony pulls me close one more time.

"So," he says, a mischievous glint in his eye, "think you might want to do this again sometime?"

I give him a quick kiss before responding. "Definitely. But next time, I want you to watch."

"Fuck, yes," he says before he deepens the kiss.

My head is spinning when he's done, and as we walk back to the party, hand in hand, I feel like I'm floating. I've discovered a new side of myself, a new depth to my relationship with Anthony, and a whole world of possibilities stretching out before us.

One thing is for damn sure: life isn't beige anymore.

The End

November Hotwife

Hotwife of the Month Club 11

Lacey Cross

Chapter 1

I sink into the pedicure chair, and warm, lavender-scented water swallows my feet. The spa's music and bubbling foot bath are already working their magic, melting away the week's stress.

"Fuck, I needed this," I sigh, wiggling my toes.

Next to me, Olivia hums in agreement. "God, yes. Nothing like being pampered."

The spa workers set us up and slip away, leaving us to soak.

I close my eyes, but my brain won't shut up. Life's become a broken record—same job, same routine with Ryan. When did I turn into such a snooze-fest? Is this what being in your thirties is all about?

"So..." Olivia's voice cuts through my thoughts. "Wanna hear about my latest adventure?"

I peek at her, catching that mischievous glint in her eye. Oh boy, here comes the juicy stuff.

"Do I even want to know?" I ask, already knowing I'm dying to hear it.

Olivia leans in, her jasmine perfume mingling with the lavender aromatherapy. "Remember that gig last weekend? Let's just say I gave the birthday boy a very...special private performance."

My jaw drops. "Holy shit! You didn't!"

"Oh, but I did." She winks. "And it was fucking amazing."

She lowers her voice, practically vibrating with excitement. "Anthony waited with the rest of the party, imagining what I was doing. Birthday boy took me to the back room, pressed me against the wall..." She wags her eyebrows. "Let's just say he unwrapped his present thoroughly."

I squirm, suddenly feeling turned on. "But aren't you worried about jealousy? Or screwing things up with Anthony?"

Olivia shakes her head. "Nah. It's actually brought us closer. The trust, the communication—it's next-level shit."

As Olivia gushes about her hotwife adventures, my mind wanders to Ryan. I remember him joking about how hot it'd be to watch me with another guy. I laughed it off then, but now...

"Earth to Nicole," Olivia teases me. "You're actually considering it, aren't you?"

I feel my face burning. "What? No, I'm just...curious."

Olivia grins. "Uh-huh, and that's why you're redder than a lobster right now?"

I kick my foot and splash some water at her. "Oh, shut up. I'm just thinking, okay? How do you even bring that up? 'Hey babe, want to watch me bang another dude?'"

Olivia laughs. "Well, maybe not quite like that. But guys can be surprisingly into it. Has Ryan ever hinted?"

I chew my lip, thinking. "I mean, he's made jokes, but I thought he was just being dumb."

"Jokes are their way of testing the waters. You should just ask him straight up. Life's too short for what-ifs, you know? Maybe it's time to add some sprinkles to that vanilla sundae of yours."

Olivia's words keep bouncing around my head as we wrap up our spa day. I can't lie, the idea gives me a little thrill. Could I actually go through with it?

I try to shake it off. It's just a stupid fantasy, right?

But as I grab my stuff, my fingers linger on my phone. For a second, I picture myself texting Ryan about all our friends joining the "lifestyle." A shiver runs through me, and it's not from the AC. I shove my phone back in my purse. Not today. But...maybe soon.

After I get home and change, I sprawl on the couch and put my laptop on my thighs. My mind's racing from Olivia's story, and my fingers hover over the keyboard. Fuck it. I type "hotwife lifestyle" into the search bar.

The screen fills with blog posts and stories. My marketing brain kicks in, analyzing the raw language. It's hot as hell. Heat pools between my thighs as I picture myself spread out, a stranger fucking me while Ryan watches.

I end up on Debra's secret blog about the "dangers" of open marriages. Debra, our group's morality police, is the wife of Ryan's college buddy. I smirk at her latest post. For someone so against it, her writing is surprisingly...detailed.

"Dios mío," I mutter, tingling as she describes a guy bending a woman over a table and pulling her hair as he fucks her. Debra should write hotwife erotica instead of pretending to be scandalized.

I giggle, imagining her secretly getting off on this stuff. It distracts me from my own mess of feelings. I was born in Spain and my parents moved to the States when I was six. That Spanish fire in my blood burns bright. The passion, the urge to live fully—it's there, even if I've played it safe most of my life.

I need to stop torturing myself. I'm happy. I have a wonderful husband. That's enough.

Hours later, the smell of paella fills our dining room. Ryan and I sit down to our usual late dinner—a habit from my Spanish roots he's embraced. I sip my wine, steadying my nerves.

"Cariño," I start, voice shaky. "I need to talk to you about something."

Ryan swallows his mouthful. "What's up, love?"

I take a deep breath. "You know how our friends are trying new things in the bedroom?" I watch his face carefully. "Well, Olivia's joined the club. She's a hotwife now."

Ryan's eyes light up. "Wow, that's what—nine of our friends now?"

"Eleven, actually," I blurt. "Not that I'm counting."

Ryan chuckles. "Sure you're not. Well, not everyone will jump on that train. Debra would probably burst into flames if she tried."

I laugh, relaxing. "God, can you imagine? She'd die from the scandal alone."

We both take a few bites, lost in thought, before Ryan speaks up.

"So," he says seriously. "Have you been thinking about being a hotwife?"

A dirty thrill courses through me, making my skin flush with longing. "I...I'm curious. I've gotten the feeling you might be into it. Am I right?"

Ryan's eyes darken. "The thought of watching you with another man is hot as fuck. But only if it's what you want."

"What if it screws us up?" I blurt out.

"We can handle anything, baby. If you want to explore this, we can talk about it."

His words make me buzz with delight. "Really? You wouldn't get jealous?"

Ryan's smile turns wicked. "Jealous? Hell no." He pauses. "Imagining you lost in pleasure, knowing I gave you that freedom...it's crazy hot."

Heat floods my body. A soft moan escapes my lips.

"Fuck," I breathe. "I've fantasized, but hearing you say it..."

Ryan smiles. "I want you to explore your fantasies."

I meet his gaze, nervous and excited. "I'd only do it if you were there. Olivia was alone while Anthony waited, but I'd need you watching. I wouldn't want to do it without you."

He laughs. "Good, baby, because I wouldn't agree unless I could watch...and tell you what to do."

Electricity shoots through me. My husband is a soft dom in the bedroom, but I never imagined he'd want to dominate me with another guy in the room. "You'd like that? Telling me how to please another man?"

"Mmm, yes," Ryan groans. "Watching you follow my commands, being my good little slut..."

My entire body ignites with desire, and my lips part in surprise. I want to be his little slut—no, I want to be his filthy whore being pounded by another guy's cock while he watches.

He grins. "Too much?"

I shake my head, cheeks burning. "No, you know I like it when you talk dirty...you could even be dirtier."

"Hmm, I'll have to remember that," he teases with a twinkle in his eye that makes my mind churn with slutty thoughts. My husband is always up for a challenge when I tell him I want something, so I bet I'm going to get more dirty talk soon.

As we discuss it further, setting boundaries and daydreaming about how we'd work my first hotwife experience, the anticipation builds. It's scary as hell to imagine embracing this wild side but also so fucking hot. I could do this—we could do this.

Later, in bed, my mind races. I think about those blogs, our friend's adventures, even Debra's secret smut. I imagine myself in those scenarios, feel ghost hands on my skin. But always, Ryan is there—watching, guiding, loving me through it all.

I turn to look at my sleeping husband, heart full. Whatever happens next, we're in this together. And that thought, more than anything, is what makes it difficult to fall asleep as I daydream about fucking someone else with my husband's permission.

CHAPTER 2

I smooth down my blue dress, admiring how it hugs my curves as Ryan walks into the bedroom. His blue eyes twinkle with that mischievous look that makes my heart skip a beat.

"Ready for this, baby?" He pulls me close, his hand on my lower back. "Remember, it's just dinner with an old friend. But if you want to test the waters and try a little flirting, go for it. Only if you're comfortable."

My stomach does a flip. I nod, not trusting my voice. When Ryan first suggested inviting Kevin over as a testing ground for flirting with someone safe, I was curious but nervous. Now? I'm a mess of butterflies and what-ifs.

The doorbell rings, and my heart jumps into my throat. I smooth my dress one last time, hyper-aware of how it shows off my body. My hands are clammy, and I try to steady my nerves. Ryan, cool as ever, strolls to the door and swings it open.

And there's Kevin, looking like he stepped out of a damn magazine. His button-up and jeans fit him perfectly. It's been years since we've seen him in person. His cocky smile and those green eyes hit me like a ton of bricks. Fuck. Kevin was supposed to be safe to flirt with, but this feels anything but.

As he steps in, I catch a whiff of his cologne—all woodsy and masculine. It goes straight to my head.

"Nicole." Kevin leans in to kiss my cheek. His lips barely touch me, but it's like he lit a fire inside me. His scent wraps around me, making me dizzy. "You look lovely. It's been too long."

"Thanks," I mumble, praying I don't sound as flustered as I feel. "Welcome back." I catch Ryan watching us, a little smirk on his face. The bastard's enjoying this.

We sit at the dining table, and I can't stop staring at Kevin. His voice rumbles through the room as he and Ryan fall into their old frat boy banter. I laugh along, but honestly? I'm too busy watching Kevin's mouth move, imagining what those lips could do to me. Ryan squeezes my hand under the table, giving me a knowing look.

"So, Kevin," I manage to say, "what made you come back after all this time?"

Kevin's eyes crinkle as he sips his wine. "Well, as much as I loved working overseas, it was time to come home. Got offered a job with a nonprofit here that I couldn't pass up."

Ryan nods. "Always the globetrotter. Remember when you almost missed graduation because you were stuck in Thailand?"

"How could I forget?" Kevin chuckles. "You were freaking out, thinking I'd never make it back in time."

"Hey, my idea to book you on three different flights saved the day." Ryan grins. "Just another example of my brilliant problem-solving skills."

I laugh. "You? The idea man? Well, I guess you do have your moments, *cariño.*"

The pet name slips out, and Ryan pulls me closer. "Oh, come on, baby," he teases, his breath hot on my ear. "You know I'm always coming up with great ideas...and I think you're enjoying one of my ideas right now."

Kevin's laugh fills me with warmth. "Your husband's definitely got a knack for creative solutions."

A thrill runs through me as my heart pounds in my ears. I'm enjoying myself tonight—the tantalizing tease of another man combined with the freedom to flirt makes my head spin.

I can't take my eyes off Kevin. His stories of far-off places and his quiet confidence make him even sexier than I remember. I catch his eyes roaming over me, and there's heat in that look that sets my skin on fire. I glance away, but not before I see his lips quirk up. Fuck, he knows I caught him looking, and that just makes it hotter. Ryan notices the exchange. Instead of jealousy, I see excitement in his eyes. I think my husband is kinkier than I realized.

The night drags on, and the sexual tension is so thick my panties are a wet mess. Kevin's hand brushes mine as we both reach for a napkin, and I swear I feel it in every nerve ending. I'm caught between wanting to jump him and feeling like the worst wife ever for lusting after my husband's friend. It's driving me crazy. But then Ryan catches my eye, gives me that warm smile of his, and I remember this is all part of our journey together.

"So, Nicole," Kevin says, his voice dropping to a sexy rumble. "Ryan tells me you've been exploring some new...interests lately."

I choke on my wine. Fuck. "Oh?" I squeak, trying to play it cool. "What exactly has he told you?"

Kevin's eyes sparkle, like he's enjoying teasing me. "Nothing too wild. Just that you've been...broadening your horizons."

I shoot daggers at Ryan, who's grinning like the cat that ate the canary. My heart's going a mile a minute. How much does Kevin know about our plans?

"Life's an adventure," I mumble, hoping the guys will drop it. They do.

After dinner, Kevin scrapes his chair back. "I should get going," he says, his voice low and husky.

I look up, and his green eyes burn into me. My breath catches. "Of course," I murmur.

He moves closer, and suddenly the room feels like a sauna. My skin prickles with heat. He reaches for my hand, and time slows to a crawl. His fingers brush my palm, sending an electric current through my body.

"Thanks for dinner, Nicole," Kevin murmurs, his thumb tracing circles on the back of my hand. My pulse races like I've just run a marathon.

I swallow hard. "Anytime. Nice seeing you again."

He squeezes my hand, and my face flushes. Our eyes lock, and the look he gives me turns my knees to jelly. The moment stretches on forever. I'm dizzy when he lets go.

"Night, Ryan," Kevin calls out. With one last smoldering look, he's gone.

I stand there, frozen. What the hell just happened? And why am I so turned on?

The door clicks shut, and I let out a shaky breath. I can't even look at Ryan without giving myself away, but Ryan notices. "Someone's all worked up," he teases, backing me against the nearest wall. "Did Kevin get you hot and bothered?"

I open my mouth to deny it, but Ryan's smirk says he knows. He slides his hands under my dress. When he rubs my pussy through my panties, I spread my legs and arch into him.

"Tell me," he growls. "How bad do you want him?"

His finger slips under my panties and brushes my clit. Pleasure jolts through me, and the truth spills out. "So fucking bad, Ryan. His hands, his mouth...god, I'm sorry—"

Ryan cuts me off with a kiss that leaves me gasping. "Don't apologize. Beg me to let you fuck him."

My pussy throbs. The idea of fucking Kevin short-circuits my brain. Even though we're just playing a twisted game, I give it my all.

"Please," I beg, grinding against Ryan's hand. "I need it. I need to feel Kevin inside me while you watch. I want to be your dirty slut. I need to taste him, to do all the things you tell me to do. Please, let me be your naughty slut. Please," I moan.

Ryan growls and crushes his mouth to mine. We tear off each other's clothes. His hands are everywhere, rough and demanding. The cold wall presses against my back as he pins me with his body.

"Admit you're a fucking slut for wanting Kevin," Ryan commands, his fingers sliding into my pussy, teasing me with slow strokes.

"I am, I'm a slut for wanting to fuck your friend," I choke out. "Oh god, I need your cock inside me. Now, Ryan."

He slaps my pussy lightly, and I yelp in surprise.

"I'm going crazy. Please fuck me!"

Ryan lifts my thigh and thrusts into me. He's relentless, fucking me like an animal. Wet slapping sounds and our grunts fill the room.

"You're so wet, baby," Ryan pants. "You love the idea of being a slut, don't you?"

"Yes," I moan, digging my nails into his shoulders. "Your dirty slut. Only yours. Telling me what to do. Please..."

My words send us both into a frenzy. Within moments, we're spiraling together. I cry out, "Ooooh fuck!" as I come, my body shivering against him. He explodes inside me, and the rapture is so intense, I cling to him as waves of bliss turn my mind to mush.

At some point, he picks me up and carries me to the bedroom. When I finally come down from my high, we're on the bed and my head is on his chest while he strokes my hair.

He murmurs, "I've got a confession. I was hoping you'd want to fuck Kevin."

I prop myself up. "What?"

"I thought Kevin would be perfect for your first time."

My head spins. "You want me to actually fuck Kevin?"

"Only if you want," Ryan says. "I trust him. He'd treat you right. And after seeing you two tonight..." He smiles.

My body lights up with pleasure. Jesus, my husband is amazing. I can't keep the happiness from my voice. "I'm agreeable to fucking Kevin."

He laughs. "How about this—we book a weekend getaway and invite Kevin to join us in the hotel room?"

My heart races. "Okay," I whisper. "Let's do it."

As much as the idea of being a hotwife scares me, I also have an overwhelming need to explore this new, naughty side of myself.

It's time to see what being Slut Nicole is like.

CHAPTER 3

I step out of the car, and cold mountain air hits my lungs. Holy shit, those peaks are something else, snow-capped monsters against a clear November sky. I squeeze Ryan's hand, my stomach doing backflips.

"Damn, it's gorgeous," I say. Ryan plants a kiss on my temple.

"Not as gorgeous as you," he smiles. "C'mon, let's check in."

The lobby's all rustic chic—warm wood, stone, and this huge-ass antler chandelier. Ryan handles the check-in while I fidget like a teenager before prom night. My heart's racing, and I can't decide if I'm more excited or terrified.

"What d'you think?" Ryan asks once we're alone in the hallway and heading to our room.

"It's amazing," I gush. "Like we've stumbled into a fancy mountain hideaway."

Our room's towards the back of the lodge, and sweet baby Jesus, it's incredible. The carpet is thick enough my feet sink into it, and the king-size bed looks so plush I want to dive in face-first. The floor-to-ceiling windows show off the wilderness.

"Ryan, look at this view!" I'm practically glued to the windows. He wraps his arms around me from behind, and I melt into him.

"Pretty sweet," he agrees. "But wait'll you see the deck."

He leads me out, and there it is: a sunken hot tub, steam rising like it's begging us to jump in. The view of the snowy mountains is unreal. I can already picture us soaking while the sun sets.

"This is perfect," I breathe, turning to face him.

His blue eyes are sparkling with that 'I'm about to get lucky' look. He pulls me in for a kiss that makes my toes curl. When we come up for air, he rests his forehead on mine. "How're you feeling about all this?"

I take a second to really think about it. "Excited," I admit. "Kinda scared, too. It's getting real now." I pause, gnawing on my lip. "Are we crazy for doing this?"

Ryan rubs my back, and it's like he's smoothing out all my worries. "We don't have to do anything, okay? You can change your mind at any moment. This weekend's about having fun, but only if you're one hundred percent down for it."

God, I love this man. I shove my doubts aside. "I know, and I am down. I want this. I want to see what it's like, with you right there with me."

I really want to see what Slut Nicole will do. I'm hoping I can relax enough to let her out. But I keep telling myself that even if I can't fully relax, tonight will still be fun. No one said the first time had to be the best.

We unpack, and with every minute that ticks by, the tension ratchets up. Kevin will be here soon, and just thinking about it makes me tingle all over. I'm hanging up a dress when Ryan calls out, "Hey, baby? Got you a little something for tonight."

I turn around and he's holding a gift box, grinning like the cat that ate the canary. Inside is the sexiest bikini I've ever seen, deep red with gold bits that'll look amazing against my olive skin.

I run my fingers over the silky material. "Wow, it's gorgeous."

"Thought you might wear it in the hot tub later," he says, his voice a low, sexy growl.

The idea sends a jolt straight between my legs. "Hell yeah."

I duck into the bathroom to try it on, and when I catch my reflection, I barely recognize myself. My cheeks are flushed, my eyes wide and bright. When I step out, Ryan's sharp intake of breath is all the validation I need.

"Damn, I love it," I purr, doing a little spin. "You chose well. You sure you want to share me?"

Ryan's eyes are all over me. "Oh yeah, you look fucking edible. Kevin's gonna lose his mind."

We laugh, and there's this electric undercurrent between us, a new excitement that wasn't there before. That more than anything is going to make tonight worth it.

Let the hotwife fun begin.

CHAPTER 4

The hot tub is ready for us, and I've thrown on a silky robe over the bikini. I'm hyper-aware of how little I'm wearing underneath. My heart's pounding so hard I swear Ryan can hear it.

Just as the sun starts to dip behind the mountains, there's a knock on the door. Ryan and I lock eyes, having one of those silent conversations. This is it. The moment of truth.

I take a deep breath and move to answer the door, Ryan right behind me. My hand hovers over the handle for a split second before I turn it, revealing Kevin in all his rugged glory. My heart does a little flip. He's all lean muscle and charm, those green eyes roaming over me like I'm a snack he can't wait to devour.

"Well, hello there," Kevin drawls. His voice hits me low in the gut. "Don't you two look cozy?"

Ryan's hand finds the small of my back. It's grounding, reminding me we're in this together. The warmth of his touch makes my skin tingle.

"Come on in, man," Ryan says, casual as hell, but I can tell by his voice that my husband is just as excited as I am.

Kevin steps inside, and that same cologne he was wearing the other night engulfs me—woodsy and sexy. We hug, and his hands linger on my hips. I'm suddenly all fluttery hands, trying to cover my nerves by offering drinks.

"Gracias, Nicole," Kevin winks, taking a glass of ice water. The Spanish makes me melt a little.

We'd previously decided to not drink tonight, despite the idea of some liquid courage helping. But Ryan said if we can't do this sober, we shouldn't be doing it, and I have to agree with him. Tomorrow morning, I want to know that I made all my choices tonight without anything dulling my senses. Somehow that makes what I'm doing naughtier.

We chat, and it feels weirdly normal. But I can't ignore the king-sized bed looming in my peripheral vision. A constant reminder of why we're really here.

"So," Kevin says, eyes darting between us. "I hear there's a hot tub with our name on it."

My stomach does a somersault. This is it. I look at Ryan, finding nothing but love and encouragement in those blue eyes of his.

"What do you say, baby?" Ryan asks. "Shall we show Kevin the view?"

I nod, not trusting my voice. We step out onto the deck, and the mountain air makes me shiver. The hot tub bubbles invitingly, steam rising into the twilight.

Kevin whistles low. "Now that's what I call a setup." He turns to me, gaze intense. "Care to join me, Nicole?"

I untie my robe with shaky hands, letting it pool at my feet. The lust in Kevin's eyes as he takes in the red bikini gives me a zip of pleasure.

"Damn," Kevin murmurs, eyes dark with desire. "You're a lucky man, Ryan."

"Don't I know it," Ryan replies, voice thick.

The men change into swim shorts, and all three of us slip into the four-person hot tub. I'm hyper-aware of every point of contact. Kevin's thigh brushes mine, sending sparks through my body.

For a moment, we just soak in silence, tension building like a rubber band about to snap. Then Kevin's hand finds my knee under the water, and I gasp.

"Is this okay?" His voice is husky.

"Yes."

Once he has my permission, his hand traces circles on my thigh, driving me crazy. I turn to Ryan, seeking...something. He smiles softly, nodding. In that silent exchange, I see his complete trust and love.

That's all it takes. I turn back to Kevin, and suddenly his lips are on mine. The kiss is nothing like Ryan's familiar touch. Kevin kisses like he's trying to devour me, his tongue demanding entrance. I moan into his mouth, hands tangling in his hair.

Kevin's hands roam my body, cupping my breasts through the thin bikini top. My nipples harden under his touch, and I arch into him, wanting more.

"Fuck, you're gorgeous," Kevin growls against my lips. He pulls back, eyes wild. "I want to taste you. All of you."

Part of me is shocked at how different he is from Ryan. But a larger part of me is thrilled, eager for the chance to explore something new.

Kevin lifts me out of the water, setting me on the edge of the hot tub. The cool air hits my wet skin, making me shiver. But then his hot mouth is trailing kisses down my stomach. The contrast between the cold deck and his warm lips is dizzying.

"Lean back, baby," Ryan commands, and I shoot a glance at my husband. Oh fuck, he did say he wanted to tell me what to do. When I obey, Kevin's fingers hook into my bikini bottoms, slowly peeling them off.

Kevin spreads my legs and admires the Brazilian wax I got in preparation for this weekend. He hums in appreciation as he pulls my pussy lips apart, and I try to embrace the vulnerability of being exposed. It's a heady feeling.

It's been years since anyone but my husband has touched me like this, but that's what makes this so amazing. Kevin buries his head between my legs, and his tongue laves my clit. I moan with delight and rock my hips. Oooh, even his tongue feels different. It's broader, and when he licks, it's like he's tasting every inch of me.

"So sweet," he murmurs, and then he's licking me like he's a starving man.

A soft pleasure radiates throughout my body as my head spins. There's nothing I can grab to keep myself grounded. I fist my hands in my hair and rock against his face as the bliss swirls in my core. Oh god, oh fuck, I wasn't expecting him to go down on me. His tongue works me into a frenzy, and all I can do is moan continuously as he increases the pressure of his tongue.

When he slides two fingers inside me and massages my cave wall, electrical shocks run through my body. The pleasure coils in my stomach as my thigh muscles quiver. I'm going to come soon.

I'm dimly aware of Ryan watching us, and the knowledge that my husband is seeing me like this, spread out and wanton under another man's touch, only heightens my arousal.

"Oh, *Dios mío.*" My hips buck against Kevin's face. "Don't stop, don't stop!"

Kevin chuckles against me, the vibrations sending shockwaves through my body. "I'm going to make you come like this. You want that, don't you? To come all over my face while your husband watches?"

I love the dirty talk, and it pushes me closer to the edge.

"That's it, baby," Ryan says, his voice thick with arousal. "Let go and come for us."

It's Ryan's encouragement that finally does it for me. I come with a cry that echoes around the deck, my body convulsing with delight as my pussy clenches around Kevin's fingers. Kevin doesn't let up, lapping at me until I'm trembling and oversensitive.

As I come down from my high, Kevin pulls me back into the hot tub, cradling me against his chest. The warm water envelops me, soothing my over-sensitized skin.

"Wow," I breathe, still shaky. "That was..."

"Just the beginning," Kevin finishes for me, his voice promising so much more.

Ryan clears his throat, amusement in his eyes. "As hot as that was, maybe we should take this inside before the neighbors call down to reception and complain."

We all laugh, breaking some of the tension, even as my face flushes beat red. Oh no, was I really that loud? As we climb out of the hot tub, I catch Ryan's eye. In that moment, a thousand words pass between us silently. I see his love, his desire, his complete acceptance of what's happening. But I also catch a flicker of something else—a hint of possessiveness, perhaps? It fills me with a warmth that has nothing to do with the hot tub.

Kevin wraps me in a fluffy towel, his touch lingering on my shoulders. "Shall we continue this party inside?" he asks, voice low and seductive.

I nod, more eager now to get his cock inside me—if it's even possible to be more eager. As we step back into the hotel room, I feel a shift in the energy. The initial nervousness is gone, replaced by pure lust. The time in the hot tub and my orgasm opened the floodgates of desire.

Kevin wastes no time. As soon as the door closes behind us, he's on me, his lips crashing against mine in a searing kiss. He pulls my bikini top off as his hands roam my body, leaving trails of fire in their wake. I moan into his mouth, pressing myself against him.

Ryan takes a seat in the armchair by the bed. There's something incredibly erotic about having him watch, knowing he's getting off on seeing me with another man.

When Ryan speaks, I'm almost surprised. "I want to see her suck your cock."

My heart skips a beat at his command, and I drop to my knees in front of Kevin. Mmm, I'll suck his cock for my husband. I look up at Kevin through my lashes as I pull his swim trunks down slowly. HIs cock is thick with prominent veins that make my mouth water.

I lean forward, my lips parting. I stop when my mouth is almost touching him. Teasing, I blow a stream of air on the tip, and Kevin groans. He moves his hands into my hair and forces me onto his cock. God, why do I love being controlled so much? As he slides into my mouth, I swirl my tongue around the head. He tastes salty and earthy, and I moan at the flavor. It's been so long since I've sucked a cock that wasn't Ryan's I was afraid I wouldn't like it...but news flash, I'm just a slut for cock.

I look over at Ryan, and our eyes meet. A bolt of lust shoots through me when I realize he's got his cock out, his hand wrapped around the shaft, stroking slowly. He didn't say he would touch himself while he watched, but I'm 100 percent down with this. Oooh, maybe I can suck on him while Kevin fucks me and call it a threesome?

"That's it, baby," he encourages, his voice strained with arousal. "Show him what that mouth can do."

Fueled by Ryan's words, I take Kevin deeper, hollowing my cheeks as I suck. Kevin's hands tangle in my hair, guiding my motions. I relax my jaw, allowing him to set the pace, to use my mouth for his pleasure. Spit leaks out the corners of my mouth, and as Kevin's cock hits the back of my throat, tears well up in my eyes. A gurgling sound comes from my throat, but he doesn't let up. He fucks my face with a single-minded intensity, chasing his own release.

When my gaze connects with Ryan's again, he's got a hungry look in his eyes and a need for control. If we're being honest, I crave him telling me what to do tonight, even if it means Kevin treating me like a whore. It's taboo and hot as fuck, and my entire body buzzes. I'm ready for whatever they want to do to me.

Eventually, Kevin pulls out of my mouth. "Lie back on the bed," he tells me, "and spread your legs. I'm not done with you yet." He looks up at my husband. "I'd say she's more than ready. Can I?"

Ryan growls. "Make her scream."

I whimper as Kevin cups my breast and plays with my nipple, pinching and rolling it between his fingers. He teases and explores my body, getting to know every curve and dip. While Kevin plays with my breasts, Ryan stands by the bed, his hand pumping his length at a slow, steady pace, his eyes never leaving my body.

I'm panting, squirming as Kevin works me over, and ready to beg him to fuck me by the time he finally settles between my legs. He positions himself at my entrance, rubbing the tip of his cock along my wetness.

Just when I think he's about to enter me, he stops. "You want this?"

"Yes," I breathe, arching my hips. "Please. Fuck me."

With a groan, Kevin presses inside me—and oh my god, the stretch is sublime. I moan and roll my hips, encouraging him to move. He starts a slow rhythm, his strokes deep and deliberate.

I plant my feet on the mattress and try to rock against him to get him to fuck me faster. I want him to pound into me and use me. If this is my only chance at fucking another guy, I want it rough and wild.

At some point, Kevin reaches between us, and his thumb finds my clit. He rubs it in tight circles in time with his thrusts, sending jolts of pleasure through my body. Ryan catches my gaze again, and the heat in his eyes is overwhelming. He's completely hard, and his movements are precise and measured. I can tell he's edging, drawing out the pleasure, savoring the sight of me writhing under Kevin.

"My slut is such a good slut," Ryan groans, and my stomach clenches at his words. Oh fuck, my husband is debasing me, and I love it. "My little whore likes to hear how pretty she looks taking another guy's cock, don't you?"

The word "whore" sizzles my brain. I didn't know he had it in him. I can only moan in response as he continues.

"Her greedy hole needed to be filled. If you hadn't fucked her, she would've begged me to bring someone else back to the hotel. Isn't that right, my sweet little whore?"

My pulse speeds up, and the tension in my body builds. Who is this man and what did he do with my husband? If this type of experience brings the filthy side out in Ryan, I'll fuck a whole football team while he watches. Maybe in the future, he'll tell me to dress up like a slut and go find someone to bring home. As I contemplate the possibility, my toes curl.

My moans grow louder as Kevin fucks me furiously. I'm trembling as he jackhammers into me. My head swirls, and I get the insane thought that I've never felt so alive or so free while being controlled by my husband and fucking another guy.

The thought is enough to make me come. "Ohhh, fuck," I scream out, not caring if the room next of us can hear, as pure joy ripples from my fingers to my toes.

Kevin doesn't stop his relentless thrusts, and grunts, "She is a hungry little slut, isn't she?"

Ryan sits down on the bed next to my head, his hard cock level with my mouth. "She is. And I'm going to feed her until she's full."

For some reason, I'm not surprised he needs me to suck on him, and I'm vibrating with happiness that I get to take both men at once. I open my mouth, and he guides his length inside. Mmmm, delicious. The familiar taste and scent of his cock fill my senses, and a jolt of bliss runs through my body as Ryan holds on to the headboard so he can drill into my mouth.

Watching me suck on my husband makes Kevin go wild. He speeds up, pistoning in and out of me. Having both men using me, sends shockwaves of ecstasy rippling through my body. I'm their fucktoy to use.

"You're such a little whore," Ryan breathes. "Look at how wide you're spread. Taking two cocks." He doesn't expect an answer—not that I could respond with his cock in my throat. "Such a pretty slut."

As Ryan's movements become more erratic, I know he's close. His eyes are locked on where Kevin is stretching me. A sense of power engulfs me and my body ripples with pleasure from knowing that they want me—and that even though they're the ones using me, I gave them permission. I'm really the one in control.

"Fuck, Nicole," Ryan groans. "I'm going to come." His cock twitches, and then he's filling my throat with his warm cum. I moan around his cock, greedily swallowing every drop.

When he's finished, I keep sucking, desperate to get every last drop. I love the taste of his cum. So delicious. He leaves his cock in my mouth until it starts to soften. When he pulls out, I open my mouth, sticking out my tongue to show him and Kevin that I swallowed everything.

Kevin suddenly stops fucking me and pulls out. Wait, he didn't come yet? Jesus, he's a machine.

He rolls me onto my stomach, and even though I've had multiple orgasms, the anticipation for more pleasure makes me moan. A moment later, his cock is pressing against my entrance again. He drapes his body over mine, his weight pinning me to the bed. I can smell the musky scent of our arousal as he slides into me.

His thrusts are shallow at first but quickly gain momentum. With each thrust, the head of his cock bumps against a pleasurable spot deep inside me, and I mewl with delight. Holy fuck, I'm going to come again!

I chant, "Yes," as waves of ecstasy crash over me. The pings of bliss shoot from my core all the way to the tips of my fingers and toes. Kevin keeps fucking me through my orgasm. The only sounds in the room are the soft squeak of the bed, my moans, and his harsh breathing as he chases his pleasure.

Ryan is sitting next to me on the bed, and he leans down, whispering, "Such a good girl." His lips brush the spot behind my ear that he knows I love. "Taking two cocks like a filthy fucktoy." The words make me whimper and clench my pussy tighter.

Kevin slams into me harder as his movements become more urgent. "I'm so close," he grunts, pounding into me. "You're so fucking tight. Your pussy feels incredible."

All I can do is moan and push back against him, meeting him thrust for thrust. When his cock swells, he lets out a strangled groan as he spills his hot seed deep inside me. A few more whacks against my pussy, and then he collapses on top of me.

For a moment, the room is silent, save for the sounds of our labored breaths. Then Kevin stirs, propping himself up on his elbow. "Fuck, that was great. You're wonderful."

A lazy, satisfied smile curves my lips as Kevin rolls off me, and I stay splayed out on the bed, relishing the bone-deep satisfaction that comes from multiple orgasms. Ryan kisses my cheek softly. "Such a good little fucktoy. Now just relax."

The filthy words make me smile in my post-orgasmic haze. I am a good fucktoy.

Chapter 5

When I wake up, my head is resting on Ryan's chest and sunlight is filtering in through the window. A quick glance at the clock on the nightstand tells me it's a little past eight a.m. But a hot tub, numerous orgasms, and a good night's sleep did wonders for my energy levels. I'm ready to face the day and fuck my husband. I need his cock.

As I cuddle against Ryan, I realize Kevin is gone. He must have left after I fell asleep. I trace lazy patterns on Ryan's chest and watch his cock stir. Is he awake? I peek at his face. His eyes are closed but his breathing is uneven. Oh yeah, he's awake and he's waiting to see what I do. Well, he can wake up a happy man.

Ryan's cock is now fully erect, and I like the idea of riding my sleepy husband. After last night, I want to service him. I slip out from under his arm and straddle him. Ryan groans, and I bite back a smile. Once I position myself over his cock, I slide down easily, taking him fully inside me in one smooth motion. His length stretches and fills me, and it feels so deliciously naughty to have my husband's cock in me again after fucking someone else last night. Slowly, I start to move, rolling my hips in a steady rhythm, savoring the sensation of his familiarity as he slides in and out of me.

"Baby," Ryan murmurs, his voice rough and his hands reaching to grasp my hips, guiding me as I rise and fall. "I...fuck."

"Just enjoy," I whisper, leaning down to plant a soft kiss on his lips. His mouth moves against mine, a low moan rumbling in his chest. Shit, he feels so good. Just the right amount of stretch, his rhythm, everything is perfect. It's more than just the physical sensations though. There's a deeper connection between us.

After a few moments, I lean back and increase my tempo, bracing my hands on his thighs as I grind down harder, taking him even deeper. My breasts bounce with each movement, and I'm aware of the delicious friction building between us, coiling in the pit of my stomach.

"Good girl," he pants and grasps my hips. "Ride my cock."

I let go and surrender to the pleasure that's coursing through me. The sound of our bodies slapping together fills the room, punctuated by our gasps and moans. We're both hurtling towards the edge.

Finally, Ryan's hips buck up, and he pulses inside me, filling me with ropes of sticky cum. I imagine it mixing with Kevin's from last night, and I explode. I ride the waves of bliss, crying out, "Oh, my god, oh, my god" over and over. The ecstasy seems never ending.

When I finally collapse onto his chest, I'm breathing hard. Ryan wraps his arms around me, holding me close. "Good morning," he says softly, a smile in his voice.

"Good morning," I echo him, my heart so full. "I love you," I whisper, looking up at him. "Thank you for last night."

"Anything for you," he replies, his eyes shining with sincerity. "I love you too. I'm glad this was a good experience."

"Um..." My body hums with pleasure, and I blush at what I'm about to ask. "Would you ever want to do this again?"

Ryan's eyebrows lift, and he licks his lip. "Let you fuck another guy, or have a threesome?"

"Hmm, both?" I'm almost afraid of his answer in case it's not what I want to hear.

Ryan nuzzles my hair. "Honestly, I've never been as turned on as I was last night. You know how I feel about seeing you come. But you taking another man's cock...shit, it was incredible."

My body lights up at his words as he continues. "It was so hot hearing your adorable, slutty noises. Seeing your pretty lips stretched around his cock like a hungry slut. Because that's what you are, aren't you?"

"Your whore," I whisper, giving myself a thrill at calling myself a whore.

He pushes me onto my back and covers me. He's hard again, and as his cock sinks into me, he asks, "Hmm, tell me. Did his cock feel good in this tight cunt of mine?"

Holy fuck, my filthy-talking husband is back. His words make me shudder, and I cry out, "Yes!"

As he fucks me harder, I know two things for certain: one, we're spending the day in bed, and two, at some point, I'm going to fuck another guy again.

I love my life.

CHAPTER 6

My phone screeches, shattering the peaceful Monday morning. I groan, pawing at the nightstand. Ryan grunts and burrows deeper under the covers. Lucky bastard.

I blink at the screen. Three-day weekend, thank fuck. No work today. But it's Debra calling. Just what I need after a mind-blowing weekend of sexual exploration—a heaping dose of judgment.

"Hello?" My voice comes out like sandpaper.

"Nicole! Oh, thank God." Debra's voice hits that pitch only dogs should hear. "We need to talk. It's an emergency."

I bolt upright. "What's wrong? Everyone okay?"

"No! I mean, yes, but our friend group...it's imploding!" Debra wails. "Did you hear about Olivia? She's gone to the dark side too! It's just you and me left, Nicole. We're the last bastions of morality in this cesspool!"

I bite my cheek, choking back laughter. If only she knew what Ryan and I had been up to all weekend. My pussy aches at the memory.

"Anyway," Debra barrels on, "I've found the solution. Sanctity of Marriage convention next month in Vegas. We should go. Show solidarity in our commitment to traditional values. You in?"

I glance at Ryan's sleeping form, his face buried in his pillow. The weekend changed everything. "About that, Debra..."

"What?" Her voice has an edge that tells me she suspects what I'm about to say.

"Well..." I drawl, unable to keep the smirk out of my voice. "Let's just say I had a very...educational weekend."

I swear I can hear Debra's brain short-circuiting as the silence stretches.

"Nicole, please tell me you're kidding."

"Nope." I pop the 'p'. "Turns out, I'm quite the slut. Who knew?"

Debra makes a sound like a stepped-on squeaky toy. "But...but...you were supposed to be the good one! My partner in righteousness!"

I lose it and have to cover my laughter with a coughing fit. So much has changed in the last few days. She's quiet until I can speak again. "Sorry to burst your bubble, Deb. But damn, the view from the dark side is fucking spectacular."

"This is a disaster," Debra moans. "What am I supposed to do now? I can't go to the convention alone."

A wicked idea hits me. "You know, if you're curious about the lifestyle..."

"I'm not," she insists. "Vincent and I are perfectly happy with our van—I mean, traditional...oh, forget it!"

The line goes dead. I stare at my phone before dissolving into giggles.

Ryan stirs and rolls on his side. "What's so funny?" he mumbles, voice thick with sleep.

I curl up against him, still chuckling. "Oh, nothing. Just enjoying being a bad influence on Debra. And thank fuck for long weekends, right?"

As Ryan pulls me close, his morning wood presses against my ass. I wiggle against him to tease him, and I can't help but wonder how long before Debra's curiosity wins out. After all, if I can embrace my inner slut in one weekend, anything's possible.

The End

December Hotwife

Hotwife of the Month Club 12

Lacey Cross

CHAPTER 1

The snow picks up just as Vincent pulls into the parking lot. I burrow deeper into my coat, trying to ignore the growing distance between us. He should be coming with me to this marriage convention, not dropping me off like some teenager catching a bus for camp—this sucks.

I'd chosen to take the bus instead of driving myself, trusting the weather forecast and banking on a professional driver's ability to handle the snow. Now, watching the white flakes thicken in the air, I wonder if I'd made the right choice.

Vincent sits there silently, one hand on the wheel, the other tapping out some rhythm on his thigh. Typical.

"Couldn't they pick somewhere closer for the bus to leave from?" I grumble, tucking my scarf around my neck. The wool scratches me, but hey, at least it's a distraction from my internal mess of emotions.

Vincent glances my way, his brown eyes unreadable. "No one is forcing you to go, Deb."

He's right, but his tone—all calm and neutral—makes me want to scream. Always the peacekeeper, even when it's just us. I used to say his unflappable attitude was a balm to my unsettled thoughts, but lately I wish he'd show some real passion for something—especially me.

"I need to go," I sigh. "Everyone is tossing their vows in the trash these days…" I trail off, my mind drifting to our friends Marilyn and James. This is all their fault. Marilyn just had to go out and sleep with someone other than her husband, and then James spilled the beans during a boys' trip to Lake Aspen. All the guys from college—the same frat, still so close—listened intently, and now it seems every couple in our circle is experimenting with this hotwife lifestyle after hearing how great James said it was. It's all spiraling out of control.

"Uh-huh," Vincent says, still tapping away. "While you're there, maybe you could—"

"Don't." The word comes out sharper than I meant, but I can't help it.

His fingers pause for a split second before resuming their annoying tap-tap-tap. "I wasn't picking a fight, Deb. I just thought maybe you could use this time to think. About us. What we need. You're clearly not happy."

Yeah, I'm not happy because my husband wants me to be a slut. I bite my tongue, holding back the flood of words threatening to spill out. Not now. Not when I need to catch the bus.

I grab the door handle and open it. The cold air bites as I climb out. "I know exactly what we need," I say, my voice clipped. "This convention will remind people what marriage is supposed to be about. You'll see."

"Have a good trip, Deb. And just think about us, okay?" He doesn't argue or follow me out to help with my luggage.

"I don't need to think about it," I huff, slamming the door. The snow muffles the sound, which is annoying. I wanted that slam to echo.

Shit, he must really be upset with me. Usually, he'd insist on carrying my bags, but today he just watches from the car as I drag them toward the waiting bus. The driver loads them underneath while I climb aboard, and I'm hit by a wall of heat. The inside smells like leather, men's cologne, and…is that garlic bread?

I yank off my gloves and look around…oh, shit.

I'm the only woman here.

The small charter bus is packed with guys, all college aged and fit. They're goofing around like they own the place. Some are glued to their phones, others are sprawled across seats. What is this, a party bus to Vegas for Christmas break?

As I move to my seat, I notice their eyes following me, and I get a tiny thrill. Something in those looks makes my stomach flutter—if I didn't know better, I'd think they were checking me out. But that's ridiculous. Sure, I check all the basic boxes—blonde, slim—but I've never been the kind of woman who turns heads. I'm the one who overthinks everything, who can't just relax and be in the moment. The wallflower who watches everyone else shine.

The worst part is how much I hate caring about this stuff. Vincent loves me, and that should be enough. But then I see someone like my friend Olivia work her magic—the way conversation dies when she passes by, how naturally she commands attention—and that familiar ache creeps in. I want to know what it feels like to walk into a room and have people whisper about how lucky Vincent is. Instead, I'm trapped in this endless cycle of comparison, measuring myself against women like her and always coming up short. It's not that any of them are trying to make me feel insecure—it's more that I want to feel as sexy as Vincent tells me I am.

So these men definitely aren't admiring me. I sink deeper into my seat and catch bits of their chatter.

"Dude, Vegas won't know what hit it!"

"You know it. Got that list ready?"

"List? What, like a bucket list? Planning to die there or something?"

"Dude, we gotta keep it lowkey though," one of them says, his tone half-joking, half-serious. "Coach Martinez will kill us if anything gets back to him."

"Yeah, no kidding," another chimes in. "Last thing the soccer team needs is another scandal."

My ears perk up at that. Soccer team? I glance over at them, trying to be subtle. It explains why they're all fit.

"For real though, we should probably set some ground rules. No strip clubs, no gambling away our scholarship money..."

"Speak for yourself, man. I'm planning to come back a millionaire!"

Their growing amusement has me questioning what chaos a team of college athletes could create in Sin City.

This is definitely going to be a long ride. But my eyes drift back to the guy who made the bucket list joke. I can't help it. His dark hair has a little curl at the ends, softening his sharp jaw. He's lounging in his seat like he's the king of the bus. There's something about him, an energy. And when he laughs? God, it's rich and confident.

I bet he'd know how to take charge in the bedroom.

My face burns at the thought. What the hell, Debra?

I whip out my phone, scrolling through emails I don't give a shit about. My mind's racing, replaying yet another infuriating non-fight with Vincent. That's our whole marriage in a nutshell—me getting worked up while he floats above it all like some zen master. Ten years of marriage and we've never had a real fight because he won't engage. He just stands there with that serene expression, making me feel like I'm being unreasonable without ever actually saying it. It's maddening. And now this crazy thing he just said...

At dinner last week, I mentioned how Ryan and Nicole had become the latest casualties in our friend group's obsession with open marriages.

"Yeah, she's a hotwife now," Vincent said casually, as if commenting on the weather.

My fork stopped halfway to my mouth. "You knew about this?"

He shrugged. "Ryan talked about it."

"Well, maybe you should spend less time gossiping with your buddies," I snapped, knowing I didn't really mean what I was saying, but it was like the crankiest version of myself had taken control of my mouth. "This hotwife trend is completely irresponsible. It's just another sign of how polyamory is destroying relationships these days."

I expected him to agree. He usually does—or says he does. But he just shrugged again. "Don't you think you're being a bit harsh?"

"Harsh?" I practically screeched. "It's cheating, Vincent. How is that not harsh?"

"It's not cheating if they talk about it in advance," he said, coolly. "And honestly? I think it's kind of interesting. If you wanted to try it, I'd say yes."

His words were like a slap. I stared at him while my mind raced—a mix of anger, betrayal, and something else. Something I didn't want to name. I lashed out, throwing every argument I could think of at him. But deep down? There was this flicker of curiosity—unwanted and definitely unwelcome.

I shake my head. Can't think about that now. Won't.

This damn bus is suffocating. The guys are still at it, their voices booming with joy. Their energy exhausts me. I stare out the window again, watching the snow blur everything. It's really coming down now.

But even as I watch the storm outside, I can't escape the one inside me. What am I doing here? Why does a part of me— the part I've spent years burying—suddenly feel like it's waking up?

And why in the hell did Vincent have to tell me he'd let me be a hotwife if I wanted?

CHAPTER 2

Two hours later and I'm not sure if I'm in heaven or hell. I'm trapped in here with a sea of fit bodies that is making me lightheaded. Their spicy cologne wafts back to my seat, and I'm distracted by every stretch and each casual flex from the guys. What the hell is wrong with me? I'm on my way to a conference about defending traditional marriage. I'm not supposed to be fantasizing about these sinfully hot college guys.

But sweet Jesus, it's impossible to focus on anything else. The bucket list jokester—Liam, I heard them call him—keeps drawing my attention. His curly hair falls just right across his forehead, and there's a tattoo teasing from beneath the short sleeve of his T-shirt. When he laughs, he tips his head back in a way that makes me imagine trailing my fingers down his throat. I force myself to look away, only to land on an equally distracting sight—two men locked in an arm-wrestling match. The way their forearms bulge... I shift in my seat, trying to ignore the heat building between my legs.

I close my eyes, hoping to block out the temptation, but it only makes things worse. My mind conjures up images of Liam's face buried in my neck, kissing and nibbling, while multiple sets of strong arms surround me—touching every inch of my body.

I snap my eyes open—holy fuck, I need to stop this. Guilt washes over me as I think of Vincent. For months, I've been running a secret blog, warning about the dangers of the hotwife lifestyle. Sure, sometimes my posts strayed into steamy territory when describing tempting scenarios, but that was just to illustrate the risks, right? Now this trip is proving exactly why it's all so dangerous for marriages. Vincent should be the only man I think about. I snatch my phone from my purse, needing something—anything—to quiet my racing thoughts, and I see a message from him.

Vincent:

> Hope the ride's going okay. Love you.

My throat tightens. How can he be so loving when he basically suggested I sleep with other men? I type out a cranky response, delete it before I send it, and try again.

Debra:

> It's fine. Stuck on a bus with a bunch of college boys. Fun times.

His reply comes quickly.

Vincent:

> Sounds like an adventure. Try to enjoy it. Maybe make some new friends?

He ends it with a winking face.

Is he serious? Before I can respond, another message pops up.

Vincent:

> I'm just kidding. But try to relax. I love you, no matter what.

I let out a shaky breath. I'm not sure if I'm annoyed or comforted by his words—maybe a little of both. Suddenly, the memory of a conversation with Marilyn comes to mind. We were having coffee last winter, and she was showing off a delicate golden anklet.

"It's from James," she'd said, her eyes sparkling. "When I wear it, it means I'm available to other men."

I'd been scandalized then, but now...Now I imagine Vincent fastening a similar one around my ankle. The metal would be a constant reminder of a world of possibility.

I shake my head to clear the image. This is ridiculous. I'm here to stand up for traditional marriage, not...whatever this is. But as I look out at the swirling snow, I wonder... am I really happy with my life?

Boisterous chuckling grabs my attention. That Liam guy is now sprawled across two seats, regaling his friends with some story. There's something magnetic about him, a dominant presence.

Suddenly, the bus lurches violently, metal groaning as the back wheels lose their grip on the icy road. Time slows as we slide sideways, and my stomach drops with that horrible weightless feeling of impending disaster.

In that moment of pure terror, only one thought crashes through my mind—if something happens to me, Vincent will always think I'm unhappy with our marriage. The truth is so far from that, and the idea of leaving him with that doubt makes me feel sick in a way that has nothing to do with the skidding bus.

The driver finally wrestles control back. My heart's still pounding when he speaks over the intercom, announcing we'll have to stop at a nearby inn due to the worsening storm.

While everyone groans about the unexpected delay, I'm still shaking, that moment of clarity echoing in my head. I pull out my phone to message Vincent. I should only tell him about the delay, but near-death experiences have a way of stripping away pretenses. My fingers move across the screen almost of their own accord.

Debra:

> I need to tell you something. I've been jealous. Of Marilyn, of Nicole, of all of them. I'm sorry I've been such a bitch about it. The truth is I'm curious about being a hotwife. Not that I'd ever do it! But I can't stop thinking about it. Is that awful?

His response takes forever. Or maybe it's just a minute. Finally, my phone buzzes.

Vincent:

> It's not awful at all. I love you. We can talk more when you get back. And hey, if you want to practice flirting in Vegas, I won't object.

I read the message three times, tears pricking at my eyes. How did I get so lucky?

While the bus travels the last few, slow miles to the inn, I fill Vincent in on my unplanned stop. According to the bus driver, the weather is going to clear tomorrow so we should only need to be here one night.

The bus finally pulls into a small parking lot in front of a quaint inn. As we file off the bus, snowflakes immediately cling to my eyelashes, and I blink rapidly.

"Need a hand?"

It's Liam. He's even more attractive up close. I feel my face flush and I'm tongue tied

"I'm fine, thanks," I croak out, but he's already lifting my bag.

"I insist. I'm Liam, by the way. Though you probably gathered that from all the yelling on the bus."

"Debra," I reply, wishing I actually remembered how to flirt so I could practice on him.

Our arms graze each other, and my skin prickles with sudden awareness. This is dangerous territory.

Inside, the inn is warm and rustic. A modest Christmas tree adorns the corner, its twinkling lights casting a soft glow over the room. Garlands of pine and holly adorn the wooden beams overhead. The innkeeper explains that they don't have enough rooms for everyone so the team will have to sleep on cots in the recreation room. Luckily, they have a private room available for me.

The innkeeper passes me the key, and I turn to retrieve my bag from Liam. When he hands it over, our fingers brush. The brief contact makes my skin tingle, and I have to force myself to step back.

"Have a good night, Debra," he says softly. "You know, if you get lonely up there all by yourself, I'd be more than happy to keep you company."

"I...that's..." The words tangle in my throat.

Liam smiles. "Just a thought. Sweet dreams...or not-so-sweet, if you prefer." He winks.

I finally manage to speak. "Have a good night."

I hurry to my room like there's a demon chasing me. As soon as the door is closed, I drop my bags and slump against the solid wood. I unzip my coat, and my pulse quickens when I trail my hands down my body. I cup my breasts and imagine Liam's mouth sucking on my nipples. I finally allow myself to experience all the emotions I have been suppressing—the desires, the curiosity, the restless urge for something more.

My eyes drift to my boots, hiding my ankles—I wish I had a pretty anklet and the confidence to flirt without second-guessing every word.

Tomorrow I'll be in Vegas at a conference full of safe people, far away from Liam and temptation. But tonight? Tonight I let my mind wander down the what-if path. What if I took Vincent up on his offer of being a hotwife? What would happen if I stopped being the good girl and explored this side of myself?

Maybe it's time to stop fighting these urges and see where they lead. After all, what happens in Vegas...

We might not be in Vegas yet, but we're close enough, right?

Chapter 3

My room is small and cozy—perfect for just one night. But it's hard to relax. My mind's on Liam and his suggestion. My body's on fire and I need to cool off. Now. A shower should do the trick.

I turn the water on and by the time I'm undressed it's ready. When I step under the spray and soap up, my hands become Liam's in my mind. I tug my nipples, moaning at the jolt of pleasure. What would Vincent think if he knew how close I am to jumping Liam's bones? He told me to flirt, sure, but what I'm daydreaming about goes way beyond flirting.

After my shower, I catch my reflection—flushed cheeks, bright eyes. Is this a woman who is on the verge of becoming a hotwife? I grab my phone.

Debra:

So something happened. One of the guys offered to keep me company tonight.

His response pops up faster than I expected.

Vincent:

Did you say yes?

Debra:

Of course not, but I wanted to. Is that crazy?

Vincent:

> Not crazy. How are you feeling about it?

How do I feel? Like I'm going to explode if I don't get a cock inside me soon. Like I'm the worst wife ever for even considering it. Like I'm more alive than I've felt in years.

Debra:

> Honestly? Really turned on. And guilty. And excited. Like I'm losing my mind a little.

Vincent:

> You know guys check you out all the time, right? You're gorgeous.

I blush as I read his words. I wish it were true.

Debra:

> Stop.

Vincent:

> I'm serious. If you want to explore this, I support you.

Debra:

> You wouldn't be jealous? I don't know if I want to actually do anything.

Liar, liar, pants on fire. I want to run downstairs and beg Liam to fuck me.

Vincent:

> Maybe start slow? See how flirting feels?

Debra:

> Slow? What if I want to take on the whole team?

I give him a laughing emoji face to show I'm joking, but a part of me thrills at the idea. All those strong, fit men focused on me.

Vincent:

> If you think you can handle that many guys, go for it. Just two conditions–send me a pic after and tell me everything.

My body flushes as I read his response, and I laugh. I married a nut.

Debra:

> Oh god, I can't believe we're talking about this. What happened to my traditional values? What would I tell our friends?

Vincent:

> You tell them whatever you want, or nothing. It's your business, and mine–not theirs. And remember, at any time, you're allowed to change your mind. About any of it.

Debra:

> If I do this, I want something from you.

Vincent:

> Anything.

Debra:

> An anklet. A pretty one. Like Marilyn's.

I cringe as I hit send, remembering how judgmental I've been for months now.

Vincent:

> You'll have the prettiest anklet I can find, babe. Promise.

I let out a shaky laugh.

Okay, I might do something tonight. I'll text you after?

Have fun. Be safe. And remember you're my sexy, gorgeous wife.

I set the phone down and I'm dizzy from the possibilities open to me. I have Vincent's permission. I could do this. I could walk out that door right now and find Liam...or I could stay here and pretend this conversation didn't happen.

I'm just so fucking tired of playing it safe.

I let my towel fall to the floor. My nipples tighten in the cool air as I dig through my luggage, looking for something that says "fuck me now." But everything says "married prude" except a short, black dress with lace sleeves. I packed it just in case there was a fancy dinner I didn't know about.

It's a little elegant for what I have in mind, but if I wear nothing underneath...

Before I can talk myself out of it, I slip it on. The soft fabric caresses my skin, and I shiver as I slide my phone and keycard into my purse. I wear the flats I brought for walking around the conference. Excitement zips through me as I open the door.

I was just joking about taking on the team. But Liam? Yeah, I'm all over that. It's time to become a hotwife.

Chapter 4

My steps falter as I spot the sign on the rec room door: "CLOSED—Emergency Housing for Stranded Sports Team Due to Weather." My pulse races as I push the door open anyway, stepping into air thick with the scent of male bodies. The heady musk makes my head swim.

Furniture has been pushed against the walls to make room for rows of cots, with Christmas lights twinkling incongruously along the edges of the room. Garland drapes across the backs of chairs, and a festive wreath hangs on the wall. My dress, which felt perfectly appropriate when I last wore it, now seems scandalously short. The hem keeps riding up my thighs, making me acutely aware that this outfit is definitely not what one should wear to a traditional marriage conference. Despite the modest neckline, I feel suddenly exposed, vulnerable. What was I thinking, coming here? My heart pounds so hard I swear it's trying to escape my chest.

As I step further into the room, an unexpected hush falls over the conversations, and all eyes turn toward me. Liam lounges on his cot in sweatpants and no shirt. "You decided to join us."

"I couldn't sleep." Right, because everyone wears a sexy dress to fight insomnia.

He sits up and pats the space next to him. "Come on over. I promise I won't bite...unless you ask nicely."

The rational part of my brain is screaming at me to turn back, but for once, I ignore its warning. Moving between the cots, I notice hungry eyes following my bare legs. The attention gives me an unexpected thrill—these men actually find me desirable.

I sit down next to Liam primly and set my purse on the floor. His hair is damp and he smells faintly of vanilla, so I can tell he took a shower too.

"So," he says softly, so the rest of the room can't hear him. "What really brings you down here?"

There's heat in his gaze. He knows exactly why I'm here. But damn him for making me say it. "I wanted to take you up on your offer."

His smile widens. "Yeah? And what offer might that be?"

He's toying with me, and instead of making me cranky, it's turning me on. "When you said you'd keep me company."

He shifts a little closer. "I'm glad you came down."

Little sparks tingle across my skin as everyone else chats quietly and stares at me. This is new territory for me—being noticed, really noticed. It's electric.

Liam rests his hand on my bare knee, his thumb drawing slow circles on my skin. "Should we go to your room?"

I'm about to say 'yes,' but then I imagine the guys watching and wishing they were in Liam's spot. I want them to want me.

A newfound courage to embrace my sluttiest side bubbles up. "No, let's play a game with everyone."

He raises an eyebrow. "A game?"

I give him my best coy smile and speak up loud enough for everyone to hear. "Truth or dare."

A chorus of whistles and cheers erupt as Liam gives me an amused, "You're on."

The game starts innocently enough. One of the guys dares another to do a silly dance. Someone else has to admit their most embarrassing moment.

But as the dares get more physical, the truths more revealing, the tension in the room increases.

Liam rumbles, "Your turn, Debra. Truth or dare?"

There's a challenge in his eyes. I expect him to ask me to do something filthy and I'm ready for it.

"Dare."

He gives me a slow grin. "I dare you to kiss me."

Heck, that seems easy enough. My eyes flutter closed as our lips meet. It's a soft kiss at first, a gentle press that makes my breath catch and my skin come alive. His lips are warm and firm, and I can taste mint on his breath.

His hand slides to the small of my back, pulling me closer. The kiss deepens, and I open my mouth to him. Suddenly we're in full-on make-out mode. He tangles his hand in my hair, holding me in place, as he explores my mouth. I can feel his hard cock pressing against my thigh, and it sends a wave of heat straight to my core.

The room erupts in catcalls and whistles, but I barely hear them. It's like nothing else exists in this moment but the two of us as I lose myself in him.

Right when I'm about ready to climb on top of him, he breaks off the kiss. My lips feel puffy and I want more. This is what I've been missing: this passion, this neediness that makes me desperate for his cock.

Liam squeezes my thigh, and his voice is rough so I can tell he's just as affected as I am. "My turn, and I choose dare."

A guy who I dub "Surfer Dude" because of his sun-bleached hair and laid-back attitude, says, "I dare you to make her come."

My eyes go round as I glance at Liam. There's a tightness in him, and I can tell he's holding back from doing what he really wants to do right now—which, hopefully, is ravishing me.

His tone is measured and controlled when he asks, "Is that a dare you want me to take?"

I don't remember the last time I wanted something as much as I want his hands on me. I don't even try to play it subtle with my response.

"Yes."

Liam's hand glides up my thigh, lifting my dress, and he groans when he discovers that I'm not wearing any panties. I spread my knees, giving him full access, and he traces the seam of my pussy with his fingers. "You're already so wet," he murmurs.

I'm spellbound and unable to speak. If he only knew I've been daydreaming about his hands on me since I first saw him.

He slips a finger inside me, and I moan as my hips jerk instinctively. God, why does this feel so good? It's not like Vincent doesn't touch me, but somehow this is different.

Liam finger fucks me slowly and circles my clit with his thumb. I rest back on the cot and let my eyes drift closed. I can't believe I'm doing this. I can't believe how good it feels.

The room is silent except for the sound of my tiny moans. I know they're all watching Liam finger fuck me, and the thrill of having their attention is more seductive than I imagined it would be. I'm probably only 10 years older than some of them, but just knowing that a whole soccer team wants me is a rush.

Liam moves his fingers faster and presses his thumb harder against my clit. The pleasure builds, it's a tight coil in my stomach. I'm getting close, and the increasing volume of my moans tells it to the entire room.

When I come, pure delight surges over me like a tidal wave. Liam strokes me through my orgasm until I'm a trembling mess.

When I can think again, I open my eyes. Everyone is staring at me—all of them—and for once, I don't want to hide. I feel powerful.

Liam pulls his finger out and sucks it clean. "You taste amazing."

I quiver with desire. I can't believe I just did that—and I still crave more.

One of the guys speaks up—I mentally nickname him Shaggy for his floppy dark brown hair and wiry frame. He keeps pushing those messy strands out of his eyes as he says, "Damn, that was hot. Your turn again, Debra."

They're skipping over a few guys' turns, but I'm not about to point that out. Not when things are getting interesting.

"Dare," I say without hesitation. Please someone, make it filthy.

Liam doesn't waste time. "I dare you to suck my cock."

I'm already nodding. Yes! I'm about to suck off a guy in front of an entire sports team. This is fabulous.

Liam stands up and pushes down his sweatpants. His cock springs free, and I take a moment to admire it. He's bigger than my husband, and his flat stomach with hair leading to his cock makes me want to lick down the happy trail and worship him. I enjoy giving blow jobs, but knowing other people are going to be watching makes me want to give Liam the best blow job of my life.

Kicking off my flats, I kneel in front of him. When I wrap my hand around his cock, the warmth of him pulses against my palm. I smile up at him as I take him into my mouth. His taste—sweet and musky—makes me hum in enjoyment. If his cum tastes half this good, I'd swallow load after load without complaining.

I grip one of his thighs to steady myself and swirl my tongue around the tip, making him groan. When I bob my head, taking him deeper with each pass, he hits the back of my throat. Yeah, he's bigger than I'm used to, but I'm taking him all in like a champ.

Liam's gaze is intense and the room is silent except the wet sounds of my mouth. Something shifts in the air between us. There's freedom in this moment—in knowing I can command this kind of attention. I want to put on a show.

Liam tangles his hands in my hair and guides my movements. I relax so I can deep throat him. He groans and forces my head to move quicker. I expect him to blow his load at any moment, and I want to taste him...except he pulls out before he comes.

His cock glistens with my saliva and I'm tempted to take another lick to see what he'd do, but he stops me with a command.

"Strip and ride me."

Liam sits down on his cot and his cock juts up, practically waving at me. With deliberate slowness, I reach for the zipper at my side. I let the dress fall, the lace sleeves caressing my skin before pooling at my feet. I'm left wearing nothing.

A collective intake of breath from the room fuels the fire building inside me, and my nipples harden. The rush of power and exhilaration is intoxicating. Every man in this room wants me.

I step towards Liam, ready to straddle him, but he stops me with a firm hand on my hip. "Face the room. Let them see how slutty you look when you come around my cock."

A delicious shiver runs down my spine as I turn, facing the room full of hungry eyes. Their gazes roam over every inch of my exposed skin, their desire almost tangible in the air. Slowly, I lower myself onto Liam, gasping as his hard cock presses against my entrance.

I ease down onto him with a moan, his thickness massaging every pleasure point inside me. Setting a languid pace, I roll my hips in slow circles. Around us, the other men watch intently, their hard cocks evident through their clothing.

Liam holds my waist as I pick up the pace. The room fills with our ragged breathing and the soft slap of flesh as I grind against him with each downward stroke. Knowing I'm being watched and wanted is a high I've never experienced before, and my skin buzzes with an energy that makes me feel invincible

I'm riding a near-painful edge, and each roll of my hips sends sparks through my core. His fingers dig into my skin, his rhythm growing erratic. The familiar pressure builds low in my belly, and I can tell by his ragged breathing that he's fighting to hold on.

"Show them," he pants against my neck. "Show them what you look like when you lose control."

The weight of their stares feeds something primal in me. When I break, my toes curl and my back arches. I pound against Liam and shamelessly chant, "Fuck me," as pleasure rockets through me in cascading waves.

Liam groans, his hips jerking upward as he spills inside me. I press down, greedy for his cum. Each roll of my hips draws another shudder from us both.

As the high ebbs, I steady myself and stand. I can feel Liam's cum trailing down my inner thighs. Something wild stirs in my chest. I'm insatiable.

I get my phone from my purse and snap a quick selfie from the chest up. My hair is mussed, I have flushed cheeks, and my lips are swollen. I look like a woman who's just been thoroughly fucked.

I send the picture and a message to my husband.

Debra:

> I did it. I just rode someone's cock in front of a room full of guys. And now I'm going to fuck them all. I'll text you afterwards. Love you!

My phone dings as I'm sliding it back into my purse, so I check it.

Vince:

> Christ. You trying to kill me? I'm so turned on right now. Go be a slut, and I want to hear every detail later.

I touch the wedding ring on my finger, and a fierce joy bubbles up inside me. Vincent gets it—gets me—in a way I never thought possible. He's given me permission to explore this part of myself, and that makes me love him even more.

I put my phone away and face the room. "All right, who wants to fuck me next?"

Chapter 5

I scan the room, and I almost giggle as the guys raise their hands as if they're in class. They all want me.

"Pick someone." Liam's demand gives me a charge. He's still perched on the cot, his curly hair sticking to his face with sweat. His sweatpants are down around his ankles and his cock glistens with our combined fluids. The wicked glint in his eyes makes my insides clench.

I'm in control. My pulse races at the realization—I'm going to be their fucktoy, their slut for the night, but I'm the one choosing this. Every heated stare, every hitched breath is because of me. I never knew control could taste this sweet, never understood why women chased this feeling. Now I get it. God, do I get it.

My eyes land on a tall, muscular blonde with a buzz cut. I remember him from the bus—he was one of the more vocal ones clowning around. But there's nothing funny about the way he's looking at me now. His confident smirk and rock-hard cock under his shorts practically make me salivate.

"You," I say, pointing at him.

His sly smile makes my stomach flip. "Then come here, slut."

I don't hesitate. My legs are shaky as I walk over, but not from fear—from pure, unadulterated lust. He bends me over the arm of a couch, and I feel the hot, blunt pressure of his cock against my entrance.

He slams into me with a grunt, and I cry out. He's not as big as Liam, but he fills me perfectly. Every thrust sends shockwaves of pleasure through my body. I can hear murmurs of approval from the room, a low hum of desire that only fuels my own.

He fucks me hard and fast. I feel every ridge, every vein, as he slides in and out of me. My body quivers with each thrust.

Liam is in my line of sight, watching us. He steps closer, fully naked, his cock already hard again. He grabs a fistful of my hair, pulling my head up to look at him.

"You like that? You like being fucked like a little slut?"

I nod as best I can, my mouth hanging open in a silent scream of joy. Liam turns to one of the other players. "Come fuck her mouth," he commands.

Mr. Muscles—as I decide to call him—doesn't need to be told twice. He holds onto my chin and positions his cock at my lips. The taste of him as he slides in, combined with the sensations of being filled from both ends, is overwhelming.

I'm lost in a haze of pleasure, sucking and licking as the guy behind me pounds into me relentlessly. Ripples of delight run up and down my body as I submit to the filthiness of the moment.

The thrusts from behind grow more urgent, and I can tell he's close. Mr. Muscles' cock hits the back of my throat, making me gag, but I don't mind. I crave it all. I want to be used and fucked senseless.

A low groan from behind signals the guy's release. I feel the hot splash of his cum filling me, spilling out as he pulls away. My moans trigger Mr. Muscles, and suddenly my mouth is flooded with his seed. I swallow greedily, not wanting to waste a drop.

As they step back, Liam grins down at me. "You're such a good little slut. Now, who's next?"

Desire ripples through me as another guy steps forward. It's Shaggy. He's stroking his cock so vigorously, I'm afraid he's going to come without fucking me.

"More," I whimper, my mind foggy with lust. "Need more cock."

Liam nods towards Shaggy. "You heard her. Take your turn."

Shaggy flips me onto my back on the couch, spreading my legs wide. His eyes darken as he takes in the sight of my well-used pussy.

"Fuck, look at that messy cunt. You're fucking dripping, slut."

The word "cunt" pings a part of my brain I wasn't aware of, and suddenly I feel like the filthiest slut who ever lived. My legs are spread and I'm inviting the soccer team to fuck me. I want to be used and filled by every single one of them. I'll probably never do anything like this again, and I revel in the feeling of complete debauchery.

This is the real me. I am a filthy slut who wants to fuck them all.

Shaggy kneels between my legs and taps the head of his cock against my clit. I squirm from the jolts of pleasure.

"Please," I whimper.

He flashes a wolfish grin. "Please what, slut? Say it."

"Please fuck me."

He pulls my legs up until my ankles rest on his shoulders, slamming into me with a brutal pace that makes me cry out in rapture. He's not gentle, and I don't want him to be. I want him to use me however he wants.

Another guy approaches, cock ready. He grabs my breasts, kneading them together. Kneeling on the edge of the couch, he leans over me to thrust between my tits. He uses the back of the couch for leverage, and with each movement, the head of his cock bumps my chin. All I can do is moan.

I'm surrounded, filled, used. And holy shit, do I love it. The room's thick with the sounds and smells of sex as I barrel towards another orgasm.

Shaggy suddenly whacks against me and shudders. I feel the hot rush of him spilling inside me as he groans, "Such a good slut."

When the guy between my tits coats my chest, I giggle in delight. I'm a mess, covered and filled with cum. And damn it, I want more.

I scan the room. There are plenty of hard cocks waiting their turn.

"More," I plead. "I need more."

A broad-shouldered guy with a hint of mischief in his eyes steps forward. "Hold her legs," he commands. Two guys immediately grab my ankles, spreading me wide. He kneels between my thighs, his cock bobbing eagerly. He rubs it between my folds, teasing. "Beg for it. Tell me how bad you want it."

I'm panting, aching with need. "Please," I whimper. "Please fuck me. I need your cock so bad."

Satisfied, he drills into me as I writhe beneath him. He's big, and the angle hits pleasure points I didn't even know I had. He moves with a feverish rhythm, each thrust igniting sparks that tingle along my nerves.

Another cock appears by my head, its owner fisting my hair. "Open up, baby. Let me feel what that mouth can do."

I part my lips, taking him in. My body quakes with each thrust, the pressure builds until I can barely think, as they both use me.

I happily gurgle around the cock in my mouth as the guy thrusts into my throat. He doesn't last long before he blows his salty load. My throat works around him as I try to clean him up.

God, my husband is going to love hearing about this. Heat streaks through me at the thought, and my orgasm hits me with full force. The convulsive waves of delight leave me shaking.

The guy in my pussy shudders against me one final time, leaving a warm trail as he eases back. I'm still quivering from my orgasm, but I'm greedy for more.

"It's my turn to use the slut." A guy with piercing blue eyes steps up. His gaze rakes over me, lingering on the mess between my legs. "Let's turn you over."

He flips me onto my stomach, and runs a hand over my ass, squeezing. "Look at this eager little thing," he growls. "I bet she wants all her holes stuffed."

I make helpless little sounds as his fingers trace their path. "Do you want that? Do you want us to fuck you in every hole and use you like the filthy slut you know you are?"

"Yes," I moan. "Do it. Use me."

He pulls me up to my hands and knees, and I barely have myself braced against the arm of the couch before he drills into my pussy from behind. Wait, I thought he was going to fuck my ass? Not that it matters—I'm so wound up, I'd beg for anything he's willing to give.

Another guy steps up, stroking his thick, curved cock. He watches the guy behind me pound away. "Part those lips, sweetheart. I want to feel the warmth of your mouth."

Holy shit. I don't even know how many men have fucked me at this point. I do as he says, and as he fills my mouth, I'm caught between them, lost in the dual sensations as they move in tandem. Their rhythmic thrusts send waves of pleasure radiating across my body. I'm consumed by them.

Liam steps closer, and there's admiration in his voice. "You're such a good little fucktoy. Look at you, taking all these cocks like you were made for it."

I nod, mouth full. Liam turns to another guy, a broad-shouldered beast with a fierce gaze. "Want to fuck her ass? She wants it."

As if by silent agreement the guys pull out of my mouth and pussy so that they can reposition themselves. Several guys pull the couch away from the wall and the guy who was in my pussy sits down. Liam helps me straddle him, and I rest my hands on his shoulders, moaning as I sink down on his cock. I can see where this is going, and I welcome it.

The guy who was in my mouth moves behind the couch, aiming his cock over the back. I lean forward so I can suck on him.

The beast steps up behind me, and I hear a squeeze bottle of lube. If my mouth wasn't so full, I would have joked about them taking lube on a trip to Vegas, but I'm way too busy. Multiple hands pull my ass cheeks apart and knowing that I'm being examined by a bunch of guys almost makes me come.

Cool lube drips down my ass, and then a thick finger works it inside me. I'm not a stranger to anal—Vincent loves my ass—but the cock that presses against that hole is bigger than anything I've ever had back there. I tense up, anticipating the burn. But Liam's there soothing me. "Relax, let him in. You can take it."

I whimper as he slides in slowly. Each inch is a delicious stretch until he's fully inside me. The guy beneath me groans, and I wonder if he can feel the guy in my ass. My body stretches to accommodate them both, every nerve ending firing at once. My head spins from pleasure.

"Make her scream," Liam orders, and the cocks all slide in and out in a rhythm that drives me insane.

Liam moves to my side. He grabs my hand, wrapping it around his shaft. "Stroke it. Make me come all over that pretty face."

Another guy moves to the opposite side and angles his cock at me. I grab it. All three holes stuffed and two guys in my hands. I am the ultimate slut.

The guy in my mouth unexpectedly comes and I'm not prepared to swallow. Some of his cum leaks down my chin and drips onto my breasts as he pulls out.

Liam removes his cock from my hand and takes the man's place behind the couch. "You look so fucking hot like this. Stuffed full of cock. Now, suck mine."

As I suck on him, I revel in the knowledge that all three of my holes are stuffed again. Another guy takes Liam's place with my free hand, so I'm pleasuring five at once. Can life get any sluttier than this? It's amazing.

The room's filled with the sounds of our pleasure—low groans and grunts as they fuck me. I'm lost in sensation, my body shaking with the force of their thrusts. Everything narrows to this moment, this feeling, as I chase the impending explosion. Each breath brings me closer to breaking.

I'm chanting, "Oh god," but with Liam's cock in my mouth, it's garbled nonsense.

When I feel the guy in my ass spasm and jerk against me, I explode. A white-hot rapture shoots from my fingertips to my toes and I scream as Liam groans and blows his load straight down my throat.

In an instant, we're all consumed by a frenzy. The guys are unloading ropes of cum into all my holes, our bodies shuddering and gasping in unison. I lose track of time as my orgasm peaks again and again.

How many guys have I fucked? Who knows.

Liam withdraws from my mouth at the same time the guy behind me pulls out. Gentle hands assist me off the guy's lap, and I find myself on my back on the couch, gazing at the ceiling where holiday lights twinkle softly. It feels like they're winking at me, as if even they know I'm a slut. I giggle at the absurd thought.

"I want to try something else," I mumble, mind hazy with lust.

Liam's kneeling next to me in a flash. "What do you want now? Say it loud and clear."

I force myself to focus, and I turn my head to direct my voice towards the room. ""I want you all to fuck me."

The guys erupt in cheers and eager murmurs. Liam laughs. "You heard her, boys. Line up and give our little slut what she wants."

And they do—even the ones who've already had a turn. One by one, they step up, cocks hard and ready. I'm fucked in every position imaginable, my body contorting to accommodate each of them. On my hands and knees as they take me from behind. On my back, legs spread, as they pound into me. On my side, knees pulled up to my chest as they fuck me deep and hard.

I lose track of time, of how many times I come. I'm covered in sweat and cum, practically mindless from pleasure. But I don't want it to stop. I want more. I want it all.

Finally, it's Liam in my mouth again. He slides down my throat as he fucks my face. His hands are tangled in my hair, eyes locked on mine. "You're such a good little slut," he praises. "Look at you, stuffed full of cock. You love it, don't you?"

I nod around his cock. I do love it. I love every filthy, depraved second of it. When Liam comes again, it's with a roar. As I swallow him all down, I can sense the night is over.

He pulls out and I slump face down onto the cot that they moved me to at some point. Liam sits next to me and brushes sweaty strands of hair from my face. "You look so fucking hot like this. Covered in cum, used and fucked."

I give him a cum-drunk grin, and I whisper, "Thank you."

God, I hope Vincent is okay with this. Oh shit. Vincent.

I wave vaguely towards where my purse is and ask Liam, "Can you take a photo of me like this. I want to show my husband later."

He gets my phone and I roll onto my back. I rest my hands above my head for the photo. Might as well make it as sexy as possible.

"Thank you," I tell Liam once he's finished.

"You're welcome. Now, let's get you cleaned up."

He helps me to my feet. My hair's a mess and my skin is sticky. I must look a sight.

Liam grabs one of the robes the inn supplied to the guys and wraps it around me gently. He picks up my purse, shoes, and dress before guiding me towards the door. The guys on the team give me a soft goodbye, and I can tell they are as worn out as I am. Liam keeps his arm around my waist, and I'm grateful for his support.

We're silent until we're outside my room. At my door, we both hesitate, the night's energy still crackling between us. His kiss is soft—nothing like the passionate ones we shared earlier. "I keep thinking I should pinch myself," he murmurs against my lips. "Tonight feels surreal."

"Good surreal?" My skin's still buzzing from everything I just did.

"The kind of surreal that ruins you for anything ordinary." He traces my cheek with his thumb. "I'm going to remember this trip forever."

He helps me inside and to the bed. He's in caregiver mode, and he brings me a bottle of water and a granola bar from the basket of provided snacks in the room.

"I'm not leaving until I see you eat and drink."

Jesus, this guy is great. By the time I'm done with the granola bar and take enough sips of the water to satisfy him, my eyes are feeling heavy.

Liam kisses my forehead. "Get some rest. You deserve it."

I nod. "Goodnight, Liam."

"Goodnight. I'll see you tomorrow on the bus."

"No, you won't. I've decided to go home," I say softly. I didn't even know I had made that decision until I say it.

He looks at me, surprised. "Oh. Well, take care of yourself, okay?"

I murmur, "I will," and he closes the door gently behind him.

My body is wonderfully sore and exhausted. I'm filthy and should shower, but I like the idea of waking up with the dried cum on me. There's just one more thing to do before I can sleep.

I attach the picture Liam took of me to a message to my husband, using Liam's wording from earlier to describe my night

Debra:

I did it. I'm covered in cum, used and fucked. And I loved every second of it. I'm not going to the conference. I'm staying at the inn. Come pick me up when the roads clear. I'm about to crash. I'm wonderful. Love you.

I hit send, wishing I could stay awake to see his response, but I can already feel sleep stealing over me.

I drift off, smiling. No matter what happens next, I'll never forget this night. The night I embraced my desires and became the slut I always wanted to be.

CHAPTER 6

It's been three days since the night of the snowstorm. I'm pacing the room like a caged animal, my heart thumping so hard I swear it's trying to escape my chest. I never saw the team again before they left, but at least some rooms freed up, and the inn hooked me up with a bigger one, so I've been comfortable while I waited...and waited...and waited some more.

My phone buzzes, and I nearly jump out of my skin. It's Vincent. He's here. Holy shit, he's actually here.

I unlock the door with shaking hands and step back, my breath catching in my throat. The door flies open, and there he is—my Vincent. His eyes lock onto mine, wild with raw need.

The door slams shut and before I can even squeak out a "hello," he's on me. I'm in his arms, his mouth crushing against mine. It's not a kiss; it's a claiming. His tongue invades my mouth, hot and demanding, and I melt against him. God, I've missed this. I've missed him.

He's already fully aroused, his cock straining against his jeans and pressing firmly against my stomach. I moan as he pulls back, his hands gripping my shoulders. "Deb," he growls, rough as sandpaper. "I need to hear it. I need to hear what you did."

I blink up at him, my brain struggling to form coherent thoughts. "I... I'm not sure I can describe it," I stammer, heat flooding my cheeks. Part of me wants to spill every dirty detail, but another part is suddenly shy. What if he doesn't like what he hears?

But then Vincent flashes a knowing smile. "Oh come on now. I know that's not true. I've been reading your blog all these months. I've married one filthy-talking woman."

My jaw drops. "You knew about my blog?"

A sharp thrill hits fast and hard, leaving me breathless. Oh god, he's read everything. Every dirty thought, every naughty fantasy...

He nods. "Every. Single. Word. Now, tell me everything."

Something inside me snaps, and suddenly I'm talking, the words pouring out of me in a torrent. Vincent's hands are everywhere, stripping off my clothes. The cool air hits my skin, but then his mouth is on me, hot and demanding, and I forget how to breathe.

"Liam...Liam fucked me first," I pant, arching into Vincent's touch. "He made me come so hard. And then the others..."

Vincent's fingers plunge into my soaking wet pussy. I cry out, my hips bucking against his hand. "Like this?" he demands, his fingers moving in and out of me at a punishing pace. "Did he fuck you like this?"

"Y-yes," I moan, my body trembling. "And then everyone else had a turn—multiple turns."

In one swift move, Vincent spins me around and bends me over the bed. I hear the sound of a zipper, and then he's slamming into me. I cry out, my fingers clutching at the sheets as he fucks me harder than he ever has before.

"Tell me," he growls again. "Tell me what they did to you."

I can barely think straight, but the words keep coming. "They...they fucked my mouth," I gasp out, my body shaking with each thrust. "They fucked my ass. They filled me completely—every hole."

The entire night spills out as Vincent hammers into me. At some point he takes the rest of his clothes off, flips me over, and pushes my knees to my chest so we're looking at each other. His desire for me matches the intense craving I feel for him, and I can tell he's beyond rational thought.

The moment he loses control, his whole body goes rigid as he fills me. His harsh groan catches in his throat as he pulses inside me, and that's all it takes—I fall apart, my body seizing with an intensity that steals my breath. My vision blurs from waves of pleasure. We crash together, neither of us holding anything back.

Eventually, we collapse onto the bed, and Vincent pulls me into his arms, pressing a soft kiss to my forehead. "I love you, Deb," he murmurs tenderly. "I love you so much."

I look up at him, my eyes stinging with unshed tears. "I love you too. More than anything. You're my man."

He smiles and climbs off the bed, reaching for his coat on the floor. "I have something for you."

He pulls out a flat black box from the pocket, and I recognize the gold lettering immediately—that luxury jeweler I always walk past but never dare enter. Inside is an anklet that makes my breath catch. The gold chain is impossibly delicate, and two tiny gems dangle from it—a sapphire and an emerald—our birthstones.

As he fastens it around my ankle, his fingers lingering on my skin, I feel a rush of love. I didn't expect him to buy the anklet before he came, but the fact he did makes me appreciate him even more.

"It's beautiful," I whisper, turning my ankle and admiring how the gems catch the light.

"It's us," he says simply. "And shows our love for adventures."

"Oh yeah?" I giggle at him. "I could probably be persuaded to fuck more guys."

We laugh together, and as he holds me tight, I feel it in my soul—this is just the start of our unpredictable future.

And honestly? I'm excited to see what kind of trouble we can get into together. I can't wait. Slutty Debra might just take on a football team next.

EPILOGUE

Hotwives Unleashed: A Confession and a Revelation

Oh, dear readers, I must confess, I have been a hypocrite. I have been a liar. I have been...a slut. That's right, you heard it here first. The woman who has been preaching about the dangers of the hotwife lifestyle, the one who has been judging and shaming, has fallen off her high horse and landed right on her knees, eager to please.

You see, I was on a trip, stuck in a snowstorm, and I found myself in a situation that I never imagined. I was in a room full of college soccer players, and one thing led to another, and...well, let's just say that I embraced my inner slut in a way that would make even the most experienced hotwives blush.

I let them use me, all of them. I was passed around like a toy, fucked in every hole, covered in their cum. And I loved every second of it. I begged for more. I was insatiable. I was a slut, plain and simple.

And do you know what? It was the most liberating, exhilarating experience of my life. I have never felt more alive, more desired, more...me.

I thought I was happy with my life, with my marriage. I thought I was content with being the good, virtuous wife. But I was wrong. I was so very wrong. I was suppressing a part of myself, a part that craved excitement, adventure, passion. A part that wanted to be used, to be fucked, to be a slut.

My husband, bless his heart, has been supportive. He has been understanding. He has been...excited. He wants me to explore this side of myself, to embrace it. He loves me, no matter what. And that, dear readers, is true love.

So, I am coming out, so to speak. I am admitting to the world that I am a hotwife. I am a slut. And I am proud of it.

I will no longer hide behind my judgment and my shame. I will no longer preach about the dangers of this lifestyle. Because, dear readers, it is not dangerous. It is not depraved. It is not wrong. It is...amazing.

So, if you are reading this and you are curious, if you are intrigued, if you are feeling that same desire that I was, do not suppress it. Embrace it. Explore it. You never know where it might lead you.

Until next time, stay slutty, dear readers.

The End